D1422981

8

09

Y

THE CORRIGAN LEGACY

Childless Maeve Corrigan is dying of cancer. She wants to leave her business empire to one of the offspring of her two estranged brothers, Des and Leo. But which young relative should she choose?

Des has four children. His second wife Judith has just left him and he's over-stretched financially. Leo, unambitious owner of a hardware store in a remote Australian town, has two children. His daughter, suffering from ME, defies him to accept her aunt's invitation to be treated in England.

Judith has met another man. But Cal has just found out he's not the biological father of his beloved daughter and his ex-wife wants to take Lily away from him.

As the younger generation begin to gather around Maeve, old secrets are revealed, new allegiances made, and there are surprises for every member of the family—because the Corrigan legacy isn't what it first seems.

THE CORRIGAN LEGACY

Anna Jacobs

WINDSOR
PARAGON

First published 2006
by
Severn House Publishers
This Large Print edition published 2007
by
BBC Audiobooks Ltd by arrangement with
Severn House Publishers Ltd

Hardcover ISBN: 978 1 405 61324 8
Softcover   ISBN: 978 1 405 61325 5

British Library Cataloguing in Publication Data available

Printed and bound in Great Britain by
Antony Rowe Ltd., Chippenham, Wiltshire

This book is dedicated to all sufferers of chronic fatigue syndrome, otherwise known as ME. I had it myself years ago and always promised myself I'd put it in a book. This is the book. I was lucky—I got better, though I'm left with severe food intolerances. I wish the best of luck to everyone else who comes down with it.

One

London. January. Heavy rain drives sideways, drivers squint through a blur of water. Pewter puddles mirror charcoal sky.

Judith Corrigan walked slowly out of the building, oblivious to the rain that was darkening her light brown hair and flattening it against her skull. When she got to her car she paused for a moment, staring blindly into the distance, then slid into the driving seat and shut out the rest of the world.

The news she'd just received wasn't a total surprise but still she'd hoped . . . foolish as that was . . . and now her last hope had just been destroyed.

It hurt.

She fumbled for the car keys, which she'd dropped into the lap of her sodden skirt, knocked them to the floor and didn't bother to pick them up. The tears welling in her eyes overflowed and with a soft mew of pain she rested her head on her hands and wept.

When someone knocked on the car window she turned her head, saw a police uniform and tried to roll the window down. But the keys weren't in the ignition, so she had to open the door to a flurry of chill raindrops.

The policeman bent down, concern on his face. 'Are you all right, madam?'

It took her a moment to find any words, so she nodded, then nodded again. 'Yes. Just—some bad news.'

'You've been sitting here for a while. Are you all

right to drive home?'

'Yes. I'm—um—coming to terms with it now.' As he nodded and stepped backwards, she closed the car door, mopping her face, twisting sideways to look at herself in the rear-view mirror and realizing suddenly how wet she was. She glanced at her watch. There was just time to get home and change before Des came back from the office. A little make-up would hide the signs of tears.

Bending down, she fumbled for the keys then, with hands clenched tightly on the steering wheel, she drove out of the car park and made her way home through a winter world so lacking in light and colour she felt as if she were trapped in an old sepia photograph.

Which suited her mood perfectly.

*   *   *

Des Corrigan didn't notice the weather or the traffic. As his chauffeur drove him home, he spent most of his time talking on his mobile phone.

When he entered the house he went straight into the living room to announce, 'We signed today. She doesn't know it, but this is the beginning of the end for my dear sister.'

Judith gave him a long, level look. 'So you decided to go ahead, in spite of all I said?'

'I told you I would. What I do in my business is *not* your concern. You're my wife, not my damned accountant.'

'I meant what I said, Des.' She stood up and walked across to the doorway. 'I'll go and pack my things.'

He followed her out into the hall, grabbed her

2

arm and dragged her back into the living room, not without a struggle that left him breathless, because she was not a small woman and she fought with the extra strength anger can lend.

As he slammed the door shut behind them, he yelled, 'We've been married for nineteen years, dammit, and you've never even met my sister. What can she possibly matter to you?'

Judith wrapped her arms round herself, rubbing the soreness where his fingers had dug into the skin of her upper arms. She could smell the wine on his breath and knew that made him reckless sometimes. Beneath the anger she felt deep sadness. This, on top of everything else! 'I don't have to meet her. It's *you* I'm leaving, Desmond Corrigan, because I don't like what you've become.'

'I won't let you leave.'

'How will you stop me? Tie me up? Set one of your security people to guard me day and night?' She could hear that her laughter was a mere rasp of sound, totally unconvincing, but it was the best she could manage. As she tucked a lock of still-damp hair behind one ear she felt her fingers tremble and made a huge effort to speak steadily. Wasn't sure she'd succeeded. 'You can't stop me leaving you any more than you could stop your first wife from doing the same thing—and she probably left you for similar reasons.'

Judith knew how few morals he had when it came to either business or his own desires. Well, she'd known it for a while, really, but it had taken time for her to admit to herself that she'd had enough of it, because he could be charming when he wanted and was very good in bed.

3

The main reason she'd stayed was not because she was still in love with him but because they had a son. Mitch mattered more to her than her husband now, far more.

Des stared at her for a moment then stabbed a forefinger towards the trio of white leather couches which had been delivered only the month before. She sat down because she couldn't fight him physically, but she hadn't changed her mind about leaving and wouldn't, whatever he said or did.

He sat on the next couch to hers, at right angles, eyes watchful. 'Stop playing silly buggers, Jude. We've disagreed before. You didn't walk out on me then.'

'Maybe I should have done. I've thought about it a few times.'

'Surely Maeve can't matter more to you than—'

'Haven't you been listening to me? I don't give a stuff about your sister. It's *you* I care about. What you're turning into. What sort of an example you're setting our son.'

His expression grew sulky. 'Maeve stole the family business from Leo and me, you know she did.'

'She paid out your shares in full. That's not stealing. And the business wasn't big enough to support the three of you then, you know that. She's the one who's made it what it is now. Besides, this all happened thirty years ago. Get over it!'

'But she *forced* us to sell them to her, cheated us of our birthright. She was determined to be top dog there. Corrigan's is known all over the world for precision engineering of small, specialist parts. And look how rich she's become on it, yet she

4

never paid us a penny for the potential. I swore then that I'd get the family business back from her one day and now I have done, or I will have once the paperwork goes through.'

Judith had argued about this before but for her own peace of mind, she tried again. 'You don't need that business, Des. And doing it this way, with trickery and lies, stinks. Does your brother know what you're doing? Have you even asked Leo if he wants the family business back? He seemed happy enough running his hardware shop when we visited him.' The unambitious one, a taciturn man more interested in his family than the world outside his small country town. Judith had only met him once, given how far away he lived, but she'd liked him and his sensible wife.

'Leo's grown old and lazy—that's what Australia does to you. Life's too easy there. Anyway, he always was too stupid to help himself. I'm not.'

'You haven't told him, have you? For all your big talk about family, you're doing this purely for yourself, out of sheer spite.' She lifted her chin to stare him out. Gone were the days when Des could intimidate her with an angry look—or make her bones melt with a loving one. He was married to the business nowadays—and to that damned mobile phone of his. Their marriage had been over for a long time, except as a useful social arrangement.

He folded his arms and leaned back. 'Just for that you'd leave me? Get real, Jude.'

'No, not just for that.' She hesitated but after what she'd heard today it was more than time to get everything out in the open. 'There is also the question of your current, live-in mistress. Your

5

previous one was, you swore blind, a temporary madness. The existence of Tiffany Jane Roberts makes infidelity seem more like an ingrained habit to me.'

After one twitch of surprise, he became very still. 'How the hell did you find out about Tiff?'

'I paid a private detective. Five mistresses you've had in the past ten years, he tells me, not to mention the odd one-night stand when the opportunity has presented—like last month in Manchester. You even *boast* about it to your business friends. They all *know* you're unfaithful to me. How do you think that makes me feel? And I'm sick to think of the diseases you might have passed on to me.' She slapped her open palm down on the couch and hurled at him, *'Years of it!'*

'Maybe I wouldn't have needed the other women if you'd been more accommodating, Judith. You're not exactly the world's greatest lover, you know. Not even in the also-rans.'

She picked up a cushion and hurled it at him before he realized what she intended. 'Your infidelity has nothing to do with my skills in bed. You're just greedy.' She paused and swallowed hard. She'd promised herself not to scream at him, to tell him quietly then leave. It was proving harder than she'd expected.

He flapped one hand sideways in a dismissive gesture. 'Ach, they meant nothing, those women. You know I've got a higher than average sex drive. It's often the way with successful businessmen—and politicians.'

'They mean nothing? This Tiffany female has been with you for five years. And your first long-term mistress bore you a child. A daughter. Whom

6

you still support. Is all that *nothing*?'

'How the hell did you find out about that?' His expression lost its geniality—its humanity, too. He looked like someone from a Breughel painting, a man with a brutal, lumpy face made insensitive by the harshness of daily life. But Judith knew that Des had not had a hard life, he had just lived life to the full.

'I wonder what we'd find if I had a detective look into *your* life?' he muttered when the silence dragged on.

'No infidelities, that's for sure.' She watched him force a smile. He could always pull out that particular smile, but she could spot it a mile off now and knew it wasn't genuine. 'You're a fine-looking man, with that head of silver hair. And you've kept yourself trim, too—'

He nodded, as if she were complimenting him.

'—but you've gone rotten inside.'

He jerked upright and glared at her. 'And you're a fat old sow. You've even let your hair go. It used to look good, now it's just ordinary.'

'You hate that, don't you? Other men have wives who don't look like stick insects—and they still manage to love them, but not you. Desmond Corrigan's wife has to be fashionable in every way, a visible sign of his success. Well, next time you marry you can get yourself a skinny young trophy wife—preferably a blonde, because you clearly prefer them. But don't forget to write it into the marriage contract that she mustn't put on any weight.'

'I don't want another wife. I want you.'

'Why? You just said I'm not the best in bed.'

'You're not that bad. We've been together

7

nineteen years and it's stupid to throw it all away on a whim. You're a good wife for a man like me. You can talk to anyone. People like you.' He gave her a sour glance. 'But you could have lost the weight. It's not much to ask.'

'I tried. Several times.'

'Well, you didn't keep it off for long.'

'No. It's not much fun living on lettuce leaves. Or eating them alone when your husband's away, which is at least half the time with you. What's more—' she stared at herself in the mirror— 'I quite like being this size. I enjoy the voluptuous feel of my body. Read the latest research, Des. Most normal men like curvy women and some people are meant by nature to be larger than size 8 or 10. Marilyn Monroe was my size, you know.'

'Well, *I* don't like all that blubber.'

'My body's firm, well-toned, and—' She bit back further protests. She'd never been able to convince him, didn't need to now, because she'd made her decision. Relief whispered through her, mingling with the sadness, and she knew leaving him was the right thing to do.

He leaned forward, his body menacing, one hand bunched into a fist. 'You'll have to fight me for custody of Mitch.'

'I won't, actually. I've already seen a lawyer about that. Our son is considered old enough to choose for himself, so the courts will let him do just that.'

'My lawyers will find a way round it.'

'I'm sure they'll try. I know you'll use any dirty trick you can think up.' Suddenly Des sickened her. She stood up so quickly his outstretched hand missed her. 'But Mitch is *my* son, too, and *I* want

8

him because I love him. You just want a son and heir to carry on your name—you've never been interested in your daughters, either from your first marriage or by your mistress—and you only want custody of Mitch to score off me. He'll be as lonely as I've been if he continues to live here with you.'

Her feet made no noise on the thick grey carpet and when she opened the door, the eavesdropper fell through it and landed at her feet.

She stared down at her son. 'Well, Mitch, I see there's no need to tell you what's happening. You'll be able to make a well-informed choice about your future.' She watched coolly as he stood up, seventeen years old, red haired, as his father had been once, six foot tall but thin and poorly co-ordinated, not yet used to his new height—which came from her side of the family, not Des's.

Mitch looked down at her from his two inches of extra height, something they often joked about. 'I'll go and stay with Gran till you two have sorted things out. I don't want to play piggy in the middle.'

From behind them Des, the smile back in place, said calmly, 'I'll drive you over there, son.'

Mitch backed away, shaking his head. 'No, thanks. I'll phone Gran and she'll come and get me.' He turned and raced up the imposing curve of the staircase as if he couldn't bear to stay with them a minute longer, banging into one of the paintings on the way and leaving it rocking to and fro on its gilt chain.

Des turned to his wife, fury twisting his face again. 'You'll be sorry, you stupid bitch! I'll make very sure of that. You're really going to miss the luxury of all this.' He gestured widely with one

9

hand at the echoing hall that reached up three storeys in the centre of the house, all polished marble floor tiles and gleaming white columns.

Judith followed his gaze and smiled. He was proud of this house, but it was an architect's kitsch fantasy designed to suit the whim of a rich man who had no taste. Des had simply indulged himself in whatever displayed his wealth most ostentatiously and mocked his wife's pleas to tone things down. 'I've never really liked this house. You're welcome to it.'

'You'll not set foot across the threshold again if you leave, mind.'

'Why would I want to? Most of my things are packed and gone already.' She realized suddenly she wouldn't have done that if she'd felt they really had a chance of healing things between them. But it had been harder than she'd expected to tell him. 'I'm not sorry I married you because we had some good years and you gave me Mitch. But I've stayed with you far too long.' Hoping, always hoping . . . that things would improve . . . that one day Des would stop lusting after money and decide he'd made enough of it . . . that they could start enjoying life *together*. He'd promised that often enough.

'You didn't mind me supporting you while you fiddled around with your painting, though, did you? You didn't mind me buying you the best of equipment or paying for those expensive private art lessons.'

'I *earned* them by acting as your hostess at those damned boring functions you're always putting on to impress rich investors. And anyway, I needed something to occupy my time while you were out with your tarts.'

She paused halfway across the hall to say, 'Oh, and by the way, I've drawn all the money out of our joint account.'

'Peanuts!' he scoffed.

'More than enough for my needs for quite some time. If you remember, I have my aunt's house in Lancashire. I'll go and live there for a while.' Her aunt May had died the previous year, dropping dead suddenly of an aneurism, the way she'd have wanted to go. Des hadn't even bothered to attend the funeral, but Judith had wanted to farewell her only aunt.

'You're welcome to that hovel.'

It wasn't a hovel. It was quite a large house, by normal standards if not by Des's inflated ideas of what a *des res* should be like. Judith had made many happy visits to the village of Blackfold and when she went round the house after the funeral she'd felt an indefinable sense of welcome. So she'd decided to keep it and rent it out.

She began to climb the stairs slowly and wearily, not even looking back at him as she added, 'And even before the lawyers start dividing things up, don't forget that one of your smaller companies is completely in my name. I think I'll be quite comfortable with the income from that, don't you? I may even decide to get involved in managing it.'

'You'll sign that over to me before you leave,' he roared. 'You've no right to it now.'

She'd known that would upset him. Very possessive about his holdings, Des was. He'd only assigned it to her for tax avoidance purposes, and she wasn't really sure whether it was hers. 'I mean to have a share of your worldly wealth, Des,

11

because I've earned it.'

Footsteps came pounding up the stairs behind her and she turned in shock. When he shook her hard, she fought back, kicking him in the shins. Yelling in pain at that, he thumped her and she felt herself start to fall, slowly, so slowly she thought she had time to grab the burnished brass handrail. But she missed it and cried out in fear as empty space whirled round her. She seemed to tumble and bounce for a very long time before darkness engulfed her.

When she came to, Mitch was crouched over her protectively and Des was sitting part-way up the stairs with his head in his hands.

Her son clutched her hand. 'Don't try to move, Mum. The ambulance is on its way. I think you've hurt your knee. It's badly swollen.'

She moved her head to look and couldn't hold back a whimper of pain at even this small movement.

Des raised his head. 'Hell, I'm sorry, Judith, truly sorry. I didn't mean to—'

She closed her eyes. Didn't speak. Didn't want to see him or speak to him ever again. Just held her son's hand and waited to be carried out of her husband's life on a stretcher.

Cheshire. A stark January day. An icy wind savages the broomstick trees. Flurries of chill drops make a vain assault on the double glazing.

Oblivious to the weather, Maeve Corrigan sat bolt upright in her favourite armchair and made her announcement to Andy Blauman in measured

12

tones.

Which jerked him out of his relaxed sprawl into instant, shocked attention. 'Ah, Maeve, no!'

'I don't want your pity, just your help, Andy. And in return, I'll—'

'You know you've no need to bribe me to help you—whatever the circumstances.' His gaze was reproachful.

While the wind whistled in shrill encouragement outside, she speared him with one of her famous looks, keeping him and his pity at bay. 'I have *always* paid my way and I intend to continue doing so until the day they carry me out of here feet first.' Which was, unfortunately, going to be sooner than she'd expected.

But when he rushed across to fold her in his arms, for a moment—just one moment of weakness—she couldn't bear to push him away, and sagged against the warmth of his young body, stroking his curly hair.

Like a teddy bear he was, this large American of Irish-Jewish descent who had come to Ireland as a young man to find his mother's family, had followed the trail of his distant relatives to Maeve in Lancashire and had stayed there for over ten years. He had a softness to him that he tried in vain to hide and when he'd first come to work for her, she'd had to teach him how to be firm with the workers. If he hadn't learned, she wouldn't have kept him on, but he picked things up quickly, did Andy. Now, well, she didn't know what she would do without him, needed him for the next two years to implement the provisions of her will and manage her legacy to her family. And as she couldn't be here, she intended to bind him to

13

herself and her heirs legally.

As she felt tears welling in her eyes she shoved him away, concentrating on the anger that had been simmering within her ever since her last trip to the oncologist. 'Get away with you!' She blinked furiously, refusing to weep in front of him or anyone. 'Sit down again, will you, and listen to what I want you to do.'

Five minutes later he was scowling. 'Maeve Corrigan, that's outrageous!'

She beamed at him, restored to good humour by her own cunning. 'Yes. It is, rather. So you'll do it for me, then, Andy?'

He was sulky now. 'What choice do I have? As if I'd desert you at a time like this!'

She smiled at that admission. She didn't intend to give him or anyone else a choice and would conduct this business of dying in her own way, as she had done everything else in her life since she had turned twenty-one. Right from her childhood she had found it deeply satisfying to make people dance to her tune. Well, why not? She always knew exactly what she wanted and the best way to get it, while other folk rarely did.

Except that she hadn't been able to bear children. That had been her one failure in life, the main thing she regretted now. But nature had denied her this privilege.

Her two brothers had children, though, five of them. And they would be her heirs. But the main Corrigan legacy, her money, would go to only one, whoever seemed the most capable of holding it together.

Two

Australia. January. A month of searing heat and bushfires. Seven o'clock in the morning and sunshine is already poking hot fingers through windows, making pampered, foreign flowers in gardens shrivel and die.

And yet Kate Corrigan woke up feeling shivery. As she got out of bed, the room wavered around her and she had to clutch the chest of drawers or she'd have fallen over. Her legs felt wobbly, her head throbbed with every movement she made, while her face—she grimaced at it in the mirror—was sickly white, in shocking contrast to the flaring red of her hair.

She looked like a Modigliani woman today, attenuated, mournful, not quite real. Felt as two-dimensional as one of his paintings, too.

Damn! She must have caught the flu that was going round at work.

In the kitchen, her partner Joe was eating his usual greasy platter of eggs and bacon. Summer or winter, he always started the day with a fry-up, the mere smell of which sickened her, for she was definitely not a morning person.

'Hey, you're late today,' he teased, not even glancing up. 'The kettle's just boiled. Get yourself an injection of good old English Breakfast tea. You'll feel better then.'

His voice seemed to echo round the kitchen of the flat they shared. It boomed inside her head, too, and she winced as she sagged against the

15

doorpost. Someone seemed to have sandpapered her throat during the night, so her words came out huskily. 'Joe, I think I've got the flu.'

He stopped eating to turn and stare at her. '*You?* You never catch anything!'

'I had a bad dose of flu eighteen months ago, just before I met you. It lasted for weeks. I couldn't seem to shake it.'

'You never told me.'

'Why should I? It was over and done with by then.' She massaged her temples with her fingertips, but that didn't prevent the bongo drums from thumping away inside her skull. 'Would you get me a cup of tea, please?'

Her asking a favour in such a hesitant voice was enough to make him put down his knife and fork and come over to tilt her chin up with one hand while studying her face. 'You look dreadful, woman. No wonder you went to bed early last night. Want me to make an appointment at the doctor's for you?'

She shrugged his hand off. 'Why bother? Everyone knows how to treat flu. Go to bed, dose yourself with aspirin and rest. If I take a couple of days off, I can—'

He turned her in the direction of the bedroom and pushed her gently along the corridor. 'Get back to bed this minute. You're as white as my shirt and you look heavy-eyed. It's a bad flu, this one. My secretary was off work for two weeks and only came back yesterday. She still felt rotten, though, and went home early, so I'll be surprised if she turns up again today.'

Kate pushed him away then had to lean against the wall to steady herself. 'Well, I can't afford more

16

than a couple of days off. Hell, I can't even afford those, really. I've a workshop to run on Friday for this new mid-management training programme.'

He said nothing, just put the kettle on. Kate Corrigan was fun, attractive and passionate. She had a fine brain and a fine body, too, slender, but soft and welcoming when you made love. But she was also the most stubborn woman he'd met in his whole life. If she was dying and decided to go into work first, she'd hire two men with a stretcher and do it.

He took her a mug of tea and a couple of paracetamols. 'Want me to bring you some toast as well?'

She covered her eyes with her forearm and shuddered. 'No thanks. I'll just—take these tablets and have a nap. Could you draw the curtains again, please?'

'Want me to ring work for you?' he called from a million miles above her head. 'Kate?'

She peered at him from the shadow of her arm. 'Of course I don't! I can do my own bloody telephoning. This is only a touch of flu, for heaven's sake!'

When she woke, Kate felt totally disoriented and it was a few minutes before she realized it was after ten o'clock and she'd not yet contacted work. Oh hell, and she'd missed her first meeting, too! She rolled over and reached for the phone.

Her head swam the minute she lifted it from the pillow and she dialled the number with great difficulty, because the keypad seemed to be jiggling about in front of her. 'I've got flu,' she croaked to the receptionist. 'Can you tell Peter I won't be in today, probably not tomorrow, either?'

'Yeah, sure. Do you have any appointments that need cancelling?'

Kate tried to think and couldn't. Her head was full of grey concrete, far too heavy to hold upright. 'Will you look in my desk diary, please? I can't seem to think straight.'

'You sound really bad. Have you seen the doctor?'

'No.'

'Well, you'd better—'

'Bye.' Kate put down the phone. She couldn't even raise the energy to argue. Which was not like her.

Next time she woke it was two o'clock and she was bursting to go to the bathroom. She sat up and immediately fell sideways on the pillows as the room whirled round her. Standing up was an act of will and she lurched from one piece of furniture to the other like a drunkard.

It was hot so she switched on the air conditioner on the way back to bed, sighing in relief as cool air began to waft around her.

When she woke again, Joe had just arrived home. Why in heaven's name did he always have to bang the front door shut so loudly?

He came to stand in the doorway of her bedroom. 'Good thing I came home early. You look bloody awful, Kate!'

'I feel bloody awful.'

'I'd better sleep in the spare bedroom tonight. Did you go to the doctor's?'

'No. I slept most of the day.'

'I'll make an appointment for you right away, then.'

Her protests fell on empty air. He made the

appointment, overrode her protests then had to support her out to the car, she was so groggy.

'A fortnight off work, at least,' the doctor said. 'Remember what happened to you last year when you didn't take care of yourself?'

We'll see about that, Kate decided on the way home. A week off work was plenty long enough. She wasn't an old woman, but a fit twenty-eight-year-old. This time, unlike last year, she'd take plenty of vitamins, really cosset herself for a few days. Sometimes you had to give in to these things. But only for a short time. It didn't do to wallow in illness. What did doctors know, anyway? She'd seen a programme on television last week which said that medicine was an art, not a science. She agreed absolutely.

*   *   *

After Judith came out of hospital, where she'd needed an operation on her knee, she moved into a luxury hotel at her husband's expense—an offer conveyed to her by his lawyer with extreme care to include no admission of Des's liability for her 'accident'. Her mother had offered to have her, but that would have involved stairs and anyway, why shouldn't Des pay for what he'd done?

She'd have to do several weeks of physiotherapy to get the knee right, which would mean staying here in London instead of settling into her aunt's old home in Lancashire.

Her son came to take afternoon tea with her after school on her first day at the hotel.

They'd avoided talking of it until now but she had to start making long-term plans. 'What have

19

you decided to do, Mitch?'

'What have *you* decided, Mum?'

'As I said the other night, I'm going to live in my aunt's old house in Lancashire—for a while, anyway. Do you fancy coming with me? You know I'd love to have you.'

As he avoided her eyes and began to fiddle with the crumbs on his plate she knew she'd guessed right.

'I can't, Mum. I've got exams coming up in a few months. The big ones. I want to do well, so I can't risk changing schools.' Suddenly he looked younger, unsure of himself. 'There's no chance of you and Dad—you know, getting back together? He's really sorry for what he did.'

'I'm sure he is. It's costing him a packet as well as putting him in a bad position for negotiating a divorce settlement. And no, there's no chance whatsoever, even if he hadn't thumped me.'

'He hasn't hit you before, has he?'

She could sense the desperate anxiety behind his words. 'No, Mitch, he hasn't. I don't think he really meant to hit me this time, either, but he seems to have been getting a bit short-tempered recently.'

He sighed in relief and closed his eyes for a moment, then opened them and asked, 'What did he do—to make you leave him? I—um—didn't hear that bit and he won't tell me.'

'The last straw was tricking his sister into selling her business to him.'

'Oh.' Long pause, then, 'What was the first straw?'

Trust Mitch to realize there was more to it. She hesitated, but decided her son was old enough to understand. 'He's been unfaithful to me—several times—almost from when we first married.' And how humiliating was that? 'You have another half-sister besides Liz's daughters. This one is twelve now.'

'Oh.'

Judith tried to make a joke of it. 'This needn't affect *your* relationship with your father. He's not been unfaithful to you, after all.'

Mitch gazed at her with a face so full of untarnished idealism that she could have wept for what life would inevitably do to him.

'When I take over the business, Mum,' he said in the tone of one swearing a solemn oath, 'I won't do anything unethical, I promise you.'

'I didn't realize you were planning to take over the business.'

'One day, yes. I like organizing things. Dad doesn't and he leaves too much of the important stuff to other people. I can do better than that, or I will be able to when I've got my MBA and gained some experience. I intend to go to Harvard for the postgraduate stuff. They have a mission to educate leaders who will make a difference in the world.'

'Sounds good. You'll have to work hard to get in.'

'I like studying.'

More silence then he finally answered her question. 'If it's any consolation, I don't plan to live with Dad. I'll stay with Gran for the next few months, until the exams are over and then, once I get to university, I'll live in. She says it's all right with her. Will Dad agree, do you think?'

'As long as I'm not getting you, I doubt he'll care.' Besides, Des got on really well with her mother.

'I'll come and visit you in the holidays, though.'

What he said next was not what she expected.

'It must be great to have parents who love one another. I'm really lucky that I've got Gran to turn to.'

Judith had to force the words out because her throat was thick with tears. 'I'm going to miss you a lot, Mitch.'

'I know. But you've got your painting. You're good at it.'

'Not good enough to make my living by it. I've known that for a while. I've tried hard and I'm competent technically, but my teachers haven't hidden the fact that there's something missing, that I'll never make a top drawer artist. So I'll have to find something else to do with my time.' She had to wipe away a tear with her fingertip.

He reached out and patted her arm awkwardly, for he was at an age where casual touching and kissing embarrassed him. 'Sorry, I didn't realize. I don't know much about art. I like some of your paintings very much, though. Can I have that one of sunset over the river to hang in my bedroom at Gran's?'

She nodded. It was her favourite, too. She'd done it a couple of years ago and her teacher had praised her so unstintingly she'd rushed home to show it to Des and tell him. After that, however, her teacher had never been quite as enthusiastic about what she produced, so she'd come to realize that the painting was the nearest she'd got to being really good.

Another pause then he added, 'We can email each other every day. You really will have to learn more about computers now.'

'All right. It's a deal. You can teach me before you leave.'

He began fiddling with his watch. 'I don't think it'll break your heart me living with Gran. I've been reading a few books about relationships, trying to understand this mess. You never give yourself fully to anyone, Mum.'

She stared back, astounded. He was too perceptive by far, this son of hers. Were all modern children this aware, or had she and Des done it to him? 'I do care about *you,* you know, Mitch,' she said, choosing her words carefully. 'Very much indeed, more than I care about anyone else.' She watched a thoughtful expression settle on his face, and refrained from adding that Des wasn't the sort of person to whom you revealed everything. She'd always known that and acted accordingly. But she hadn't realized she'd been guarded with Mitch as well.

'You care about me in your own way, on your own terms,' he went on. 'Not enough to let me spend much time with my sisters or have them round at our house.'

Not that old complaint again! 'Half-sisters, actually.' And why should she encourage it? Whenever he visited them, he came back dissatisfied, angry about not seeing them more often, frequently taking that anger out on her, since his father was rarely around. Des's first wife didn't really want Mitch visiting them, either, and was quite rude about it on the phone sometimes, but Liz hadn't stopped him going there.

It was strange how well he got on with them, his older half-sisters, how the three of them schemed to meet and spend time together. When Lacey got married in a couple of months it'd be even easier for them to meet, because she'd have her own home. Mitch would be going to the wedding with his father now, because Judith was no longer in the picture for such family occasions. She sighed. She'd never had Liz's touch for bringing children up, showering them with open affection, crawling around the floor with them when they were little, sitting for hours with them on her knees, from all she'd heard.

But though Mitch was right, it was partly Des's fault. He'd been very demanding of her time when they were first married and hadn't paid much attention to their son. He said they had a nanny for that. She should have gone against Des's wishes and taken a bigger part in the daily tasks of raising Mitch, she saw that now.

It was too late to remedy matters. Too late to remedy a lot of things.

Judith sat and chatted with Mitch until it was time for him to go back to his grandmother's for the evening meal, enjoying his company, agreeing to start computer lessons soon.

It wasn't until later, after the staff had cleared away her half-eaten room-service meal and wished her a good night's sleep, that she let herself weep about moving north, away from her son and mother. There was no one here to see her weeping, after all.

But she couldn't, just couldn't stay near Des or he'd never leave her alone. He hated to lose control of anything.

Tomorrow she would get on with building herself a new life, go down to eat in the hotel restaurant, call her friends, start arranging for the move. She wasn't sure exactly what she'd do with herself in Lancashire, wasn't sure what she'd be like at living alone, but even if she didn't stay there, it'd give her a breathing space to get her head together again—and to find something to do with the rest of her life.

Three

Central London. Tourists, ancient monuments, museums. Chill winds, moist air threatening rain. Buildings, sky, pavements, roads—all toned perfectly in shades of grey.

Cal Richmond strode through the streets, avoiding people by instinct as worry etched away at his thoughts, worry about his twelve-year-old daughter, Lily. His ex was up to something, he knew it as surely as he knew his own name. Kerry was beautiful, capable and not to be trusted an inch where her own interests were concerned.

Why this summons to her lawyer's? What the hell else could she want of him? Why couldn't she have told him what was wrong when he'd picked Lily up for his fortnightly access visit the previous weekend? He paid maintenance promptly and willingly, took his daughter out whenever he was allowed, had her to stay with him for extra weekends whenever Kerry wanted to get away with her latest boyfriend. What more could a man who loved his child do?

Have her with him all the time.

The old longing crept unbidden into his mind, as it so often did. He knew Kerry was an efficient mother who cared properly for all Lily's physical needs, but she wasn't a demonstrative person. He'd rarely seen her cuddle Kerry since their daughter grew out of being a toddler and had been surprised when she'd insisted on custody. That was the only thing they'd quarrelled about, but mothers seemed to have an advantage in the legal system when it came to bringing up little girls.

The waiting area was overheated and he loosened his overcoat, unwinding the long, multi-coloured scarf Lily had knitted for him. When the receptionist called his name, he stood up thankfully. One way or the other, this would soon be settled and then they could get on with life until Kerry's next crisis.

In the office, his ex-wife was sitting primly at one side of the lawyer's desk, dressed in the black outfit she used to impress the authorities on solemn occasions, more conservative than her usual outfits though as flattering as all her other clothes. She was wearing well, didn't look thirty-nine. In fact, in the six years they'd been divorced she seemed to have thrived. Well, it had been plain almost from the start that they were a mismatch, but they were expecting a child and had agreed to try to make it work. And he'd been useful to her, looking after Lily so that she could go out to work as a publicity officer, a job she loved.

He looked at her outfit again. It shouted that it was an expensive designer creation. Not for the first time he wondered where she was getting her money from. Surely her job didn't pay for such exquisite clothes?

He nodded to her but she stared back at him stonily, as if he were a stranger.

'Please sit down, Mr Richmond.' The lawyer hesitated, took a deep breath then said, 'It's bad news, I'm afraid.'

'Oh?'

'Your wife has had DNA testing done on Lily, which proves conclusively that the child is not

27

your daughter. Ms Foster is therefore . . . Mr Richmond! Please sit down.'

Cal stared at Kerry in horror. 'I don't believe you! Of course Lily's mine.'

'She doesn't even look like you, with that red hair!' Kerry snapped. 'I'd have thought you'd be glad. It means you won't need to pay any more maintenance.'

'I've never resented paying maintenance for Lily and well you know it. How the hell did you get a sample from me?'

'You cut your finger when you were fixing that shelf in Lily's room.' Kerry gave him one of her tight, smug smiles.

He had often wanted to shake her and tell her to stop playing games, but never had the desire burned as fiercely as it did today.

The lawyer intervened. 'Please sit down, Mr Richmond. That's better. Now, let's discuss this in a civilized manner.'

Cal ignored the man's bleating and addressed his wife. 'You're trying to take Lily away from me. Well, I won't have it. She's mine in every way that matters and I love her.' He watched Kerry's lip curl in that sneer she did so well. 'Anyway, I don't believe you.'

'She's not yours. I've always suspected it, so in the end I had the tests done.'

'I don't care two hoots about your tests. Whatever they prove, *if* they prove anything, she's my daughter because I've helped bring her up.'

'She's *not* yours. I'm marrying again and Wayne's adopting her then we're all moving to the States. I'll pay you back the maintenance, if you like, and I apologize for deceiving you. I wasn't sure . . . I'd hoped . . .' She gave her lawyer a help-me look.

Comprehension roared through Cal. She wanted to move away from England and knew he'd never let her take Lily away from him. This was a trick, it must be. 'I insist on new tests being done, tests where I can see the provenance of the samples. I won't believe anything until I see that.' *It couldn't be true. Dear God, it just couldn't!*

She gave an exaggerated sigh and looked at the lawyer.

'Since Mr Richmond didn't willingly provide a sample, it's a reasonable request, Ms Foster. The courts will also need to be sure of the provenance of the samples.'

Scowling, she turned back to Cal. 'Very well. But it won't make any difference. I'm telling you the truth. You're *not* Lily's father. I've always known it. Why do you think I rushed you into marriage?'

He felt sick to the stomach because her words had a ring of cold truth, but he wasn't giving in so easily. 'I *am* her father, whether biologically or not. And if you try to stop me seeing her this weekend, I'll go straight to the children's court for access.'

She glanced at her lawyer again.

'Unless you fear he'd harm the child, it's a reasonable request, Ms Foster.'

'Oh, very well. But you're not to upset her.'

'Have you told Lily?' Cal asked.

'Yes.'

'How did she take it?'

'She got a bit upset. But children get over these things very quickly.'

Cal bit back hot words of protest. Lily wouldn't get over him quickly, he was sure, any more than he'd get over her. He'd loved her from the minute she was born—and she loved him too, far more than she loved the mother who could hardly be bothered to listen to her these days and who had little idea of their gifted child's hopes and aspirations. Then he remembered something else. Lily had been born a month early. He felt sick to the core. It couldn't be true, could it?

The lawyer stood up. 'I'll be in touch about the tests, Mr Richmond.'

Cal walked outside, his soul in torment. If they took Lily away from him, he didn't know what he'd do. He could see why the legal system drove men to desperate measures, but he'd never hurt his child, or anyone else for that matter.

He had to see Lily, talk to her, make her understand that whatever the outcome of the tests he would still consider himself her father in every way that mattered.

*   *   *

Cal couldn't pick Lily up until Saturday, his usual visiting day, because Kerry refused point-blank to give him access sooner, or even allow him to speak to their daughter on the phone. But she forgot about email and he was able to contact Lily as soon as he got home, telling her he loved her whatever the damned tests showed.

Her reply was unlike her usual chatty emails. Short. Guarded.

I can't think straight about this, Dad.
Can we just go back to your place on Saturday and talk?

Lily

He had tears in his eyes as he read this and typed his agreement to do whatever she wanted.

*   *   *

When Saturday came Cal arrived half an hour before his usual time. Lily ran out immediately without looking back or waving farewell to her mother, and flung herself into his car. Kerry came to stand on the doorstep, arms folded. He knew that look. She wasn't happy about this visit, was plotting something.

He forgot about her as he looked at his daughter, her swollen eyes, her unkempt hair, her down-curving lips. 'I love you,' he said softly. 'Whatever anyone says or does, I love you Lily. And I *am* your father.'

'She says you're not.'

He drew round the corner, drew over to the kerb and stopped the car, then pulled her to him in a cracking hug. 'Do I feel any different? You don't.'

She blinked at him, tears welling in her eyes, then buried her face in his shoulder.

After a moment or two he said, 'How about I drive us home and we don't talk till we get there? I'm upset too, you know, and I don't want to cause an accident. This is the worst thing that's ever happened to me in my whole life.'

'Me, too.'

In the house they went into the kitchen and he made hot chocolate, her favourite comfort drink. They carried the cups into the sitting room and sat close together on the sofa.

31

'Did you know you weren't my—my biological father?' she asked.

'No. I hadn't the faintest idea.'

'She said you always suspected something, that you'd asked her before and she'd been too afraid of you to admit it.'

Disgust rolled through him at Kerry's cunning, making him feel physically sick. 'That's not true! I never suspected a thing. And she was never, ever afraid of me. I'm a geek, not a macho man. If anything, I was always too soft with her.'

'She's going to try to stop us meeting after today. I overheard her talking to Wayne. We're supposed to go and live with him in Texas, but I won't do it, whatever she says. I want to be near you and—' she hesitated then added quietly—'I'm English and I'm staying English.'

When her hand crept into his, Cal held it tightly. 'I don't know what to think, what to advise, but you have to remember that she's going to put her own spin on the facts whenever she says anything about me. Everyone does.'

Lily rolled her eyes. 'It's more than that, Dad, and you know it. Mum's an expert at twisting the truth. You should hear what she says to Wayne about you.'

He sighed. He hated to blacken Kerry in her daughter's eyes, but his ex sounded to be working against him already. 'Well, don't believe anything about me until you hear it from my own lips.'

Lily sniffed and took another sip of her chocolate drink. 'She may be able to stop us meeting or talking—and I think she definitely will, because she's taken my mobile phone away from me already—but she can't stop us emailing. If she takes away my computer, there's always an Internet café or I can email from my friends' houses. I've already arranged with Karen that if I pass her a note, she'll email it to you for me. I'll get myself an online email address, so that you can send messages there, not to the home computer.'

He was aghast. 'Is all this necessary?'

She turned a knowing gaze on him, a woman's look not a child's. 'You know it is. This isn't a time to be thinking the best of people, Dad. We have to make plans.'

'How can I do anything till I know the facts? We have to get the results of the new tests. Maybe there's been a mistake.' But the words sounded lame even to his own ears.

'The tests will only slow her down. She's got everything planned, believe me. She always does have.'

'You shouldn't talk about your mother in that tone.' He hesitated. 'Did she—tell you who your biological father was?'

Lily shook her head. 'It's not Wayne. She's only known him for a year or so. When I asked her she said it's none of my business who my father is. Can you believe that? *None of my business!*'

They spent the day at Cal's flat, watching DVDs of movies they'd seen and loved before, but paying little attention to them. Talking. Thinking. Just hanging out together.

'You're too cynical for your age,' he said, giving her a hug. 'And you shouldn't have to face all this.'

She shrugged. 'I've always been old for my age. I wonder what my biological family background is like.'

This new hard edge to her tore at his heart—it

showed a resemblance to her mother, though Lily had a sweetness to her nature that Kerry didn't. But the girl was only twelve, for heaven's sake, she should have nothing worse to worry about than school, what to wear and her friends.

When it came time for her to leave, Lily lost all her assurance and burst into tears, clinging to him, weeping, begging him to let her stay with him.

'Sweetheart, you know I daren't. It'd give your mother more ammunition. We'll do what we said, stay on email, make plans, see if we can persuade her—'

'To do what? Wayne's rich. She's really excited about going to live with him in America. They're talking about marriage, you know.'

'Do *you* get on with him?'

'I don't not get on with him. He gives me presents, chats while he's waiting for her. But he doesn't really see me. He only sees her. His tongue's hanging out all the time he's round our place. It's gross.'

Cal gave her another hug and looked at his watch. 'We really do have to leave now, sweetheart.'

'You'll see a lawyer, find out where you really stand? Promise me. Don't take her word for anything,' Lily said urgently as he drove her back.

'Yes, of course. As soon as we get the results from the tests.'

When they got there, Kerry came to the door. Wayne was standing at the living-room window, watching. She sent Lily inside and glared at Cal. 'She's been crying.'

'She'd been crying before I picked her up as well. She doesn't want to leave me. Kerry, why

34

don't you let me have custody? You know I'll look after her properly.'

'No way. You're *not* her father.'

'I'll fight you all the way, you know that.'

'With what? You have no grounds to challenge me on what I do about Lily.'

She said that so confidently. Could she be right? Surely they wouldn't be so cruel to him?

When he got home he tried to work, then gave in and wept. Men weren't supposed to do that, but he couldn't keep a stiff upper lip about losing Lily.

*   *   *

Kerry's lawyer had a letter hand-delivered the very next day, since Cal worked mainly at home. It set up an appointment for the taking of DNA samples from him and Lily, and stated that owing to the child having been upset the previous day, further access meetings would be suspended pending a decision by the courts.

He gave the DNA sample, watched as they took one from Lily and managed to hug her before Kerry could stop him. Then he waited until the lawyer's clerk, who'd been there as an observer, had left. He was pretty sure the laboratory, part of a well-known chain, wouldn't let the samples be tampered with.

Afterwards he saw a lawyer of his own, who took notes about his 'case' and said he'd better not do anything to rock the boat until the test results came back and they were more certain of exactly where they stood.

But the man did admit that the legal situation wasn't as black and white as Kerry had said, not by any means. Cal tried to take some comfort from that, but it was all so chancy, with so many ifs and buts that he couldn't see his way clearly.

After that the test results were all he could think about. His work suffered. It was hard to design clever web pages when his heart felt torn apart, when he had no weekend visit from Lily to look forward to, when the ground felt to have shifted beneath his feet and further earthquakes still threatened.

*   *   *

It was two months before Judith's knee was well enough for her to move to Lancashire. During that time she stayed at the hotel, reading a lot, trying to get used to the new laptop computer she'd bought, seeing as much of Mitch as she could. While she relished the idea of what her stay was costing Des, she was increasingly frustrated by her physical limitations and wished desperately that she was in her own home.

She didn't press charges of assault against Des but made sure her lawyer had evidence that it had happened—just in case.

In case of what? She wasn't sure. Des had never thumped her before. It seemed so unlike him, though during the past year or so his temper had been more chancy than usual. Well, he wouldn't get the opportunity to thump her again, she would make sure of that.

Various friends visited her at the hotel, curious as to why she wasn't recuperating at home. 'Des and I have split up,' she told them, always adding, 'but I don't intend to discuss the reasons for that with anyone.'

She hated the thought of her private pain being paraded for everyone to pick at, so usually turned the conversation towards the village she was moving to in Lancashire and her intention of spending more time on her painting. 'Once I'm settled in, you must come and visit,' she told one or two particular friends—but only those whose husbands were not dependent on doing business with Des. She didn't want to expose anyone else to his business spite.

Four

March. Snow one day, immaculately white. A week later, golden sunshine and the first daffodils dance lightly across the land, challenging winter's greyness.

Eventually the time came for Judith to arrange her move. She informed Des's lawyer of the coming move, saying she hadn't fixed on an exact date yet.

Des turned up at the hotel the very next day. She was so stunned to see him when she opened the door that he'd walked in before she could protest.

She remained where she was, didn't even try to close the door. 'Go away.'

'I want to talk.'

'Well, I don't.'

When he came towards her, she flinched, couldn't help it, even though she hated herself for doing it.

He took a step backwards, spreading out his hands. 'For Christ's sake, woman, it was an accident. I didn't mean to knock you down the stairs. I've never hit you before, have I? I lost my temper. Can't we even *talk* now?'

'What is there to talk about? I've left you. Period.'

He put one arm round her, slammed the door with his other hand and drew her over towards the couch. 'That's what I want to talk about.'

She was horrified at her own reaction to his touch, for her body was responding to him as it always had. For a moment, she desperately wanted him to touch her, hold her—even persuade her to stay. She hated herself for that, so she pulled away and repeated, 'What's to discuss?'

He pushed her gently down on the couch and sat next to her. 'I'd like to discuss whether it's really necessary for us to split up, Judith. We were a family and we can be again. It's you who's driving this and not only is it not good for Mitch, it's not what I want either. Ah, come back home, darlin'.'

Anger began to bubble up in her. The Irish accent only crept into his voice when he was conning someone, because he'd left Ireland when he was seven to live in Lancashire. But oh, a man had no right to be so attractive at the age of fifty-eight. 'If you'd said this to me last week, I might have listened, Des. I was thinking about returning. So . . .' She let the word hang in the air for a minute, then said bluntly, 'I had another report done on you by my detective friend.' She paused as she saw understanding begin to dawn in his face, then tossed at him, 'You're still seeing her. I won't be part of a *ménage à trois*, not now, not ever! It's over between us, Des. Get used to it.'

Anger darkened his face and all the easy charm vanished.

She got up and moved towards the door. 'I'd like you to leave now, please.'

'Not so fast, you stupid bitch!'

He had such anger burning in his eyes that terror slammed through her and she dived for the bathroom, just managing to slam the door on him and lock it. As he pounded on it and roared at her to come out, she leaned against the wall, shaking from head to toe, shocked at how physically afraid of him she was now. The door shook against her body and she backed away from it. It wouldn't hold him for long. What was she going to do?

Then she caught sight of the wall phone. She'd wondered why they bothered to put them in hotel bathrooms, now she blessed whoever had thought up the idea. With a hand that shook, she picked it up.

'I have an unwanted guest in my room and he's turned violent. I'm locked in the bathroom.' The noise Des was making, banging on the door and shouting, must be audible, surely? 'C-could you please send someone quickly to get him out?'

'I'm *not* leaving till you come out and discuss things properly!' Des roared from outside the door, doing some more thumping. A wooden panel split beneath his fist.

She didn't answer, couldn't, just sat on the toilet seat and covered her face with her hands. She couldn't believe they'd come to this, that she was terrified of Des. But she was. He'd changed in so many ways lately. Judith hadn't even noticed what was happening at first, putting his irritability down to his being so busy. It had begun to sink in eventually, however, that this was what he had become—not only unfaithful, but domineering and sharp-tempered.

It seemed a long time till someone knocked on the door of the suite. She heard Des shout, 'Sod off!' then the outer door open. This was followed by what sounded like a scuffle and the words, 'But I'm her husband, dammit! I'm paying for this room, so I have every right to be here.'

When someone knocked on the bathroom door and said, 'Ms Horrocks?' Judith's maiden name, which she was using now, she couldn't hold back a

40

sob of relief. She opened it to see Des standing there, still radiating anger, with two burly men standing between him and her.

'Do you wish this gentleman to leave, madam?' one of them asked.

'Yes. Yes, I do, please. And so I told him.'

Des breathed in deeply 'Look, this is just a lovers' quarrel. I'm sorry if we disturbed the peace. It won't happen again.'

She said quickly to the concierge, 'I don't want him to stay. He may be my husband, but we're separated and he won't leave me alone. I'm going to have to take out a restraining order against him.'

The two men moved towards Des, who threw up his hands and asked the ceiling, 'Does anyone understand women? She opened the door to me and invited me in, you know. I can't figure what's got into her lately.' His Irish accent was back.

'It's easy enough to understand that a woman whose knee you injured recently in a fit of anger doesn't want to risk something similar happening.'

There was an audible intake of breath from the uniformed concierge, and the other man glanced quickly from one guest to the other.

The smile vanished from Des's face. 'You'll be sorry for that, you stupid bitch.' He turned on his heel and left. One man followed him.

Judith collapsed on the nearest couch, tears running down her cheeks.

'Can I get you something, madam?' the concierge asked.

'No, thank you, but I'm grateful for your help. I'll be very careful who I open the door to from now on, I promise you.'

41

That evening Judith's mother rang. 'All right if Mitch and I come to see you tonight?'

'Yes. I'd love that.'

'Is something wrong?'

Judith sniffed back a tear. 'Des came here today. He—was pretty nasty.'

There was a long silence.

'Mum? Are you still there?' She was weeping, couldn't hide it, was still so upset by what had happened.

'It's his age, probably. I was reading an article about it only last week, how their hormones change and it makes some men grumpy. They can fix it *if* the man will seek help.'

'I can't see Des admitting he needs help. You know how he hates doctors and hospitals.'

'No, I can't either. Well, shall I see you about half past seven?'

'Yes.'

That evening one of the concierges escorted her visitors upstairs himself.

Mitch waited for the door to close then asked, 'What happened with Dad this time?'

'Do you want to sit down before we discuss it?'

Shrugging, he sprawled on the bed. 'Well?'

'How do you know anything happened?'

'Because he came to Gran's in a fury and it seemed to be because of you. He said I shouldn't come to see you unless I wanted to be treated like a criminal, but wouldn't explain what he meant by that. What happened today, Mum?'

'Oh, he came here ranting and raving and

wouldn't leave. He wants me to go back to him, but I won't because he's still seeing the other woman. He started shouting and I got a bit nervous, so I locked myself in the bathroom and called for help.'

They both looked automatically at the bathroom door, one panel of which had a long split down it.

Hilary gasped and covered her mouth with one hand for a moment or two, then whispered, 'Dear God! What's got into the man?'

Mitch came and put his arm round his mother, something he didn't often do.

Judith leaned against him for a moment. 'I don't want you involved in our quarrels, love.'

'I'm part of it all, whether you want it or not.' Mitch hesitated, then added, 'Gran says I should keep out of it, only Dad keeps saying things to me about you.'

She could feel herself stiffening. Des playing dirty already! 'Well, I'm not going to start blackening his name to you. I shall keep to the facts, and only those you need to know.'

After another thoughtful pause, Mitch said, 'I ignore most of what he says about you, but I will ask you if there's something I really want to know your side of. You'd better get on the Net as soon as you settle in, then we can email one another. How's it going?' He nodded towards the laptop.

'I'm getting pretty good at it. I'm starting to enjoy surfing the Net, actually. Thank goodness this hotel's connected in all rooms.'

'Good. It's such an easy way to stay in touch. There's always time for a quick email, even if it's only a one-liner. I'm a bit busy with my studies just now but *he* doesn't seem to understand that.'

'No. He's not very understanding about other

43

people's needs.'

'Will you be all right in Lancashire?'

'What do you mean?'

'Well, living on your own. I think you should get someone to share your house, Mum. It'd be much safer. Preferably a strong young guy.'

'My aunt's house is in the country, in a village not an urban ghetto.'

'Still . . . better to be safe than sorry.'

When they'd gone she couldn't get Mitch's remarks out of her mind. Surely Des's dislike of anyone besting him wouldn't make him reach out so far to get back at her?

*   *   *

The private investigator looked at Maeve, his face expressionless. 'You want me to send someone all the way to Australia, Miss Corrigan?'

'Yes. Someone very skilled and circumspect. I have a niece and nephew there whom I've never met. I want to know what they're like, but I don't want them to know I'm having them investigated.'

When he pursed his lips, she said nothing more, waiting for him to consider what she'd asked him to do. She'd employed Mark Felton several times, then had helped him set up his own business. He was intelligent and tactful, able to do more than just find out facts.

'That'll cost a lot of money, Miss Corrigan.'

She brushed that aside with a wave of her hand. 'You'll do it?'

'Yes. It may take me a few days to find someone suitable, though.'

'You couldn't go yourself?'

He stared at her, giving nothing away, then a slow smile warmed his face. 'I'm due a holiday. Why not?'

'There are a few other things I want looking into here in England as well. For that I require someone very capable to take your place.'

'All my employees are capable. I'll put James at your disposal.' Mark had been thinking of offering his deputy a partnership, taking life a little more easily now his business was thriving. He was getting the urge to find a life partner, settle down, but he didn't seem to meet many single women and he wasn't into clubs and pubs.

Australia, end of a long, hot summer. Sydney is full of dust, fumes and heat. Sweaty, sleepless nights send tired people into streets and offices. The sky is cloudless. No prospect of rain.

It was cooler that day, after a five-day hot spell, and people were smiling as they walked along the street. Kate stared at them and wished she could feel the same *joie de vivre,* but she was on her way to the doctor's and all she could focus on was the results of the latest tests. Surely they'd show *something* this time, something that could be treated, because she still felt terrible?

The waiting room was full and she slumped down in the nearest chair without even the energy to pick up a magazine from the pile on the table, let alone read it.

As soon as she was ushered into the consulting room she asked, 'Well, what do the tests show?'

Dr Smithers consulted her computer. 'That

you've had a virus. But it's nothing specific, like Ross River or glandular fever. There's not much we can do about viruses anyway, I'm afraid.'

Kate swallowed hard. She was determined not to weep in front of the doctor today as she had last time.

'How are you feeling?'

'Pretty lousy. This fluey feeling just won't go away. And my head feels as if it's stuffed with cotton wool.'

Dr Smithers looked at her sympathetically. 'It's been going on for what—nearly two months now? We should start calling it post-viral syndrome, I'm afraid.'

Kate glared at her. 'I don't care what you call it, I just want to get better. There must be *something* you can do!'

'I'm afraid not. The main advice I can give you is to take time off work—have a really long holiday and continue resting.'

'And will that get me better?'

Another hesitation, then, 'I don't know. Sometimes it helps, sometimes it doesn't.'

'I want to see a specialist.'

'What sort of specialist?'

'How the hell do I know what sort? You're the doctor. You tell me what sort deals with post-viral bloody syndrome. I'm running out of money. I can't *afford* to stay off work any longer.'

There was a silence, then Dr Smithers looked at her patient, who had been bad-tempered and uncooperative all through this illness, who had twice tried to go back to work—against her advice—only to collapse and have to be taken home again before the morning ended. She had to make this young woman realize how serious this could become. 'There's a possibility now that you may be suffering from chronic fatigue syndrome and—'

Shock held Kate rigid for a moment, then she clutched her handbag with both hands. 'But that's a crippling disease! No, I can't have that! *I won't!* I'm finding myself another doctor. You don't know what you're talking about.'

She slammed out of the consulting room, storming through the reception area without trying to pay for the consultation. But she had to sit in her car for a few moments before she could drive off because she felt so exhausted she could hardly lift her hands to grip the steering wheel. But she did *not* have chronic fatigue syndrome!

When she got home she went and lay down on her bed because she simply couldn't stay upright a minute longer. But her last thought as she drifted off to sleep was that it wasn't chronic fatigue, couldn't be. She had a friend who'd been ill for two years with that. No, she couldn't, wouldn't have it! It must be something else.

Joe woke her later with a cup of tea and she stared at him in shock. 'What are you doing home at this time of day?'

'I always come home at five thirty.'

She struggled to sit up. 'It can't be that time already.'

' 'Fraid so. What did the doctor say?'

Kate blinked furiously, but the tears wouldn't be held back. She fell against him, sobbing, 'She says it could be chronic fatigue syndrome.'

He went very still.

She looked up to see pity on his face. She didn't

want his pity, she wanted his love, wanted them to go out and have fun at the end of a long day's work, as they had done before.

'I was afraid of that. A cousin of mine went down with it a few years ago, so I've seen what it can do to people. I reckon it's more widespread than the authorities will admit. I'm sorry, Kate. So sorry.'

He held her until she had stopped weeping, then coaxed her into drinking the now lukewarm tea.

'What am I going to do, Joe?' she asked afterwards as she lay on the bed holding his hand. 'I'm not a permanent employee, only on a temporary contract. I've used up most of my savings and I can't even finish this contract.'

'I told you. I can pay the rent and buy you a few groceries till you sort something else out.'

But she hated the thought of being dependent on anyone, even him. And besides, that didn't really solve her problems. Some days she felt as though her skull were dense fog and—even more frightening—couldn't even remember what she'd done the day before. And though she slept for ten hours or more most nights, she still needed a nap or two during the day, because she simply couldn't stay awake.

On bad days it was a major achievement to wash the dishes. Or get dressed. Even on good days she couldn't do all that much.

She would go mad if this continued.

Five

An inner suburb of London. The early morning urgency is over and the sun is shining. Somewhere nearby traffic hums. In this street elderly folk stroll along, mothers push babies and cats sun themselves in sheltered nooks.

Cal picked up the envelope that dropped through his letter box, letting out a long, shuddering breath as he saw where it came from. As he read the results of the new DNA tests, fear sat like lead in his belly. He had hoped . . . but this proved that Lily wasn't his, not biologically anyway. Feeling gutted, he sank down on the nearest chair and stared into a bleak future.

When he went back to his computer there was an email from her, sent from an Internet café.

Mum told me about the tests, but I still love you, Dad. And you *are* my dad, whatever she says, the best dad ever. She's bought me a new mobile phone to cheer me up but I've had to promise faithfully not to ring you on it. As if a new phone makes any difference to how I feel.

We'll find a way to be together. We have to. I'm not going with her and Wayne to the States.

Love ya!
Lily-Pilly

Cal was filled with warmth at the thought of how much Lily still loved him, but he knew how implacable the law could be—and Kerry. He

49

wasn't sure any longer that his lawyer could handle such a ticklish case, but it seemed there were complexities and something called parental responsibility to be decided before they went any further.

He went online and downloaded everything he could find about it. There were web sites which seemed to be run by angry men who'd lost their children. There were lawyers' web sites that tangled him in articles full of legal complexities, ifs and buts. Only they all seemed to deal with biological fathers in marriage break-ups, not cases like his. He tried every combination of words in the search engine, scouring the Net until the small hours of the morning, but found little to help him understand his own options.

He didn't think the law would really allow Kerry to take his daughter to the States, preventing him from seeing the child again, because it seemed children had a say in these matters, especially children over twelve, like Lily. The trouble was, he was torn every which way. He didn't want to make his daughter the subject of a bitter custody battle. And actually, he didn't want to stop Kerry re-marrying. Not if it made her happy.

If only he could believe that going to Texas with Kerry would make the child happy, he might have stood back a little, heart-breaking as that would have been, in return for a guaranteed annual visit in the summer holidays. But he didn't believe it. He knew how Lily felt about it, he'd never seen her so upset, and also how self-centred his ex-wife was. Kerry would be engrossed in her new husband and life.

And why should Wayne care for Lily? It was

Kerry he was interested in.

He emailed back:

I love you too, Lily-Pilly. Untold. I'm going away at the weekend, just for a couple of days to think about things, taking the Hog. I'll email when I get back.

Dad

He sent off the email to her new address and wandered round his flat, unable to settle.

When he was upset, he always went back to his roots and that's what he intended to do now. They'd knocked down the terraced village house where he'd grown up, but the rolling slopes of the moors that separated Lancashire from Yorkshire never changed and he loved them. He'd live there if it weren't for the need to stay near Lily. Several times a year he mounted his Harley-Davidson and simply took off for a refresher break in the north. Only this time he took a bottle of whisky with him.

It wasn't refreshment of the soul he needed, but a wake to mourn the loss of a daughter who might not be flesh of his flesh, but was the child of his heart.

He didn't love Lily any less, of course he didn't, but he had cherished that blood and bone connection between them, been proud to have fathered such an intelligent and affectionate child.

And now he knew he'd fathered no one. He, who had wanted a family and children so desperately, had been glad Kerry was pregnant when they married.

*   *   *

51

The following day Judith rang her former housekeeper to tell her she would be collecting her car that afternoon.

'I think you'd better speak to Mr Corrigan, madam.'

'Why? It's the car I need. I won't have to come inside the house.'

'The car isn't here any more.'

So Judith rang Des's office.

'What car are you talking about?' he asked.

As if he didn't know. '*My* car, the Mercedes you bought me for my birthday.'

He chuckled. 'That's a company car, not your personal possession. It's being used by an employee of the company now. I don't like things to go to waste.'

'You're a bastard, Des Corrigan.'

He was laughing loudly as he put the phone down.

She rang up her lawyer, but he could do nothing to help her get the car back if it really had been a company car.

'Your financial situation will take some time to sort out, I'm afraid, Mrs Corrigan. It's rather complex.'

'How long?'

'Well, your husband is being awkward about quite a few things, so I'm afraid it's going to drag on a bit.'

'I see. Then I'd better buy myself a new car.'

'Yes. Best thing to do. And about the company you thought was in your name . . .'

'Mmm?' She waited, sure there was another nasty surprise in store.

'There is some doubt about your owning it. It seems that it's owned by the family trust. Rather a complicated tax avoidance set-up, perfectly legal, of course, but complicated. So you'll not be receiving any income from that until everything is—'

She finished it for him, '—sorted out.'

When she'd put the phone down, she sat down to do some calculations. She had the money she'd taken from their joint account, but wasn't sure how long it'd last. It had been a good many years since she'd lived frugally. She had her jewellery, of course, but she didn't really want to sell her bits and pieces. Most were antiques that she'd searched for until she found exactly the right thing. Des had never understood that it was the beauty of the pieces that mattered to her, not their antiquity or value.

Damn him! He could well afford to make her an allowance, wouldn't even miss it. But she wasn't going to beg for it.

*   *   *

The next day she received a letter from Des's lawyer informing her that since she had now recovered from her unfortunate accident, they wouldn't be paying for her hotel room as from Thursday morning. That was tomorrow, she thought, looking round. Right then, she'd need to get cracking.

She went out to buy herself a car, a second-hand one. She was lucky enough to find one that suited her, a silver Ford Focus. It seemed very utilitarian after the Mercedes, but it would be economical on petrol, and that was the important thing now.

She paid for two more nights in the hotel rather than move somewhere else. After all, she was on a cheaper, long-term rate. She could have saved money by staying with her mother, but that might make difficulties with Des, who was still popping in to see Hilary, so she didn't even suggest it.

The bed seemed harder that night and her knee was aching because she'd been on her feet a lot. She tossed and turned, worrying about money, about Mitch, about the future.

And creeping in to settle like a fat ugly toad on her shoulder, was a feeling of apprehension about what Des would do next. She was quite sure he wouldn't just let her go in peace, not when she had been the one to end it. He enjoyed paying people back for what he saw as slights, and could be very inventive about how he did it.

In the morning she phoned her mother and asked if Mitch could come to the hotel to say farewell.

'Des just rang me, Judith. He said he doesn't want the boy going near you again on his own. I'm to be with the two of you at all times, so that you don't poison his mind against his father.'

'You won't stop Mitch coming to say goodbye, surely?'

'Certainly not. I'll drive Mitch to the hotel myself, give him half an hour alone with you, then join you both, if that's all right. I want to say goodbye too, darling, even though you're only going up to Lancashire. I fully intend to come and visit you there, by the way. I only have one daughter.'

'Thanks, Mum.'

54

'That's my pleasure. And Judith? If Des withdraws his financial support from me, I'll still have enough to live on, you know.'

'Not in such comfort. And that house you're living in belongs to him.'

'I still own my unit. I didn't take his advice about selling it, but rented it out. So do what's necessary for your future happiness, love.'

'You're the best, Mum.'

Judith went to repair her face, feeling warmed by her mother's support. Hilary had always got on well with Des, and he seemed fond of her, too, but the fact that she was prepared to give up her comfortable home to stick with her daughter meant a lot.

Only—if Hilary did move back to her tiny one-bedroom unit, where would Mitch stay?

What a sad tangle this was!

Later on, the concierge rang her room. 'Ms Horrocks?'

'Yes?' It still felt strange to be called by her maiden name.

'There's a Mr Mitchell Corrigan to see you. All right to send him up?'

'Yes. And thank you for being careful about who comes to my room.'

'Our pleasure, madam.'

She didn't mention her financial problems to her son, but Mitch raised it with her. 'Dad said you tried to pinch the company car.'

'Is that what he calls it now? It was a birthday present to me, if you remember.'

He nodded. 'Of course I remember. It came tied with a big bow. Is he being difficult about money?'

She nodded.

'Tell me.'

'I can't get a penny out of him until things are settled legally about the company I thought I owned. Luckily I've some money saved, but I'll have to be a bit careful and I'm afraid you'll be totally dependent on him financially. I can't help you much till it's all sorted out. But I don't want you to get involved in our quarrels, so don't discuss it with him.'

'I *am* part of this, whether you want it or not. But I appreciate the way you haven't tried to blacken Dad to me.'

It wasn't that she hadn't been tempted! she thought bitterly.

Half an hour later the concierge sent her mother up. Hilary came across to fold Judith in her arms. 'You look tired, love.'

'I didn't sleep very well.'

'We came by taxi, so let's have a bottle of champagne to launch you in your new life. My treat. Mitch is old enough to help us drink it, don't you think?'

So they sat and reminisced, then drank to Judith's future.

When they'd gone she felt bereft, wanted to run after them and drag them back.

Didn't, of course. She was determined to stand on her own feet from now on. But what could she do to earn a living? She wasn't good enough to be an artist, even though she still loved to paint. She was going to be dependent on Des at first, whether she wanted it or not. She'd given up everything to marry him.

How stupid she'd been! She should have finished her studies. Would at least have her teaching qualification now. Only he wouldn't have waited for her, she'd known that.

*   *   *

A week or so after Kate's visit to the doctor the doorbell rang. Joe was out so she went to answer it.

'Why didn't you tell us?' her father said by way of a greeting. 'You look dreadful.'

She held the door open and her parents walked in. If she'd been dressed, she might have tried to brazen it out, but she wasn't. It hadn't seemed worthwhile, when the effort of putting on clothes would only tire her out and send her back to lie on top of the bed. Her hair needed washing, too. She looked a mess and she knew it.

She followed them back inside and sat down beside her mother on the sofa.

Her father began to pace to and fro. 'Joe says you've been ill since February. *Since February!* And not a word to us!'

Her mother took her hand and held it, patting it gently as she had when they were children and upset about something. That brought tears to Kate's eyes. It was tempting to throw herself into her mother's arms and allow herself to be cosseted and comforted, as if she were a child again. Too tempting. She pulled her hand away and forced herself to sit upright. 'I didn't want to—bother you.'

'Well, now we're more than bothered.' Her father slapped one hand against his thigh. 'And you're coming home with us so that your mother can nurse you better.'

'I can't. I have to get back to work and—'

57

'Joe says your contract has expired. You're unemployed. Living off your savings.'

She scowled at the floor. 'He's been saying too much, then.'

Her mother raised one hand, a gesture that had stopped traffic in its time and always stopped her father, who had a bit of a temper. He closed his mouth and let her take over now that he'd vented some of his anger. He liked an easy life, Leo Corrigan did—and had found it.

Her mother turned to her and said, 'The point is, Kate: how can we best help you?'

It wasn't the words, but her loving expression that did it—and the extra pat on the hand. Kate couldn't hold back the tears any longer. 'I don't know what to do, Mum. I can't even think straight. And—and I'm not getting any better.'

'Seems to me you'd better come home for a while, then, love. Have you seen a doctor?'

'Yes, but she said there was nothing she could do, so I was going to find another one.'

'We'll take you to old Dr Ramsay. If he can't help you, no one can.'

Her mother's Lancashire accent reminded her of childhood. Her mother's hand was warm in hers. And heaven help her, Kate couldn't say no to them. She was at the end of her tether.

When Joe came back, she was packing and her parents had just got back from shopping for winter clothes, making the most of their visit to Sydney.

She glared at him. 'Why didn't you tell me you'd contacted them?'

'You'd have thrown a fit. But you won't see another doctor and you're not looking after yourself. You definitely won't get better if you don't eat.' He held up one of her arms. 'Look at you! Skeletal. I don't have time to care for you properly . . .' He hesitated. 'And . . . well, I haven't told you yet, but I'm being transferred to Melbourne next month.'

'So that's it. I'm inconvenient when I'm like this, so you need to get rid of me.' Anger pounded through her. 'Well, good riddance to you, too, Joe Carvalli. I'll be better off without you.'

'Kate—'

She pushed him away then collapsed on the bed, sobbing.

Her mother came in and murmured something. Joe left the room.

'I'll do the packing for you, love. Joe says he'll clear your household bits and pieces out for you when he moves and send them up to Callabine.'

'He's ditching me, Mum,' she whispered. 'Going to Melbourne.'

'Yes. He told us about it when he phoned. That's what trouble does, real trouble. It either brings you closer or it tears you apart. Better to know the truth about what he's like now, don't you think, than after marrying him?'

It didn't feel better, Kate thought. Definitely not. She couldn't think what to say and was glad when her mother didn't dwell on Joe's defection.

'Let's get on with this, then, love. No need to prolong the pain.'

Kate tried to think what else she should take with her, but the grey fog that had plagued her almost from the start of this illness was expanding inside her head, blotting out the capacity to think clearly, and all she could do was subside on the bed and let her mother finish packing her clothes,

59

make-up, books and computer.

When they went back into the lounge, Joe came towards her. 'Kate, I—'

She stepped back to avoid him. 'You're a shit!' Then she tried to push past him.

'Look, wait—I found this in a bookshop. It might help.'

Kate thrust the book to one side as she passed.

Her father glanced at the title *Chronic Fatigue Syndrome: A Hidden Epidemic?* and took it from him.

'I'm sorry, Kate,' Joe called after her. 'I can't cope with an invalid. I don't have the—the stamina, whatever you call it. But I *am* sorry.'

She didn't even turn her head.

Six

Cars are strung like coloured beads on an abacus all along the motorways. They dodge in and out, now speeding up, now slowing down, as their numbers add to and subtract from the grand vehicular total.

Judith didn't sleep well on her last night at the hotel, then fell into a heavy sleep in the small hours of the morning, not waking till eight o'clock. By the time she'd had breakfast and paid her hotel bill, it was past ten o'clock, a chilly morning but fine at least.

She took the M40 out of London, finding traffic moderately heavy. When she turned on to the M5, traffic was much heavier and everything began to slow right down as she approached the junction between the M5 and the M6. She spent well over an hour driving a mere couple of miles. By then her knee was aching, but there was nothing to be done about it.

Her thoughts skipped here and there as she drove a hundred yards, waited, drove a little further, stopped and waited again. Her mind couldn't seem to settle on anything for long and she felt utterly disoriented, suspended between her old life and her new. Well, at least she had her Auntie May's house to go to, a place where Des had never even set foot. That seemed important now.

A few months ago, when he'd started working secretly to regain the original Corrigan's from his sister, Judith had begun to think that if things went seriously wrong between them she might need a refuge. She'd shied away from that thought for a while, then faced it squarely and contacted the agency who managed her house, asking them to keep the tenant on one month's notice from then on.

After her accident she'd asked the agents to give the tenant notice and make sure the power and phones were connected in her name. There was some furniture in the house, left over from her aunt's day, but she'd no doubt need to buy more, as well as doing a lot of re-organizing and decorating. That would keep her nicely busy for the first few weeks. Then she realized she wouldn't be able to afford it, not till the settlement came through and she knew where she stood financially. Damn you, Des! she thought. You're only delaying things to get back at me.

She stopped at the next services but didn't fancy anything to eat, so bought a cup of coffee and took it back to the car. She didn't want to be surrounded by people, not today.

When she set off again, traffic was moving slightly faster and soon she was circling Manchester on the ring road, getting closer and closer to her destination. She felt exhausted now after her sedentary life of the past few weeks.

In Rochdale, the town centre had changed so much she had to stop to ask the way out to the village of Blackfold. The accent of the woman who offered directions, the way she called Judith 'flower', brought back vivid childhood memories. Her aunt had spoken in the same way. Judith's father, however, had been ashamed of his accent and had modified it to what he considered 'better

English'. But his sister had laughed at the way he spoke and continued to use her long slow vowels and dialect words with relish, exaggerating it when her brother and his family visited her—which wasn't often.

He'd died at fifty, Judith's father. So young. Why, she was less than ten years from fifty herself! That thought made her shiver.

She arrived at Blackfold around four in the afternoon. Since she hadn't been here for some time, she parked near the centre and studied the amenities—a minimart, a few small shabby shops and three pubs. It pleased her that nothing had changed much since her last visit and she smiled as she drove slowly along the main street. She remembered it so well from her childhood visits.

The house stood on an acre of land at the far end of the long, narrow village, backing on to fields that were bright with the promise of spring. The moors were only a hop and a skip beyond them, within easy walking distance of her new home. The Gatehouse, it was called, no one knew why, because it had never guarded the gates to anywhere. The house itself looked unchanged, but the front garden was untidy and unloved, as it had never been in her aunt's day.

The Gatehouse was built of local stone, once golden, blackened now by two hundred years of exposure to the elements. It was a solid, square building, looking as if it'd put down deep roots and intended to stand there until the last trump sounded. It was three storeys high, with weaver's windows along back and front of the top floor, a whole row of them to let in as much light as possible. They'd be the devil to clean with all those small leaded panes, but Judith remembered how lovely they looked from inside, fracturing the light on sunny days and sending it shimmering round the walls. Maybe she could make herself a studio up there? Even if you weren't good enough to earn a living from your painting, you could still enjoy it, couldn't you?

The house had been built long before garages were needed, so she parked the car on the gravelled space in front and stood for a few moments looking up at the moors then back along the main street. The fresh, damp air felt so invigorating after the car fumes on the motorway and she breathed deeply in appreciation.

There were some outbuildings at the back of the house: long, low buildings, quite substantial and appearing to be in a reasonable state of repair. She'd look round those tomorrow. They'd been full of junk when she was a child, but who knew what they'd contain now? Perhaps nothing. Perhaps even more junk.

When she had trouble opening the front door, she frowned and examined the keys again, but she was definitely using the right one—it even had a label attached to it saying *Front Door* in ornate italic script. Only the key didn't fit the hole at all and when she studied the lock, she realized that it was brand new.

She went round to the back, getting the heavy, old-fashioned key ready—but again there was a new lock and she couldn't get in.

Bewildered, she went all round the house, checking whether there was a window open. There wasn't. Why had the estate agent not told her he'd changed the locks? Why hadn't he sent her the new keys?

She got back into the car and called him on her mobile.

'We haven't changed any locks, Ms Horrocks. We paid a security firm to drive past every day or two and check that the house was all right, as you asked, and of course someone from the office went out there regularly to check the inside. Perhaps you've been sent the wrong keys? I'll drive over straight away with the correct ones. I do apologize profoundly. I'll set off immediately and be there in about half an hour.'

When he arrived, they both stared at the keys in bewilderment because the sets were identical. He tried to open the doors with his keys, but they wouldn't go into the holes. 'The locks must have been changed. I can't understand why, though. We definitely didn't authorize this and when someone checked the house only two weeks ago, she had no trouble getting in, so it's quite recent.'

She knew then who'd done this and a shiver ran down her spine. Des, of course. Who else could it be? And who else had keys to these new locks? She didn't feel comfortable about moving in now, which was just what he'd intended, of course. 'It can only be my ex, trying to make trouble for me.'

The estate agent stared at her in shock. 'Surely not?'

'I'm afraid so. He can be very—spiteful.'

Even when the locksmith came and put in new and very secure locks, unease was still skittering up and down her spine about staying here alone. *Damn you, Des!*

By the time the locksmith had finished, it was dark and she was ravenously hungry, so she drove into the village to buy some food at the minimart, enough to tide her over for a day or two.

'Staying in Blackfold, are you?' the lady behind the counter asked.

'Yes. I'm May Horrocks' niece.'

'Ah, you'll be living at the old Gatehouse, then. Nice place, that. Lovely outbuildings too. There was a man wanted to buy the outbuildings and land at the back and do a barn conversion on them, only your aunt would never sell. Nice fellow, he was, became quite friendly with her.'

It was amazing how much the woman knew, Judith thought, and would no doubt be spreading the word about her arrival.

When she got back, she found the gates closed, which worried her. Had Des sent someone else to hassle her? She opened them, looking round her all the time, but could see no sign of anyone. Still filled with trepidation, she drove her car into the driveway, hesitated, then left the gates open in case she had to drive away quickly.

The front door opened easily with the new key and she hastily carried the shopping inside. Suddenly the fact that the house had three storeys worried her and she knew she'd have to have a security system installed if she was to sleep soundly at night.

Heart pounding she made her way up to the attics and searched the whole house from top to bottom, leaving no cupboard, no wardrobe out. There was no one there, of course, no sign of disturbances, but she'd needed to be sure of that. When she got down to the kitchen she felt more comfortable.

She looked out of the window and for a moment

thought she saw a glimmer of light down at the end of the garden, but decided she must have been mistaken because when she blinked and looked again, there was only darkness. After eating a sandwich, she opened a bottle of Chardonnay and poured herself a glass, then spent a pleasant hour reading the novel she'd bought at the minimart. Eventually a gigantic yawn interrupted her reading and when she looked at her watch, it was nearly eleven o'clock.

As she was about to switch on the light in her bedroom she caught sight of what looked like a light further down the garden, and this time it didn't go away when she blinked. She walked across to the window without putting her own light on and stared out. Surely that was—yes, the big shed at the end of her garden was definitely lit up! Was Des playing some other nasty trick on her? She got her mobile out to call for the police, then anger surged through her. Whatever it was, whoever it was, she was going to deal with it herself. Des was *not* going to spook her.

Besides, of one thing she could be certain. He didn't intend to kill or physically hurt her. He'd far rather keep her alive and make her suffer. But just to be sure she was able to defend herself, she went downstairs and picked up the living-room poker, a solid piece of iron with a brass handle. Then she went into the kitchen, switched off the light and opened the outside door quietly. Step by careful step she crept down the garden towards the shed.

*   *   *

That evening Mitch picked up the phone and

listened for a moment, before calling to his grandmother, 'It's Dad, for you.'

She came out of the kitchen pulling a face and thrust a spoon into Mitch's hand, whispering, 'Keep stirring the sauce.'

Des's voice boomed in her ear. 'Well, Ma-in-law, I've just concluded a rather nifty deal and since I no longer have a wife to celebrate with, I'd like to take you and my son out for dinner.'

'Oh, dear! I've already cooked something and we're just about to eat.'

'Save it for another time. I'll be round to pick you up in half an hour.'

She stared at the buzzing phone, then slammed it down and went back into the kitchen. 'Oh, he's such an infuriating man! Sorry, Mitch. I tried to fend him off but he's insisting on taking us out to dinner. Says it's to celebrate some business deal.'

'That's a new one. Since when does Dad need us to do his celebrating with? I've told him I can't afford late nights. Doesn't he *ever* think of anyone else?'

She spread her hands helplessly. 'I'll ring back and suggest he eats here with us. I can get out a bottle of wine.'

Mitch hesitated, then shook his head. 'No, don't. You know how he loves lavish meals in restaurants. It'll put him in a bad mood.'

'Let it.'

'I'd rather not. He can get a bit shitty if you stop him doing something he's set his mind on.'

She stared at him. 'Are you by any chance frightened of your father, Mitch?'

He was tracing patterns on the vinyl flooring with his toe. 'Not exactly—well, I wasn't before, but since he thumped Mum, I've realized how strong he is physically. You should have seen the expression on his face when he hit her, Gran. Sheer fury. And you and I both saw what he'd done to that door at the hotel. So I'd rather not cross him just now. I'm not as strong as he is and well, I'm dependent on him. I'll need financing for university next year.'

Which made her thoughtful, because she too was dependent on Des and would live a very meagre life without his help. She'd told Judith that didn't matter, but it did really. When you were over sixty, you valued your comforts and being able to afford outings with friends. So if she could keep Des happy without betraying her daughter, she would. But if push came to shove, it was Judith who mattered most—and Mitch.

With a sigh she switched off the cooker and began to put the food away, planning what to wear. If Judith rang to say she'd arrived safely, as she'd promised to do, she'd find only the answer phone.

*   *   *

That evening Des was so expansive and talkative that Hilary began to wonder if he was taking some sort of drug. He hardly glanced at her but he looked at Mitch a lot, and gloatingly too. He also seemed to be nursing some secret amusement. What was he up to now?

But he didn't raise any objections when they insisted they had to get home early so that Mitch wouldn't be too tired to study the next day.

'Ambitious little sod, aren't you?' he said to his son, his speech just the tiniest bit slurred because

69

he'd drunk most of the bottle of expensive wine he'd ordered, plus a double cognac afterwards.

'I want to get a good degree, Dad. That sort of thing matters these days.'

'Yeah, well, you go for it, lad. I'll put up the money for the university fees. And *she's* out of the picture now, so you'll not be messed around any more.'

Mitch and his grandmother both went to peer out of the dining-room window as Des sauntered back to the car. The chauffeur hopped out smartly and opened the door, then it purred off down the street.

Hilary gave her grandson a hug. 'Well, that wasn't too bad. Look, there's a message on the answer phone.' She pressed the button and her daughter's voice echoed round the room. Mitch came across to listen with her.

When the message finished, they stared at one another.

'That's why he was so smug tonight,' Mitch said bitterly. 'What a rotten trick to play. Poor Mum. And whatever Dad says, I'm definitely going up to see her in the summer holidays.'

'Don't tell your father that. We'll work something out together, fool him.'

He looked at her and sighed. 'I suppose we'd better. I'll feel a coward, though.'

'At your age you've no power and no money, so it's the sensible thing to do, the only thing really.' And she would have to tread just as carefully—up to certain limits. She wondered if Des would push against those limits or whether he really was as fond of her as he pretended.

70

*　　　*　　　*

'Drive me to Pearton Gardens,' Des told his chauffeur.

'Yes, sir.'

'Then you can go off duty. I'll take a taxi home later.' He leaned back, looking forward to seeing Tiff.

She was sitting watching television in the luxury flat he paid for, dressed in one of the expensive negligées he'd bought. Blond and slim, exactly twenty years younger than him, and fun without being clingy. He'd never met a woman whose company he enjoyed more. He kept careful checks on her, of course, but she'd never strayed since he began supporting her, not once.

'Des, darling! I didn't know you were coming tonight.' She held out her hand.

He joined her on the couch, indulging her in her favourite programme, enjoying her rich chuckles. When it was over he began to kiss her.

'Here or in bed?' she asked.

He was getting too old for contortions on the sofa. That's what had gone wrong last time, he was sure. He'd twisted his spine. 'Bed, my pet. I like my comforts.'

But he could feel his nerves growing taut as he followed Tiff along the corridor. She and his doctor were the only ones who knew about the difficulties he'd been having. Last time he'd used Viagra, and it had worked all too well, but he hated the damned stuff and anyway, it didn't wear off when you wanted it to. Tonight things would go fine, he was sure. He was relaxed and had a gorgeous woman to arouse him.

71

She led the way into the bedroom and they helped one another out of their clothes.

Ten minutes later he rolled off her and covered his face with one arm, ashamed that once again he'd been unable to finish what he started.

She said nothing for a few moments, then reached for his hand and raised it to her lips. 'It's all right, Des.'

He didn't turn to look at her. 'It damned well isn't! This is turning into a habit.'

She squeezed his hand. 'Perhaps you'd better see a specialist, not just for those tablets, but for a good check-up? That's what your doctor wanted you to do last time, wasn't it?'

He couldn't hold back a growl of anger at the thought of going back and telling a man he knew socially that he still couldn't maintain an erection.

She pulled him round to face her. 'I'm not with you just for the money, Des, or for the sex. We'll sort this out together.'

He lay scowling at her, then closed his eyes and sighed. 'You're a nice girl, Tiff.'

'I'm thirty-eight. Hardly a girl.'

'You won't tell anyone?'

'Did you really need to ask that?'

He pulled her into his arms and buried his face in the soft skin of her shoulder. 'No.'

But he didn't dare try to make love to her again, and shortly afterwards he left.

Seven

A chill wind whines across the moors, clouds tease the moon, hoar frost whitens the grass. Winter has suddenly sneaked back for one last thrust of the icy dagger.

Walking on the grass so as not to make a noise, Judith crept through the darkness towards the light, which was coming from the furthest part of the long brick shed. The intruder was making no attempt to hide his presence. But what would anyone be doing there at this hour of the night? Surely there was nothing worth stealing?

She was so angry about this second intrusion into her refuge that she kept going, muttering, 'Just you wait, Des Corrigan.' The light was coming from a small window in the stone-built shed, two dirty panes of cracked glass festooned by cobwebs. To her annoyance, they were too high for her to see through, so she crept up to the door and listened.

Silence.

Was it a trap? She didn't know, only that she wasn't going to cave in and leave her house. Nor would she crawl back to Des, whatever he did or said to her. Taking a firmer grip on the poker, she hefted it in her hand. If someone leaped out at her, they'd get more than they'd bargained for. She reached for the handle, sucked in a deep breath and flung the door open. It bounced back on its hinges, creaking loudly, and thumped against the wall, rebounding so that she had to push it back again.

By the light of a single bare bulb hanging from the ceiling she saw a man slumped forward across a rickety table with his head on one arm. His other arm was flung out next to an empty whisky bottle. He moved his head, grunted and settled down again.

She took a quick look round, puzzled. The place looked lived in, with odd pieces of furniture, even a computer and a bed. She hesitated. If she had any sense she'd back out, lock herself in the house and call for the police.

She had no sense. She stayed.

From the direction of the table came a gentle bubbling snore. There was no sound apart from that, no traffic noises, no sound of people's voices. They could have been alone in the universe. A minute or so later another snore followed the first and the man twitched, muttering something in his sleep. He was unshaven, his clothes crumpled, but he didn't look like a tramp. His shoes were new, even if they were muddy, and the leather jacket he was wearing was of good quality, showing few signs of wear and tear.

Was she dreaming? What had this man been doing drinking himself senseless in her shed?

She took another step forward, then a final movement brought her right next to him. On a sudden decision she shook his shoulder hard. 'Wake up!'

'Go 'way.'

His voice was husky and when he raised his head slightly his eyes were unfocused. Even as she watched he laid his head down and closed his eyes again. *He was blind drunk!* Had he consumed the

74

whole bottle of whisky?

Anger made her shake him harder and shout, 'Don't go to sleep!'

'What?' He blinked at her, looking like all the mock drunks she'd ever seen in plays and films.

'Who—are—you?'

'Cal.'

She didn't let him put his head down again. 'Get up and get out of here, Cal. This is *my* shed.'

This time he seemed to consider what she was asking of him, she could see understanding dawn slowly, but then he shook his head. 'Can't.'

'What do you mean, you can't?'

It took a long time for the next words to emerge. 'Broke down.'

Then she saw the motor cycle helmet on a chair beyond the table, the heavy leather gauntlets beneath it.

'Even the Hog let me down,' he repeated, closing his eyes, an expression of pain on his face. 'Everything's gone wrong.'

That didn't seem like a reason to empty a bottle of whisky, but as he muttered something indistinguishable and closed his eyes, she gave up and backed out, not allowing him a chance to jump her. But he didn't. He didn't even stir.

When she'd closed the door she swung round quickly and set her back to it. But the garden was quiet, even the row of daffodils looking colourless in the darkness. And the wind was getting up, a damp, icy wind that promised rain. Fine spring weather this was! Shivering, she returned to the house, unlocked the back door and hesitated. He'd be cold in that shed.

That wasn't her business.

75

But what if he died of hypothermia?

No, you didn't die of hypothermia in April. Did you? Anyway, it wasn't her business. She didn't know him from a bar of soap. He might be a dangerous lunatic or someone working for Des. But still . . . she watched her breath cloud the air . . . it had got cold quickly, and the weather forecast said there was a possibility of snow on high ground.

She couldn't leave him there.

With a sigh she retraced her steps, shook the man until he was more or less awake, then hauled him to his feet. He seemed bewildered but docile, and when she tugged him forward, he stumbled along obediently beside her.

' 'S'not fair, you know,' he said suddenly.

'What's not fair?'

'Taking my daughter away from me. It's just not fair.'

He said nothing more, but she couldn't get what he'd said out of her mind. Was that why he'd been drinking? She knew how it hurt to lose a child because in one sense Mitch had been taken away from her, though he'd have gone anyway in a few months. But she'd have fought like a wildcat if anyone had tried to take him away from her when he was little.

Horrible things happened between divorced couples and children suffered from it. This man certainly didn't look like a habitual drunkard, because he was scrupulously clean, apart from not having shaved. But stubble on the chin was fashionable these days, wasn't it?

She propped him against the house wall while she unlocked the back door, then guided him

76

inside.

'I'm cold,' he announced suddenly.

In the light she could see that his face was white and when she tugged him forward again, she touched one of his hands and found it clammy. She wasn't cold because the exertion of getting a tall, drunken man into the house had warmed her up. One look at her companion and she decided not even to try the stairs, leading him into the sitting room instead, where she eased him down into an armchair and switched on the heater. He was clearly far too tall to sleep on the couch, so she dragged the cushions off it and laid them on the floor.

He leaned his head back, closed his eyes and sighed. His expression was sad, even now, but there wasn't a hint of aggression about him. It was utterly stupid to have brought a complete stranger inside, but she didn't feel at all threatened by him. He simply didn't look aggressive.

She went to find sheets and blankets for the makeshift bed. The blankets smelled a bit musty, but were of good wool, so would keep him warm. She made it up and tried to persuade him to lie down. The trouble was, he put his arms round her and pulled her down beside him. For a moment her body responded to his touch, just for one crazy moment. He made sounds of pleasure, nuzzled her neck then rested his head against her breast and fell instantly asleep.

Smiling, she eased herself away from him. There was something very appealing about his face, which was narrow and elegant beneath dark hair lightly touched at the sides by silver. What had upset him so greatly that he'd had to drown his sorrows? Why had they taken his daughter away from him?

And what on earth had brought him to her shed?

* * *

It was one of Maeve's bad days. She felt weak and insubstantial, hardly stirring from the sitting room. They were getting more frequent, days like this. She hated the way her strength was declining because she'd always been a strong, energetic woman. It was feeling like this that had driven her to the doctor in the first place. She went to stare out of the window at the immaculate grounds of her house, her eyes blind with tears, then sniffed them away and shouted, 'Damn them all!' She would *not* give in to self-pity!

Picking up an ornament she had always hated, she hurled it into the fireplace. It made a very satisfying smashing sound, so she prowled round the room, finding another that was just as ugly.

The door opened and her housekeeper rushed in, only to stop dead at what she saw.

Maeve grinned at Lena and hurled the second ornament into the fireplace with all her force before reaching for another.

'Maeve, what *are* you doing?'

She looked at the ornament she'd just picked up, a numbered edition that had cost rather a lot of money and drew a long, shuddering breath before setting it down on the mantelpiece with a hand that shook. 'I was feeling bad. Took it out on those stupid things. Sorry. You can clean up the mess later.' Though she wasn't really sorry. She'd enjoyed smashing them. But two were enough.

She'd lost the desire to weep, at least.

Lena gave an indignant snort. 'Well, if you have any other ornaments you don't like, let me know. I'll be happy to buy you some cheap ones to smash and I'll take the good ones off your hands.' She picked up a shepherdess's head, stroking it with her fingertip. 'I'd always liked this piece, too.'

'I'll remember that next time.' Maeve watched Lena hesitate and guessed what was coming. They had grown up together and she didn't feel the need to treat her as an employee, though Lena was very correct in her behaviour when other people were around.

'Was it—bad news from the doctor, then? You've not seemed yourself for a while now.'

'Yes. Bad enough. I'll be telling you about that later.' She couldn't keep it secret from Lena much longer, but her old friend knew how to keep her mouth shut. 'How about a snack? I'm not too ill to enjoy a cup of tea and one of your scones.'

After she had drunk three delicate china cups of finest Earl Grey tea and forced a scone down to please Lena, Maeve leaned back and closed her eyes. This was the way she'd planned all the major events in her life—drunk a few cups of good tea, then sat comfortably with her eyes closed and worked through whatever the current problem was in her mind. She'd planned what she wanted in a husband by this method, then chosen one who fitted the criteria. Ha! Fat lot of good that had done. She hadn't even considered the possibility that *she* would be the one who couldn't have children.

She'd divorced Ralph when she found out, of course, because for all his protestations of loving

79

her, he desperately wanted children and he'd have left her sooner or later to gain them from another woman. Blood was what counted, he'd always said whenever he saw a programme on adoption—your own, not other people's. So she had told him to get out, not wanting to see his affection for her fade.

He'd been so damned understanding that she'd been furious with him for weeks. But he hadn't tried to persuade her to change her mind. He'd been a realist, like herself. She couldn't have married a man who wasn't.

Father Michael had been furious, had scolded her for years about it, told her she was still married in God's sight, whatever that bit of paper said about a divorce. Then Ralph's sudden death had shut the parish priest up.

Her ex hadn't made old bones, despite his magnificent physique and regular exercise. She'd far rather have had a sudden heart attack as he had done than face cancer and a slow decline—as she was doing.

Ralph had left two sons behind from his second marriage, though, damn him. Why had she been denied a child and he given two?

Ah, think of something else, you fool! Don't go down those same old tracks.

The business. Yes, that was better. It was something to be proud of. She'd started by building up the ailing family firm to a thriving and efficient concern. Not too big for comfort, but big enough to give her a nice income. Then she'd invested this, and done rather well. She smiled. Extremely well, actually. She had a magic touch when choosing shares.

Her smile faded. She'd kept Corrigan's for

sentimental reasons but now the machinery was becoming obsolete. She'd always had the knack of seeing into the future and diversifying, making changes before the blow fell. This time she hadn't bothered to do that. Instead she'd let her brother Des buy her out sneakily. She smiled at the thought. As if she hadn't known all along who was behind the takeover.

She must have dozed off because the telephone startled her and for a moment she couldn't think where she was. She stared at it across the room. Did she want to answer it? No. Let the damned thing ring itself out.

But of course Lena picked it up and then came to see if she was 'in'.

She shook her head vigorously and made shooing movements with one hand. She was most definitely not in. Not to anyone. She still had a lot of thinking to do, then some detailed planning. She wasn't going to just fade away; she was going to leave some sort of legacy behind her. She'd already made her mark on the business world—now she was going to make it on the next generation of Corrigans.

She might not have any children of her own, but she'd got other blood relatives, hadn't she? Both her brothers had children from their various marriages, five in all. Surely one or two of them would be worth bothering with, worth leaving her money to? She smiled. Her detective had already sent her a summary of what her brother in Australia was doing with himself. Not much, it seemed. Leo owned a hardware store which sold farm supplies as well in a small town in New South Wales. He had owned the same store for twenty years, built it into a thriving business, but was more interested in coaching the town's junior soccer team, it seemed, than taking it further and making a fortune. Typical of Leo!

He had two children. A son and a daughter.

She'd always liked Leo better than Des, even though she'd considered him too soft to keep on as a business partner. She wondered what his children were like. Soft—or with the same Corrigan shrewdness and drive as herself?

As for Des and his family, she'd had an eye kept on him for years for her own protection. He'd made a lot of money from his business, but she'd been better at saving and investing her money, while he'd always spent lavishly. He'd been a lazy devil as a young man, always chasing skirt, but he'd wanted the family business quite desperately. Well, so had she, and she'd won it. Leo had been more interested in the family home, but he'd never have had the money to maintain it, let alone restore it as she had.

Des had one broken marriage behind him and it seemed his present wife had just left him as well, again because of his infidelity. It now turned out that there was an illegitimate daughter somewhere, though that wasn't a fashionable term to use nowadays. *Still chasing skirt, Des!* She'd told the detective agency to find out where the second wife had gone, what she was doing with herself, and to locate the illegitimate daughter and see what she was like.

'Can't keep 'em happy, can you, Des?' she muttered. 'Well, let's see if you've produced anything worthwhile in that son of yours, or those three daughters.' The son was, it seemed, doing very well at school. And wasn't living with either parent. Why not?

Well, they said Maeve would have time enough left still to find out. The game wasn't over yet. That made six children, one of whom would inherit a substantial legacy from her.

Oh, yes, she'd definitely leave her mark on those who were left behind. She smiled. The Corrigan legacy! It sounded like a film, one full of dark deeds and suspense. She wished she could be here to watch it play out to the finish. She couldn't, so she'd have to make her plans very carefully . . . Tie things up legally so that Des couldn't get his hands on any of the money that was to be offered to his children.

Doing all that would give her an interest for these last few months.

*　　　*　　　*

Kate went to see the specialist physician their family doctor in Callabine referred her to. She had to get her mother to drive her to the nearby town of Berriman to do that and by the time they got there she was exhausted.

Mr Knowles was grey-haired and plump, and from the beginning he spoke to her as if she was mentally deficient.

'I think what you're really suffering from, young woman, is depression.'

She'd done her homework. 'I'm not. I've looked it up on the Internet and—'

He held up one hand to stop her. 'We'll have no amateur doctoring here. I'll prescribe you some antidepressants and you can come back and see me in six weeks.'

'I'm not taking them. I'm *not* in a clinical depression.'

He looked at her mother. 'She isn't thinking clearly. Perhaps you can see that she takes the tablets, Mrs Corrigan?'

Kate's mother looked at her, then back at the doctor. She picked up the prescription Kate had shoved away. 'Come on, love.'

When they went out, she made an appointment for six weeks' time while Kate stood scowling at her from near the door.

'It's no use coming to see a specialist if you don't do as he tells you,' Jean said when they were in the car. 'I'll just stop at the chemist's and have this made up.'

'Mum, how can I say it more clearly? I'm *not* taking those things. I'm *not* clinically depressed.'

'He's a specialist. He must know better than you.'

'There's no need to get them. I won't take them.'

When they got home, her father listened to their combined explanation of what had happened.

'The doctor was rather autocratic,' her mother admitted, 'and I didn't like the way he spoke to Kate, either. But we're not paying him to be our friend. We're paying him for his expertise.'

'I want to see someone else, someone who really knows about chronic fatigue syndrome,' Kate said stubbornly. 'I'm *not* taking those things.' She stood up to leave the room and her father blocked the way.

'Sit down, Kate.'

Fuming, she did so.

'You're not getting any better. Would it hurt to take the tablets and see if they help?'

She opened her mouth.

'I'm asking you to try, that's all. We're doing all we can to help you. I think you should play your part.'

'I want to see someone else.'

He slammed down his hand on the table. 'There *is* no one else near here! And you haven't even tried. One month. Give it one month.'

Her mother looked at her pleadingly.

Kate felt so tired she caved in. 'It won't work.'

'One month,' he repeated. He picked up the packet and popped out a tablet, then offered it to her, and got her a glass of water.

She looked at it, her mind a blur of tiredness, and with a sigh she swallowed it.

For the next few days she dutifully took the tablets but she hated the way they made her feel, as if there were a layer of heavy insulation between herself and the world. She couldn't even think straight when she was on her computer and made the silliest mistakes.

After one week, she waited till her father was at work and her mother shopping in town, then she flushed the rest of the tablets down the toilet.

At tea time her mother went to get her a tablet and she confessed to what she'd done.

They both looked at her as if she'd lost her wits.

'That's not the way to treat chronic fatigue syndrome,' she said, as she'd said so many times. 'Truly it isn't. That physician is old-fashioned.'

Her father's face was red with anger. 'You didn't even give it a month.'

'I can't bear the way those tablets make me feel.'

He got that stubborn look on his face. 'Well, young woman, I'm not paying for you to go to see any other specialists if that's the way you treat what they say.'

She stood up and left the room, in tears but too proud to let them see. She didn't always think clearly with this mind-fuzz that seemed to overwhelm her sometimes, but they hadn't even tried to look at the research she'd found online. The best thing to do was rest and gather her strength, then find out the name of a specialist in Sydney. She could stay with her friend Jen for a day or two and spend some of her remaining money on seeing one.

But she couldn't do it yet, because she was too weak to travel there on her own and her father was so furious, she was sure he wouldn't let her mother take her.

She locked her bedroom door and lay down, wondering yet again what she'd done to deserve this.

Eight

Shreds of mist curl across the tops of the moors, raindrops bounce off windows, cows plod silently across a field, full udders swaying, heads marking time. The man following them pulls his hat down further against the rain and hunches his shoulders.

Judith woke early, pulled away the chair that she'd prudently jammed under the door handle and wondered as she took a quick shower if the man she'd rescued was still there.

He was.

She stood in the doorway of her aunt's shabby sitting room and stared across at him. He was sound asleep, spread-eagled half on and half off the seat cushions. With a shrug at her own rashness she went into the kitchen, making no attempt to keep quiet, smiling as she wondered if he'd remember anything about the previous night.

When she heard him stirring she went back to stand in the doorway. He was sitting up, staring round with a look of utter bewilderment on his face. The minute he noticed her, he blinked and became very still. 'How the hell did I get here?'

'I found you in my shed, dead drunk. I couldn't rouse you properly and didn't want to leave you outside on such a cold night, so I brought you into the house.'

'You must like taking risks. I might be a mass murderer, for all you know.'

'That's what I told myself. But you didn't seem threatening, could hardly stand up, and I couldn't

87

reconcile it with my conscience to leave you out there in the cold.' She smiled as she added, 'Though I did keep a poker handy, I will admit.' His answering smile lit his whole face and made her breath catch in her throat at how attractive he was.

'Thank you. I'm very grateful. And I'm not a mass murderer, actually, though you'll have to take my word for that.'

She chuckled. 'I feel much safer now you've told me. Look, there's a shower room across the hall and I've put out a towel. Breakfast will be ready when you are.' Her aunt had had a downstairs suite created when she grew too old for the stairs, but somehow, Judith hadn't wanted to put the stranger in May's bed. That would have seemed too intimate.

He moved as if to stand up, winced and closed his eyes, rubbing his temples.

'Hangover?'

'Yeah.'

'A cup of coffee and a couple of paracetamols might help.'

'Please. I won't be more than a few minutes.' He threw aside the covers and got to his feet, sucking in his breath a couple of times as if moving about hurt.

She went back into the kitchen, smiling wryly. So far, her guesses had been correct. Her intruder spoke in educated tones and was very attractive in an understated way. She stopped dead at that thought because she wasn't used to finding other men attractive, then shrugged mentally. Well, she was officially separated from Des now, knew she would never go back to him and she certainly didn't intend to stay celibate for the rest of her life. In fact, it had been a few months since Des had made love to her. That was what had alerted her to the fact that he was cheating on her again.

When her visitor joined her, he was pale, smelled of soap and his hair was damp. He'd also put on a pair of spectacles. He looked good in them, too. She nodded towards the table. 'Help yourself to coffee. I think you should eat something before you have any tablets.'

He poured a cup and sat down to cradle the mug as if enjoying the warmth, then sipped from it and sighed with pleasure.

'I'm Judith Co— I mean, Horrocks,' she prompted.

'Cal Richmond. And I apologize for trespassing last night. When May was alive she used to let me sleep in the shed. Last night my bike broke down a few hundred yards from here, so I left it and plodded along on foot.'

'I'm her niece, Judith.'

'She's shown me photos of you. They didn't do you justice.'

His eyes were warm and admiring. A shiver of response ran through her.

'I got to know your aunt quite well, wanted to build a weekender up here, but she refused to sell me her shed and end section of land, said it didn't do any good to split up properties or everyone wound up with only a bit more than nothing.'

'Sounds like her. She kept all the family photographs too, right back from the 1860s. I was instructed in her will to keep them together and hand them on to my son intact. I don't think she'd understood that you can scan them in nowadays

89

and make copies for every member of the family who wants them.'

He nodded, then set down his empty cup and looked at it wistfully. 'All right if I get another?'

'Of course.' She stole a glance at him and decided to ask the question that was puzzling her. 'You'd been drinking heavily, though why you'd choose to sit in a shed to do that puzzles me. Surely a pub would have been more comfortable— or even your own home?'

After a brief hesitation he said, 'I wanted to find a place where no one would see me or talk to me— or be able to tell people I'd got blind drunk.'

She could see pain flaring in his eyes again. 'So you broke into the shed.'

'I still had my key, so technically I didn't break in, just trespassed.'

'And how did you get hold of the whisky?'

'I'd come prepared. It was in my pannier.'

Cal took another sip of coffee, avoiding his hostess's eyes because she seemed to see too deeply into him. He'd been half mad with the pain of losing Lily, if truth be told, and hadn't been thinking straight. He'd had a desperate need to blot out the world for a few hours, but had been worried in case Kerry was keeping him under observation. He didn't want her reporting him to courts and solicitors as an unsuitable man to have parental responsibility . . . just in case there was the faintest chance of him being with Lily again.

He looked up, studying his good Samaritan. She was a great-looking woman, voluptuous in a way he'd always found attractive, not stick-thin like Kerry. When he smiled, she smiled back at him and somehow the warmth in her face eased the pain a little.

'You seemed very upset,' she said softly. 'You muttered something about your daughter, that they'd taken her away from you.'

He hadn't realized he'd said anything so specific. 'I thought I was well out of it last night.'

'I stirred you into moving and helped you into the house. That's when you said it.'

'What exactly did I say?' Oh, hell, he hadn't wept all over her, had he? Guys weren't supposed to weep, especially guys about to turn forty.

'You didn't say much, just something about it not being fair to take her away from you. I—um— had a fellow feeling because circumstances have just separated me from my son.'

He could see a sadness in her face that mirrored his own feelings. 'Divorce?'

'Yes. And Mitch's educational needs mean he must stay in London, near his father, while I only have this place to live in so I had to come north. But I'm going to miss him like hell.'

Cal nodded, but didn't volunteer any more of his story and to his relief she didn't press the point or share any more of hers. It was established that they had something in common. That was enough to form a tentative bond.

'Bacon and eggs? Toast? Marmalade?'

'You're a very generous hostess. Could I get my bike first, then take you up on your offer of food? It's a Hog—Harley-Davidson—and I don't like to leave it lying around for someone to pinch.'

'Sure. Your things are still in the shed.'

He drained his cup and went to get his helmet and ignition key. She watched him, deciding his walk had a lazy grace that was attractive. Des either stumped along as if he were off to do battle or strutted as if he'd just won a battle.

Quarter of an hour later Cal returned. 'It's working now. Go figure.'

She started cooking. 'You were a friend of my aunt, you say?'

He smiled, 'I like to think so. She was a feisty old lady.'

'Did you grow up round here? I was born in Rochdale, just down the road, but my parents and Aunt May didn't get on, though she was my father's sister, so I didn't see much of her till I grew up. My mother died in a car accident when I was thirty. My father was lost without her and moved about a bit. He died a couple of years ago.

'I met May again at the funeral and we kept in touch. I lived in London, but she came down sometimes to shop and I came up here to see her once or twice. I never thought she'd leave the house to me, but I'm grateful now that she did.'

He smiled reminiscently, leaning against the wall in a position from which he could look out of the window at the moors. 'I grew up in the village and I think it'll always be home to me. Your aunt caught me scrumping her apples once when I was a lad. She read me a lecture then turned and twisted her foot in the grass, so I helped her back to the house. Somehow I kept coming back. She treated me like an adult, let me read her books, talked to me. My mother was widowed, worked all hours to support the two of us, so I was lonely, I guess. She lives in Norwich now with her second husband.' He stopped talking, amazed at how easy he found it to confide in Judith. The silence continued until she broke it.

'Breakfast is served.'

He went to join her at the table. 'Sorry to be such poor company. I keep—losing track of what I'm doing.'

'I'm a bit that way myself lately,' she said softly. 'Disoriented.'

They ate mostly in silence, but it was a comfortable silence. To his surprise he found he was ravenous.

Just as they were finishing, the doorbell rang and Judith went to answer it. As she opened the door, she wrinkled her nose at the pungent smell of dung that wafted in and looked in puzzlement at the man standing there.

'Can someone move that ruddy great motorbike from round the side, missus? I can't get the trailer round to leave this where they said.'

She stared beyond him to a van with a trailer which appeared to be laden with manure. 'I haven't ordered anything.'

'Name of Horrocks?'

'Yes.'

'Well, someone's ordered some garden manure.'

'It isn't me, so please take it away again.'

'But it's been paid for!'

And then she guessed—Des again. How utterly puerile of him! A flash of light from across the road made her look up to see a man standing beside a car, grinning at her, a camera in his hand.

Cal came out to join her. 'Problem?'

The camera flashed again.

'Another of my ex's nasty little tricks, I should think.' She gestured towards the trailer then at the man standing on the road outside her gates. 'A gift from him. And a photographer to show Des how I

93

react.'

Cal let out a scornful puff of laughter. 'He must be a prat. Hasn't he anything better to do with his time and money?'

'He's a shrewd businessman but he has a very juvenile sense of humour. He had all the locks changed here so that I couldn't get in when I arrived yesterday. Knowing him, I should think there'll be more nasty tricks coming.'

Her companion's smile faded. 'One or two nasties is par for the course in an acrimonious split, they tell me. I hope you're wrong about others following. If not, you should let the police know he's harassing you.'

'I doubt I'm wrong, but I don't want to bring the police in. It's bad enough for my son us splitting up. I don't want him to see us brawling publicly.'

'You may have to do something if it goes on.'

'Yes, I suppose so. But I'll wait and see first.'

Cal looked at the manure and then back at the man who'd brought it. 'What sort is it?'

'Horse manure, sir. Best thing there is for vegetables. It doesn't come cheap.'

'Des never does things by halves,' Judith commented sarcastically.

Cal turned to her. 'Are you intending to reinvent the garden at some point?'

She looked round. 'I suppose so. One day. But I'll not be digging in manure myself for a while. I'm still recovering from an accident to my knee, have to take things a bit carefully.' She suddenly remembered her financial state. 'Though it might come to my doing it myself. Des is rich, but he's delaying giving me an allowance because I emptied our joint account. I have to be a bit careful with money until he's played out all the stalling tactics his lawyers can devise.'

'Why don't you accept his gift, then? If you have the manure dumped as far towards the rear of the garden as you can, I'll come back in a few days and spread it out for you wherever you want to grow things.'

His wry smile made her heart suddenly thump in her chest. 'I couldn't ask you to do that.'

'You didn't. But I owe you big time for last night.'

'Oh. Well. All right, then. And I do have a spare bed, so you can sleep in more comfort this time.'

'Actually, I wonder if we could come to some arrangement about the shed instead, to give me a bolt hole?'

The man with the manure, who'd been watching them with increasing impatience, intervened. 'Sorry to interrupt you two but I have a business to run, so if you've decided what you want to do, can you tell me whether to take the stuff away or not? If you want me to leave it, you'll need to move that motorbike. My instructions were to dump the manure on the back patio. All right?'

Judith looked at Cal. 'You're on.'

He nodded and turned to the man. 'I'll move the bike, but we want the manure dumping right down at the back of the garden, as far away from the house as you can get.' He pushed his Harley off its stand and wheeled it to one side, then came across to Judith. 'Do you want to give your husband something to think about?'

'Yes. But what?'

'This.' He pulled her into his arms, smiling warmly at her, and began to kiss her. After an

95

initial jerk of surprise she let him, would have smiled if her mouth hadn't been otherwise engaged. But after a moment or two she forgot about Des and lost herself in the kiss.

When he pulled away, they both stared at one another in shock.

'Where did that come from?' he asked.

She couldn't frame a single word, so shook her head and went back inside to clear up the breakfast things. Cal Richmond was a very attractive man. *Richmond.* She stopped with the kettle in her hands to wonder where she'd heard that name before, but couldn't bring it to mind. It'd come to her later, no doubt, once she'd stopped thinking about it.

In the meantime she should forget the kiss, which had just been a spur of the moment thing to torment Des with.

Only—Cal had been as affected by the kiss as she had. And as surprised.

She smiled again at the thought of Des seeing a photo of a man he didn't know kissing her. Let him work that one out if he could!

When Cal came in again, she was still smiling.

'Something nice happen?'

'What? Oh. No, not really. I was just wondering what Des would make of that kiss and you.'

'Who cares? I doubt I'll ever meet him. Now, about that shed of yours . . . could I rent it for a holiday home?'

She goggled at him. 'You can't mean that?'

'I do. I used to stay there every now and then, and paid your aunt for it by doing little jobs around the place, because I'm not a rich man like your husband—'

'Ex-husband.'

'Sorry—ex-husband. But I gather you're short of money so I could pay you a small retainer, say ten pounds a week and something towards the electricity.'

'But the place is a hovel.' She saw his eyes stray towards the window and the moors.

'It keeps the rain off and there's an old toilet out there as well, which is still in working order, so you don't need to worry that I'll intrude on you. It's just . . . I love to get out of London and up on the tops. I get my best ideas up there. When your leg's stronger, I'll show you some great walks if you like and—' He broke off and smiled wryly. 'Sorry. I'm rushing things, aren't I? But you feel it too, didn't you, the attraction between us?'

She nodded.

'I'd like to see you again. You seem like an old friend already. Your aunt was the same, a very warm person, easy to talk to.'

Judith was won over by his simple honesty. You couldn't doubt that he meant what he said with an open face like that. She held out one hand. 'It's a deal. But I couldn't accept money.'

'Then I'll do jobs for you, if you like. I'm fairly handy.'

'Will you have time? Don't you have your living to earn?'

'I work for myself. I'm a web developer. So I come and go as I please.' He sighed. 'I was going to bring Lily up here to walk the tops now she's big enough—only I'm not even sure now that I'll be able to have her at weekends any longer.'

Judith watched his smile vanish and the strain come back into his face, and spoke without

97

thinking. 'If you bring her up here, you can both sleep in the house. There are several spare bedrooms.'

'Thanks. I might take you up on that if they let me. You'll like her. She's a great kid.'

Nine

In New South Wales, the long dry summer has burned the grass to a crisp beige and even autumn has brought no relief. Gardens are patchily green, favourite plants gifted with buckets of water, others left to struggle alone.

The day started badly, with yet another phone call from Joe, which Kate refused to take. Things got worse when her father brought the mail home from town at lunch time and slammed two envelopes down on the kitchen table in front of her. He stabbed a finger at the top one. 'What's she doing writing to you?'

She stared at him in shock then picked up the envelope. Its expensive linen weave paper was crumpled as if it'd been screwed up and then straightened out again. She turned it over and saw the sender's name and address, sucking in her breath in shock.

Maeve Corrigan
Saltern House
Witherford
Cheshire
England

'I don't know.'

Her father leaned his hands on the table, towering over her threateningly. 'You'd better open it. I want to know what she's up to.'

'Leo!' her mother chided. 'Kate isn't a child and

99

her letters are her own business.'

'She's living under my roof and I want to know how long she's been corresponding with my—damned—sister.'

Kate fingered the letter. 'Why do you hate her so? You've never told us why, just expect us to hate her because you say so. You didn't even tell us we had an aunt till I found those letters in the attic.'

'I hate her because of what she did, sent me away from Saltern House and because—' his voice broke and he had to fight for control—'there hasn't been a day since I left that I haven't wished myself back there.'

Jean gasped. 'You never said, Leo. All these years and you never once told me you felt like that about your old home.'

He turned to her, his face softening a little. 'What was the point in worrying you, Jean? Would it have taken me back again?'

'We could have started up a business in England, as we did here. You'd maybe have been happier if we'd stayed. It was you who insisted on coming to Australia.'

'The only place in England that could be home to me is Saltern House itself. It didn't matter to Des where he lived, but it did to me. I was the eldest—I should have had the house, at least—but she wouldn't even allow me that! And she was right about one thing: I didn't have the money to look after it, but I still loved it.' His words choked in his throat and he turned to Kate. 'If you care about me, you'll throw that letter away unopened and forget about Maeve.' He shoved his chair back so hard it fell over. As he strode out into the garden, he averted his head from them, but not before they

100

had both seen the tears glistening on his cheeks.

Jean stared at Kate pleadingly.

All she could say was, 'I have to see what she says, Mum, and it's not fair to ask me to do otherwise.'

'Then you'll break your father's heart.' Jean followed him outside without a word.

Kate turned the envelope over, then over again, smoothing out the creases as if they mattered. She was annoyed at her father's assumption that he had control over her correspondence and guessed he'd screwed this up to throw it away, then thought better of it.

She could hear them talking as she walked along the corridor, her father's voice still sharp and angry, her mother's soothing. What was her aunt writing to her about? She'd never met the woman, for heaven's sake. And yet her father was right about one thing: Maeve had already stirred up dissension in the family.

Finding her paper knife, Kate slit the envelope neatly, pulling out a single sheet of paper.

Dear Kate,

I know that your father and I haven't spoken for years, but I hope you'll give me a chance and hear me out.

I'm having a little trouble with my health and I'm thinking of making my will. As I have no children of my own, I'm interested in meeting my nieces and nephews, with a view to one or more of them benefiting. I can't come to see you, so perhaps you could come to see me in England?

All your expenses will be paid for the trip and

visit. And while you're here, we'll see if there's a specialist who can do something about your chronic fatigue syndrome, only we call it ME in England.

Since you're not well, I've asked a colleague of mine, who's been doing a job in Sydney, to escort you. His name is Mark Felton and he'll phone you in a week's time, so that you can think about my offer and deal with your father's reactions.

Sincerely yours
Maeve

Kate gaped at it, re-read it, then shook her head. This sort of thing happened in novels, not in real life.

Go to England! All expenses paid!

She'd always wanted to go there, but had been too busy building a career for herself. Only how would she cope with the trip in her present condition?

And how much money was Maeve talking about? Was she really dying? Or did she want her nieces and nephews to dance to her bidding in the hope of inheriting?

Remembering the other letter, Kate picked it up. Her heart sank when she saw it was from the Social Security office in nearby Berrabin. She opened it reluctantly, because letters from them never contained good news. She was right. Her case was up for a three-monthly review and an appointment had been made for her for the following week. No question of whether the date was convenient for her. It was an order to attend, however politely phrased.

Tears slipped down her cheeks at the mere thought of it. When she'd applied for sickness benefit, they'd treated her like a malingerer, reducing her to tears because she cried easily these days. She'd been dreading the review. Angry at herself for this weakness she snatched a tissue, wiped her eyes and blew her nose hard, then went back to the letter from her aunt, studying it again.

When she was more in control of herself she took it back into the kitchen where her parents were eating their lunch in a heavy silence. She'd made her point about her correspondence being her own business, now she wanted to see what they thought of this offer, because she was tempted, very tempted . . .

She held the letter out to her father. 'Read it and tell me what you think.'

He held it as if it was contaminated, scanning it quickly. 'What the hell does she think she's doing? You don't *need* her money. *We* can look after you.'

Her mother took it from him, read it then looked at Leo.

Tears were thickening Kate's throat and she swallowed hard. She wasn't going to let her father bully her about this. 'You can look after me, yes, and I'm deeply grateful for all you've done. Deeply. But I'm still lacking two important things, neither of which you can give me—and perhaps my aunt Maeve can.'

'Oh?'

'My health and with it my independence.'

He breathed in slowly, then let the air out again accompanied by a growling sound in his throat. 'You won't be independent if you're dancing to her tune. There'll be some trickery involved. Nothing

103

is ever simple with Maeve. And how did she know where you were, or that you'd been ill? Tell me that, eh? She must have had us investigated.'

'I wonder if Jason has had a letter too.' Her mother looked from one to the other. 'I'll phone him tonight and ask him.'

'I'll ask him when I get back to the shop,' Leo said. He pushed his plate away. 'I'm not hungry. I might as well go back to work.'

When he'd driven off, Jean looked at her daughter. 'Surely you'll not go to England, love?'

'I don't know. It's tempting.'

'It'll upset your father more than you'd believe.'

'I know. But . . . Well, I'll have to think about it.' She knew suddenly that she wanted to go, would do anything that would get her away from here and out of her present miserable state. She was going quietly mad in Callabine.

Her mother stood up. 'I've arranged to see Noelene about the fête. If you're too tired to clear up, leave it till I get back.' She left without another word.

As Kate began to clear the table, tears welled in her eyes, because she knew she'd hurt both her parents. But even as she wiped them away, she knew she would go, whatever they said. This offer might give her back her life again. If Maeve was rich, if she could get Kate the best help available . . . surely a specialist who really understood her problem would be able to help her? You had to lose your independence to realize how much it mattered.

*   *   *

104

'Jason's coming round this evening at eight o'clock,' Leo said as the three of them sat down to their evening meal.

'Did he get a letter too?' Kate asked.

'Yes. Nearly the same as yours, apparently, except she offered to pay for his wife and children to go to England as well.'

Kate picked at her food, not feeling at all hungry. There was going to be an almighty row when they found out she intended to accept her aunt's offer of a trip to England.

'You're not eating enough to feed a sparrow,' Jean complained as she watched her daughter push the food aside. 'How do you expect to get better if you don't eat?'

Kate fiddled with her dessert spoon. 'I'm not even sure I will get better properly. According to the research, some people never recover.'

'Of course you'll get better,' Leo said harshly. 'You're already better than you were when we brought you home. Give it another year and you'll be back to your old self.'

She smiled at him, knowing his brusque ways hid a genuine concern for her. 'Just a small piece of apple pie, Mum.'

When Jason and his wife arrived, they were sitting in front of the television watching a quiz programme and studiously avoiding the topic of Maeve's offer.

He passed round his letter.

'Well?' Leo asked, giving it back.

'I'm not going. It's tempting to hope she'd leave me some money, but on the other hand there's no guarantee. Anyway, our second store is doing well and I enjoy running it. I don't *need* her money.'

It seemed to Kate that her sister-in-law didn't agree with this decision, but she said nothing, just sighed.

'Good lad!' Leo said.

They all turned expectantly to Kate.

'I'm sorry. I don't want to hurt you, but I'm going to accept the offer.'

Her father glared at her. 'After all we've done for you!'

'Leo!' Jean laid a hand on his arm and he shook it off.

Kate tried to explain, but knew her words wouldn't take away the sting of what she was going to do. 'I badly need a change. Whether my aunt leaves me anything or not, I'll get a trip to England and maybe that will help me shake off this . . .' Words failed her and she waved one hand, then found to her dismay that she was crying. Again.

Her mother was there instantly. 'Come to bed, Kate. You're white as a sheet tonight.'

And she went, glad to be cosseted a little. 'I don't want to hurt Dad—or you, Mum. But I want to meet her, see what she's offering, and see if someone there can help me get better. That is the main reason I'm going.'

'We'd have paid for a holiday for you.'

'She's rich. She'll not miss the money. You're not rich. You should be saving for your old age— and you shouldn't have to help a daughter my age.' And the tears that had come so easily ever since she became ill started falling again.

When her mother put her arms round her and rocked her, making shushing noises, she laughed through her tears. 'You'd think I was still a child.'

'You always will be to me.'

Jean walked back to the living room, shaking her head in response to Leo's unspoken question. 'It's her decision. Let her make it in peace.'

'But—'

'It's not her quarrel, Leo. And she's very depressed, whatever she says. I think a trip might be just the thing for her.'

'Then *we'll* pay for it!'

'She wouldn't take it from us. Now, let the subject drop. How are the children, Jason love?'

*   *   *

Lily walked slowly down to the sitting room where her mother was waiting for her. She could guess what this was about and felt shaky inside as she stopped just inside the door to stare across the room.

'You can't stand there all day. Come and sit down beside me.' Kerry patted the couch.

Lily walked across to a chair instead and sat down opposite her mother, hands clasped, waiting.

'Can't you make yourself look a bit tidier? Wayne's coming round soon.'

'He won't care what I look like.'

'But I will.'

'You're too fussy about appearances. Anyway, he won't be looking at me, he'll be staring at you. He always does.'

Kerry smoothed down her skirt. 'It's in a woman's interest to look her best. Keeps her man interested.'

Lily didn't point out that at twelve she was hardly interested in finding a man. Her mother was old-fashioned about that sort of thing, seemed lost without a man in her life and only dated ones who were rich and could treat her to the best of everything. Goodness only knew why she and Lily's father had ever married, because Dad didn't really care about money. He was more interested in people and computers, had interesting friends all round the world whom he met at conferences or on the Internet.

'Are you listening, Lily?'

'What? Oh, sorry, Mum. What did you say?'

'I said: Wayne and I will be getting married as soon as possible, then we'll all be moving to Texas, so we'll have to start looking at what we need to take with us.'

Lily took a deep breath. 'You and Wayne will be moving there. I won't.'

'You'll go where I tell you, young woman!'

'How will you get me there? Drag me screaming every inch of the way?' She had the satisfaction of seeing her mother gape at her for a moment or two, clearly lost as to how to deal with her.

'The courts will insist you go with me.'

'Even if I want to stay with my father?'

'Cal is *not* your father.'

'Who is, then? Maybe I should go and live with him.'

'That's my business.'

'It's mine too. I'll ask the court to find out who my real father is. I'm sure you know.'

'You'll not be appearing in any court. We'll settle this on our own, in a civilized way.'

'We might have to go to court and my friend says they ask children of my age what they want these days.'

Kerry stared at her. 'That's ridiculous. As if you

know what's best for you.'

That's when Lily began to wonder whether her mother was just counting on her dad's vagueness about business matters to push things through in the way she wanted. Well, Lily would make sure he did things properly this time. It was too important. She realized her mother was still talking so reluctantly switched her mind back.

'. . . and anyway, your biological father won't want you, so that's a non-starter. He was married, had other children, wanted me to have an abortion and when I wouldn't, insisted your existence be kept quiet. He's never even tried to see you, not once.'

Lily dug her fingernails into the palms of her hand at this hurtful news. 'Well, I'm still not going to live in Texas. I'd never see Dad if I did. Besides, I'm English and I want to live in England.'

The doorbell rang. 'That'll be Wayne.' Kerry jumped up, glanced at herself in the mirror and went to answer the door.

Lily let out a long, careful breath. It was scary stuff, defying her mother, who didn't take kindly to being answered back or disobeyed, and would no doubt ground her for a million years, but she definitely wasn't going to Texas. She sighed as there was the sound of whispering in the hall.

When they came in, Wayne had his arm round her mother's shoulders and Kerry was dabbing at her eyes with a handkerchief. He guided her to the couch as if she couldn't find her own way. Lily watched them in disgust. It was gross how her mother played helpless for him. She was one of the least helpless females you could ever meet.

He went straight into the attack. 'Kerry tells me

you've got some strange idea about not coming to Texas with us.'

Lily used the tricks they'd taught her at school in human relations lessons on standing up for yourself firmly and with dignity. Who'd have thought those boring lessons would have come in useful? 'I have nothing against you, Wayne, and I hope you and my mother will be very happy together, but I want to stay in England and live with my father.'

'He's not your father, honey. You know that.'

'He is in every way that counts and I love him.'

'He doesn't love you now that he knows,' Kerry snapped. 'He's just doing this to annoy me.'

'That's a lie!'

'Don't speak to your mother like that!' Wayne snapped. 'Apologize to her at once.'

Lily looked at him and shivered, because suddenly he didn't seem half as friendly as before. But she wasn't going to be bullied, not by anyone, so she pressed her lips together. Why should she apologize? And how come her mother got away with telling so many lies and she got in trouble for telling the truth? It wasn't fair.

'Well?' He stared at her. 'I'm waiting.'

She stared right back. 'My mother's not telling the truth about my father so I've got nothing to apologize for.'

'The sooner we get her away from his influence, the better,' Kerry said, with a hint of a sob in her voice. 'He's always encouraged her to defy me.'

Lily gazed at her in shock. 'He's never done that and you know it!'

They ignored her.

'Once she's in Texas, she'll settle down, honey. I

110

know a really good boarding school where she can make friends with people whose families matter, and we can arrange for her to get some counselling.'

So Lily said it again, broken record trick it was called, repeating your statement firmly and quietly as many times as it took. 'I'm *not* going to Texas.'

'You'll do what your mother tells you, young lady!' he shouted. 'And I'll be behind her one hundred per cent.'

Lily lost it then and yelled, 'You'll have to drag me forcibly on to the plane and I'll scream every inch of the way. They'll stop you taking me out of the country.'

He smiled and so did her mother. 'We'll be going on my own executive jet, not a public carrier. No one will question what state you're in when you're taken on board. If you need a sedative because you're afraid of flying, then so be it.'

Lily felt icy dread creep down her spine. Suddenly she could see the ruthless man behind the normally soft-spoken Texan and wondered if her mother realized what Wayne was really like. She knew then that she'd have to run away, but first she'd find out if she could get help from the children's court or whoever it was you had to see when your parents split up. People had to understand that Cal was her real father. There was a kid at school who'd been through a custody battle recently. She'd ask him to tell her exactly what happened, who to go and see.

She pulled herself together and repeated, 'I'm *not* going to Texas.' After that she folded her arms and refused to answer any more questions or even talk to Wayne. What was the use? They'd not change their minds.

But neither would she.

'Go to your room,' her mother said at last. 'And don't switch on that computer of yours. You'll not be allowed to use it again till you see sense.'

Lily blinked hard to try to clear the tears from her eyes at this worst of all possible threats, but of course they noticed and *he* smiled. She hated him then, which she hadn't done before.

Wayne jumped to his feet. 'I'd better come up and get the computer. I don't think we can trust this young lady an inch, Kerry. She needs firm handling and that's just what she'll get in my house.'

Lily said nothing, walking slowly up the stairs behind them. It had started.

When they'd left her alone in her room, she sat down and pretended to read a book in case they looked in, but actually she was trying to plan what to do next. She didn't allow herself to cry until after she'd gone to bed, and didn't do it for long, because she'd no intention of them seeing her with eyes swollen from crying.

*   *   *

Two days later Maeve listened to the specialist in silence and stared into space for a moment or two, willing herself to stay calm, not to hope for too much. 'You—um—think this new treatment may help?'

'It could prolong your life by a few months, a year even, but I'm afraid it can't cure what ails you, not with that sort of cancer.'

'A few more months of life would be very

welcome just now. It'd allow me to set my affairs in better order.' She slapped her hand down on the chair arm. 'I'll do it.'

'The treatment won't be pleasant. One of the side effects is severe nausea—and hair loss is very likely.'

She shrugged. 'I'm not feeling wonderful anyway.'

'Some people find it comforting to know they'll be contributing to research, thus helping others.'

She shrugged again. 'I'm not that altruistic. I'm concerned more about myself at this stage than about others. Please arrange to get things started as quickly as possible. And tell them that if they take me into this programme, I'll make a substantial financial contribution to their research funds.'

'You can get into the programme without doing that. You're exactly the sort of guinea pig they're looking for.'

'I've always paid my way and I don't intend to stop now.'

'I'm sure they'll be grateful for your contribution. I'll make an appointment for you, then, shall I?'

When Maeve went back into the waiting room, Andy stood up and hurried across to her. 'All right?'

'Yes. Let's go out to the car before we talk.' Andy had wanted to come in to see the specialist with her, but she wasn't going to allow that.

He escorted her down to the car, but she noted with wry amusement that he didn't make the mistake of trying to help her. She hated that, however exhausted she was.

When they were both seated he put the keys into the ignition and turned to her without attempting to switch on the engine. 'What did he say?'

She explained.

'Oh, Maeve, that's wonderful!'

She swallowed hard and blinked her eyes, unable to speak calmly in the face of that genuine caring. It'd been a long time since she'd allowed anyone to get so close to her, except for Lena.

'I'll drive you to and fro for treatment.'

She nodded, wondered if it'd be safer emotionally to hire a chauffeur instead, then allowed herself the small luxury of claiming Andy's time and support. After all, the company wasn't going to need him for much longer, as it soon wouldn't belong to her. She should be feeling sad about that, but she wasn't. The company had had its day in the sun and now she was far more concerned about making the most of the time she had left than worrying what Des was doing.

'Thanks, Andy. I'd like that. And after the company's gone, you'll stay on as my personal assistant, won't you?'

'I'll welcome having more time with you. I'll be glad when we've handed Corrigan's over to the new owner. He's coming up on Monday. Will you be there to meet him?'

'No, you do it.'

'OK.' He hesitated. 'Lena and I were talking and we were wondering if I should move into your house—for the time being. To be there for you.'

Maeve considered this, then gave him a wry smile. 'My live-in toy boy, you mean?'

'More like your live-in adopted nephew, if I may presume?' He lifted one eyebrow, waiting.

114

Pleasure filled her, followed by the unusual feeling of love for another human being, something she hadn't experienced for a long time—or in the case of Andy, hadn't allowed herself to admit to feeling. Now—well, she'd damn well do as she pleased for whatever time she had left, even become sentimental. But the most she could admit aloud was, 'Yes. Good idea. Much more convenient. And I'd like a nephew.'

Andy was surprised at how easily she'd agreed, but he kept that to himself. He and Lena had debated for days about how to broach it with Maeve and here she was agreeing without any quibbles whatsoever. He didn't look at her or say anything else, not wanting to push his luck, but he couldn't hold back a smile as he started the car.

Not an easy woman to love, Maeve Corrigan, but worth it. She was more a mother to him than his own had ever been. He didn't want to lose Maeve, still couldn't believe that such a vibrant person would die so young, at not quite sixty.

Ten

Outdoors bright sunshine glints off the parked cars and formal flower beds flourish a cheerful salute to summer, perfuming the air. Indoors air whispers quietly through the monochrome offices, served always at a constant temperature, with no perfume.

The following Monday, Andy waited in the main office at Corrigan's for the man who would be in charge of the takeover processes. Raymond Tate was Director of Finance, second in command of DC International, Maeve's brother's company, and the two of them had met several times during the course of the negotiations. Tate was always perfectly civil, but Andy hadn't taken to him. That was how it went. Some people you trusted on sight; others you didn't.

He looked out of the office window to see a large car purr into the executive parking area and roll to a halt. A uniformed chauffeur jumped out and hurried round to open the door for a man whom Andy recognized from photographs in share brochures as Desmond Corrigan. So the big boss had come out of hiding now about buying the company!

The brother and sister weren't much alike. Maeve was slim and restrained, though you couldn't help being aware of the power she wielded so skilfully. This one looked like a farmer dressed up for a day out in London. The suit was expensive, you could see that at a glance, but although Corrigan wasn't overweight, he had a florid complexion and his face looked a bit puffy. Maybe he was a man who spent a lot of time out of doors—or who drank a lot? Probably the latter.

What had brought him here today? Did he want to gloat over his sister? Well, he'd be disappointed.

With a sigh, Andy put away the papers he'd been sorting through, because Maeve's instructions were very clear. Nothing was to be left behind that wasn't absolutely necessary.

The executive secretary knocked on the door then poked her head round it to say, 'Your visitors are here, Mr Blauman.'

'Show them in.' Andy braced himself.

Corrigan strolled in first, looking round with a proprietorial air. 'Nice office.'

Tate made the introductions and the two men shook hands. 'Mr Corrigan is actually the new owner.'

'I know.'

They both stared at him in surprise.

'How?' Corrigan asked.

He avoided the question. 'We've known for a while.'

Corrigan breathed deeply for a moment or two, then looked round. 'Where's my sister?'

'At home.'

Des grinned, the sort of knowing, triumphant smile that made Andy want to punch him in the face. He couldn't remember when he'd taken such a dislike to a person on sight. No, he'd disliked him long before then—because Andy was the one who had found out about the convoluted trickery of this take-over.

'I'd not have thought she was afraid to meet me.'

'Maeve isn't afraid to meet anyone, but she's not

well.'

Des smiled. 'Yes, of course.'

Andy didn't say anything because Maeve had strictly forbidden him to mention what was wrong with her. However, half an hour later, when they came back from a quick tour of the works, Corrigan made yet another snide reference to Maeve avoiding him.

'Miss Corrigan *is* ill,' Andy said curtly. 'I give you my solemn word on that.'

Des stared at him, still with a half-grin on his face. 'I hope it's something serious.'

Andy closed his eyes for a minute, trying to hide his anger then opened them to see Corrigan looking at him, eyes narrowed. 'That's her business.'

'It *is* serious!' Des's smile faded. 'Don't bother to deny it, I can see from your face.'

'Can you?'

'You're fond of her, aren't you?'

'Everyone here is fond of Miss Corrigan, who has been an exemplary employer.'

'Well, give her my best wishes for her speedy recovery.'

'Yes. Now, about the handover arrangements . . .'

Before they left, Corrigan took Andy aside. 'It'd make things a lot easier if you'd come and work for me. I'm prepared to give you a substantial rise and good fringe benefits.'

'I already have a job, but thank you for the offer.'

'It's still open if you should change your mind.'

Andy kept a smile pinned to his face until the door had closed behind them, then sat down in his

118

chair with a low groan of relief. As if he'd ever work for a man like that! Well, only a few more days and he'd be through here. He'd expected to be sorry to leave, but helping Maeve was so much more important that he wished he could walk out this minute. On that thought he got up and went back to checking the master files, keeping some, discarding others, which was a job only he or Maeve could do.

If she was well enough, though, he hoped to bring her here for the farewell party on Friday. Everyone wanted to see her, say goodbye, thank her.

She wasn't the only one who was leaving. Several staff members had taken the offer of early retirement she'd made to them. Corrigan would find some important gaps in the ranks of management and technical skills.

*   *   *

Back at the hotel, Des paced up and down, frowning, not speaking to Tate, who sat quietly studying some figures. 'Has there been any word about my sister being ill?'

'No.'

'Find out about it. Even if you have to hire a whole squad of detectives, I want to know exactly what's wrong with her.'

'Very well.'

The phone rang. Tate picked it up. 'Someone for you, waiting in the lobby. Says his name's Smith.'

'I'll go down to him.' Des shrugged himself into his jacket and left without another word.

119

In the lobby he went across to the man he'd hired and took him into the coffee lounge. 'Well? Did my dear wife appreciate her present?'

'She intercepted it and had it dumped at the rear of the garden instead, so presumably she had some use for it.'

'I thought I told you I wanted it dumped on the rear patio, as close as possible to the kitchen window.'

'There was a motorbike blocking the way. The delivery man couldn't get round there.'

Des stiffened. 'A motorbike?'

'Yes. A Harley-Davidson. I got a photograph of it. The owner of it was in the house with her. He came to join her at the door. I got a photograph of them both standing there. It was rather early for visitors and he had bare feet and rumpled hair, so my guess is he'd been there all night. And then I took this one.' He passed across the photo of them kissing.

His employer's face turned deep puce. 'Any idea who he is?'

'No. But I have the number of the motorbike, so I can find out.'

'Do that.' Des held out his hand for the print-outs of the rest of the photos, nodded dismissal and stayed where he was. He ordered a cappuccino and studied the photos again, then pulled out the one showing the kiss. The fellow definitely had bare feet. Dammit, she *had* been having an affair, for all her fine words! She hadn't had time to meet anyone since she left him—unless it was someone she'd met at the hotel?

Either way, he'd soon find out what was going on.

*   *   *

Kate stared out of the window as a sleek new car pulled into the drive then scowled as Joe got out. What was *he* doing in Callabine? He lived in Melbourne now, too far away to just pop in and see her. He looked too well for her peace of mind, with those dark good looks and an air of physical fitness and energy. She'd looked like that once, been full of beans from morning to night. She and Joe had been good together, both in bed and as companions—and it still hurt that he'd abandoned her like that.

She went to open the door and stand barring the way in with her arms folded across her body. 'What are *you* doing here?'

'I had business in the district so I thought I'd stay on a bit longer and call in to see you.'

'Then you've wasted your time. I don't want to see you.'

When she turned to close the door, he stuck out one hand to hold it open. 'Can't we at least be friends, Kate?'

'I don't feel very friendly towards someone who left me when the going got tough.'

He gave her one of his level glances. 'The new job meant a lot to me. I couldn't have done anything to help you and you weren't getting any better. You're looking a bit better now, though you're still pale.'

She shrugged. She was still a long way from her old self. She saw that every time she looked in the mirror, felt it every time that bone-melting tiredness swept through her. 'You made your

121

choice then and I'm making mine now. Go and call on someone else, Joe. I'm busy.'

He didn't budge. 'Why won't you ever speak to me on the phone? I really wanted to keep in touch.'

'Kate Corrigan, you're never turning an old friend away.' Her mother pulled her out of the way and held the door wide. 'Come in, Joe. Have you driven far? Would you like a cup of tea?'

As Kate turned towards her bedroom, her mother grabbed the back of her tee shirt, hissing, 'This is *your* friend.' Within minutes she had the two of them sitting on the back veranda with a tray of tea and scones.

Kate didn't attempt to argue. Her mother had set views about hospitality—and this was her mother's house. Her parents kept reminding her of that, not so much in words as by their insistence on her doing things their way, as if she were still a child. And in one sense she was, because she couldn't afford to move out on her own, so was dependent on them for the roof over her head.

Joe concentrated on stirring sugar into his tea. 'Tell me how things are going. Really.'

'How do you think? I'm still not well enough to work. If I didn't have my computer and the Internet, I'd go mad. Maybe I've gone mad anyway. My father certainly thinks so.'

'Why?'

'Never mind. Tell me about your new job.'

When she realized they'd been sitting chatting for over an hour, she gave him a wry smile. 'We always could talk, couldn't we?'

He nodded. 'You're looking tired now, though.'

'It's been rather a fraught few days.'

122

'Still don't want to tell me why?'

She shook her head.

He stood up. 'I'm staying overnight in Berrabin. Want to come out for a drive tomorrow?'

She hesitated, very tempted to accept, but annoyed with herself for that. Had she really forgiven him that easily? But the thought of getting away from her parents for a few hours tipped the balance. 'It'd make a nice change to get out of Callabine.'

'Is your car being repaired? It's not outside.'

She shrugged. 'I sold it. Couldn't stay awake to drive very far at first and Mum lets me borrow her car when she isn't using it.' Her father had offered to pay for running her car, but she'd refused out of sheer pride. They'd done enough for her. Besides, she'd got a good price for it and would use the money later to buy a less expensive one, when there was a reason for it. Living here meant she could actually save money from the sickness benefits, which was important to her now.

Joe's glance was sympathetic but thank goodness he didn't comment on her lack of a car. She stood in the doorway waving to him but couldn't face her mother's smug smile, so went to her room and switched on her computer.

Over the evening meal she refused to discuss Joe's visit with them and didn't mention the outing planned for the following day. You had to guard any shred of privacy fiercely in the Corrigan household—even when you were twenty-eight years old.

By seven thirty that evening she was exhausted, as usual, so went to bed with a book. Thank heaven for libraries!

Around ten she woke with the light still on and her book lying on the pillow beside her, its pages bent. She felt desperately thirsty but as she reached the kitchen door, she heard her parents chatting quietly and hesitated. She didn't want another lecture. Or an interrogation about Joe.

Then she heard her father say triumphantly, 'Joe came, didn't he? All it took was one phone call. And if I have to pay to keep him coming, I'll even do that. I'm not having my daughter taking Maeve's leavings, if I can prevent it.'

Sick at heart, Kate turned round and crept back to her room, switching off the light and huddling beneath the sheet. Joe wouldn't have come but for her father's prompting. The humiliation of that left her beyond tears and she lay staring up at the ceiling for a long time. She had worried about alienating her family by accepting Maeve's invitation, but if anything had been needed to help her keep to her decision, this was it.

At six o'clock the following morning she rang up the motel where Joe would be staying, because it was the only one in Berrabin. She was savagely glad she'd woken him up. 'I don't know what my father said or did to get you down here, Joe Carvalli, but you can bloody well go away again. I definitely won't be in if you call.'

'Kate, please—'

She slammed the phone down. When it rang she let her mother answer it.

Her mother came into the bedroom without knocking.

'I accidentally overheard you and Dad talking last night,' Kate threw at her. 'It's humiliating to have you asking someone to come and see me.

124

How did you do it? Play on his guilt and pity? Pay his travel expenses?'

Jean sighed and leaned against the door frame. 'I told your father it wouldn't work. I'm sorry, love.'

'But you still let Dad do it, didn't you? He talks about his sister manipulating people, but he's tarred with the same brush.'

'Kate!'

'Go away and leave me in peace. There's nothing you can say or do now to change my mind. I'm definitely going to England.'

She stayed in bed until her father had left for work, didn't get her breakfast until her mother had gone to the regular weekly meeting of the Country Women's Association. Well, she was never hungry these days.

She hoped this Felton man would ring soon and get her out of here.

*   *   *

The next day at school Lily gave her friend Rosemary a message to email to her father, then asked to see the counsellor, telling her teacher it was an emergency and sobbing that she couldn't bear things any longer. It wasn't hard to cry on demand, she found, because she felt upset all the time at the moment, but even as she wept she was watching herself and trying to do this properly. She'd watched herself like that for as long as she could remember. She studied other people too, trying to work out why they did things.

The counsellor sat Lily down, provided tissues and talked gently to her as she told Mrs Gipson exactly what had happened the previous day.

'But Lily, if your mother has custody of you, I can't see how you'll be able to avoid going with them. Where would you live if you didn't?'

'With my Dad.'

'I'm not sure that would be approved if he's not your real father.'

'He *is*! He's the one who brought me up, has always been there for me. Don't *I* have any choice about my life?'

'Well, the courts will ask for your opinion, since you're over twelve, but still . . .'

'So you'll let my mother drug me and take me forcibly out of the country, then dump me in a boarding school? I thought you were here to *help* me!' She began sobbing again.

'I think you're exaggerating about them taking you forcibly out of the country, Lily.'

'I'm not. Wayne has his own plane and he's very rich. He said they'd sedate me and carry me on board if necessary, pretend I'm afraid of flying.'

There was a long silence, then Mrs Gipson looked at her severely. 'I hope you're not exaggerating about this, Lily.'

'No. I'm not. That's exactly what he said they'd do, so now I'm afraid of him. And he said they'd be putting me in a boarding school over there, so why take me anyway?'

'I'm sure you've mistaken what they said.'

'Why will you not *listen*? I'm telling the truth. He said *sedate.* He said *boarding school*, too. So it's not even as if I'd be with my mother. I'd be in a strange country, away from everyone I know.'

Mrs Gipson made some notes then looked up. 'I think you'd better go home for the rest of the day,

Lily. We'll talk about this again tomorrow.'

'I'd rather stay at school. If I had my choice, I'd never go home again, not to *her* anyway.' She stood up. 'Thank you for listening to me. And please— don't let them take me to America.'

'I'll talk about the situation to someone. Come back and see me tomorrow before school if you're still upset, otherwise I'll make an appointment to see you in a week's time.'

'Yes, Mrs Gipson. Thank you.' Lily made sure she walked out slowly, shoulders drooping. She was very quiet in all her classes, not answering unless the teacher asked her something directly, instead of volunteering as she usually did. She sat quietly at lunchtime, too, not eating much so that the prefect in charge of her table asked her if she was feeling all right.

Letting the tears well up again, she left the table hurriedly. But it was a while before she could stop crying. She didn't know any more where pretending to be upset ended and real weeping began.

Rosemary said afterwards, 'I've never seen you like this, Lily. You're usually so strong and confident.'

'I've never felt like this before.' She blinked her eyes furiously and opened her locker to take out her books for the next lesson. 'I'm not going to America, though. I'll run away first.'

'They'll only bring you back and force you to go.'

'We'll see about that.'

Lily skipped athletics practice after school and went straight home, getting back over an hour before her mother usually returned. She put her things in her room, set out a biscuit on a plate in the kitchen and ate half of it, filled a glass with orange juice and drank half of it, then began her search. Her mother's computer was now password protected, so she couldn't email her dad. No doubt Wayne had done that. Her mother wasn't very good with technical stuff.

She began going carefully through her mother's drawers in the desk where the business papers were kept, hoping to find a clue about who her real father was. Maybe *he* would help her—if only to keep her quiet.

Why hadn't he wanted her? Even if he was married, he could have come to see her from time to time. Only—if *he* had still been hanging around her mother, she wouldn't have her dad, who was better than any stranger could ever be.

She heard her mother's car drive up and the automatic garage door open, so she put the papers back in the desk carefully and went into the kitchen to sit in front of her half-eaten biscuit.

'There you are, Lily dear. Did you have a nice day at school?'

She stared at her mother, surprised by the endearment and gentle tone of voice. 'No. I was too upset.'

'We'll have to cheer you up, then. I thought we could go shopping at the weekend for some new clothes. You've been growing again and you'll want something smart for our wedding.'

'No, thank you.'

Her mother swung round. 'What do you mean by that?'

'I mean, I don't want to go shopping. I can wear my blue dress for the wedding. I've only worn it once. And I keep telling you: I'm *not* going to Texas with Wayne.' She saw her mother's face tighten and added, 'What's more, there's nothing you can take away from me now that I care about, so how are you going to force me to go shopping with you? I'm twelve, not two, so you can't carry me. I have a mind of my own, you know, and I have my own plans for the future, too.'

'You're still dependent on me, however.'

'I'm not. My dad pays for my keep. I want to go and live with him.'

'I keep telling you he's *not* your father.'

'And I keep telling you he *is* and always will be. And what's more, he's a better father than you're a mother, so—'

Her mother slapped her across her face, something she hadn't done for years.

Seeing a face at the kitchen window, Lily jerked away and began to scream, 'Don't hit me! Don't hit me again!' just as there was a tap on the back door.

Kerry swung round to see their neighbour from next door staring through the glass panels on the door as Lily cowered back against the wall. She turned to her daughter. 'You'll regret this. Stop play-acting at once!' She flung the door open, but Mrs Baxter was already backing away.

'I'll—er—come back later, Kerry. When you're not—er—busy.'

After the gate had clanged shut, Lily straightened up, smiled at her mother then walked out of the kitchen and up to her bedroom.

Kerry glared after her. 'You little bitch!' she muttered under her breath. She went to pour herself a glass of white wine and sank down at the kitchen table, sipping it, trying to work out what to

129

do about this. Lily wasn't going to win. She was coming to Texas and that was that.

And not just for the obvious reasons. The marriage with Wayne might or might not last. Kerry suspected it wouldn't because he'd had three other wives already. But she intended to give it a good go and if not, come out of it with money. You could rely on money. People only let you down, usually when you most needed them.

* * *

Cal waited impatiently for someone to pick up the phone. 'Kerry?'

'Oh, it's you.'

'I want to see Lily.'

'Seeing you upsets her.'

'Stop playing games, Kerry.'

'The answer is no. She's not your daughter and you have to accept that.'

'Never!'

'Anyway, we're taking her down to Brighton for the weekend. A break will do her good. Perhaps the following weekend?'

Frustrated and afraid of doing something that would jeopardize his chances of remaining in his daughter's life, he put down the phone. He continued to email Lily every day but there had only been one email from her friend on her behalf. That could only be because Kerry was keeping her away from computers. He felt helpless, needing to fill the weekend with something, someone . . . but at the moment he didn't want to see his other friends, most of whom were either happily married with children or shacked up together testing out

130

the possibility of marriage.

The happiness of such friends made him wish he had someone special in his life. On that thought Judith's face came into his mind and he shook his head to banish it. How stupid could you get? He'd only met the woman once. But the memory of her warm smile wouldn't stay banished and he was enjoying their email exchanges. She understood what it was to be separated from a child and seemed to be missing her son a great deal.

He would, he decided on the Friday morning, make an appointment for the following week to see someone at the Children's Department about his legal position with regard to Lily. If necessary he'd then get his lawyer to do whatever lawyers did in these cases—take out an injunction to stop Kerry taking Lily out of the country perhaps. He should have done something before but had been terrified of being told he had no rights whatsoever.

Kerry seemed so confident about her ability to take her daughter away from him and she didn't usually make mistakes about things like that.

In the meantime hard physical labour like spreading out a trailer load of muck would be an excellent way to work off some of the tension. He picked up the phone . . .

*   *   *

Judith spent a peaceful week, with no more tricks being played on her. The manure was a pungent reminder of her ex, though, and she didn't lower her guard about security, closing all the windows as well as locking the door every time she went out. She ordered a new security system to be fitted,

131

resenting the money it cost, but needing it to stay comfortable in her own home.

Thank you, Des!

Cal emailed her on the Monday, thanking her for her hospitality and asking if there had been any more incidents. She replied and before she knew it they were emailing every evening about their daily lives. She visited his web site and it seemed to be a reputable business. Indeed, it was an elegantly simple site, unlike some of the cluttered, fussy ones she'd seen. She liked it artistically. She liked him too, had never taken to someone so quickly. It was as he'd said: it felt as if they were old friends.

Still feeling that she was marking time with her life, she started going through the house, doing what she could to set it in order without spending much money. Her aunt had let it get very run down as she grew older but Judith had sneaked out some furniture from her old home before she split up with Des. She must have been prescient! In storage in London she had the furnishings and equipment from her studio, every single thing, and also the stuff from a small sitting room they never used because Des said its colour scheme looked faded. She'd bet he'd not even noticed the things had gone, because he never went into either room.

The removal men who brought her things carried the old suite from the living room out to the shed for her. Her new suite looked perfect and she moved the smaller pieces of her aunt's furniture around until she was satisfied that her sitting room looked attractive in a comfortable, understated way.

The kitchen was extremely old-fashioned but that would have to wait until she reached a settlement with Des. She hadn't cooked for years and was starting to get her hand in again, had forgotten the sheer pleasure of making a dish that was exactly what you wanted. Her aunt had some lovely old-fashioned cookery books which didn't pretend that fat was a dirty word.

Mitch emailed her most days, too, amusing little messages telling her the latest jokes, mentioning some of the highlights of his week, giving her Gran's love, but saying little about his father. She missed her son greatly and sent him long emails in return, telling him all about her new house. She phoned him a couple of times too and they agreed that he and her mother would come to see her during the summer holidays.

When Cal repeated his offer to come and spread the manure for her at the weekend she hesitated, waiting several hours before replying. But after a week of solitude interrupted only by a visit to a physiotherapist to check how her knee was going, she was tired of being alone.

In the end she emailed back to say she'd love to see Cal, then wished she hadn't because she didn't want to give him ideas.

Or were the ideas simmering already in both of them? She couldn't help remembering, with a little shiver in her belly, how attractive he was.

*   *   *

James, who was Mark Felton's second in command at the private investigation agency, reported to Miss Corrigan on Thursday. He had quite a lot of news for her this time.

'Your brother's wife has gone up north to live in

133

Lancashire and *he* is seeing a lot of Tiffany Roberts, his mistress of several years.'

'Is this Tiffany person of interest to us?'

'I shouldn't think so. She's not borne him any children. She's good-looking, another blonde—he does go for them, as you said—but unlike the other women, she seems genuinely fond of him.'

'I want to hear more about his son.'

'Mitch is well liked, not very good at sport, which upsets your brother, but ambitious and academically gifted, a straight A student. He's aiming for Oxford or Cambridge.'

'Does Des see much of him?'

'No. He took his son and mother-in-law out for dinner on the day his ex-wife moved up north, but hasn't seen them since.' James put a photograph on the table in front of her. 'This is quite a good one of Mitch.'

She picked it up with a hand that shook. 'Dear heaven!'

'Is something wrong?'

'He looks just like Leo as a boy, even to the red hair. I'd like to meet him. I think I'll write him a letter. Could you get someone to deliver it to him in person?'

'Is that wise, Miss Corrigan?'

'None of what I'm doing is wise, but see if you can arrange it anyway. What of my brother's other children?'

James put photos of each daughter down on the table as he summed them up. 'Lacey, the elder girl from his first marriage, is getting married next week. Big wedding, father paying for everything. She seems a nice young woman, is fond of her half-brother, but she's not nearly as intelligent as

Mitch. She's quite good at golf and tennis, though, and Des has been paying to have her privately coached. Her sister Emma is doing well at university and is going on to do a postgraduate degree in Biochemistry. She might bear watching, too, for your purposes.'

'Fine. What about the illegitimate child?'

'She lives with her mother. Des doesn't seem to have visited her or even met her, but he pays very handsomely indeed for her keep.'

'Hmm. I'll leave her for the time being.' Maeve leaned back, thinking about her options, knowing James would wait patiently. All Mark Felton's operatives were patient. 'I think I'd like to meet Mitch's mother before I contact him. It wouldn't be fair to make any offers to her son without telling her.'

'Do you think that's wise?'

'You keep using that word. It's not a concept that matters much to me now. I'll do what's necessary to make sure my hard-earned money isn't wasted and I'll do what pleases me.'

'Sorry, Miss Corrigan.'

'It's all right. One begins to think very differently when one's days are numbered.'

When he'd gone, she sat mulling things over, praying she'd have enough time left to make a sensible disposal of her wealth.

She hoped Leo's daughter would accept her offer to come to England. She felt a certain sympathy towards anyone trapped by illness and had asked Andy to research chronic fatigue syndrome for her and find out the best specialist dealing with it.

As for Leo's son, from all reports Jason was

exactly like his father, content with moderate achievements, living for his family. She'd bet he'd not accept her offer to come to England.

How fecund her brothers were, damn them!

*　　　*　　　*

That evening Maeve shared her plans with Andy. 'I intend to write to Des's wife Judith, inviting her to come and visit me. Could you bring her here without him finding out? He's having her watched twenty-four hours a day, apparently.'

'Are you sure that's—'

Maeve held up one hand. 'Don't *you* start asking me if it's wise! I've finished being wise. I intend to be selfish and self-indulgent for what time I have left. And I intend to leave my mark on my family! They're not just getting my money, they're getting a few prods in the right direction.'

He grinned. He'd been the recipient of her prods early in their association, and was truly thankful for them when he looked back and saw how much stronger he'd grown because of her tutelage. 'They won't know what's hit them. But wise or not, I'll do whatever you wish and well you know it, you manipulative woman.'

She smiled at him, taking that as a compliment.

'When you write to Judith, tell her to phone me on my mobile and I'll arrange a meeting.'

Her hand rested briefly on his. 'Thank you.' Then she leaned back in her chair, looking tired again. 'I need another damned rest.'

He left the room quietly, hoping the new treatment was helping fight the cancer. She looked almost transparent, but she'd never looked as beautiful, and she'd lost some of that hard edge which had sometimes upset him. But then, he was too soft, he knew.

*   *   *

On the Friday Judith heard something fall through her letter box and went to pick up the envelopes from the hall floor. Two were bills, the other was cream in colour and looked expensive. She rubbed her finger across it, enjoying the texture and feel. She'd tried paper making once so could recognize quality.

In the kitchen she slit the envelope carefully because it was too beautiful to tear and spread out the single sheet of paper inside. It was from an address in Cheshire, not one she recognized, so she quickly scanned the letter, gasped in surprise and read it again more slowly.

My dear Ms Horrocks,

You may be surprised to hear from me, but I'm your ex-husband's sister and I'd like to meet you. Our meeting could lead to financial advantage to your son—but I must request that you don't mention this letter or anything that stems from it to Des, given his feelings about me.

I'm not in good health so cannot come to you. I wonder if you'd kindly come and visit me at your earliest convenience. If you ring the number below, my personal assistant, Andy Blauman, will make the necessary arrangements.

Maeve Corrigan

137

Judith stared at the letter, re-read it then stared into space. Des had never had a good word to say for his sister and if Maeve was using her to stir up trouble, then Judith didn't want to get involved. But she'd seen for herself how spiteful Des could be, so maybe his sister wasn't as bad as he said and . . . Oh, hell, she didn't need anything else to worry about. She'd just ignore this letter.

But the words *financial advantage to your son* kept repeating themselves in her mind and in the end she dialled the phone number she'd been given. She put the receiver down again after one ring. No, she'd be foolish to get involved.

An hour later curiosity got the better of her and she pressed redial.

'Mr Blauman? Judith Horrocks here.'

'Maeve will be delighted you rang.'

'I'm still not sure whether to come and see her or not. I don't really want to get involved in my ex's family feuds.'

'The feud is on your husband's side only.'

'Yes, but—'

'Look, Miss Corrigan hasn't long to live. She has cancer, though we'd be grateful if you'd keep that to yourself. She's a wonderful, courageous woman and I'm sure she won't waste your time.'

Judith frowned. This put a new perspective on *financial advantage* for Mitch. And the way Andy spoke of his employer said a lot about her, too. She doubted any of Des's employees would praise him so unstintingly. Well, she knew for certain they wouldn't. He regarded all of them, except for Raymond Tate, as expendable and interchangeable. 'Very well. If you'll give me the address, I'll drive over to see Miss Corrigan.'

'There's a small problem. Are you aware that your husband has you under 24-hour surveillance?'

'*What?* No.'

'We'd prefer that he didn't know about this meeting.'

'So would I!'

'Then I suggest you drive to the Wheatsheaf Shopping Centre in Rochdale and I'll meet you there. You can leave your car in the car park and I'll drive you to Cheshire. Would next Monday suit you?'

'Yes.'

'Shall we meet at nine o'clock outside the bookshop?'

'Yes. How will I recognize you?'

'Trust me. I'll know you.'

When she put the phone down Judith didn't move for a moment or two. *Trust me,* he'd said. She wasn't sure she trusted anyone linked with the Corrigans. What the hell was she letting herself in for? If Andy Blauman knew her by sight, then it meant that someone else had been watching her as well.

But she had to admit she was curious to meet Maeve, after all Des had said about his sister.

Besides, Judith's new life was a bit lonely and not once had she been in the mood for painting.

Eleven

As the setting sun lengthens the shadows, ancient drystone walls pattern the lower slopes of the moors. Trapped between them, sheep punctuate the landscape.

Of such evenings were masterpieces painted Judith thought, gazing eastwards out of the kitchen window towards the moors. For the first time in many weeks she itched for her paints. She'd unpack them tomorrow, sort out the attic, make a studio for herself.

No wonder her aunt had loved this place. She tore herself away from the view that daily blessed her eyes and nipped upstairs. But she forgot to change her clothes and couldn't bear to switch on the light, because another view greeted her here, just as beautiful, and she could only stand at the window looking out at the gilded clouds floating across the western sky. Beauty, whether in large or small doses, never failed to move her.

It was not until she was drawing the curtains on the landing that she noticed the car parked on the road outside her gates. Same dark car, again with a solitary occupant.

That brought her back to reality with a thump and as she realized what its presence meant, she grew so angry that she forgot any questions of safety and ran downstairs. Flinging open the front door she marched across the road to rap on the tinted window of the vehicle. 'Get out! I'd like a word with you.'

She couldn't see his features clearly through the darkened glass, but she could see the lighter crescent of his teeth as his mouth dropped open in surprise.

While he was doing what she'd asked, she suddenly saw the camera lying ready on the dashboard and thinking of him taking sneaky photographs of her daily life or visitors was the final straw to send her anger blazing up to white heat. Snatching the camera, she hurled it as far as she could into the field beyond. 'Tell my husband he can go to hell! I'll do as I please and he can't stop me,' she yelled, then turned and marched back into the house.

From the bedroom window she watched in great satisfaction as the man clambered over the dry-stone wall and began searching through the tussocky grass for his camera. It took him a long time to find it.

*   *   *

Cal arrived in Blackfold just as dusk was blurring the landscape. The village street was quiet, except for the central area near the three pubs and chip shop. He drove through, smiling at the sight of groups of young people talking and gesticulating, some in couples, some standing alone, one trio sitting on a wall like carrion crows—why did so many of them wear black? He liked young people, had allowed one or two to spend time with him on work experience, and hoped he'd helped them. Most of them had been full of wonderful energy and enthusiasm.

At Judith's end of the village he saw a flash of

141

light in one of the parked cars as someone lit a cigarette. After parking the bike, he looked in his rear-view mirror and realized that the car was ideally placed to see who came and went. That must be her ex having a watch kept on her.

When she answered the doorbell, she said only, 'Cal!' and smiled at him.

For a moment he stood smiling back at her, saying nothing.

She took a step backwards and gestured gracefully with one arm. 'Come in. I have a bottle of wine opened.'

'I'd better not. There's a man over there watching the house.'

'I know.'

'You do?'

She glared towards the car. 'Yes. I'd rather you came in openly. I don't want Des thinking he can stop me seeing people. He and I are permanently separated and I intend to do what I like with my life from now on. In fact,' she leaned up to kiss his cheek, 'I hope he takes more photos of us.'

'If you're sure . . . ?'

'I'm very sure.'

'Then I'll park the bike in its usual place and unload it. Did you put the blankets back in the shed?'

'No. I'm not having a friend sleeping out there when I've got several spare bedrooms empty here. I mean it.'

He grinned at her. 'You're in a stroppy mood today.'

She smiled back. 'I certainly am. I went across the road earlier and threw that man's camera into the field. It took him ages to find it again.'

Cal threw back his head and let out a shout of laughter.

'While you're getting your things I'll pour you a glass of wine. Red or white?'

'White.'

'Come in the back way. The kitchen door is open.'

Still smiling, Cal went to roll his bike round to the back of the house, unable to resist the temptation to flourish a mocking bow towards the watcher in the car first.

*   *   *

'Go and get ready, Lily,' Kerry said sharply. 'We're leaving in a few minutes.'

'Can't I just pick up my emails first? You can read them. You'll see for yourself then that Dad still cares for me.'

'Wayne and I have checked. He hasn't sent any emails either yesterday or today. We'd have printed them out for you.'

'I don't believe you!'

Her mother shrugged. 'Believe it or not, it's the truth. Now, go and get ready!'

Lily was tired of saying she wasn't going to Brighton with them, that she didn't want to go anywhere but to her dad's. She didn't believe he hadn't tried to contact her. He emailed every single day, never forgot, sending the emails to both her addresses. He must be worrying about not hearing from her, but her mother had kept her home from school for the past few days, so she hadn't been able to give her friend any more messages for him.

Yesterday her mother had gone on and on at her about their new life till Lily lost it, screaming at her to shut up and leave her alone.

She went upstairs, wondering if she could barricade herself in her room but knowing that wouldn't work for long. Wayne was a strong man. He'd soon break down her door.

As she looked out of the window, he drove up and her mother rushed out to meet him, flinging herself into his arms. When they started kissing, right there beside his car, Lily realized this was her chance, grabbed her jacket and backpack, took her father's door key out of its hiding place inside a CD cover and slipped downstairs. She went out through the kitchen door and climbed over into Mrs Baxter's back garden. The dog gave a sleepy woof, wagging its tail at her, but she didn't dare stop to pat it as she ran across to climb over the far fence on to the cycle path that curled between the houses.

A bus came round the corner just as she reached the next street and she put on a sprint to catch it, smiling in delight at this good fortune, which seemed like an omen. Leaving the bus at the nearest tube station, she took a train to her father's. She knew she shouldn't be doing this, didn't want to get him in trouble, but couldn't think of anywhere else to go. He'd probably take her straight back home, but at least she'd have seen him, hugged him, talked to him, and made him promise not to give up on her, whatever her mother said.

Outside his house she stopped dead at the sight of the security light winking, disappointment pinning her to the spot. He was out! She started moving again, walking past, fighting against tears. Was he out for the night?

What was she going to do now?

*   *   *

Kerry called up the stairs, 'Lily! Come down and say hello to Wayne.' When there was no response, she went up and flung open the door of her daughter's bedroom. 'What are you—' She broke off and stared round the empty room, her eyes going immediately to the hook on the door where Lily always hung her favourite casual jacket—it was gone—and the shelf where she kept her backpack. That too was gone, though the new mobile phone was lying on the desk, half-hidden by some papers.

A quick search of the other bedrooms, then a rapid tour of the downstairs rooms and Kerry said to Wayne, 'She's got out, run away.'

As he took her into his arms and held her gently, she leaned against him pretending to need his support. But her mind was racing furiously. Where had the stupid child gone? Obviously to her father's. Well, Lily would soon find that she'd only delayed their departure today.

'Is it all worth it, honey?' he asked.

'Yes. I'm not having *him* bringing her up.' And anyway, Lily's real father paid Kerry a handsome sum each month because of her—and without asking for an accounting, too. She hadn't told Wayne any of the details.

He smiled. 'If that's what you want, I'm with you all the way. She's putting up a stronger fight than I'd expected against coming with us, though.

145

What's her real father like? Does he have red hair too?'

'He did when he was younger. But he couldn't care less about Lily. He made that clear from the start.'

'Who is he?'

She bit her lip.

'Kerry?'

She could see no way of getting out of telling him. She'd already learned that when he spoke in that tone of voice, Wayne meant business.

He stared at her in surprise. 'I know him.'

'Well, don't tell *her* who he is! She'll be going off to look for him and I'm not having her hurt by him.'

He put his arms round her. 'He hurt you, didn't he?'

She shrugged but she knew she wasn't fooling him—or herself. She'd been badly hurt when Lily's father had dropped her just because she wouldn't get rid of the baby, and she'd never forgive him for that. She would never let herself care for someone that much again, and she'd make sure he continued to pay handsomely for Lily until she grew up. By then Kerry would have a very nice nest egg behind her, what with Cal's money as well.

*   *   *

Judith and Cal sat up late. She made him a Spanish omelette with crusty bread and a salad, then produced the first cake she had baked in years, a rich fruit cake, and they ate some of it Lancashire fashion, with sharp, crumbly local cheese.

They shared the bottle of wine, sipping it and

chatting like old friends. When she yawned she looked at the clock. 'Goodness! I hadn't realized it was so late.'

He glanced across at it, pulled his glasses off and rubbed the bridge of his nose. 'Eleven o'clock's early for me, but I must admit I'm tired today. It's been an uncomfortable sort of week.'

'You should have found out from the authorities where you stand.'

He sighed. 'I suppose so. But what if I have no rights whatsoever?'

'Then at least you'd know.'

He shook his head and his voice was tight with anguish as he added, 'I can't bear the thought of losing her completely, just can't *bear* it!'

Judith picked up his hand, intending only a gesture of comfort, but the currents that had been whispering between them all evening suddenly grew stronger and desire burned through her. She hadn't felt like this in years, not just roused sexually but roused emotionally too. It would be so easy to care for Cal. He was an attractive man, tall and rangy, with a lean face and beautiful blue eyes magnified into mesmerizing prominence by the spectacles. Even his hair was beautiful, soft and dark, with just a few threads of silver. It had a hint of a wave and was too long at the moment, nearly jaw level, but that suited him. She'd seen an advertisement for spectacles with a guy in it who wasn't half as attractive as Cal.

Then she stopped thinking as he raised their joined hands to his lips and kissed her knuckles. Desire lurched in her belly and she couldn't help sucking in her breath. It had been a long time.

He took off his glasses and set them down

147

carefully on the low table in front of them. When he pulled her back into his arms, she leaned willingly into his embrace, wanting to see where these feelings would lead. The kiss was curiously gentle, as unlike Des's kisses as anything could be, but it went on and on until she felt the world around them fade and was conscious only of Cal, his lips, his body. When he drew away she let out a little moan of protest.

'Is it too early for us to go to bed?' he asked.

She didn't pretend to misunderstand him. 'This morning I'd have thought so. Now, I think maybe it's the right time. Have you—got something to protect us?'

'Yes. I always was an optimist.' With one of his devastating smiles, he stood up and pulled her to her feet. Another kiss made her knees go weak then it was she who took the initiative. 'Let's go upstairs. I'm too old to lie on the floor.'

Without a word he followed her, picking up his spectacles and holding them dangling by one sidepiece, leaving his jacket behind.

The bedroom was old-fashioned and still smelled slightly of mothballs, though she'd had the window open each day. He moved to put his spectacles down, then turned to smile at her again. She opened her mouth to apologize for the smell, but his kiss stopped the words. She wanted to touch him, wanted him to touch her, moved willingly as they began to remove each other's clothes, then felt suddenly shy as she stood in bra and panties.

He noticed and stilled at once. 'What's wrong?'

'I'm too fat. I'm embarrassed.'

He stood back, lean and splendid, unfazed by his

148

own nakedness. *'Fat?* Judith, you have got to be kidding!' He watched her and said in surprise, 'You're not kidding, are you?' He took hold of her hand and held her at arm's length. 'You're beautiful, just how a woman should be, soft and curved and—ah, Judith!' He pulled her into his arms as tears welled in her eyes. 'Did *he* tell you you were too fat?'

She nodded against his shoulder.

'He must be a fool.' He chuckled softly into her hair. 'My ex was too thin and bony, still is. I've been with one or two other lovely women since her, not many, but not one of them was splinter-thin. I like comfortable women, real women. This—' he slid her bra strap down and cupped the fullness of her bosom—'is perfect.'

His mouth stopped her speaking again and somehow they were on the bed, caressing one another, not rushing into love, but moving gently towards it in a way that was new to her . . .

Afterwards, as she lay in his arms, she felt tears trickle down her cheeks.

He wiped them away with his fingertip. 'What's wrong?'

'Nothing. In fact, something inside me feels better than it has for a long time.' She laughed self-consciously. 'I'm crying because I'm so happy.'

'Your ex is a fool to throw away something as valuable as you.'

She gave another shaky laugh and hugged him suddenly. 'You're a lovely fellow, Cal Richmond. And I—' She broke off because she'd suddenly remembered where she'd heard the name.

'What is it?'

'Nothing.'

'There is something. If you don't want to tell me, that's all right, but please don't pretend with me.'

'I suddenly remembered where I'd heard your surname before.'

'Oh?'

'You're probably no connection.'

'But . . . ?'

'I had my ex investigated a while back and it turned out he had an illegitimate daughter. Her name was Richmond too.' She laughed. 'No, of course it's not you. The girl's name was Maria, not Lily.'

Cal stiffened against her. 'Maria is my daughter's first name. We called her that at first but when I left Kerry, the girl decided she wanted to be called by her second name, Lily. She can be a stubborn little devil when she's set on something and she won out in the end, even against her mother, from whom she inherits her stubbornness.'

Judith sat in stunned silence. Such a coincidence wasn't possible! Couldn't be. Only—it had happened. 'This won't make a difference to us, will it?'

His voice sounded tight when he replied, the gentleness gone from it now. 'I didn't want to know who Lily's biological father was, and now that I do, well . . . it's thrown me, I must admit.'

'I shouldn't have blurted it out like a fool.'

He brushed her hair back from her forehead and planted a kiss there. 'I had to know sometime. Though if he's never bothered with her, I don't suppose it'll make much difference to anyone now.'

Judith watched him lie back against the pillows.

150

He was frowning slightly and had withdrawn from her, she could sense it. Not completely, but he was thinking more of his daughter now than of her.

His next words proved her guess to be right. 'I can forget Lily for a time in your arms, or when I'm driving, and I truly enjoy your company, think about you when I'm away from you. But she's so important to me, Judith, and this is a crisis . . . one so terrible that it messes me up for giving any other relationship the attention it deserves till Lily is sorted out. I'm sorry, but I can't go to sleep yet.' He sat up, still frowning, and put on his spectacles. 'You snuggle down. I'll go downstairs and—have a think.'

She rolled over on to one elbow, saying nothing as she watched him pick up his clothes and slip out of the room. She didn't follow him because it was clear he didn't want her with him. After he'd gone she lay down and covered herself up, but it was a long time before she could sleep because he didn't come back.

When she went down in the morning Cal was lying on the couch, fully clothed, looking as if he'd been sitting there and simply fallen asleep.

At least he was still there.

Damn Des! Were the ripples he made in the world going to pursue her for ever?

And why was he having her watched? She didn't have money to spend on lawyers to find out if she could stop him, and he probably knew that.

Twelve

Rows of houses stand guard on their contents, windows blind and uninviting. Streets are littered with cars. Wind blows the day's debris around. Neon flashes in the distance.

Lily walked round the streets wondering what to do, hating the thought of going tamely back home to face another row and, no doubt, some form of punishment. That was all her life seemed to consist of these days.

As she turned the corner of the street she saw Wayne's car pull up outside her father's house so slipped behind a parked car. She watched as her mother hammered on the door, waited, foot tapping impatiently, and hammered again.

The neighbour came out and said something then her mother got back into the car, which drove away.

They'd guessed where she'd go, but she couldn't face the thought of going home to them because they'd know she'd failed to find her father.

The neighbour came out and walked briskly down the street in the opposite direction. Lily realized this was her chance. She hurried along to her dad's home, looked up at the security light blinking away, smiled and went up to the door. Using her key to let herself in, she punched the secret number into the keypad, then punched the perimeter security system button, which would keep the light winking outside.

Sighing in relief she wandered through the

house. It was as if her dad's presence still lingered here and she felt comforted by that. But she wished he was here in the flesh.

In the kitchen she made herself a cup of drinking chocolate, sitting at the table to drink it. 'I had no choice, Dad,' she said aloud. 'They're not being fair to me. And I'd have gone mad spending the whole weekend with Wayne. He probably keeps a whip in the cupboard, that one.'

When she'd finished the chocolate, she went upstairs to her bedroom where she had her dad's old computer to use when she came round if he was busy. With a sigh of pleasure she went online and picked up her emails from the new address, finding that he'd sent her a message every single day. They'd lied to her about that and had probably deleted them on the computer at home, so it was a good thing she'd got this new account. They'd probably lied about other things too. That thought brought tears to her eyes.

He'd said he was going to Lancashire, was probably there now, so it was no use her staying.

When she went downstairs she was so hungry she decided to make herself a quick sandwich. She sat down in the living room to eat it, enjoying the peace with no one growling at her or telling her to smarten up or talking about dragging her away from everything she knew.

She moved across to the big recliner rocker her dad used, snuggling down in it, closing her eyes just for a minute . . . and woke up to darkness except for the small green and red lights on pieces of electrical equipment. She moved across to switch on the overhead lights then realized that this would give her away to the neighbours, so went into the kitchen and switched on the cooker light instead.

It was two o'clock in the morning! How could she have slept for so long?

She wasn't stupid enough to go out on her own at this hour. Should she ring her mother to fetch her?

No!

Perhaps her dad had his mobile switched on. Half the time he forgot, though. She dialled his number but couldn't get through.

She put her fingertip on the button that was a short cut to her home phone number, to let her mother know where she was, then stopped. She could imagine exactly what would happen. Even though it was the middle of the night, her mother would come round, furious. Probably Wayne would be with her and they'd both go off their heads at her. They'd be mad at her dad, too, blaming him, perhaps using this against him.

Still in the darkness Lily went upstairs to her bedroom and lay down on her own bed, expecting to find it difficult to sleep. But it wasn't. She'd been sleeping badly lately, but here she felt safe.

She didn't wake again until a stray beam of sunlight fell across her eyes.

She rolled over and yawned, stretching and coming awake slowly at her own body's speed, a rare treat. She was tempted, very tempted indeed, simply to stay here. She'd love a weekend on her own without anyone scolding her. But she'd better not. They might bring in the police and if she said where she'd been, they'd take away her key to this house. She'd better hide it more carefully when she got back.

After writing her dad a note she let herself out, sighing as she caught the tube, then had to wait ages for a bus. She went from the cycle path into Mrs Baxter's garden and hid the key to her father's house on the ledge above the neighbour's shed window. Then she went back to the street.

As she approached her own house she nearly turned back, then told herself not to be such a wimp and walked quickly up to the front door. It was flung open just before she got there and her mother stood glaring at her.

'Where the *hell* have you been?'

'Can I come in or must we have the Inquisition here on the doorstep?'

Kerry slapped her across the face then grabbed her arm and dragged her into the house, shoving her into the front room where Wayne was standing. He looked rumpled, as if he'd slept in his clothes. And angry. No, more than that, furious.

Lily faced them both, rubbing the cheek which her mother had slapped because it stung.

'Well?' Kerry demanded. 'Where have you been?'

'I went round to a friend's. Her parents were away and we just chilled out. I was going to come back after tea, but I fell asleep. She was going out so she left me there. She thought I'd wake up and come home, but I didn't stir till two o'clock in the morning, so I stayed there.'

'Why didn't you ring me? Didn't you know I'd be worried sick?'

Lily looked at her, surprised that her mother's voice had broken and there were tears in her eyes. 'I thought about it, but I didn't want to get her in trouble and I didn't have my mobile with me.'

155

'I don't believe you.'

Lily shrugged.

'You've been round to your father's. I'll report him to the Children's Officer.'

'I haven't been near him. What's the point? He's out of town this weekend visiting a friend. He told me that last week.'

'Why don't I believe you?' Kerry picked up the phone and pressed the shortcut button, holding it to her ear, foot tapping impatiently as she waited for Cal to answer. But all she got was his voice mail message.

'Dad isn't involved in this,' Lily repeated. 'He wouldn't keep me overnight without phoning you, you know he wouldn't.'

'Is she right?' Wayne asked.

Kerry grimaced. 'Probably. I guess Cal would have phoned me.'

Lily tried not to show her relief as her mother turned to glare at her again.

'Go up to your bedroom and stay there. You've ruined our weekend away and you're permanently grounded from now on. You don't leave the house unless I'm with you. I'll take you to school and pick you up every day, or Wayne will. We'll make very sure this doesn't happen again.'

Lily went upstairs, lay on her bed and stared at the posters on her ceiling. When her eyes filled with tears she let them roll down her cheeks, rubbing the sore cheek again.

She hated her mother.

She hated Wayne too, now.

And she wasn't going to America with them, whatever they said or did.

In the house next door Nancy Baxter sat and

worried about Lily. That was the second time she'd seen Kerry hit the child, and hit her hard too. What was going on?

Lily looked so unhappy lately. Everything about her drooped and her eyes had dark circles round them.

You couldn't interfere between parent and child, but something wasn't right next door.

*   *   *

On the Saturday morning Cal took Judith for a walk on the tops, showing her a place he particularly loved but one which wasn't too hard a climb. She strolled beside him, breathing deeply, her eyes sparkling and her cheeks rosy.

'Sorry about last night,' he said.

'That's all right. I shouldn't have blurted my thoughts out like that.'

'I'm glad you did.'

When they got back he hesitated, then asked, 'Do you have any photos of him?'

'Yes.' She wasn't so warped about her marriage that she'd cut Des out of the photos, as she'd heard some women did. 'I'll get them.'

He studied the photos in silence, not saying anything. Then he pulled a tattered photo out of his wallet and laid it beside one of Mitch and Des. 'She looks a bit like him about the eyes.'

'She's got a look of Mitch, too. Same hair colour.'

'Well, he is her half-brother.'

'Yes. We must introduce them one day. He gets on really well with his other two half-sisters.'

'If I'm allowed to keep seeing her.'

157

After lunch Cal fiddled with his coffee cup then looked at her across the table. 'I'm sorry. I can't seem to settle. Would you mind if I went home now? I have a lot to think about.'

Judith tried to hide her disappointment that he hadn't said anything about seeing her again. Was he going to vanish from her life after one sexual encounter? Had that been all he was after? She'd thought they were becoming friends. Maybe she was too naïve. Des had taunted her with it a few times.

Worried, she watched Cal gather his belongings and go towards the front door. Pride kept her head high as she followed him outside, watched him settle his things in the panniers.

He came across and pulled her into his arms for a long hug. 'I'll come back again, if I may. I really do want to get to know you better, even if our timing on getting together isn't the best.'

She pushed back slightly against his chest, looking into his eyes, trying to work out whether he was just spinning her a line. He looked sad beneath the smile. 'You'll always be welcome . . . and I hope things go well for you and your daughter.'

'I hope so too.'

'You'll—let me know you've arrived safely?'

'Of course. And we'll email one another until we can meet again. Won't we?'

She nodded.

He walked out, turned and came back to plant a light kiss on her cheek. 'I do want to see you again, Judith.'

She looked at him doubtfully.

'I don't tell lies.'

So she nodded and forced a smile. 'Good. I want

to see you too.'

But she felt bereft when he'd gone, walked round the house, couldn't settle. Fancy missing someone you'd only met twice! Fancy making love with him! She needed her head looking at.

But he was a lovely fellow, so gentle and caring—and sexy, though he probably didn't realize it. He didn't have an intrusively macho ego, unlike Des. It was very refreshing.

Thirteen

Rain falls quietly on city streets, then drifts away to baptise the countryside. It leaves cars gleaming with moisture and runnels of water chasing each other down their paintwork.

When Cal got home he knew at once that Lily had been there, even before he found her note, from the small disturbances she always left behind. She was incurably untidy while he always kept the place tidy, because he found that easier than cleaning up a mess. Frowning, he read the note, wondering how soon it would be before Kerry rang to harangue him. He read it several times, trying to see behind the words, upset that Lily was being driven to such deceit.

I came round to see you, Dad, and I didn't mean to stay, but it was so lovely and peaceful I fell asleep till two in the morning, so then I couldn't go home till it was light.

Please don't tell Mum I was here or she'll never let me near you again. I'll say I went to a friend's and fell asleep there.

And Dad, please, please, PLEASE will you see a lawyer and find out where we stand? I think Mum is trying to pull the wool over our eyes about this. I think you do have some rights to custody.

<u>YOUR</u> Lily!!!!!!!!

X X X X X X X X X X X X X X X X X X X X X X X X

He smiled at her row of kisses, then the smile faded and he frowned. He hated lying. If he had a philosophy of life, it was to do as you would be done by, and do it openly and honestly. How was he going to deceive Kerry anyway? He never had been able to before.

When the phone rang and he saw from the caller ID that it was his ex, he took the coward's way out and didn't answer.

He couldn't get the thought of Lily out of his mind. A child of that age shouldn't crave peace the way she did lately, shouldn't have to face all these upheavals in her life, either. That set him thinking about her biological father. How ironic that it should be Judith's husband. What sort of a man was he? There must be some good in him to father a child like Lily, surely?

And yet there were two reasons to despise Des Corrigan: the way he had ignored his daughter all her life and the way he was treating Judith now. Cal wondered how the man dealt with his son, what the son was like.

With a sigh, he collected his emails, replying to those dealing with business. When a new one plopped into his mailbox, he hesitated. Judith. He'd not been fair to her, he knew, keeping his thoughts to himself, leaving so abruptly. He closed his eyes for a moment, praying that she wasn't emailing to say goodbye, then clicked to open the email. To his relief, it was simply a friendly query, asking if he'd got home safely.

He didn't answer it then, couldn't string two words together, let alone make them tactful. Going back to the job he was working on, he immersed himself in coding, fairly mindless work but you had to pay great attention not to get details wrong. That kept his worries at bay for a while, but he knew they'd resurface when he stopped work.

He hoped that unconscious part of his mind, which sometimes continued working while he did the coding, would have some answers by then.

*   *   *

Des went round to see Tiff because if he sat at home and thought about his problems, he would drink too much. Even though he saw nothing wrong in a few drinks, ever since Judith had left he'd begun to realize that he was drinking too much, because there was only him emptying the bottles in the marble-topped bar. He'd recently seen a business colleague go downhill rapidly because of alcohol and didn't like the thought of following that path.

Tiff greeted him with her usual sunny smile, which always cheered him up, and he sat down beside her, feeling better already. After a few minutes he pulled out his notebook. 'Look, I've tried several times to do this and I can't seem to get it right. It's my speech as father of the bride. This isn't something I can farm out to a professional speech writer, it has to be more personal. Lacey wouldn't thank me for a meaningless gabble of words! Could you . . . ?'

'We'll go through it together. Maybe you just need a sounding board.'

An hour later they had a short but witty speech prepared and he gave her a big hug. 'I didn't know you had such a way with words, Tiff.'

She looked at him, pressing her lips tightly together in that way she had when she was wondering whether to say something.

'Go on. Spit it out.'

'You know I'm trying to write novels, so wouldn't you expect me to have a bit of a way with words?'

He stared at her, frowning slightly. 'Yes. That's why I bought you the computer. But I didn't know you were that good.'

She rolled her eyes. 'Heaven grant me patience, Des! I told you last time I sent the first few chapters of my latest effort to a publisher and they liked them so much they asked me for the rest. That means the writing was good.' She gave him a mock punch in the arm. 'It's not flattering for you to look so surprised, Des. You're a selfish sod sometimes.'

'Sorry. What's it about, this story of yours?'

Another punch, harder this time. 'It's a romance. I keep telling you, I like writing *romances*, because they always end happily. And if you ever looked at the titles in my bookcase, you'd have noticed that they're mainly romances too. I don't just sit here and wait for you to phone me, you know. I do have a life of my own.'

'Sorry, Tiff.'

'So you should be.'

He put his arm round her shoulders and tried to think how he could make up for his clumsiness. 'Can I read it?'

'No.'

'Why not?'

'Because you'll only mock me. This is women's stuff and you wouldn't like it at all.' She stared

163

back at him, eyes narrowed, 'And don't start thinking about using your money to give me a helping hand. I'll get published on my own merit or not at all.'

He grinned. 'How did you guess that was what I was thinking?'

'We've been together for a while now. I know you pretty well, far better than you know me. You're amazingly generous with money, too generous sometimes.'

He shrugged. 'It's nice to have plenty. Why not enjoy it?'

That discussion made him thoughtful on the way home. What did she mean, saying she knew him better than he knew her. It wasn't true. He knew Tiff really well, of course he did. Though he'd been a bit busy lately, not paying much attention to anything except buying back the old family business.

He smiled involuntarily. She was great, Tiff was. If he hadn't been married to Judith, he'd probably have married Tiff. She was much easier to live with.

*   *   *

Late on Sunday morning Mitch's father turned up unexpectedly, strolling in with an air of proprietorship that infuriated his son, who couldn't help noticing how tense his Gran became lately every time his father visited them.

'Your mother's got herself a man,' Des announced. 'Didn't waste much time, did she?'

'I hope he makes her happy,' Mitch said. 'You've got another woman, so what's the difference?'

Des turned a frowning, assessing look on him. 'Leave Tiff out of this! And just so you understand: this separation thing with your mother is only temporary. I'll reel her back in when I decide it's time.'

Mitch couldn't believe his ears. 'What do you mean "reel her back in"?'

'What do you think I mean? Bring her back home.'

'And if she doesn't want to come back?'

'She'll come anyway. She suits me, knows how to deal with all sorts of people. She's worth a fortune as a company wife.'

'That's a disgusting way to talk about Mum.'

Des shrugged. 'About time you got more realistic, Mitch.' He roared with laughter at his son's expression. 'Surely you don't still believe in true love and happy ever after? God, you're wet behind the ears. She's over-protected you. Well, I'm not having a son of mine grow up into a naïve prat anyone can take advantage of.' He paused and looked from one to the other before saying in a quieter tone. 'Get your glad rags on. We're going out to lunch.'

Mitch glared at him. 'I can't. I have studying to do.'

'Do it later.'

'It's tricky stuff. I need to do it now, while I'm fresh. And anyway, I don't want a fancy hotel meal at this time of day. I prefer something light.'

Hilary intervened hastily. 'Why don't you have lunch here, Des? You always say you like my cooking.'

'I do, but we're meeting some people for lunch, you, me and Mitch here. And I'll *not* take no for an answer. A businessman sometimes needs to produce a family, especially for earnest Americans like these. It soothes them. So since your dear daughter has abandoned her duties, it's up to you to fill her place *when I need you.*' He glared at them both.

'I didn't realize it was—important. We'd better go and change.' Hilary looked pleadingly at Mitch as she spoke.

He walked upstairs behind her in silence to change his clothes.

However, later on after his father dropped them at home after a rather boring lunch, he turned to his grandmother and said quietly, 'I'm going up to see Mum next weekend. I don't intend to be on call for Dad like this.'

'You can't. It's the wedding.'

'Oh, hell! I'd forgotten. The weekend after, then.'

'Do you think you should?'

'Yes. I miss Mum. In fact, I'll phone her tomorrow to arrange it. Now, I've still got that studying to do.'

He went upstairs and didn't join her to watch television that evening. When she peeped into his bedroom, he was lying on his bed, arms folded behind his neck, frowning into space, his lips moving as if he was reciting something to himself. He gave her a quick smile but didn't speak, so she went downstairs again.

After some thought she decided she too would go away the same weekend so that Des couldn't turn up at the last minute and harangue her about where Mitch was, or expect her to abandon everything again to do what he wanted. She had

166

always quite liked Des, but was beginning to see another side of him now. He was like a juggernaut when he wanted something. It didn't even seem to occur to him that other people had needs. For Mitch's sake, she'd try to keep the peace, but didn't intend to jump to Des's bidding for ever. She had a life of her own to lead, though no one seemed to think of that.

'I'll go and visit my cousin Gracie the weekend you're away,' she said over breakfast. 'I rang her last night and arranged it.'

He grinned. 'Good thinking, Gran. And we won't say a word about any of it to Dad. After all, he gives us no warning about taking us out. I emailed Mum and asked if it was all right for me to go up and see her the weekend after the wedding, told her I need to chill out a bit. I could even stay till the Monday. It's only sport on Monday mornings and I'm never going to be good at that, however hard I practise.'

*   *   *

The next day Des popped in at Tiff's flat on his way to work because he'd had an idea, wanted to run something past her. He rang the bell, then used his key to open the front door. 'Hoy, Tiff, where are you?' He stared at her in surprise when she came out of the bathroom, because she was still in her dressing gown and looked distinctly wan. 'What's the matter? You don't look well. Do you need to see a doctor?'

She hesitated. 'Just feeling a bit sickly. It'll pass.'

'How about a cup of nice strong coffee?'

She clapped one hand to her mouth and raced

167

back into the bathroom. The sound of her vomiting had him fixed to the spot as an unwelcome suspicion crept into his mind. But when she came out to join him, she looked so pale and wobbly, he put an arm round her and guided her into the living room. 'What can I get you?'

'A glass of water and a plain biscuit.'

He brought them back and sat opposite her. 'Surely you're not . . . ?'

'I'm pregnant. The Viagra was extremely effective, if you remember.'

'But you're on the pill!'

'I've been a bit preoccupied lately, got careless. I'd not have thought missing two days would be enough to let me get pregnant, but the test showed positive.'

'It's early days. Won't be a problem to get rid of it.'

'No.'

'Tiff, you know you've never wanted children—especially now that you've got a publisher interested in your book.'

'I didn't want children before but now it's happened, I've changed my mind.' She pressed one hand to her belly. 'I'm nearly forty. The old biological clock's ticking and I might not have another chance to have a child, so I've decided I want to keep this one. And you, Des Corrigan, can like that or lump it.'

He scowled at her and stood up. 'Why do I always get mixed up with crazy women who want to ruin their bodies having children?'

She shrugged, then asked in a hesitant voice, 'You'll pay maintenance for the baby, at least?'

'If you can prove it's mine.'

She shoved him away from her hard. 'I don't have to prove it. You *know* I've not seen anyone else since I've been with you.'

He could see the tears in her eyes and felt guilty. 'Oh, hell, Tiff! I'm sorry. Of course I know you haven't been with anyone else, but I don't need this.'

'It could have been better timed, I will agree. Why did you come round so early anyway? It's not like you.'

'To invite you to the wedding.'

There was a long silence then she said slowly, 'But I don't join in your family events.'

He went and put his arm round her shoulders, guiding her to sit with him on the couch. He'd been thinking during a wakeful night and had surprised himself by realising suddenly that he wasn't at all sure about getting Judith back. 'Maybe you should start doing so—as my official partner.'

She was quiet for so long that he turned to look at her and saw tears rolling down her cheeks.

'What the hell are you crying for?'

'I cry rather easily at the moment.'

'And . . .'

'This is the first time you've asked me to be your official partner at a function. In over five years, the first time—and just when we both know the relationship's over.'

He grunted, fiddled around with her fingers, then looked sideways at her again. 'I don't want another baby, I will admit, but I don't want us to split up, either.'

'I won't change my mind about having it.'

He let her hand drop and slumped back. 'Could we just—carry on as we are for the time being? Till

I can see my way. Till we're sure about that.' He gestured towards her stomach.

She fumbled for a tissue in the box next to the couch and failed to pull one out.

'Here, let me!' He thrust one into her hand and watched as she sobbed into it. Women! And of all the ironies, to get her pregnant the only time he'd been able to manage it recently. That was a turn-up for the books. He waited a minute then said firmly, 'Stop crying now. We have to go out and buy you a knock-'em-dead outfit for the wedding. You're not sick all day long, are you?'

'No. Just in the early mornings.'

'Thank God for that! I'll pick you up this afternoon and we'll go shopping.'

They walked to the door together, his arm round her shoulders. His kiss was gentler than usual. She clung to him for a moment. She didn't usually cling.

As he walked out to the car, he began to grin. Well, at least no one would suspect what his problem was now.

*   *   *

The phone rang one evening exactly a week after the letter's arrival and Leo picked it up. 'Just a minute.' He turned to his wife and daughter. 'It's for me. I'll take it out on the veranda.' He closed the door carefully behind him, glared at the phone and snapped, 'I have only one thing to say to you. Tell my sister than none of my family want anything to do with her.'

'I'd like to hear that from your daughter. May I speak to her, please?'

170

'No. She doesn't want to speak to you.'

'It'll take only a minute, but I must hear it from her own lips.'

Leo disconnected the phone and waited for a minute, breathing deeply, trying to control the anger. When he was calmer, he went back into the family room and put the phone in its socket.

Five minutes later it rang again.

'Don't answer that!'

Kate and Jean looked at him in surprise.

The phone continued to ring.

Kate got up and he blocked her way. 'I said, don't answer it.'

'It's him, isn't it? Mark Felton?'

'No.'

But his tone was unconvincing. Jean looked at him pleadingly. 'Don't do this, Leo.'

The phone stopped ringing.

'It's my house,' he said, taking it off the hook, 'and I'll do what I bloody well want with my own phone.'

'You're despicable.' Kate went into her bedroom and slammed the door on them.

*   *   *

The following morning Kate was woken by her parents quarrelling in the kitchen. They started off in low voices, but their final comments were loud and sharp.

'You've run mad, Leo. How am I going to manage without a phone in the house?'

'It'll only be for a day or two. I'm *not* letting our Kate get into Maeve's hands, and you'll not persuade me otherwise.'

171

When the sound of his ute had faded into the distance, Kate got up. 'What's he done now?'

'Taken all the phones in the house with him to work. And he's done something to the point in your bedroom too, so I'm afraid you won't be able to get on the Internet today.' Jean shook her head. 'He said he would last night, but I didn't believe him. I've never seen him so determined about anything. When he gets in this mood, you might as well try to change night to day as change his mind.'

'I've got my mobile if you want to call out, but Mark Felton won't know its number.'

'Thank you, dear. I'm sorry.'

'It's not your fault.'

'I should have been able to stop him. He's being ridiculous!'

'He's only making me more determined than ever to go to England, Mum, even if I have to pay my fare myself. I have Aunt Maeve's address.'

'That would hurt him badly. Are you sure it's worth it?'

'Yes. He's treating me like a child, trying to control me. I'm ill, Mum, not stupid, and I'm twenty-eight, not eight!' She turned and went into her bedroom, leaning against the door and fighting against tears of sheer frustration.

*   *   *

Just before noon a car pulled into the drive and Jean peeped out of the window. She saw a man get out—slim, neat, with nothing remarkable about him or his vehicle. She guessed who he was and her heart sank as she went to answer the door.

172

'I'm Mark Felton. I'm looking for Kate Corrigan.'

Torn between two loyalties, she hesitated for a moment then held the door open. 'Come in. If you wait here, I'll fetch my daughter.'

Kate was sitting on the back veranda, staring out across the valley.

'It's the man who phoned yesterday. He's come to see you. Wait a m—!'

But her daughter had pushed past her and gone running into the living room. 'I'm Kate.'

'Mark Felton.' He offered his hand and then his business card.

'I don't know what my father said to you last night, Mr Felton. He's physically stronger than I am and he wouldn't let me answer the phone.'

'He said you weren't interested in Miss Corrigan's offer.'

'He was lying. I'm very interested indeed. I want to accept it and come to England.'

'She'll be glad to hear that.'

From the doorway Jean watched them. Her daughter's face was alight, as it hadn't been for months. It was that more than anything which convinced her she'd done the right thing. She moved forward to join them. 'My husband will be back for lunch soon. Perhaps you could go for a drive somewhere and come back in two hours, Mr Felton? Kate can pack her things and leave with you before Leo comes home tonight. I think it's best we avoid a confrontation or he may say things he'll regret later.'

Kate nodded, so Mark left the house. But as he was getting into his car, a battered ute pulled into the drive and an older man got out. Leo Corrigan.

Mark sighed. No getting out of a confrontation now.

Leo strode across to the car. 'Who are you?'

'Mark Felton.' He offered his card, but it was slapped aside and went fluttering across a flower bed.

'You're not wanted here. Get off my property.'

Mark looked across at Jean and Kate questioningly.

'Leo!' Jean's voice was sharp. 'You can't do this.'

'Just watch me.' He turned to his daughter. 'Get inside the house.'

Kate didn't move. 'You can't order me around like that, Dad.'

'I can while you're living here.'

'In that case, it's a good thing I'm moving out today, isn't it?' She took a deep breath and spoke in a softer voice. 'Dad, *please,* let's not quarrel about this.'

'I'm not quarrelling, just setting the ground rules. You can choose between me and my sister, but you can't have us both.'

Jean put her arm round her daughter's tense shoulders. 'Leo, that's not fair.'

'I'll do whatever is necessary to protect my family.'

Kate reached up to pat her mother's hand then moved away. She turned to shout across to Mark. 'Can you come back in an hour? I need to pack.'

He nodded and started up his car.

She looked once more at her father, saw the grim resolution on his face, and went back inside the house.

As she was packing, her parents again quarrelled fiercely in the kitchen. Before she'd finished sorting out her clothes, she grew so dizzy she could hardly think straight and sank on to the bed. This was what happened to you with CFS, in a crisis you were useless. She jumped in shock at the sound of her mother's voice next to her.

'You look dreadful, love.'

'I feel dreadful, can't seem to think straight. Where's Dad?'

'Going back to town in a huff.'

'And you're stuck in the middle. Poor Mum.' She felt the room swirl around her. 'Could you help me finish my packing? I'm feeling dizzy again.'

'Yes, of course, love.'

There was the sound of the ute starting up and when Jean moved forward to the suitcase on the bed, Kate saw that her mother had tears in her eyes.

'I'm sorry. I didn't mean to cause trouble.'

'I know. And *you* didn't cause it. At your age, you're perfectly entitled to do whatever you think best, and so I told your father.' She hesitated, then added, 'But I want you to promise me one thing.'

'What?'

'If Leo ever shows any sign of—of wanting to heal the breach, you'll not hold this against him.'

Kate hugged her mother close. 'I can easily promise that.'

'It's the one thing he's totally unreasonable about, his sister. But even I didn't know how much it had hurt him to lose his old home. Now, let me see what you've got here.' Deftly she pulled the jumble of clothing out of the suitcase and laid it on the bed, taking underwear out of drawers, asking Kate about her preferences, working with her usual efficiency. When the suitcase was full and

175

closed, she looked at her daughter again. 'Will you be all right?'

'I don't know. But she said—Maeve did, that is—that she'd try to get me medical help. I'll not get better sitting here, Mum. I have to take advantage of this opportunity.'

Fourteen

Cloud shadows drift lightly across the moors. Shadows of buildings sit heavily across whole streets. Shadows of passers-by jerk across pavements in a twitching parody of life.

Judith set off that Monday morning to meet Maeve Corrigan, feeling like a conspirator as she parked her car and walked into the shopping centre. Once inside, she stopped and peered back out to see if her shadow was following her, but the man was leaning back in his car seat lighting a cigarette, knowing she had to return to her vehicle, which was close to his.

Much relieved, she went down to the bookshop and stood outside, scanning the passers-by. A tall, well-built man with short curly hair and an engaging smile stood up from a seat nearby and came purposefully towards her.

'Judith Horrocks?'

'Yes.'

'I thought so.' He held out one hand. 'Andy Blauman. I parked outside in the street, so that we wouldn't need to go back up to the car park.'

His eyes crinkled up at the corners, the lines there hinting at many smiles given and received. He reminded Judith of a big teddy bear Des had once bought her.

He pretended to glance furtively over his shoulder. 'It's like playing cops and robbers, isn't it? Perhaps I should have worn a cloak and false moustache.'

She chuckled. 'Yes.' But then she felt her smile fading. 'Only it's not exactly playing, it's more serious than that, if Maeve is so ill.'

His smile faded and his face sagged into sad lines. Judith wished she hadn't said that so bluntly. He must be very fond of his employer.

It took over an hour to get to Maeve's home in Cheshire. As they drew up at some big barred gates in a high wall, Andy pressed an electronic gadget and the gate slid sideways. He waited until it had rolled back across the gap before driving slowly along the drive, glancing at her expectantly.

Judith realized why as soon as they came in sight of the house, a small manor house built in black and white panels. 'What a stunning building!'

'Yes. Maeve's father bought it originally and she loves it. She's had a lot of work done on it, because there was some subsidence, and it's been exquisitely restored inside and out.'

'I didn't like my old home at all. My husband chose it and it's one of those crass modern places, looking like a jumble of boxes from the outside, built mainly to show off someone's wealth.'

He smiled. 'And you're an artist, so you should know.'

'Not a good enough artist. Not nearly good enough to earn money from it.'

'Who's been telling you that?'

'My tutor. A while ago now.'

Andy pursed his lips and drew to a halt in front of the main door, not moving for a moment as he asked, 'Are you sure he was telling you the truth?'

She could feel herself freezing and after a moment or two realized her mouth was open. 'I never thought of that.' Never, not once. No, not even Des would do that to her, be so cruel. 'Why—' Her voice broke and she had to take a deep breath and start again. 'Why did you say that?'

'We—ah—made enquiries about you and people seemed to think you were rather talented.'

'People?'

'I can get you their names, but I don't remember them off hand.'

'I'd appreciate that. I can't believe Des would—'

'I'll tell you up front that Maeve has a very low opinion of her brother Desmond. She's kept tabs on him for years—on him *and* his family, just to make sure he wasn't getting up to anything that might harm her. So we know quite a bit about you and your clever son.'

'And yet Des managed to buy her business without her realizing it was him.'

Andy's grin returned. 'Not at all. She knew perfectly well what he was doing, but she wanted to sell, so she let him pay above the odds for it.'

Judith shook her head, at a loss for words.

'Maeve's a very intelligent woman, but she's utterly honest. If she offers you anything today, makes promises, you can trust her absolutely. Oh, and I'd better warn you, she's being treated for cancer, has lost her hair and refuses to wear a wig.' He opened the door. 'Come inside. I'll take you in to see her and later we'll all have lunch.'

Judith followed him into the house, pausing for a moment in the hall to marvel at how exquisite the interior was. Yet it was homely and welcoming, too. She realized Andy was waiting for her near a door on the far side of the hall and pulled herself together, gesturing around. 'Sorry. I was just

179

admiring it.'

'People usually do.' He opened the door and stood back to let her go inside.

Maeve was sitting by the fireplace, a rug across her knees in spite of the warmth of the room. She looked as fragile as spun glass, fey almost. Her head was completely bald, but that only served to highlight her fine bone structure and beautiful green eyes. They were eerily like Des's, yet they had a direct look to them that his didn't.

'Come and sit down, Judith—you don't mind if we use first names, do you?'

'Not at all, Maeve.' She took a chair opposite her hostess and folded her hands in her lap.

'I'll get Lena to bring you some tea.' Andy left them alone.

'So you've separated from my brother. Is that permanent?'

'Yes.' Judith tried to hide her surprise at this blunt personal question from a near stranger. 'Actually, except for his business functions, we've been living separate lives for some time now.'

Maeve grinned as if she understood exactly what her guest was thinking. 'Sorry. I haven't much energy. Don't want to waste what I do have on small talk. Would you mind telling me why you left him?'

'His infidelity and—well, his unscrupulous business practices. I should have left him sooner, when I first found he was being unfaithful, but there was Mitch—and Des swore his first infidelity would be his last. He didn't keep that promise. In fact, he's been seeing his latest woman, this Tiffany person, for years now. She seems to be a permanent fixture.'

180

'I gather he knocked you down the stairs, hurt your knee. Had he beaten you before?'

'No. He's never even threatened to, but he's been rather grumpy for the past year, touchy, unlike himself.'

'Is he paying you an allowance now?'

'He's stalling.'

'In the meantime you have to live. I'll give you an allowance, if you like, and you can pay me back when things are settled legally.'

Judith gaped at her and it was a minute or two before she could speak. 'Why should you do that?'

'Because you're Mitch's mother and I want to make sure he has somewhere else to go if he falls out with his father. We both know how suddenly Des can quarrel with someone.'

'But why should that concern you when you're . . .' She broke off, realizing what she had almost said.

'When I'm dying? That's easy. I have plenty of money that I can't take with me. I only kept the old family business for sentimental reasons.' She laughed suddenly. 'And if I'm honest, because I knew it galled Des. What I'm really good at is playing the stock market and I've made my real money that way. I'd like to keep the money in the family when I go, except for what I leave to my staff and Andy. There'll be nothing for Des, obviously, or for Leo either. Well, Leo's a plodder and he couldn't cope with a fortune. But the next generation is different . . . I'll leave them all something, though I'm not leaving big money to a fool. I think I've still got time to get to know them a little and work out who deserves a more substantial legacy from me.'

181

'I can see that you'd be interested in Mitch, but not me, so I don't understand why I'm here today. Is it you who's having me watched? I'd thought it was Des.'

'It's both of us, but Des's man is clumsy. The people I employ are rather more discreet and I certainly don't feel a need to keep an eye on you every minute of the day, or even every day of the week. I apologize for doing it, but I needed to find out what you were like, you being Mitch's mother. And when you moved to the north, it seemed a good thing for us to meet. I'll say up front, though, that I'm not intending to leave *you* anything.'

'I wouldn't expect it.'

There was a knock on the door and a plump, grey-haired woman came in wheeling a trolley containing delicate china crockery and a plate of what looked like home-made shortbread. She nodded a greeting to Judith then said firmly to her employer, 'You need to eat something, Maeve. Do I have to stand over you or will you keep your promise this time?'

Maeve spread her hands apart in surrender. 'Ah, you're an old nag, Lena.' She reached obediently for a biscuit, took a bite and waved the rest at the other woman.

Judith was surprised at how warm and loving Maeve's smile was after the crisp tone she'd been employing until now.

'Two pieces,' Lena said.

'Two, then. Even if they choke me.'

When they were alone, Maeve indicated the trolley. 'Please help yourself and I'd like a cup of tea, if you don't mind. Black, slice of lemon, no sugar. Milk makes me nauseous lately.'

Judith served them both, going back for a second piece of shortbread and offering the platter to her hostess, who took another piece with a grimace and ate it quickly and impatiently before resuming the conversation.

'I want to meet Mitch. Could you invite him up for a visit and then let Andy bring him across to meet me. Would you do that for me?'

Judith considered the request, then nodded. 'Yes. But the money is only a secondary reason.'

'Oh? What's the primary reason, then?'

'To set the record straight about his father's family, so that he at least knows you and his other relatives too, if possible. He hasn't met his Australian uncle and cousins, either, though Des and I went once. We could easily have afforded another trip out there. I think Mitch hungers for family, actually.' She'd never fully realized how much until now, talking to Maeve.

'My Australian niece has accepted an invitation to come and see me. I'll make sure the two of them meet.'

'That'd be good.'

'Why did you never go back to visit Leo? He and Des didn't quarrel.'

'Des hates to be torn from his business and he's not fond of flying. Are there any other relatives lurking in the background I should know about?'

'One or two cousins in Ireland. I'll make sure Mitch has their details.' Maeve leaned her head back against the chair and the cup she was holding tilted without her noticing.

Judith got up. 'Let me take that for you.'

'Thank you. I'm ridiculously weak. It's a new combination of treatments and they think it'll give

183

me several more months of life.'

'But not cure you?'

'No. Unfortunately. But cancer has some strange compensations. Life is very sweet and when you know you've not got much time left, you relish every single second of it, seeing more clearly, speaking more honestly, just—living every moment to the full. When you're not sleeping, that is.' After a moment's silence, she added, 'I'd better take a rest now, then I'll join you for lunch.' She pressed a buzzer that was standing on a small table next to her chair. 'I'll leave you in Andy's care until then.'

'Could I look round the house and grounds? It's so beautiful.'

Maeve gave her another luminous smile. 'Isn't it? I love this place. Where better to end my days? I have to work out who among the younger generation will love it as I do.'

Andy arrived, took in the situation in a glance and rang the buzzer twice before showing Judith out. 'She gets tired very quickly and she's due a rest, but she wanted to talk to you alone first.'

'She said she'd join us for lunch.'

He frowned. 'She shouldn't but I daren't try to stop her.'

'You're very fond of her, aren't you, Mr Blauman?'

'Andy. And I'm more than fond of her, I love her. She's become like a favourite aunt to me. Now, come and see the gardens while it's still fine.'

Over lunch Maeve asked questions about Mitch and Judith talked willingly, showing the photos of him as a child that she'd brought. Her hostess studied them, smiling, but was monosyllabic in her comments and questions. She seemed like a wilting flower with only willpower keeping her upright.

In the end she pushed away her plate. 'I'm glad to have met you, Judith. My brother didn't deserve you.' She turned to Andy. 'Would you help me . . . ?'

He went round and scooped her up, carrying her swiftly out in spite of her protests.

When he came back, Judith said bluntly, 'I've never believed the cliché before, but she really does look as if a breath of wind would blow her away.'

'Yes, but it wouldn't dare!' He chuckled, studied her, then asked, 'Shall you do as she asks?'

'Definitely. I'd like Mitch to be independent of Des, though I'm not sure a large legacy would be good for someone his age. People should have to struggle to achieve something, don't you think?'

Andy gave this some thought, then nodded slowly.

'But most of all, now that I've met Maeve, I'd like Mitch to meet her too, then maybe he'll understand that being a Corrigan isn't all bad. His father's example hasn't been a good one and I've been a bit tied up with my own problems.' It still hurt her to remember Mitch's accusation about that. 'I think I should have paid my son more attention, but Des was very demanding when we were first married and—it's easy to be wise after the event, isn't it?' She sighed and stared blindly into space for a minute then looked at Andy. 'Sorry. What were we talking about?'

'Your son meeting Maeve. Sooner rather than later, I'm afraid. We hope she'll live longer than the first prognosis, but she's not recovering from this treatment as quickly as they'd expected.'

185

'I'm sorry. I like her.'

'Most people do. Her staff adore her.'

'I'll ring Mitch tonight.'

'You can always reach me on the same number to make arrangements. We can even use the same subterfuge for eluding your watcher, if you like.'

'It might be better not to do things openly, for Mitch's sake, though I hate all this deceit. He's still dependent on his father financially and Des can be bloody minded when he takes a huff about something.'

There was her mother to think about as well. Hilary was treading a difficult path at the moment and Judith worried about her.

Soon after she got home it began to look like rain so she went to sit in the kitchen and stare out of the window. She watched the clouds descend and gather just above the moors, the lowest wisps of ragged white seeming to caress the rolling curves of the tops. She had a lot to think about, needed the peace of this place.

When the phone rang, she hesitated, not wanting to be disturbed, still trying to come to terms with her visit to Maeve. Then, with a shrug, she picked it up.

'Mum. It's Mitch.'

'I do still recognize your voice.'

'Can I come and visit you the weekend after next? It's Lacey's wedding this weekend, or I'd come then.'

'Of course you can. I'd love to see you. How did you know I was going to ring up and invite you?'

'Dunno.'

'I'm missing you dreadfully.' She smiled into the ensuing silence. He always went monosyllabic

186

when emotions were discussed.

'Look, Mum, I can skip the last two classes on the Friday if you'll send me a note, and then I'll travel up to see you straight from school. I hope the trains are good.'

'Does your father know you're coming?'

'No.'

'He'll find out. He's having a watch kept on me. There's someone in a car outside my house every time I look out and they've started to follow me everywhere.'

'Dad can be a sod, can't he?'

'What's he done now?' She listened to her son's explanation, not saying much, surprised that Des was taking this Tiffany person to the wedding but not really caring. Judith was only surprised that Tiffany had stayed with him for so long. She was welcome to him.

*   *   *

With the greatest reluctance, Cal made an appointment to see another lawyer, because the first one hadn't been much use. This one had been highly recommended by a friend of his. Pete had gone through an acrimonious divorce a couple of years ago.

Time to get the facts straight and take action.

He came away shocked to the core, unable to believe that Kerry could have been so deceitful and tried to pull the wool over his eyes like that about his legal rights. She must think him stupid. He stopped and considered this. No, she didn't think him stupid, but absent-minded and impractical—and he had been.

Only how to deal with this without putting Lily at the centre of a tug of war battle was more than he could immediately work out.

The first thing was to try to contact his daughter. When he rang Kerry asking to speak to Lily, she told him it would upset the child too much and put the phone down on him.

He tried emailing but his messages to Lily went unanswered.

He contacted the school's guidance officer, but she said Kerry had rung in to say Lily was ill and would be off all week. So he asked to speak to her about his daughter, but she preferred to wait until the child was better and check that Lily didn't mind her speaking to him.

When he shared his worries with Judith, she suggested hiring a private investigator to find out what was going on. He stared at the phone and couldn't at first answer.

'Cal? Are you still there?'

'Yes. I was just—surprised. I don't know any private investigators.'

'Neither do I, but I know someone who'll help us. Hold on. I'll ring you back when I've contacted him.'

Judith put the phone down and went for Andy's mobile number, relieved when he answered straight away. She explained the situation, almost explained that Lily was Des Corrigan's daughter then decided not to rock the boat for Cal at the moment. 'Can you give me the name of someone my friend can contact?'

'Yes, of course. Hold on a minute.'

He read off a number and she scribbled it down.

'Let me know what happens.'

188

*   *   *

Andy didn't put the phone down but rang through immediately to the firm used by Maeve. He explained the situation and asked that Cal Richmond be given priority and helped in any way possible. Then he went to tell Maeve, sure she'd agree he'd done the right thing.

'Does Judith know Lily Richmond is Des's daughter?' Maeve wondered.

'I don't know.'

'Keep an eye on things, Andy. And find out what this Cal Richmond is like, what his relationship is with the child.' She shook her head, making a muffled noise of irritation in her throat. 'There are so many things to sort out and I can't keep up with them.'

'We're not doing badly.'

She leaned her head back. 'I trust you, Andy. If you ever have to take any decisions without me, remember that.'

'Do you suppose Des knows what's going on with Lily?'

'I doubt it. He's ignored the child all his life, except for paying maintenance.' She smiled. 'I don't know whether this Kerry has broken the law, taking maintenance from two men, but she's definitely been unscrupulous. In fact, this is all very interesting.'

*   *   *

As Mark drove her away from the small town of Callabine, Kate sighed and closed her eyes, leaning back against her seat. 'Sorry about all that.'

'It's not your fault.'

'Dad's usually fairly reasonable, if a bit old-fashioned. He just—has a thing about his sister.'

'I'm sorry to hear that. I find her an admirable woman, though she can be very determined if she wants something.' He glanced sideways at her. 'You don't look at all well. You're chalk white.'

'Stress. It makes everything worse. Trouble is, I get bored living a quiet life, so that stresses me out too. Can't win sometimes, can you?'

'I've been researching ME. I believe there are several ways of treating it nowadays.'

'Not in Callabine, there aren't.' Her voice was bitter.

'Have you seen *any* specialists?'

'The GP sent me to a physician in Berrabin, but he was quite old and I'm sure I knew more than him about what was wrong with me from my research on the Internet. All he wanted to do was put me on antidepressants.' She gave him a wry smile. 'Dad and I had a sharp disagreement about that as well. I didn't have the energy to pursue other avenues at the time. I thought if I took things easy for a while . . . and I *did* get a little better . . . then later on I'd try to find proper help.'

'Couldn't your parents have pushed matters further?'

She grimaced. 'They know the local doctor socially, have great trust in him, and he took the physician's side. Dad said they wouldn't do anything else unless I tried the antidepressants, because the doctors knew best. As if! So I tried them and they turned what's left of my brain off. I was just a zombie so I stopped taking them. Dad

190

said if I wasn't prepared to give them a fair go, it wasn't worth trying anywhere else. And Mum never goes against him, not when he's set his mind on something.'

'That must have been tough.'

She nodded, pressing her lips together.

'If you're up to it, I'll drive to Sydney and book us into a hotel there until we can get a flight to England.'

'I'll be fine. I'm just sitting here.'

But she wasn't fine. When they stopped for refreshments, she stumbled and would have fallen but for his arm round her.

'Sorry. I get—disoriented, dizzy.'

Mark waited for her outside the Ladies and guided her to a table, bringing her some food and insisting she eat.

'I'm really not hungry.'

'You won't get better if you don't eat.'

'You sound like Mum.'

'No one's ever accused me of being maternal before.' He grinned at her as he turned to his own food.

She looked at the plate, sighed and forced as much as she could down her throat, then saw him watching her.

'Good girl,' he said softly, taking her hand for a moment.

She was sorry when he let go. The simple warmth of a human touch was so comforting.

When they set off again she felt sleepy, so he stopped the car and insisted she get in the back so that she could spread out.

She woke to find they were driving into Sydney. 'I can't have slept so long!'

'You did. I was glad to see it.' He stopped outside a large, expensive-looking hotel. 'Wait here.'

She spent the time tidying herself up.

'I've booked a two-bedroom suite,' he said as he handed over the keys to the parking attendant and waited for her to get out of the car. 'If you need any help during the night, you'll be able to call out.'

'I don't usually need help. It's just that I've pushed myself too far today. All I want to do is sleep.'

'I'm going to insist on you eating something first.'

'I'm not hungry, Mummy dearest.'

He chuckled. 'I know. But humour me, please. If I can't show Miss Corrigan I've done all I can to look after you, I'll never dare face her.'

She looked at him, surprised into another smile. 'Somehow I don't think you're afraid of anyone.'

He considered this, mouth pursed, head on one side. 'You're probably right.'

In the suite, which was more luxurious than anywhere she'd ever stayed before, he carried her suitcase and laptop into her room, but insisted she stay in the living area between the two bedrooms. 'What do you want to eat, or shall I just order for you?'

Kate studied the menu and tried in vain to work up some enthusiasm. She couldn't so pushed it towards him. 'You order.'

'We'll have steaks. Can't beat red meat for iron and energy.'

'Whatever.'

'How about a glass of red wine, too?'

When the food arrived, he coaxed her into eating half the steak and drinking a full glass of red wine. By that time the world had blurred around her and she felt totally exhausted. 'I can't stay awake any longer.' She set down her glass carefully and pushed herself to her feet. When the room whirled around her again, he was there to help her to bed.

'Never mind about undressing, Kate. Just go to sleep.'

And she did, slipping happily down into the warm, peaceful world that was her only escape from feeling rotten. She didn't stir for ten hours straight.

*   *   *

Once Mark was sure Kate was asleep he looked at his watch, calculated the time differences and picked up the phone. 'Andy? I'm in Sydney. I've got Kate with me and I'm bringing her to England as soon as I can get a flight. She's not at all well. Can you arrange an appointment with a specialist in ME? As soon as possible, I'd say.'

'I'll get on to it as soon as places open for business.'

'How's Maeve?'

'Struggling. The treatment's very aggressive.'

'Give her my best. I'll ring back when I've booked our flight.'

After he'd let Andy know the flight details, Mark peeped in again at Kate and only then did he go to bed himself.

How could Kate's father try to stop her getting the help she needed just because it was from

Maeve? It must be awful being so ill at her age. Her life had come to an almost complete stop in Carrabine.

His last thought as he fell asleep was: she'd be pretty if she didn't look so wan. She still had a beautiful smile.

Fifteen

Sunshine after rain. People turn up their faces, eyes closed, as they enjoy the warmth. Flowers turn up their faces too, bobbing a humbler greeting to the sun.

The day of Lacey's wedding dawned bright and clear after a stormy night. Mitch got up early and managed to do some studying before he donned the hired morning suit. He grimaced at the sight of himself in the mirror, ruffled up the tangles of his gelled hair so that they stood even higher, and went to find Gran. She was struggling to fasten her necklace, so he did it for her, then stood back to study her appearance.

'Very smart, but didn't Dad buy you a new necklace to go with your wedding outfit, Gran?'

'It's far too flashy for me. Besides, I always wear this one for weddings. It's my lucky piece.'

He grinned at her. 'Rebelling against him?'

She smiled. 'Just a little.'

He pointed at his hair. 'My little rebellion. Dad'll hate this.'

She looked at him, head on one side, a slight frown creasing her forehead. 'Yes, he will. Look, Mitch, try to remember that your father wasn't always like this. I don't know what's got into him lately, but he used to be fun.'

'Too much testosterone. He's like a stud bull snorting defiance at the world.' Mitch scowled down at his shiny new shoes. 'What about this new woman he's bringing today?'

'Must be someone important to him, or he'd not

bring her to Lacey's wedding. You *will* be polite to her, won't you?'

He shrugged. 'She'll be beautiful and mindless, a trophy doll to flaunt in front of us all.'

'Wait and see. Don't always think the worst of him.'

'I wonder if this one is the reason Mum left him?'

'Does it matter now? I'm quite sure Judith won't go back to him. He's pushed her too far and Mitch—' she debated for a moment the wisdom of being frank then said something she'd been thinking for a very long time—'I never did think he was right for her, never. He stifled her.'

'Do you think so?' Mitch had a think about it. 'In some things, maybe he did. He does like things to be done his way. But he did encourage her to paint, don't forget.'

'Only as a hobby. They had quite a few disagreements about it when she got serious. But her tutor said she wasn't quite good enough to paint professionally, so she backed off on that one.'

He thought of Mum's painting, hanging on the wall of his bedroom now, and some of the others she'd done. 'I can't see why he'd say that. Her paintings are beautiful, and I'm not just saying that because she's my mother. They—' he waved his hands about, searching for words—'show you something beautiful you'd not have noticed.'

'I think so too, and I told her so, but she said I was biased.'

'Anyway, it's hard to go against Dad.' He couldn't hold back a sigh.

'You won't always be dependent on him.'

He scowled. 'I'll have to work with him when

196

I've finished studying, though, won't I?'

'Well, let's go downstairs. The car will be here for us soon. And remember, this is Lacey's day, so whatever you think of this new woman, keep it to yourself.'

'All right, Gran. Message understood.'

*   *   *

Tiffany took a deep breath and went to answer the door. Des let out a long, low whistle of appreciation at her appearance and she gave him a nervous smile. 'I'm not sure this is the right thing to do. Are you certain you still want me to come with you today? I won't be upset if you've changed your mind.'

He held her at arm's length. 'Of course I want you to come. You look absolutely wonderful, Tiff. Never seen you look so good.' He frowned then rolled his eyes at the ceiling. 'It's being pregnant, isn't it? Some women seem to get a glow on their faces. Judith didn't. She was sick all the time and she not only got fat, she stayed fat afterwards.'

'I've told you before, size 16 isn't fat and it suits her to be voluptuous.'

'You women always stick together. But it doesn't suit me to have a fat wife! I'm glad you haven't put on weight. No one would think you were . . .' He patted his belly and winked.

'I'm lucky. I never put on weight. And they would know I was pregnant if they saw me throwing up in the mornings.'

'I think we ought to see a specialist about that.'

'I've already seen my GP and she said morning sickness is perfectly normal at this stage. It passes

197

after an hour or two, anyway.'

'What does a GP know?'

'Enough for me, especially since she's had three kids herself and truly understands what it's like.'

'We'll see about that later.' Des glanced at his watch. 'Are you ready?'

'Just got to get my hat.' She took a deep breath as she fitted it carefully on. She wasn't ready, really. She didn't know what Des meant by this invitation, never had felt sure of him, had always schooled herself to think of their relationship as something finite. Especially now. And let's face it, she was using him as much as he was using her, because with him paying her bills she was able to write full-time. She'd been quite open about that when they made their bargain and he didn't mind, said it kept her out of mischief.

As she emerged from the bedroom, he tucked her arm in his. 'You're a real beauty, Tiff. I'm proud to be seen with you.'

She shrugged. She sometimes wished she wasn't, so that people could see the real person behind the mask, the one who wrote stories about love and happiness, who wanted all the usual things in life: marriage, a husband, home and family. No, not any husband. Des Corrigan. It wasn't easy to love someone like him and she often wished her fancy had settled on someone else. Only it hadn't and that was that, so she would take what she could of him while he wanted her, then sort out a new life for herself . . . afterwards. She liked to think of herself as a survivor, after the sort of life she'd led. Taking a deep breath and schooling her face into the regal look that had once made her a successful photographic model, she took his arm and let him

198

lead her out to the shiny white limousine.

There were two people sitting in the back already and she stopped dead. 'You didn't say we were going with someone else.'

'That's only my mother-in-law and son. They don't bite.'

She hung back. 'Des, no! Your mother-in-law will hate me.'

'Hilary isn't the sort to hate anyone.' He pulled her forward, waited as the chauffeur opened the door and helped her inside. 'This is Tiffany. Tiff—meet Hilary and Mitch.'

The boy nodded stiffly. The older woman studied her face, seemed mildly surprised and said, 'Nice to meet you, dear. Do you prefer Tiffany or Tiff?'

'Tiffany. But try telling Des that.'

He laughed. 'You can be Tiffany to everyone else, but you'll always be Tiff to me.'

She felt tears start in her eyes and turned to look out of the window, blinking furiously. *Always!* How long was that with Des? She caught Hilary watching her with sympathy and understanding written clearly on her face and thought that, in other circumstances, she might have got on well with his mother-in-law, who had a kind face.

The son hadn't even looked at her since the introductions, let alone spoken, and was staring fixedly out of the window. He'd be good-looking when he grew into his body, but at the moment he was bony and had a spot on his chin.

She felt relieved when they arrived at the church, but the feeling didn't last long. There was a murmur among the guests as Des escorted her along to the front. He didn't sit down with her,

199

though, just bent to kiss her cheek.

'I've got to pick up Lacey now and do the father stuff.'

She'd forgotten that he'd have to escort the bride in and give her away. She *definitely* wouldn't have come today if she'd realized she'd be sitting alone.

He touched her cheek gently. 'Tiff? You were miles away. I was just saying that Hilary will look after you till I get back. Only I wanted to settle you here myself first.'

Did that mean he was making a public statement about her? Tiffany wondered. When he'd gone she cast an anxious glace at the older woman. 'I'm sorry. I didn't know he'd be foisting me on you.'

'That's all right.' Hilary hesitated then said, 'You're nervous, aren't you?'

'Very.'

'You're not at all what I expected.'

'You thought I'd be a tart?'

'Yes.'

The words were out before Tiffany could stop herself. 'I'm with Des because I love him. I'm sorry about your daughter, really I am. I didn't want to hurt anyone . . . but I do love Des.'

'He's luckier than he deserves.'

Tiffany could see Mitch listening. He was still glaring at her. He had his father's green eyes but his hair was auburn not silver. It was just like Des to dump her with two people who had every right to hate her. She picked up the wedding programme and bent over it, pretending to study the order of service.

Why on earth had she agreed to come today?

The answer to that was easy. Because once, just

once, she wanted to be seen openly with Des.

Oh, she was a fool, an utter fool! Why not ask for the moon? It'd be far easier to get than what she wanted.

*   *   *

Judith picked up the phone, recognizing Andy's voice immediately.

'I've found out the information you wanted about your painting tutors . . .'

When she put the phone down she stood there feeling numb, unable to move as she tried to take in what Andy had said.

Was he telling the truth? Had Des really bribed her private art teachers to play down how good she was? Reluctantly, she came to the conclusion that she believed it. Des had been very insistent on finding the art tutors for her, which had surprised her. Now she understood why.

She reached out to pick up the phone and tell him what she thought of such a nasty trick, then remembered it was Lacey's wedding today, so she went upstairs to the top floor, running her fingers lightly over her boxes of painting equipment. If only she'd known! She'd slowed down, stopped doing as much painting, tried to interest herself in other things. Hadn't succeeded.

Suddenly tears rolled down her cheeks and she plumped down on the floor, clutching a bundle of clean paintbrushes to her breast and sobbing. She cried for a long time.

What Des had done to her dreams and hopes was cruel.

When she was cried out, she wiped her eyes and

stood up. Working carefully she began to set out her materials, feeling hope swell inside her once again.

Then she pulled out her unfinished canvases one by one, studying them carefully.

'My life isn't over yet, Des Corrigan,' she muttered. 'One day I'm going to rub my success in your face.'

*   *   *

The wedding reduced Tiffany to tears, as she'd feared it would. As she tried to flick the moisture away without Des seeing, he turned his head and grinned, miming a boo hoo. She fumbled in her tiny, beaded bag, hoping desperately that she'd put in enough tissues. Hilary passed her a handkerchief and she nodded her thanks.

When it came time to leave the church, Des pulled Tiffany's arm firmly into his and led her outside. 'Do you always cry at weddings?'

'Invariably.'

'Women!' But his voice was gentle, his expression genial. 'Lacey looks beautiful, doesn't she?'

'Very.'

He nodded as if the compliment had been made to him. 'Takes after her old man.'

The photography session seemed to take a long time, with Des involved in several of the main shots. He dragged Tiffany into a couple of the mass shots, though if looks could kill, the bride and her mother would have become murderers on the spot.

'You shouldn't have brought me, let alone

shoved me into the photos,' Tiffany whispered. 'It's not fair to your daughter.' She saw Mitch looking at her as if surprised by what she'd said.

She was seated next to Des at the high table, another embarrassment. An older woman a couple of places away from her kept making loud and scornful remarks about people who traded on their good looks to push in where they weren't wanted. 'I suppose that's all some people have, their looks,' she finished.

Des's face took on an angry flush.

Tiffany had had enough. 'Oh, I'm not a model now,' she said loudly, as if in response to someone. 'I'm an author. In fact, I just heard today that my first novel has been accepted for publication.' She'd waited for a lull in the conversation and her voice carried clearly down the table. Everyone turned to stare at her, including Des, but she held up her head and stared right back.

'Oh, well—er—congratulations,' someone said, and others echoed the words.

'You didn't tell me!' Des complained in a low voice as the talking started up again.

'I didn't think this was a day for blowing my own trumpet, only that woman over there has been making such nasty remarks that in the end I let fly.'

He grinned. 'I've seen you do that once or twice before.'

They exchanged smiles as they both remembered their first meeting, when she'd put a sleazy photographer firmly in his place.

Des squeezed her hand. 'You're right to defend yourself. And congratulations. This is the book you were telling me about the other night, the romance?'

'Yes.'

'Do they pay much?'

'I don't know yet. You get paid in dribs and drabs and it depends on how many copies are sold.'

He was looking at her thoughtfully now. 'You're a dark horse, Tiff.'

'I'm not. I've been perfectly open with you about my writing. No one else needed to know except for my friends online, whom I haven't told about my acceptance yet.' Her expression grew sad. 'My mother will be scornful about it because it's a romance and my father won't care.'

'Well, I'm proud of you. You always have been more than a beautiful face.'

She looked at him in surprise.

'I mean it. You've got guts and I admire that.'

Someone else claimed Des's attention and then the speeches started. Tiffany sat quietly listening to what people were saying, feeling a warmth inside her at Des's unexpected compliment.

She looked along the table and wished it were her in that white dress, wished she had the sort of family who cared what you did. Oh, she was being silly! It was her hormones, which were all out of kilter lately, or else why would she keep wishing for the moon?

By the time they got back to her flat she was exhausted.

'I'd like to stay over,' Des said, 'but I'm not in the mood for anything but sleep tonight.'

'I'm not, either. Why don't you stay anyway? I don't just care about the sex, you know. I care about you.' Which was as far as she dared go in admitting that she loved him.

To her surprise, when they got to bed, he held

her close. 'You did well today, Tiff.'

'Thanks. It was—a bit difficult at times.'

'Yes. That old aunt of Liz's always was a cow, never speaks well of anyone.'

'Hilary's nice, though. She came over to talk to me once when I was alone and someone had whisked you away. I was really grateful for that because everyone else was avoiding me like the plague.'

'Good for her. I've always liked Hilary, though I'm not sure she ever approved of me as a husband for Judith.'

Tiffany made a non-committal noise.

'About this baby of yours—'

'Yours too, Des.'

'Yes. It's thrown out my calculations.'

'Has it? Well, it's thrown mine out too, but now that I'm getting used to the idea of it, I'm glad.' She wouldn't be alone again, whatever happened to Des.

Silence, then, 'I'll have to work out what to do.'

'It's me who'll be doing most from now on,' she said with a chuckle. 'Your main part's been played.'

'Yes, well. I don't want to be a stranger to it this time.'

She meant to ask him what he meant by 'this time', but she was so tired she stopped struggling and let herself slide into sleep.

When she woke Des was still there, lying on his back, hands crossed behind his head.

'I woke early and I've been thinking . . . I reckon we might as well get married, Tiff.'

She closed her eyes, then opened them again, swallowed hard and tried to think what to say. But even as she opened her mouth, the familiar wave

205

of nausea swept over her and she had to rush to the bathroom.

When she got back to creep shivering beneath the bedcovers, he wasn't there, but he returned shortly afterwards carrying a cup of weak tea and a dry biscuit.

'Thanks, Des. I'd have killed for that.'

' 'S'all right.' He got into bed and fidgeted with the covers. 'You didn't say anything.'

'What about?'

'I just proposed to you, woman!'

'Oh, that. Well, as you're already married and as you didn't sound particularly enthusiastic, I didn't take you seriously.'

He scowled at her.

She snuggled down and closed her eyes. 'If you can't whip up more enthusiasm, I don't think we should even consider getting married. Anyway, we're all right as we are.' The expression of shock on his face pleased her greatly. But she meant what she'd said. She wasn't tying herself to him if he was half-hearted or expected her to be grateful for it.

She wanted love and the whole damn thing!

*   *   *

On Monday morning Lily went downstairs ready for school, only to find her mother and Wayne having an earnest discussion in the kitchen. They broke off when they heard her on the stairs, which made her wish she'd made more effort to eavesdrop. She would do in future. Her dad might view the world through rose-coloured spectacles but she knew you had to be very aware of what was happening to deal with her mother. 'Am I interrupting something?'

They exchanged glances in a way that said they'd been discussing her.

'I'm sorry if I am, but I need to get my breakfast now or I'll be late for school.'

Wayne held up one hand to stop Kerry speaking and turned to Lily. 'You won't be going to that school again. Since we're leaving for the States on Sunday, you might as well enjoy a week's holiday.'

She gaped at him then looked at her mother for confirmation.

'It's for the best,' Kerry said, 'though I'd hoped to break it to you more gently.'

'But I won't be able to say goodbye to my friends.'

'You can email them from Texas,' Wayne said.

Lily folded her arms. 'I'm not going.'

He smiled confidently.

Her mother bit her lip.

Feeling sick inside, Lily tried another tack. 'What am I supposed to do all day? I don't even have my computer any more.'

'You can pack your things and help your mother clear out the house.' Wayne looked at her. 'Unless you want us to pack for you? Oh, and in case you're thinking of trying to escape, either Kerry or I will be here at all times and you'll not be allowed to close your bedroom door in the daytime.'

Lily looked at her mother and let the tears overflow. 'How can you do this to me?'

'It's for your own good.' Kerry tried to put her arm round her daughter, who shook her off.

'I haven't figured out why you're doing it yet, Mum, but it's definitely *not* for my own good. There has to be some other reason.' She knew she was right when her mother went red. She'd have to find a way to escape. Maybe when they were both asleep.

But a man arrived that afternoon to fit a security system on the ground floor.

Wayne gave her another of his smug smiles. 'Just in case you try sleep-walking.'

She didn't let her thoughts show. Anger had taken over from everything else now—and with it determination to escape.

Whatever it took.

On that thought she went up to her bedroom and hid most of her money behind her books.

Sure enough, her mother came in a short time later and took her purse away.

Sixteen

A cool summer's day. Clouds form, threatening rain. The sun pushes them aside briefly, then they pile up again. Even the flowers seem less colourful in this light.

Maeve decided to stay in bed. 'It's just for today,' she warned her two helpers. 'I'll be up and about again tomorrow.'

Neither Andy nor Lena said anything until they were down in the kitchen, then they exchanged anguished glances.

'It's a bad sign,' he said quietly.

'Yes. I've never known her stay in bed before, not even when she had the flu so badly.' Lena pulled out her handkerchief and wiped her eyes.

He put his arm round her. 'We mustn't let her see how worried we are. She'd be furious.'

'I know.' After leaning against him for a moment, Lena pulled herself away, blew her nose with a defiant trumpeting sound and turned to stare round the kitchen. 'It's about time I cleared out these cupboards.'

He didn't say that her kitchen was always immaculate and he doubted there was a need. He wished he had some cupboards to clean out himself.

*   *   *

Upstairs Maeve lay against the pillows, feeling too exhausted to lift a fingertip. Was she dying? she

209

wondered. Was this the beginning of the final slide into oblivion?

'No!' she said aloud, but even she could hear that her voice didn't have its usual decisive tone.

I'm just resting, she concluded in the end, gathering my strength, that's all. And I'll stay in bed for however long it takes. Silly to push myself so hard when what I need most now is rest and recovery time.

After taking a nap she rang the bell. Andy answered.

'I need something to read, something light and happy.'

'I'm not sure we've got much fiction in the house. You don't usually—'

'Then go out and buy me a few books. Anything will do, as long as it's got a happy ending.'

He went back to the kitchen. 'She wants something light and happy to read. I'll have to visit the nearest bookshop.'

'No, wait! I've plenty of light fiction in my room, romances, mostly. I'll take her up a few, see if they'll do.' Lena snapped her fingers suddenly. 'I know! Georgette Heyer. She'll love them.'

She went up to Maeve's room. 'Try *Friday's Child*. It's one of my favourite books.'

When she tiptoed up to listen at the door half an hour later, she heard Maeve chuckling and went down to report the good news to Andy.

He gave her a hug. 'You're a miracle worker.'

'I'll take another couple of books up with her lunch tray.'

*   *   *

Lily was in despair. Not only was her mother or Wayne in the house at all times, but they didn't leave her alone except to sleep, and they made sure the security system was switched on downstairs when they went to bed. She tried going down the first night to test it out and set off alarms that screamed. Wayne came leaping down the stairs.

She stood in the kitchen, arms folded. 'I only wanted something to eat.'

'In future you'll have to wake one of us, or better still, we'll put some biscuits and water in your bedroom and you can stay put.'

She went and got a couple of biscuits and a glass of orange juice, though she wasn't in the least hungry. Back in her room she sat up in bed, arms crossed round herself, feeling desolate.

She was trapped!

After that, from the minute she got up in the morning till bedtime (the hour of which was dictated by Wayne) she was always with one of them, packing, clearing out cupboards, never given a minute to think or even sit peacefully reading.

She retaliated by speaking as little as she could, answering in monosyllables, never making a comment or starting a conversation.

One morning her mother tried to put an arm round her, 'Lily, can't you—'

She shook the arm off. 'Don't *touch* me! I can't bear you pretending to care for me.'

'I'm not pretending. I do care for you.'

'Then you choose a strange way of showing it, dragging me off to America against my will, separating me from Dad—who is my father in every way that counts and always will be. How

211

many times do I have to tell you that? You've changed, Mum, and I don't feel I know you any more, don't even want to. You're a gaoler not a mother. So don't touch me any more and especially don't tell *lies* about loving me.'

She had the satisfaction of seeing her mother shrink away from her.

But of course the following morning Wayne cornered her after breakfast. 'If you upset your mother again, young lady, I'll do something about it.'

'What else can you do to me? You're taking away everything I love, my father, my country.'

'Oh, I'll find some way to get through to you, believe me.'

'I'm sure you will. Sadists always do. I don't know what she sees in you.'

He slapped her across the face.

She stood her ground, even though she could feel her knees trembling. 'Very brave of you. I'm what—half your weight and size? You could beat me up quite easily if you get your kicks from that sort of thing.'

'Sit down and shut up!'

She judged it best to do so.

When Kerry came home she noticed Lily's red cheek. 'Did you bump yourself?'

'No. Wayne hit me.'

Her mother stood open-mouthed and stared at her. 'I don't believe you!'

'Whatever. I wonder why I thought he slapped me. Perhaps it was a cupboard door that jumped out and hit me.'

Kerry grabbed her arm and swung her round. 'Tell me the truth.'

Lily could feel tears in her eyes and blinked furiously. She'd vowed not to cry in front of them. 'I did tell you the truth.'

'What on earth did you say to provoke him so much?'

'What does it matter? He'll probably say I'm lying and you'll believe him.' She pulled away from her mother. 'I need to be alone sometimes, you know. This is—it's cruelty.'

'We can't trust you.'

'I feel exactly the same about you.' She went and sat on the window seat, staring out at the front garden but seeing only a blur of colours as she tried to blink away the tears. But they would fall in spite of her efforts.

When her mother came to stand beside her and said more gently, 'It really is the best thing for you to come with me, Lily. You'll have everything money can buy, a beautiful home, a wonderful lifestyle.'

'That's what *you* want. What *I* want is my father.' To her horror, she began to sob, couldn't hold it back any longer. But she thrust her mother's arm away. 'I told you not to touch me. I hate you! And I don't care if he hits me again for saying that.'

When she ran upstairs, her mother didn't follow and she was allowed a whole half hour to herself. She sat by the window, letting the peace and silence wash around her. Then Wayne came home again and her mother called her downstairs.

But the incident had shown her a slight weakness in her mother and she wondered if she could exploit it. She went to look out of her bedroom window, wondering how long it would take her to open it and climb down a knotted sheet. She didn't dare cut up a sheet in advance, though, that was the trouble.

Next time she was in the kitchen alone she pulled a pair of ancient scissors out of the bag of things to be thrown away and stuffed them down her sock, where they were hidden by her jeans. As soon as she could she went up to the bathroom and hid them in the cistern of the toilet.

She wasn't at all sure she would manage to escape, though, because Wayne was terrifyingly efficient in his arrangements. He seemed to have a hold over her mother that was beginning to worry her. Did her mother really love him? No, she probably just loved the fact that he was rich. She was always going on about money and security.

Every night Lily vowed to try her best to escape the next day, to be alert for the tiniest opportunity. But as the long slow hours crawled past and Sunday drew closer, no chink became evident in the walls surrounding her. Hope began to fade and her spirits got lower and lower.

She didn't even try to hide her reddened eyes from her mother in the mornings any more.

*   *   *

Judith squeezed the first half inch of colour from the tube with a hand that trembled. It was so long since she'd painted, months now, not since before Des had hurt her knee. She'd only sketched a bit, and that half-heartedly. Hesitantly she dabbed paint on the canvas, working slowly and carefully.

When she stood back an hour later she could see no life in what she'd done. Maybe they didn't

214

have to lie to Des about my talent, she thought. Maybe I really don't have what it takes to call myself an artist. She felt very sad at that thought.

Going downstairs, she made herself a cup of coffee and sat sipping it near the kitchen window, gazing out at the view she loved so much. Suddenly galvanized, she rushed upstairs, piled a few things together and set up her easel on the paved area at the back, looking straight across at the slopes of the moors, the undulating tops and the glorious cloud patterns above them.

This time she didn't dab cautious blobs of colour on the canvas, she slathered it on with big strokes, trying to capture the clouds, the shadows, the faint curls of mist near the tops of the slopes, the zig-zag patterns of the drystone walls.

When the phone rang inside the house, she ignored it. She didn't intend to let anything interrupt her today. It rang again a bit later, she didn't know how much later because she always took her watch off to paint.

It wasn't until a drop of rain fell on her face that she realized the weather had changed. Looking up she saw drops whizzing down at her, laughed as they hit her face, and began to carry her things into the house. By the time she'd finished, it was pouring down and she was wet through.

The day's post lay on the floor in the hall. She gathered the letters up and dumped them on the hall table, shivering now but feeling on a high. It was always like this when her painting went well.

She didn't look at what she'd done until she'd had a hot shower and made herself a mug of coffee. Only then did she allow herself to study the canvas. She froze at what she saw, feeling as if she'd never seen it before. Was this really her work? It was *good*! Well, promising, anyway. Putting the mug down on the nearest surface, she folded her arms and studied the canvas. She didn't move for a long time, not until she'd imprinted it on her brain and decided what to do to it the next day.

This painting had promise, it really did. Tears of joy came into her eyes. She'd found her purpose in life now.

Just wait till she saw Des! That thought made her pause. There had been no more nasty tricks played, not for a few days. Did that mean another one was brewing or that he'd given up?

If she knew him, there would be something else brewing. He never gave up if he really wanted something.

*   *   *

Mark had asked for a wheelchair for Kate and it was waiting for them when they got off the plane at Heathrow. He saw her staring round and murmured, 'This has to be the ugliest airport there is.' He watched her nod and try to summon up a smile, but she looked so wan he felt sorry for her.

A chauffeur-driven car was waiting for them and took them to a large hotel, where another suite had been booked.

'I could get used to this sort of luxury.' Kate gestured round the sitting room.

'Miss Corrigan always treats people well. Ah!' He pounced on a letter that was propped up on the table and ripped it open. 'You have an appointment tomorrow afternoon with a

216

specialist.'

'So quickly!'

'Yes. I hope it's not too soon for you? We can always postpone it if you're too tired.'

'The sooner the better.' Her voice came out choked as she added in a near whisper, 'I daren't hope.'

He couldn't help it. He went and put his arm round her, even though he knew this wasn't a professional thing to do. 'Why not? They've made great strides these days in treating ME.'

She leaned against him with a sigh. 'I know. And I've only been like this for a few months. What about the people who've spent years struggling to get better?'

'We won't let it last for years with you.'

'Mmm.' She didn't move, just stayed in his arms.

He felt protective. 'Are you tired?'

'Yes. I know I slept on the plane, but I never seem to get enough sleep.'

'Food first, then I'll leave you in peace.'

'You're a bully.'

She looked up at him with a teasing smile and for a moment he caught a glimpse of the pretty, lively young woman she must have been before, then the smile faded and he realized how white she was. He frowned. 'Do you always go so pale when you're exhausted?'

'Yes. I used to be quite rosy, though you'd never believe it now.'

'Don't forget to tell the doctor that.'

'Will you come in with me?'

He was startled. 'Me?'

'I need someone with me because my brain gets even fuzzier when I'm tense. I say the wrong thing, can't think straight.'

'I'll come in with you.'

He watched her force some food down, then trail across to her bedroom as if each step was a huge effort. He hadn't realized how badly ME affected people.

*　　　*　　　*

Cal went to the house again, banging on the front door until Wayne opened it. There was no sign of Kerry.

'I want to see my daughter.'

'She's not your daughter.'

'We can have this argument every time we meet, but it won't change the fact that I helped bring her up.'

Wayne tried to close the door but Cal put his foot in the gap. He looked at the other man, saw chill anger in his eyes and suddenly felt even more worried for Lily, couldn't bear to think of her under the control of such a cold fish. He tried to speak more temperately. 'I've been to see my lawyer and I definitely have a right to see her because I've acted as her father for all these years and because I've paid maintenance. My lawyer will be contacting you about that if you keep refusing access.'

'I'll wait for the letter and refer it to *my* lawyer. Don't hold your breath.'

There was a noise in the back of the house and the door at the far end of the hall banged open to show Lily struggling against her mother.

'Daddy! Ow!'

Kerry dragged her away again by her hair,

218

slamming the kitchen door behind them. Wayne took advantage of Cal's shock at this violence to shove him backwards and slam the front door in his face.

He stood there on the path, breathing heavily, wanting to smash his way in again and stop them hurting his daughter. Then common sense took over and he made himself stand still. It'd do his case no good to cause trouble. He yelled, 'I'll be back, Lily' several times, as loudly as he could, then turned and strode back to his car. It would be better to see his lawyer and get that court order granting him access. Being reasonable had got him nowhere.

It hurt him to remember Kerry handling Lily so roughly, to hear his daughter calling for him, to be so utterly helpless.

In the garden next door Mrs Baxter shook her head, upset by the screaming and shouting. And when the sound of sobbing drifted out of the sunroom a short time later, she felt tears rise in her own eyes. She never could bear to see children upset—or beaten—and Lily was such a nice child. What was going on?

*   *   *

Inside the house Lily was sobbing, curled up in a ball on the old couch. 'You could have let me *speak* to him, at least!' she threw at her mother. 'How mean can you get?'

'Darling, it's best to cut the tie. He's not your father and you'll not be seeing him again after this week. Why prolong the agony?' Kerry sat on the other end of the couch and tried once again to put

219

her arm round her daughter.

Lily threw her off and looked at her with loathing. 'I don't know you any more. I don't *want* to know someone who's so unkind.'

Wayne came into the room. 'I've told you before, young lady. Mind how you speak to your mama.'

'Or what? You'll hit me again.' She jutted her chin out at him. 'Go ahead. What does it matter?'

He took a hasty step forward. Kerry jumped between them. 'No, Wayne!'

'You let her run rings round you, honey. And I can't bear to see you so upset.'

'I wonder why no one cares whether I'm upset?' Lily asked the air above her head.

'Give her a few minutes to recover,' Kerry said and threaded her arm in his, pulling him out of the room.

The minute they were outside, Lily tried to control her sobbing to listen where they went. Into the kitchen. Seizing the opportunity, she tiptoed out to the hall and opened the front door as quietly as she could. As she was stepping through it, Wayne grabbed her from behind. She wriggled out of his grasp and began to run down the path, screaming at the top of her voice, but he lunged for her and began to drag her back into the house.

She kicked and screamed all the way and had the satisfaction of seeing Mrs Baxter next door standing by the fence watching them, her mouth open in shock.

He shoved Lily along the hall towards the kitchen. 'Don't try that again, young lady!'

She said nothing, but vowed she would try to escape every single time she saw an opportunity.

Surely she'd manage it? Surely they wouldn't succeed in taking her out of the country? She began sobbing again, not because of the thump he'd given her but because she kept remembering her father shouting that he'd be back. He didn't know they were leaving and she had no way of telling him.

She didn't go down for the evening meal and when her mother came up and tried to persuade her, she shouted, 'Why don't you drag me downstairs by my hair since you seem to enjoy hurting me.'

'Of course I don't.'

'Then you'd better send Wayne up to do it for you. Is that what he's going to do in America? Beat me into submission?'

She had the satisfaction of seeing her mother wince.

'You can't win, Lily. I don't know why you won't admit that and make the best of things.'

'It's *you* who can't win, *Mother*. If you want me to hate you, you're going exactly the right way about it.'

'Don't be stupid! You'll forget all about this once you're settled in your new school?'

'Did *he* tell you that? Ha! *You* ought to know me better.'

Her mother spread out her hands in a helpless gesture and left the room. No one came up to see Lily.

She was very hungry, but she wasn't going down willingly, not now and not in the morning either.

What she was going to do was make a plan.

She went to open her bedroom window and looked down, trying to work out how long a rope

221

she'd need to make.

Someone had nailed the window shut.

She lay down again, her stomach growling with hunger, despair filling her. Wayne seemed to think of everything.

When she went to use the bathroom, she checked the window there and to her surprise, found it still opened. It wasn't very big, but she was sure she could get through it. It'd be dangerous. She might fall. But this could be her only chance of escape.

Seventeen

Birdsong ebbs and flows around the house, while a bright summer dawn gilds the edges of the hilltops. It is the very best of mornings.

Judith woke early, went to stand by the window on her way back from the bathroom and enjoy the day's promise. She stretched, feeling lazy and happy, then decided to have the luxury of another few minutes in bed.

She awoke two hours later to another sort of noise, one she couldn't quite place though surely there were men's voices somewhere close to the house? She went to look out of the landing window at the front of the house and discovered a van and trailer parked on the road outside while two men were hard at work, digging up her drive. She gaped at the scene for a moment, unable to believe it was real, then slung on her dressing gown and marched outside.

'What the hell is going on here?'

'You reported a blocked water main. Just investigating. We tried to contact you yesterday, but no one answered the phone, so we shoved a card under the door to say the water would be switched off. Didn't you find it?'

'No.' She'd been enjoying her painting so much she hadn't even looked at yesterday's post, let alone opened or read anything. 'But I didn't report anything.'

'Someone must have. They don't send us out for nothing.'

And then she realized. 'It's my ex. He's played a few nasty tricks like that on me since we split up.' She looked across the road. Sure enough, the car was there. She pointed. 'That's one of his employees, who comes to take photos of me every time a trick is played so that my ex can enjoy the sight of me getting upset.'

Even as they watched the man waved a mocking hand at her and raised his camera to take another shot.

The men looked at one another. 'So you're not having any problems with water?' the one who seemed to be in charge said.

'I wasn't till you switched it off.'

'I'd better ring my foreman.'

There followed at least ten minutes of waiting while the man listened and pressed numbers on his phone. She watched him impatiently. These automated systems were inefficient and like everyone else, she hated being kept waiting.

He gave her an apologetic look. 'The receptionist says the foreman's dealing with someone else then he has another call to answer. It'll be my turn after that.'

While he was waiting, she went inside and flung on some clothes then picked up her camera and marched down the drive, holding it out of sight behind her. She pulled the camera out and took a quick photo of the man sitting in the car, catching him before he could wind up his window. Then she took a photo of his number plate.

'Evidence for my lawyer!' she called cheerfully as she walked back up her drive.

'I'm here on general surveillance, that's all,' he called back.

'Tell that to the judge.'

Once she'd put the camera away she decided to use the age-old method of getting the two workmen on side. 'I think I've enough water left in the kettle for three cups of tea. Would you like some?'

They both brightened up and nodded. 'Very grateful,' one said.

'How do you take it?'

Two hours later the hole had been filled in and Judith watched them leave. Her drive now looked a mess, the pattern of the trench they'd dug showing clearly. She was furious with Des.

When was he going to stop doing these childish things?

Switching on her new computer, she sent him an email warning that if he played any more nasty tricks on her, she'd take out an injunction against him, then she printed it out for evidence. She should probably have taken legal action when he first started messing her around, but she hadn't because of Mitch.

At the thought of her son, she smiled involuntarily. He was coming up to see her at the weekend and she couldn't wait! She'd made all sorts of plans for showing him round the places she used to live as a child, which included taking him into what she called the 'border country', meaning the Pennines between Lancashire and Yorkshire.

* * *

Des looked at the report and photos that had been emailed to him that afternoon by the man on surveillance. He'd forgotten that he'd arranged this. For a moment he took pleasure in seeing how angry he'd made Judith. Serve her right! Then the pleasure faded to be replaced by an image of Tiff, looking soft and beautiful. He'd expected her to jump at his proposal of marriage. Was it because he was having difficulty making love to her that she'd not accepted him?

Shame flooded through him at that thought. He couldn't imagine what had gone wrong with his body. He'd always been able to 'show an interest' as he called it to himself, given even a small encouragement. Until this past year.

He swivelled his chair round to stare at the magnificent view of the Thames beyond his office window. Usually that gave him pleasure too. But today he couldn't summon up more than a mild interest in it.

When he turned back to his computer he noticed an email from Judith. He read it and realized suddenly that he didn't want to play any more tricks on her. Didn't want her back, either. What he did want was the sheer comfort of Tiff, who was the most restful and undemanding person he'd ever known—and who was carrying his child.

He was too old to raise another child, really, but if Tiff was set on having one, he could always arrange for a nanny. Should he move Tiff into his present house or buy somewhere else for them to live? He'd make a more romantic proposal this time and—

The phone rang. He shook himself out of his daydreams and picked it up to hear Raymond Tate's voice.

'Reporting in from Cheshire, Des, but you're not going to like it.'

226

'What do you mean? What's gone wrong with the takeover?'

'Nothing. It's going very smoothly, but we've now found out that several key operatives had taken early retirement and there are serious gaps in the skills portfolio.'

'Find someone who can do those jobs and hire them. You shouldn't need me to tell you that.'

'That's just it. It's a dying set of skills and they're not easy to find. People have been replaced by automated systems, only this factory isn't tooled up for computer controlled production.'

'Then tool it up.'

'It'd cost more than it's worth.'

He could hear that there was something else Tate wasn't saying. 'And?' he prompted.

'I'm not sure the orders would justify it.'

'We checked the order books. They were full.'

'That was last year when we were starting our buyout operation. This year—well, the order books aren't full any more. And . . .' He paused again.

'Stop hedging about. I pay you to tell me how it is.'

'I think we've been sold a pup, Des.'

Suddenly he knew Tate was right, knew it instinctively, in a way that had guided him to riches and success. But he hadn't listened to that inner voice when he was trying to take over the family firm, only to the sweet siren song of vengeance. 'Don't do anything yet. I'll have a think about it.'

He put the phone down with great care then slumped back in his chair, eyes closed. If what Tate was saying was correct, Maeve had won again. And Tate was a shrewd analyst. He cursed long and fluently under his breath. She always won, that

227

bitch did!

Mentally, he began calculating and knew he'd knocked a big fat hole in his finances to buy back the family firm. He'd have to retrench, be careful about his spending—and try to do it in a way that wouldn't betray the fact that he'd be scrabbling for money for some time to come.

If he had Maeve here, he'd strangle her. Only he didn't have her. And if what they told him was right, Maeve was seriously ill. Maybe this was her swan song?

He picked up the phone and contacted the fellow who was watching Judith. 'Stop working on that job. This is what I want you to find out . . .'

Then he rang Tiff. 'Something urgent's cropped up and I'll be busy. Probably won't be round for a day or two. Are you going to be all right?'

'Yes, of course. What's wrong, Des? You sound stressed.'

'Got a few business problems. I'll tell you about it next time I see you. Got to go.'

*   *   *

Tiffany put down the phone, wondering if this was the beginning of the end. Had she mortally offended Des by not accepting his proposal of marriage? She put her chin up defiantly at the mere thought. She'd like nothing better than to marry him—but not when the offer was tossed at her as an afterthought. And anyway, he hadn't started divorce proceedings against Judith yet, so talk of marriage was premature.

She picked up the publishing contract she'd just received through the post and forgot about Des.

The contract was eighteen pages long and complicated. She wasn't stupid, but she simply didn't understand the legal jargon. For all she knew, the publisher could be taking advantage of her ignorance. Perhaps there were clauses that could be improved, should be improved. How could she know?

She went to get the book she'd been studying carefully then opened her email program to send a message to her favourite writers' list. She'd belonged to the Romantic Novelists' Association for years and had learned so much from the published authors on the email list, and from submitting her early efforts to their New Writers' Scheme.

Her message read: 'Just received my first contract and am wondering about getting an agent to translate it for me. Does anyone have any information about the following literary agents: Jane Ferringer Associates, Peter Castorill or Felix Nemerson?' It felt wonderful to be able to talk about publishing contracts. She was still mentally dancing on the ceiling every time she thought about her book being published.

She had her first reply within minutes. 'Felix is my agent. He's a sweetie. Shall I introduce you?'

Within half an hour she had an appointment to see him.

Someone posted a warning about one of the other agents and sharp practices, so she crossed that one off her list.

Not bad for a day's work, she thought, and opened the file containing her new story. She was dying to get an uninterrupted run at it.

It wasn't until evening, as she was sitting alone

229

in front of her television, that she wished Des were there. She ought to be used to being alone by now, but ever since becoming pregnant she seemed to need company, particularly his. Did he really want to marry her or was it just for the sake of the baby? Perhaps he'd changed his mind about it by now. Business problems didn't usually take up the evenings as well as the days. Did they?

She shook her head. How could you ever tell for certain what people were thinking? Des had had two marriages break up so he had to be a bad risk. She smiled. She knew all that, but when did reason ever stop you loving someone? He was fun, cared for her in his own way—to her he was just Des, the man she loved.

She'd miss him dreadfully if he didn't stay with her, but she wasn't going to marry him unless she was convinced it was what he really wanted and that he'd give it his best effort this time. She knew she was easy-going to a fault, but she had her sticking points, as he'd found out once or twice in their five years together.

*   *   *

Maeve spent three days in bed, reading, relaxing as she hadn't done in years, but most of all sleeping.

On the fourth day she got up, surprising Lena in the kitchen.

'I thought you were staying in bed.'

'I feel a bit better today, so I thought I'd have breakfast in the garden room. Has Andy eaten yet?'

'No, but I heard him stirring a few minutes ago.'

'Ask him to join me when he comes down,

would you?'

When Andy came in, she smiled to see how anxiously he looked at her.

'Should you be up, Maeve?'

'Yes. Eat your breakfast then we'll talk.' Until he'd finished his meal she kept the conversation light, chatting about how much good it had done her to rest, and how much she'd enjoyed reading Lena's books.

She watched him clear his plate and pour a second cup of coffee then said quietly, 'Let's go and sit in the conservatory.'

He followed her out and fussed about whether she was comfortable. She patted the seat next to her. 'Stop fussing and sit down.' She hesitated then allowed herself to take his hand. She seemed to need a human touch lately, need it so badly. 'The other day I got to thinking what if I never got up out of that bed again? So I made a few plans.'

He nodded and clasped her hand in both his, waiting for her to go on.

'We've already agreed that Kate and Mitch are the two most promising from the next generation of Corrigans, and I'll soon be able to meet them. But there's one that I know hardly anything about—Des's illegitimate daughter. I want a report on her, and as quickly as possible. Can you get things moving?'

'Yes, of course.'

'And arrange for me to meet Mitch?'

Another nod. 'What about Kate? She sounds to be in a bad way, Maeve.'

'We've got her the best available help. She's young, has only had ME for a few months, so we have to hope she can be cured. And even in her

231

weakened state, she defied her father to come here, while that brother of hers rejected even the idea of meeting me—and not politely, either. From the reports, he sounds to be very like Leo.' She pulled a face. 'Too much of a plodder for my purpose, and he's a bit old to allow his father to make his decisions for him.'

He looked down at the hand he was still holding and surprised her by raising it to his lips. 'If I do all this, Maeve, will you continue to take it easy?'

'Yes. Resting has done me a lot of good. Oh, Andy, I'm not stupid.' She sighed and for once let down her guard. 'I want to live as long as I can. I'm too young in the head to die without kicking and fighting all the way.' She tried to laugh, but it was unconvincing and her voice broke on the final word.

He pulled her into his arms and gave her a hug. 'I'll fight and kick alongside you every last inch of the way.'

That brought tears to her eyes. She didn't push him away, but laid her head on his shoulder and they just sat there for a while until the distant tinkle of a phone made her raise her head and say gently, 'Go and find out about Lily for me now. And Andy . . .'

He turned to look at her.

'Thank you.'

*   *   *

Cal rang his lawyer. 'I need to get a court order to allow me to see my daughter. I called at the house today and they wouldn't even let me speak to her.'

The lawyer rang back later. 'We've got a hearing

for Monday.'

'Can't you get one sooner?'

'Sorry. Unless you can prove it's an emergency.'

'I don't suppose a day or two will make that much difference.'

'I think you have a very good case and I'm sure you'll get access.'

*   *   *

At Dr Upson's, Kate had to fill in a long questionnaire before she went in to see the doctor. She felt nervous and foggy-brained but she struggled on, ticking the boxes.

Dr Upson studied the questionnaire, nodding and pursing her lips as if it was meaningful to her. 'Now, tell me exactly what's been happening to you, Kate.'

When she'd finished explaining, she leaned back, feeling the room swim around her.

'The pattern is very typical of chronic fatigue,' that quiet voice said. 'Your Australian doctor was quite right about that diagnosis, I'm sure. And it's a serious, debilitating illness, make no mistake about that. There is no instant cure, it takes a year or two to get your body's biochemistry back on an even keel, so you're going to have to be patient and accept incremental progress. But the good news is that we're having a lot more success nowadays, especially with a nutritional approach. I'd like to run a few tests, but I'm fairly certain we can improve some things quite quickly, that foggy brain for one.'

Kate stared at the doctor, unable to believe what she was hearing. 'You can—do something?'

233

'Oh, yes. Though I can't guarantee a full recovery. I think you'll prove to have an iron deficiency, hence the extreme weakness. As for the fuzzy brain, it's likely that you've developed a wheat intolerance, possibly one to milk as well. It quite often happens in these cases, especially in those with Irish ancestry.' She reached for a pad. 'Let's get the tests done as quickly as possible and we'll bring you back in as soon as we get the results to discuss what else we can do. In the meantime, do you think you can give up eating wheat?'

Kate nodded.

'It'll mean reading all the labels. Wheat is in more products than you'd believe. But you can get rice bread in any health store.'

As they walked out, Kate stumbled, and again Mark's arm was there to support her.

She looked at him and smiled, in spite of her tiredness. 'You've been a tower of strength. Thank you.'

'Looks like you're about to get better,' he said quietly. 'Now, let's go and get those tests done.'

When they got back to the hotel afterwards, she turned to him and dared say it herself. 'Dr Upson sounded so confident that she could help me.' And then tears were running down her cheeks and she was sobbing against him.

Hope, she found, was as hard to bear as the lack of it.

Eighteen

Early morning mist drifts across the moors, rags of it trailing down the slopes. Sheep huddle in clusters near the walls. No sign of the sun today, no blue in the sky even.

Judith woke feeling apprehensive. She couldn't have said why. Yesterday she'd been full of hope and enthusiasm. Today it had all evaporated and she had a feeling something was about to happen. The phone rang just as she was setting out her painting materials. She hesitated but decided to answer it because she didn't want any more workmen turning up unannounced.

'Hi, Judith. Andy here. Have you a minute to talk?'

'Of course.'

'Maeve's not been well this week. She's very keen to meet Mitch as soon as possible—and Lena and I are keen to give her whatever she wants.'

There was a pause and she heard him taking a deep breath, as if the subject was painful. She waited patiently for him to continue.

'You said he was coming up this weekend. Could we build in a visit to Saltern House on Saturday, do you think?'

'Of course. I was going to show him round this part of England and it'd be good for him to visit his father's old home.'

'Maeve will be pleased.' He chuckled. 'Though it wasn't their home until they were in their early teens.'

235

'From the way Des talks about it, his family had lived there since the middle ages!'

'No. Maeve's father bought it after he made some money. It was quite tumble-down then.'

'Des doesn't talk much about his childhood or his family. I'm sure Mitch would love to chat to Maeve about the Corrigan side of the family.'

'I'll tell her. She's had some genealogical research done which goes back quite a long way. So, do you want to use the same ploy as last time to avoid your watcher?'

'He isn't here this morning and if he stays away, I'll just drive straight over on Saturday. It's only for Mitch's sake that I'm even bothering to keep the visits secret. I don't want to get him into his father's bad books.'

'All right. Let me know what you decide to do.'

She put the phone down, glad she'd answered it. When it rang again she picked it up automatically, thinking Andy must have forgotten to tell her something.

'Judith?'

Her heart sank. 'What do you want, Des?'

'I need to see you, to talk to you.'

'Well, *I* don't need to see you. No doubt you're planning some other nasty trick. When are you going to grow up?'

There was silence at the other end of the line, then he surprised her. 'Maybe I have done.' He let out a mirthless bark of laughter as he added, 'Or maybe I'm just growing old. Look, I'm sorry about the tricks I played on you.'

'Oh?'

'Really I am. I was annoyed at the way we parted. But it was a waste of time, really. I should

236

have just got on with my life.'

'I can't believe I'm hearing this from you.'

'Well, there you are. Look, things are a bit full-on for me at the moment—I've got a few business problems. Could you come down to London, do you think? We can meet for lunch. I'll send a car up to fetch you.'

She didn't know what to say. Was this another trick? Or was he starting to act reasonably about their divorce?

'Please, Jude.'

'I shan't come back to live with you.'

'I wasn't going to ask you to.'

She made a quick change of plans. 'Well, I was thinking of going down to see Mum and Mitch, so I can come this weekend and see you on the Friday. But I'll drive myself, so don't send a car. Where do you want to meet?'

He named his favourite restaurant and put down the phone.

She was baffled. He was usually full of himself and his doings, but this time he'd sounded serious, sincere even. And quiet. Des Corrigan, quiet? Something must have gone wrong.

Unless this was another trick . . . Only how could it be? She'd be driving herself, only meeting Des in public.

She wondered whether to contact Cal, perhaps even go and stay with him on the Thursday night, but he'd only sent her a couple of short emails in the past three days, so she decided not to. If he didn't want to see her, she wasn't going to cling to him or pester him. Pity, though. She really liked him, had thought they might even have a future together. Silly of her, really. People were into casual sex these days, not marriage. She was old-fashioned, wanting it to be more. Only . . . he was a lovely man.

She went back to her painting, trying to capture the dull undertones you got when it was going to rain, but she couldn't settle.

It wasn't until she went to prepare lunch that she realized how little she had in the fridge. She needed to do some serious shopping unless Mitch had changed. He always ate like a horse—two horses.

Wandering round the shops and market in Rochdale was as good a distraction as any, but she kept wondering what Des needed to see her about and then wondering why Cal had stopped emailing her.

*   *   *

Kate lay awake for over an hour in the middle of the night as her body tried to persuade her that it was time to wake up, but eventually she got back to sleep again. When she woke to daylight, she looked at her watch and gasped. Ten o'clock already! She was wasting her life sleeping!

She peeped into the sitting room and saw Mark working on his computer. He looked up and smiled. He had a serenity about him, though that wasn't usually how you described a man his age. But nothing ever seemed to upset him. He was so easy to be with.

He lifted his fingers off the keyboard. 'How are you this morning?'

'One of my better days, I think.'

'You've no medical appointments today, so we

can either go up to see Maeve and stay there for the weekend or we can stay in London till your test results come through. Whichever you prefer.'

She looked out of the window at the sunshine. 'I've never been to London, though I'm sure I won't have the energy to do much sightseeing. Could we go and see a few things today, do you think, then go to Maeve's tomorrow?'

'Sure. We can get a car and drive round, which shouldn't tire you too much. Then we'll go up to Cheshire tomorrow.'

'Would my aunt mind us doing that? She's been so generous. I don't want her to think I'm taking advantage of that.'

'Maeve says to do whatever will make you happiest. But you do need to eat breakfast before we set off.' He gestured to a package on the table next to him. 'I've been out and bought some rice bread and a couple of other things for you.'

She went across to examine the special bread, pulling a face at its dryness. 'Not like the real thing, is it?'

'No. They told me at the health store that it's best toasted. Now, go and get yourself ready. I'll order breakfast and let them toast a couple of slices of this stuff for you.'

She couldn't resist teasing him. 'Right, Mumsie dear.'

But she had an appetite this morning and didn't have to be persuaded to eat.

When they went out, a large comfortable car, complete with chauffeur, was waiting for them. And she managed to see some of the sights she'd dreamed about for years: Buckingham Palace, the Thames, the Tower of London. She knew they were trite old tourist places, but still, she wanted to go there and see them for herself. She looked wistfully at the beautiful shops they drove past but knew she'd never stand up to a tour of them even if she'd had some money to spare, which she didn't.

Mark brought her back to the hotel at one o'clock for a snack and a rest, then took her out again, ending the evening with an early dinner at a restaurant which had no prices on the menu. She didn't dare ask how much it had cost.

The next morning she woke up to find that some of the fog had lifted from her brain. 'Can it really be that easy?' she asked Mark over breakfast.

'I doubt it will be the final answer to your problems, but each step along the way ought to see an improvement from what Dr Upson told us.'

'I can't remember clearly what she said. That's why I wanted you with me. Thank you, Mark. You've been like a fairy godmother to me.'

He gave her a long, slow smile. 'Actually, I don't feel at all godmotherly where you're concerned.'

His steady look promised . . . something. Or was she fooling herself? She hoped not.

'But for the moment, it's my job to look after you, help you get better and take you to Maeve.'

'I'm looking forward to meeting my aunt.'

'I'd better warn you that she's being treated for cancer, has lost her hair and is looking very frail. Don't show your surprise. She hates it.'

'It seems terrible to discover an aunt, then lose her.'

'She's not dead yet. She'll have a few surprises for everyone yet, if I know Maeve.'

'Do you know her well?'

'I ought to. She helped plan and fund my

business when I started it up.'

'That was kind of her.'

He laughed. 'Kind? No way. She didn't do it out of *kindness*. It was a shrewd investment and has paid her well. I'm good at what I do.'

'Private investigations?'

'Done with tact and delicacy, along with anything else that's needed.'

'Like looking after me.'

'That's a pleasure as well as a job.'

'Oh.' She felt herself go a bit pink and bustled off to pack. Only when she was closing her suitcase did she realize that she'd done it all herself this time. She was tired now but not exhausted beyond reason. In fact, she really did feel better. Could going without wheat be helping her foggy brain?

Please, let it last! She didn't think she'd ever prayed more fervently for anything in her whole life.

*   *   *

Hilary heard Mitch put the phone down. He'd just asked his mother not to tell Des he was going up to visit her, and that upset Hilary. She didn't like to see a son treading so carefully round his father.

He came into the sitting room and flopped down on the couch beside her.

'Why do you suppose Dad wants a face to face meeting with Mum?'

'I'm hoping he's going to ask her for a divorce.'

'She's already told him she wants a divorce, so it can't be that.'

'Well, you'll find out tomorrow, won't you?'

He shrugged, stretching his legs out, sitting in a

241

position that would have given her backache. Oh, for a supple young body again! she thought. 'We'll have to pack your things tomorrow, then your mother can take them with her on Friday and pick you up from school after her lunch meeting. Could you go up and check there's nothing needing washing?'

'Sure.'

'I'll not be back till about eight o'clock on Sunday evening.'

He turned to grin at her from the doorway. 'I think I'm old enough to look after myself now, Gran.'

'Of course you are. I just didn't want you worrying about me.'

She sat staring at the TV, seeing nothing but a blur of colours and movement. Mitch was such a good lad, too good she sometimes thought, as if he did nothing without working out in advance the best way to tackle it. He had a few friends, but didn't usually bring them back here. It was as if he kept his life in several separate compartments, like his relationships with his half-sisters. Judith had been wrong not to encourage that. In Hilary's opinion, the lad was hungry for relatives. A pity her side had so few.

But when she thought of the things some lads his age got into, drugs and stuff, she could only be grateful that Mitch hadn't gone down that path. She'd miss him when he went to university. She didn't really like living alone.

Maybe she wouldn't have to. She hadn't told anyone, but the friend she was going to visit this weekend was a man. Glen had been married to an old school friend of hers who'd died last year, and they'd met at a dinner party a few months later. Since then she'd been seeing him fairly regularly, though that had eased off a bit when Mitch came to live with her because she didn't want her family to know. She enjoyed Glen's company and he'd suggested they marry, but she wasn't sure, felt a fool at her age to be even considering it.

She wondered if Judith would remarry, hoped she would and to someone more suitable this time, someone kind, with a loving nature.

*   *   *

Judith packed carefully, wanting to appear her best for her lunch date with Des. Twice she went and picked up the phone to ring Cal, and twice she put it down with the number only half dialled. He hadn't emailed last night, either, not even a quick reply to her last post.

When she got down to London, she gave in to temptation and drove past her old home because it was almost on the way to her mother's. Goodness, the place looked huge! It was exactly like a child's pile of boxes. She'd never liked that sort of architecture. Des was welcome to keep it.

Her mother came out to greet her, looking at her face searchingly. 'Are you all right, darling?'

'Never better, Mum. But I'm dying for a cup of tea.'

'Just nip up to the tiny bedroom with your case while I put the kettle on.'

As they sat and chatted, she told her mother about Maeve and how she was taking Mitch to see his aunt.

'Good idea.'

'How is Des? Really.'

'He never changes.'

'What about this woman of his?'

'To my surprise, I liked her.'

'You didn't!'

Hilary nodded. 'Yes I did. She behaved impeccably in a difficult situation and although she's very beautiful, it's not that. She's got a kind expression in her eyes, as if she really likes people. She used to be a model, apparently, very successful too, Des says. At the wedding some great-aunt of Lacey's was rude to her and Tiffany put the old hag in her place very cleverly. Did you know she was a writer?'

'I've never discussed her with Des, beyond finding out her name.'

'Well, she's just had her first novel accepted for publication. A romance. She hadn't told him and he looked as surprised as anyone when she announced it to prove to the old aunt that she wasn't just a pretty face.' Hilary smiled reminiscently.

Bitterness welled up in Judith. Des hadn't stopped Tiffany from fulfilling herself, just his wife. She looked at the clock and changed the subject firmly. 'I'm looking forward to seeing Mitch.'

Half an hour later he was there and Judith surprised herself as well as the others by bursting into tears as she gave him a big hug. 'I'd forgotten how tall you'd grown. I've missed you dreadfully.'

He gave her another hug, then swung her off her feet. 'I missed you, too. I think of you every time I look at your painting. I'm glad I've got it.'

She bit back an angry denunciation of Des and

how he had cheated her about her artistic potential. She didn't want to put barriers between Mitch and his father. 'So, what are we going to do tonight to celebrate?'

'Go out for a curry?' he asked. 'I'm pining for one.'

'Gran doesn't like them,' Judith pointed out.

'I don't mind mild ones,' Hilary said. 'A friend is training me and I've found there are some milder dishes which I quite like.'

Mitch let out a yell of triumph and waved his fist. 'Yessss! Shall I ring and book a table?'

*   *   *

The following morning was a mad scramble to get Mitch off to school in time and make sure he'd packed all he needed for the weekend. Then Judith sat and chatted to her mother, keeping an eye on the clock.

'You're on edge,' Hilary said. 'Surely you're not afraid of Des?'

'No. I just keep wondering why he wants to see me, and feeling it'll be bad news.' She didn't tell her mother about Cal. Well, he might be history now. She was stupid to keep thinking about him.

As she parked outside the restaurant, making sure she was a full five minutes late, she admitted to herself that she did feel nervous. She'd been married to Des for twenty years, for heaven's sake. He'd not have grown horns and a tail in the months since they'd split up!

He was sitting in a corner, swirling red wine round and round in a glass, frowning at it. When he saw her approaching, he stood up and she was

245

sure that was an expression of relief on his face. He looked as if he'd put on a bit of weight and his colour was too high, but otherwise he was much the same.

She allowed the waiter to seat her and hand her a menu.

'You're looking good, Jude.'

'I'm feeling good, thank you.'

'The north must suit you.' He looked down at the table for a minute, fiddling with the edge of his napkin, then said gruffly, 'Sorry about the dirty tricks. I was angry at you.'

'I'm angry at you for a lot of things, but I've not acted so—so *childishly.*'

He shrugged it off in his usual manner and drained his glass, reaching out for the bottle, a movement forestalled by the attentive waiter. 'Do you want something to drink, Jude?'

'Just a fizzy mineral water with a twist of lime.'

'Given up the booze?'

'I'm driving back to Blackfold this afternoon and I don't want to be done for drink driving, do I?' She waited and when he didn't say anything, prompted, 'Well? What was so important that you had to see me face to face?'

'Let's order the meal first.'

When the waiter had gone, he said abruptly, 'I want a divorce and I need it quickly, if you don't mind. So today I want us to agree on division of goods, custody of Mitch, all that sort of thing.'

'We should have met at my lawyer's, then. I'm not agreeing to anything without his approval.'

'I appreciate that, but we can agree on broad principles today, can't we? The lawyers will only charge us an arm and a leg to do that.'

'We can try. Depends what you want.' She frowned at him. 'Why the sudden hurry?'

He moved uneasily in his seat. 'You're not going to like it.'

She waited.

'Tiff's pregnant. I want to marry her.'

As the waiter brought the food, Judith sat back, shocked by this, then suddenly the humour of it struck her. How many times had he said he didn't want any more children, thank you very much, and three were enough for anyone? 'I bet you didn't get her pregnant on purpose.'

'No. But she wants to keep it. She's getting on, thirty-eight, says it may be her only chance to have a child.'

'And you agreed?'

He shrugged. 'I didn't have much choice. She'll keep the baby whatever I say or do and I—' He hesitated, then finished in a rush, '—want to keep Tiff.'

'You love her?'

'Mmm.'

They spent most of the meal discussing the division of their possessions, then when they'd finished, he said, 'You could have taken me for more than that if you'd been greedy, Jude, except I don't have more as it turns out. I've had a few business upsets lately, thanks to my bloody sister.'

'I don't need more than I've asked for from you. And what's Maeve done to you now?'

'Tricked me. The family business was failing, but she made me pay through the nose for it, knew what I was doing all along. Ironic that that was the final straw between you and me, isn't it?' After another mouthful of wine, he added, 'She always

247

was a manipulative bitch.'

'You don't usually drink so much at lunchtime.'

'Well, today I feel like it and what do you care now, anyway?' He emptied the rest of the bottle into his glass. 'Maeve's ill, though. I think it's cancer, though I can't find out any details. Her staff are damned close-mouthed.'

'Serves you right for trying to trick her.'

His scowl reappeared. 'Might have known you'd be on her side.'

'I'm not on anyone's side, but I always thought you were being stupid about that family business.' She watched him roll his eyes, looking just like Mitch for a moment, and that took the edge off her anger. 'I don't want to get into a quarrel. Let me jot down what we've agreed and you can check it.' She took out her notebook and scribbled down the details, showed the list to him then looked at the clock. 'I need to get going. Thanks for the lunch.' She picked up her handbag.

'Good luck with the new fellow.'

She turned to stare at him, surprising a smug smile on his face. 'He's not a permanent fixture.'

'Well, good luck with your painting or whatever you're doing with yourself.'

At the mention of painting the anger returned. She leaned over him and said in a low, tight voice, 'I nearly didn't come today when I learned that you'd tricked me about how good an artist I was, especially when I found you'd let this Tiffany person do her writing until she was good enough to be published. Why did you stop *me*, Des, and not her? You knew how much it meant to me.'

He wriggled uncomfortably. 'I needed your help with entertaining business colleagues, you know I did. And anyway, it would have been embarrassing to have you hawking your paintings round town, as if I couldn't afford to keep you in style.'

'And you won't need *her* help with your colleagues?' Judith tried to control her anger, but couldn't help adding, 'That, Des Corrigan, was the meanest thing of all, and it will always rankle with me. I'm being civilized about our split because of Mitch and because I'm not greedy. You don't deserve my forbearance, though, so here's something to remember our last meal together by.'

She picked up his glass of red wine and tipped it over his head, then walked out.

'You stupid cow!' he yelled across the restaurant.

She turned at the door and smiled at the sight of the red wine dripping down his face and staining his shirt. It was a childish thing to do, as childish as the stupid tricks he'd played on her, but it felt good.

Now, perhaps, they could both move on.

*   *   *

When they arrived in Blackfold, Mitch insisted on a tour of the house before he went for a walk around the village while Judith prepared tea. When he came back, he ate as heartily as ever, then washed the dishes, something that surprised her.

'Gran says you either cook or clear up,' he informed her. 'I don't know much about cooking, though she's teaching me, so I usually wash up.'

Afterwards they settled down in the living room and she offered him a glass of white wine.

'It's nice not being a child any more,' he said thoughtfully.

'How grown up do you feel?'

He shrugged. 'It varies from day to day.'

It was such a lovely evening she didn't even consider switching on her computer and looking at her emails. She wanted to spend every moment she could with her son. Besides, she felt tired after two days with long drives. 'Did you know your dad's new woman is pregnant?'

Mitch gaped at her for a minute, then grinned. 'Got to give it to him, he's a lively old sod.'

'Not so much of the old. He's only fifty-eight.'

'Fifty-nine next month, seventeen years older than you. You look more like his daughter than his wife sometimes, especially lately.'

'I do?'

'Yes. You look younger, more casual and relaxed, since you left him. He's drinking heavily and leaving too much to Raymond Tate.'

'Are you still intending to study business at university?'

'Yes. I've told Dad and he's cool about paying for it, says he's glad I don't want to do one of those useless arty courses.' He chuckled. 'When you think how badly I draw, I'm surprised he even considered that a possibility.'

'I don't think he knows about it.'

'No, just about how poor I am at sport. Once I leave school, I'm never going to play any sort of sport again. What I like best is going for long walks and watching birds and animals.'

'I like that, too.'

Later she said, 'Tell me about the wedding—and about *her*. Mum says she's not as bad as we'd expected.'

'I suppose not. If she weren't shacking up with my father, I'd not mind her, but I think it's weird the way he goes for skinny blondes. And it's embarrassing that she looks even younger than you.' He smiled mischievously. 'I like them more curvy.'

'I hope not too many of them.'

'No, just one or two, here and there. I'm not interested in guys, in case you were worried.'

'I wasn't.'

He sat staring at the fire for a moment or two, frowning, then burst out, 'I don't know what Tiffany sees in Dad, but you can tell she loves him from the way she looks at him. How does he do it? How does he pull so many women?' He let out a snort of disgust. 'Bet he leaves her as soon as her belly starts to puff up.'

'He told me he's going to marry her.'

Mitch groaned. 'How gross! Third wife!'

She changed the subject and got him talking about cars, because Des had promised him a new one as soon as he passed his driving test, and being Mitch he'd already started researching what was available. In some ways, he was very much a rich man's son, and she wished she could make him better understand the value of money, because he didn't, not really.

They didn't go to bed until after midnight. And when they got to the top of the stairs, he gave her a quick hug and said gruffly, 'I've missed you, Mum. Gran's great, but she's not you.'

Nineteen

Clouds roll in from the west, threatening rain. A short, sharp shower darkens roofs and batters young flowers into submission. The temperature drops and the storm builds slowly, inexorably, confidently.

Kate and Mark arrived at Saltern House mid-afternoon. She stared at it in delight. 'What a beautiful house! I can see why my father was upset about his sister getting it.'

'It wasn't like this when Maeve took over. I've seen photos. She's done a lot to restore it.'

'She never married?'

'Yes. But they divorced. She couldn't have children.'

'How sad.'

The car drew up and Mark got out and came to help her. 'You're looking a little better.'

'I'm feeling better. Tired, still, but not so fuzzy-brained.'

'Come and meet Maeve then. I'll unload the car later.'

She swallowed hard. 'I'm a bit nervous.'

'You'll like her. Everyone does. Except for cheats and hypocrites. She has a sharp way with them.'

The door opened and Lena stood there, staring at Kate as if she was seeing a ghost.

'Is something wrong?'

'You're so like her when she was young, even to the colour of your hair. I can't believe what I'm seeing.' Then a gust of chill wind blew around

252

them and she clicked her tongue in exasperation at herself. 'What am I doing, keeping you on the doorstep? Come in, come in. I'm Lena, Maeve's housekeeper.'

'And friend,' Mark added.

Lena led the way towards the back of the house and opened the door to a small, exquisitely furnished sitting room. A woman was sitting staring into the flames of a gas fire, seeming lost in thought. 'She's here,' she announced.

Maeve turned round and looked at Kate in surprise. 'Goodness!'

'Isn't she like you as a girl?' Lena said. 'Will I bring you some tea?'

'Yes, please do.' Maeve held out her hand. 'Please excuse me for not getting up to greet you properly, Kate.'

She went to grasp her aunt's hand and bent to kiss her cheek. 'You've got green eyes, too.'

'It seems rather a dominant trait. We all have, Leo, Des and myself.'

'My brother has brown eyes and hair.'

'There! I knew he wasn't a true Corrigan when he spurned my offer without even meeting me.'

Kate smiled sadly. 'He's very loyal to Dad. Those two have always been close.'

Maeve looked at her sharply, but didn't make the obvious comment. 'Come and sit down. Mark, would you mind if we ladies had a quiet chat together?'

'Not at all. I'll bring Kate's bags in and cadge a cup of tea from Lena.'

Kate sat on the couch, feeling tired but more cheerful, for some reason she couldn't fathom. After all it was too early to see whether she could be cured.

'You don't look well.'

'Neither do you.'

They looked at one another solemnly, then Maeve leaned forward and said, 'It's a damned nuisance, isn't it? Let's hope they can sort you out, at least. Now, tell me about yourself—and about that stupid brother of mine. As if he could have run our engineering works!'

'He runs his hardware store well enough.'

'I'm sure he does. He always did like fiddling round with tools. But he'd not have liked big-scale accounting and managing a large staff.'

'No. I can't see him doing that sort of thing, I must admit.'

'Did you think I took the business away from them on a mere whim? Leo would have let it run down still further. And Des—he'd have indulged in a few sharp practices once he found out how bad things really were. He always was impatient.'

'They hated you for taking over the business.'

Maeve shrugged. 'We quarrelled all through our youth. It was no different as adults. We couldn't have worked together so one of us had to take over. Some families don't know how to live in harmony. Ours was one of them. Now, tell me about yourself, your hopes and ambitions.' She looked at the clock. 'I have one hour then Lena will be nagging me to rest, so don't waste time.'

Kate leaned her head back. 'I think when you rest, I will too.'

Maeve chuckled. 'We're well matched, then.'

The door opened and Lena came in pushing a small trolley. 'Mark phoned to tell us about the wheat, so I went out and bought some wheat-free

254

things. I'll soon get the hang of it.' She studied them and added, 'And I want to see a difference to this trolley when I come back for it. You both look as if you need feeding up. Maeve, don't forget you'll need a rest in an hour.'

When she'd gone, they laughed.

'Better eat something or she'll nag us to death,' Maeve said.

*   *   *

Furious at Judith for making a scene in a restaurant and embarrassed that it was in this particular restaurant, one of his favourites, Des went round to Tiff's flat to change his clothes. He let himself in, calling, 'It's only me.'

She peered out of the smallest bedroom, which she used as an office, and gaped at the sight of him. 'What happened?'

'My damned wife is what happened. The bitch tipped a glass of red wine all over me.' He saw amusement in her face and growled, 'It's not funny. This shirt will never be the same.'

'You'd better wash and change, then put the shirt to soak in cold water. I have to get back to work.'

As she turned away he pulled her round. 'I need some company, Tiff.'

'I'm just in the middle of writing a crucial scene. I'll see you later.' She walked back into the office and shut the door.

He stared at it in annoyance. She'd never done that before, had always been attentive to his needs.

She'd never been a published author before, either. He wished she wasn't now, wished she was still absolutely dependent on him.

After cleaning himself up, he made a cup of coffee and sat sipping it. Should he insist Tiff come out and talk to him? After all, he was the one paying for this place. On the other hand, she'd been very determined about going on with her writing.

Moodily he switched on the TV, then switched it off again and stood up. 'I'm going back to work!' he yelled. 'I'll see you this evening.'

'All right. Bye.'

He wasn't good at understanding modern women, wished they hadn't got all bolshy and liberated. But he didn't want to lose Tiff. Or later on face the humiliation of a third marriage breaking up. So he had to tread carefully. He had enough problems with the business.

'Sodding feminists!' he muttered under his breath as he hailed a taxi. 'They've got a lot to answer for.'

*　　　*　　　*

Lily lay awake until very late on the Thursday night plotting how to escape. It'd be best to do it while Wayne was out, because her mother let her spend the odd half hour by herself and *he* never did. But her mother still kept popping in to see how she was, or using the excuse of bringing her up a cup of tea to check on her, so even that wouldn't be safe enough.

In the end, she decided to fake an upset stomach so that she could take refuge in the bathroom, but wondered how she could convince them about this, since they were all eating the same sort of food.

On the Friday morning, while Wayne was out, she said casually, 'Could we get some takeaway tonight? I'm fed up of eating green stuff.'

Kerry looked at her. 'You know Wayne doesn't like cheap takeaway food.'

'Well, I do and I haven't had a pizza for a million years.'

Kerry wrinkled her nose in disgust. 'I don't know how you can eat that stuff—or why you don't get fat on it. Cal pandered to your low eating habits more than I ever will.'

Lily felt her eyes fill with tears at the mention of his name and didn't try to hide that from her mother. Then she swung round and went to stare out of the window, making sure her shoulders drooped. 'I can't bear it,' she said in a choked voice. 'The thought that I'll not see Dad again until I'm old enough to leave home, is—' She let her voice falter to a halt and wrapped her arms around herself.

Kerry came over to stand beside her. 'Darling, it will get easier, I promise you.'

'No, it won't! *You* don't care about him any more, but I do and I always will. He's the only father I've ever had. And I promise you this: as soon as I turn eighteen—at one *second* past midnight!—I'll be leaving you and going back to him. What's more, I know for certain he'll still want me.' She had the satisfaction of seeing how shaken her mother looked, so let the tears overflow some more and ran up the stairs, sobbing.

It wasn't all faked, either.

When Wayne's car drew up, she waited for the call from her mother to come downstairs, but it didn't happen. He entered the house then there was silence, which probably meant they were talking about her in hushed voices.

Ten minutes later, her mother called up in that bright, artificial tone Lily hated, 'Darling, why don't you come down and join us for lunch?'

It was an order more than a request, so she wiped her eyes and went downstairs, keeping sad thoughts in her mind.

She fiddled with her salad, while Wayne brewed himself some fancy coffee. That man was certainly into caffeine.

'We'll get you a pizza tonight to cheer you up,' her mother said. 'Special treat.'

'Really?'

'I said so, didn't I?'

'Thanks. I'd like double cheese with all the trimmings.' She saw Wayne grimace and shake his head disapprovingly. Well, let him! He could crunch something healthy with those big white teeth of his, but when you were feeling sad, unhealthy food was what hit the spot.

The pizza was delicious and she was relieved that it was a small size so that she could eat the lot and leave no 'evidence'.

She waited until twenty past midnight to rush noisily along to the bathroom and pretend to throw up. Her mother called out from outside, wanting to be let in.

'I'm all right.'

'You're not. You've just been sick.'

'Well, I'm not doing a public performance, thank you very much.' She stuck her fingers down her throat until she retched and pretended to be vomiting again, flushing the toilet to hide the fact that she wasn't.

When she came out, her mother was waiting for her. 'How are you?'

She shrugged. 'Better, I guess. I got rid of it, anyway. I feel a bit shivery, though.'

'I'll get you a hot water bottle.' Kerry went downstairs, forgetting to switch off the alarm system and a siren shrilled out.

With a curse, Wayne rushed out of their bedroom and ran down to fix it, but he had to ring the people who monitored the security and prove who he was.

Lily sat up in bed, hugging her knees and grinning. This was better than she'd hoped.

Hearing footsteps coming up, she slid down under the covers, letting one hand lie across her face.

Her mother passed her the hot water bottle and felt her forehead. 'Do you want me to stay with you?'

'No, thanks. I'm old enough to manage on my own.'

'You'll call if you need anything? I'll leave our bedroom door open and you must do the same.'

'All right. And Mum . . .'

'Yes?'

'Thanks.'

Lily took great pleasure in waiting until they were asleep, with Wayne's gentle bubbling snores wafting along the landing. Then, taking a deep breath, she pounded along to the bathroom and did a repeat performance, making sure it was shorter this time.

After assuring her mother she was all right, she went back to bed and enjoyed a sound sleep, not waking until nearly nine o'clock. A glance through the landing window showed that Wayne's car was gone, so she went downstairs.

Her mother was in the kitchen. 'Want something to eat?'

Lily was ravenous but shook her head. 'No. Just a cup of tea.'

'Perhaps a piece of dry toast?'

'No, thanks. Honest. I'm still feeling a bit queasy, if you must know.'

As she sipped the tea, she asked, 'Where's Wayne? I thought you were going out this morning and he was staying on guard duty.'

'He had an urgent business call and had to go into the office.'

'Oh.' Lily drank the tea and went to get dressed, choosing practical clothes suitable for climbing out of bathroom windows. Now that the time had come to act, she felt nervous. And hungry.

When she came down, she sat slumped in a chair, rubbing her belly. 'I've got a pain.'

'That time of month?' Kerry looked at the calendar. 'No, of course it isn't.'

'I think I've got an upset stomach. Do you suppose the demon pizza is going to hit me at both ends?' She let out a small grunt and clutched herself again.

'Could be.'

'I think I'll go up and—um—stay near the bathroom.'

Lily went up and pulled the sheet off the bed, stuffed her purse into her pocket then locked herself in the bathroom. Taking the old scissors out of the cistern, she tried to cut the sheet. They were rather blunt, but she managed to get a start with them on cutting the hemmed edges. She flushed the toilet and ripped the sheet quickly into strips under the cover of the cistern refilling, then began knotting them together as quickly as she could.

Her mother's voice outside the door made her jump in shock.

'Are you all right, Lily?'

'Yes. Just an upset tum. Not too bad, but I think I'll stay in here for a bit.'

'Call out if you need me.'

When her mother had gone downstairs, Lily opened the window then tied the makeshift rope round the bath taps and let it unroll down the wall outside. It wasn't as long as she'd expected, but she could jump the last bit. She'd jumped off higher walls than that.

Flushing the toilet again, she began to wriggle out of the window. This was the most dangerous part of the escape. She had to cling to the window frame and the makeshift rope as she eased her body out.

She had been worrying that one of the neighbours would see her and come round to tell her mother, but soon forgot that because it was all much scarier than she'd expected and the drop seemed huge from where she was crouching.

She lowered herself over the edge, hanging on to the makeshift rope for grim life. The wind was blowing hard now, and when she tried to get a purchase on the sheet, her feet kept slipping. It was far harder to keep a foothold on a flat piece of sheet than it had been on the ropes in the gym at school—and she'd never been good at climbing those.

Taking a deep breath she began moving down again, but it hurt her arms. To her horror the rope jerked suddenly and dropped her a few inches, jerking her feet loose. When she looked up she saw that the first knot had slipped. Even as she looked, it slipped again.

It began to rain, a sudden, slashing downpour that beat against her head without mercy while thunder rumbled in the distance. Her hands were cold and wet. Rain was trickling down her neck and the wind was banging her body against the brick wall.

Then, without any warning, the knot gave way and she let out an involuntary yell as she fell.

*   *   *

On the Friday morning Cal realized he'd been neglecting Judith and tried to ring her, but got only her answering service. So he sat down and wrote her a long email, explaining why he couldn't come up to see her this weekend, assuring her that he really wanted to keep seeing her, and telling her about the trouble he was having with Kerry, how he couldn't even speak to Lily now.

He didn't know why he was staying here in London this weekend, but felt that he had to be as close to Lily as he could, in case . . . in case what? No way was Kerry going to let him see his daughter. And yet some instinct still told him to stay.

When he'd sent off the email, he didn't know what to do with himself. He fiddled about for a while with the design for a new web site he'd been contracted to set up, but could get no inspiration.

262

When your heart was sore and you were worried sick about your child, it was impossible to be creative. Well, it was for him.

In the end, he decided to clean the whole house from top to bottom, something he'd been neglecting lately. If Lily had been here they'd have done it together and it would have been fun. On his own it was merely a grim determination to do something to fill the long, slow hours.

Outside it began to rain, a real downpour. Thunder rumbled as he peered out of the window. He needed to buy some groceries, but he'd wait until later.

He kept looking at the phone, expecting it to ring.

'You're losing it, Richmond!' he muttered and since the house was as immaculate as it ever got, he went to play solitaire on the computer.

*   *   *

Lily hit the concrete path hard and pain shot through her right ankle. She knew she'd yelled out as she fell and was terrified her mother would rush out of the back door. But nothing happened, so she figured the thunder had muffled her cry. She tried to stand up and yelped as she put her weight on her bad foot. Gingerly she tested it and decided it wasn't broken, just sprained. But it hurt to walk, it hurt so much!

She didn't know how she managed it but she hobbled across to the fence and got herself over into Mrs Baxter's garden, crouching there for a moment, shivering and whimpering with pain. At least now she was out of sight. But how was she to get to a phone and call her father?

Her mother might come out at any moment, so she didn't dare wait. She began hopping grimly across the neighbour's garden, hoping to hide in the thick bushes behind the greenhouse. Through the foliage she watched as her mother peered out of the bathroom window, looking from one side to the other, searching all the gardens for a sign of her. She waited till her mother had pulled her head back inside, then stood up. She had to get to a phone, however much it hurt to walk on the ankle. If she didn't escape, she'd not see her father again for years.

As she turned round, she nearly bumped into Mrs Baxter and flinched. 'Don't let them find me. *Please!* Don't let them find me.' She couldn't help it. She began to cry.

*   *   *

Maeve had taken to having breakfast in bed every day, but got up mid-morning and pottered about the house. She refused obstinately to lie in bed all day doing nothing. Other people might call it 'resting' but she called it being bored. Today she read for an hour or so, finishing a book with a nod of approval. Then she took a fancy to sort out her photograph collection, to make sure the next generation would know who everyone was.

'I've got all the family photos from the mid-nineteenth century onwards,' she told Andy as he helped her get it out. 'Des was furious when they were left specifically to me, but my father didn't want to break up the collection.'

'It wouldn't matter nowadays. You can scan

264

them in and make copies.'

'Perhaps that's what I should do, send copies to Des and Leo.'

'Or I can do it for you.'

'No, show me how to do it. I've avoided computers for too long.'

'You can use mine.'

'Why should I? Go out and buy me one of my own, the best you can find, then teach me to use it.'

'I can buy one online and have it delivered by this afternoon. I know a place that'll do it for me.'

She beamed at him. 'Good. I'll have my first lesson as soon as you've set it up. I'm fed up of playing the invalid.'

'I'll get on to it right away.'

She turned and staggered as the room spun round her. He caught her just in time.

'Just a bit of dizziness.' But she let him help her across to the sofa and left the photograph collection for the time being.

When he'd gone, she leaned her head back and cursed the weakness that was slowing her down so much. If you had to die at such a ridiculously young age, then at least you should be able to make the most of what time you had left, not spend it sleeping or damned well resting.

Anger at the unfairness of it all welled up and burned through her, until she felt aglow with it. She didn't try to stop it. She had a right to be angry and by hell, she would exercise that right.

*   *   *

Saturday morning was fun. Mitch was so eager to get out and start exploring, in spite of the chancy

265

weather, that they grabbed a quick, early breakfast and left everything in chaos.

'I want to see an old cotton mill working,' he said. 'I've been checking online and there are several that you can visit.'

'When I was young, there were still mills with steam engines working for real,' she said, 'though some were on shortened working weeks. But by the time I'd grown up, most of them had shut down. It's very sad, because cotton is what made Lancashire great in the nineteenth century.'

'The only certainty in life is that things will change.' His voice was solemn, as if he was the first to enunciate that. She'd noticed several times her son's barely concealed scorn of the previous generation, but hadn't commented, because that was natural to people his age. She realized he was making further pronouncements and forced her attention back.

'Things change in modern businesses as well. I don't think Dad plans for that like he should. I shall when I take over.'

'You're going to take over, are you?'

'One day. He's not as young as most fathers, so I have to be prepared. I can't afford to muck about.'

So that was what was driving him. He was very like his father in some ways, single-minded about what he wanted. But he was too young to be so solemn, so she ruffled his hair, enjoying his annoyance and the mock scuffle that followed, even though he won and ruffled her hair in retaliation.

'Pax!' she called, weak with laughter. 'Come on, Mitch. Let's go. I want to show you so much and we don't have much time.'

266

'But we'll have other weekends, won't we?'

'As many as you like.'

Only when they were well on the way did she remember her emails. Well, too bad. If Cal had sent something that needed a reply, he'd have to wait, as she'd been waiting for the past few days. *If he'd written . . .*

Twenty

Thunder booms along city streets like bass drums, rain plays timpani with the window panes, water makes tinny music in the drainpipes then joins the choruses in the gutters.

The back door of the next house crashed open again and Kerry yelled. 'Lily! Come back this m—!' Thunder cut off her last word. 'Stop—messing—around—Lily! You know you can't get away.'

Hair plastered flat against her skull, water running down her face, the girl looked pleadingly at Mrs Baxter, who hesitated then gestured to the bushes. Unable to believe her luck, Lily limped across and hid again.

It didn't matter that it was raining and cold water was running down her face, because hope flooded through the girl as she crouched behind the bushes. She could hardly believe that Mrs Baxter, of all people, would be hiding her, especially when she remembered all the times their neighbour had complained about the noise of her sound system or the thump of her netball against a wall. That made her feel guilty now.

'Come into the house once your mother has gone inside again,' Mrs Baxter said quietly, then opened the door of the shed, picked up a bundle and banged the door shut loudly.

Kerry ran out into the rain to peer over the fence. 'Lily?'

'No, only me.'

Her mother's voice sounded shriller than usual.

'Mrs Baxter, have you seen Lily? She's run away again.'

'Why should she do that?'

'Oh, she's just being silly, doesn't want to go and live in America. You know how girls of that age get these fancies. She'll settle down once we're living there.'

'Are you going permanently?'

'Yes. But please don't tell anyone. We're having a lot of trouble with my ex about it.'

'I see. Well, good luck with your hunt. Dear me, I'm getting soaked standing here.' She hurried into the house.

Lily watched her mother stare across the garden. Could she see her through the bushes? Her mother went back to the house, but Lily didn't move until she heard the back door slam shut. Then, crouching low, she limped across the garden as quickly as she could, terrified that her mother hadn't really gone into the house and would look over the fence and see her. She slipped inside, shutting the kitchen door behind her and leaning against it, shivering violently, dripping water everywhere, unable to move for sheer relief.

'Come closer to the Aga, dear. You need to get out of those clothes and have a warm drink before we talk,' Mrs Baxter said in her thin, old woman's voice.

It was such a comforting, everyday sound after the loud voices that seemed to have filled Lily's days recently. She tried to say something and couldn't, tried to smile but her face felt stiff with cold so she moved closer to the big stove, still shivering.

'Stay where you are and I'll fetch you a dressing

gown.' Mrs Baxter was back two minutes later with a man's dressing gown, stroking it absent-mindedly as she said, 'This was my husband's. Nothing like wool for keeping you warm. Now, go into the utility room and get those wet clothes off, all of them. Put them in the washing machine and I'll spin them, then tumble them dry.'

Moving slowly, still unable to believe she had escaped, Lily did as she was told. She returned to the kitchen, naked now under the woollen gown, unable to stop her teeth chattering.

'I've made you a cup of hot chocolate.'

She sat down on one of the high stools, cradling it in her hands then sipping it gratefully. The chocolate drink seemed an omen that she would get to her dad. Warmth ran through her and she found she could speak again. 'Thank you.'

'I'll deal with your clothes then we'll have that talk.'

Mrs Baxter vanished and there was the whine of a washing machine spinning from the small utility room off the kitchen. She came back to ask, 'Are you hungry?'

'Ravenous. I haven't eaten since last night.'

'Aren't they feeding you?'

'I was pretending to have an upset stomach so I could climb out of the bathroom window this morning.'

'I saw you. Of all the dangerous things to do! My heart was in my mouth. Did you hurt yourself when you fell?'

'Yes, but it's only a sprained ankle. I can manage.'

'Food first, then I'll strap the ankle up for you. You should have tied reef knots, you know, but

270

they don't teach children such things nowadays.' There was a clunk and a chiming sound. 'Just a minute.' She disappeared into the utility room again and transferred the damp clothes into a tumble dryer. When she came back she made a huge beef and salad sandwich for Lily, who fell on it, murmuring in delight as she wolfed it down. A piece of home-made fruit cake followed it.

Not until her unexpected guest had finished eating did Mrs Baxter fix her with a determined glance and say, 'Tell me everything, dear, then we'll decide what to do. I don't like deceiving your mother, but I've seen with my own eyes how she's been treating you lately.'

When Lily had finished her tale she crossed her fingers for luck and looked at the old woman. Everything depended on her now.

'I'll need to confirm with your father that he wants you.'

'He does, I know he does!' Relief shuddered through Lily so violently that she started crying, couldn't help herself.

When Mrs Baxter put her arms around her, she leaned against their neighbour and sobbed loudly. It went on for a long time and in the end, Mrs Baxter had to hold her at arm's length and give her a little shake. 'Stop it now! You have to stop if we're to get you away. Let's have a look at that ankle of yours.'

Lily gulped and hiccupped, eventually managing to calm down.

'I don't know what they do to children these days,' the kind old lady muttered. '*You* need someone to love you, that's for sure, and I've seen your father's face when he's called for you. *He*

271

cares about you. That new fellow of your mother's has a nasty face. I never did trust men with heavy eyebrows.'

'I have the best father in the world, even if I'm not really his.'

'Of course you're his. He's made you his own. Not his, indeed! Whoever said that was wrong. You're his daughter and don't let anyone tell you differently. Now, give me his phone number. That American fellow went out a few minutes ago and he might be bringing in the police, for all we know. I couldn't go against them.'

Which sent worry shivering through Lily again.

*   *   *

The phone only rang once before Cal snatched it up. 'Yes?'

'Mr Richmond?'

'Yes.'

'I'm Lily's neighbour, Nancy Baxter. I have your daughter here with me. She's run away from her mother. Do you want me to bring her to you?'

'Of course I do. Is she all right?'

'More or less. She hurt her ankle climbing out of the bathroom window.'

'Hurt? Do we need to get her to hospital?'

'No, I've strapped it up. I've done first aid and I can tell a sprain from a break. I don't like to interfere between parents and children, but it worries me that they're taking her to America on Sunday.'

'They're doing *what?*'

'You didn't know about that?'

'No. I'm applying for an injunction to stop them

taking her out of the country, but I couldn't get it to court until Monday.'

'I see. Well, I think I'd better bring Lily to you. They'd recognize your car if you drove up to my house. She's a very unhappy girl and she needs you. Have a quick word with her.' She passed the phone to Lily.

'Dad? Oh, Dad!'

'Darling, hang in there. I'll get you away from them.'

'You do want me?'

'Did you even need to ask?'

'No. Not really. But Mum kept saying you'd change now you know you're not my biological father.'

'I'll never change, Lily. I love you. Put Mrs Baxter on again, will you?'

Cal could feel tears filling his eyes and he smeared them away with his forearm, saying in a thickened voice, 'Mrs Baxter, I can't thank you enough for helping us.' He heard a noise and looked out of the window. 'Wait a minute, please! Don't hang up! Wayne's just arrived at my house. Damn! Kerry must have phoned him. Still, I suppose this would be the first place they'd look.'

'They're very determined to get her back, aren't they?'

Cal thought rapidly. 'Look, can you bring her to meet me somewhere? I'll come on the motor bike. It'll be easier to avoid them on that.' He didn't usually drive fast, but he'd push the Hog to the limit to get Lily away. What had Kerry and Wayne been doing to upset her so? She never cried normally.

When he put the phone down, he stood for a

273

moment, getting his order of action worked out in his mind, then he went and crammed some clothes into a bag, including some of the things Lily kept here.

The doorbell rang three times while he was doing that, but he ignored it, working as quickly as he could. When he went out of the back door he slid the bike off its stand and rolled it, not without difficulty, to the end of the back garden. Just as he was pushing it through the little-used back gate, he heard a voice yell, 'Hey? Richmond! I need to speak to you.'

He turned to see Wayne climb over the side gate and run down the garden. There was no way he could get his bike started before the man reached him, so he stopped and forced a smile to his face. 'That's an unusual way to come in!'

'I rang the doorbell several times. Didn't you hear me?'

'No, sorry. Been working on the bike in the garage. The extension bell mustn't be working.' He glanced at his watch. 'Look, I'm just going to see someone about a new contract, so if you can make this fast . . .'

'It's about Lily.'

'Is she all right?'

'She was when I last saw her.'

Cal improvised rapidly. 'Look, this is a rather special contract I'm signing for. It'll bring in half my income for the coming year and I'm running late as it is. If it's really important I can come round to Kerry's in about an hour and a half. You know I've been trying to see Lily. We can talk then.'

'You haven't seen her today?'

'That's a strange thing to ask.' He looked at Wayne. 'Has she run away again?'

'Yes. But we'll soon find her.'

'She probably just wants some time to herself. All children do.' Cal swung his leg across the bike and switched on the motor, keeping his expression calm. 'I really do have to go. See you in about an hour and a half. We'll work out what to do about Lily then.' He paddled his way out then lifted his feet off the ground and drove carefully down the rutted back lane. When he turned on to the street at the end, he thought he'd got away with it, then he saw Wayne's big four-wheel drive turn the corner and accelerate after him. He smiled grimly. He'd back his Hog against a car any day, but he didn't need to speed to get away this time.

He drove to a street he knew to be a cul-de-sac. When he got to the turning circle at the end, he slowed down so that he could get his bike between the bollards that blocked off access to cars and then drive off along a pedestrian walkway. For once he didn't care if the bike got scratched. There was nothing as important as getting to Lily, nothing!

A quick glance behind showed Wayne standing beside his vehicle looking angry and pulling out a mobile phone.

Cal prayed that Mrs Baxter had got Lily away. He knew where he could take his daughter. Well, he hoped he did.

Then he'd come back and face the court on Monday.

He'd tried very hard to keep things amicable between himself and his ex, but now it was time to fight for his daughter. It took a lot to make him this angry, but Kerry had pushed him into his anger zone now.

He frowned as he threaded his way carefully through the busy streets. What he couldn't understand was why Kerry was insisting on taking Lily with her. It wasn't as if she was devoted to the child, though he guessed she loved her in a cool, Kerry kind of way. But she'd often let Cal have Lily for weeks on end when she was in the throes of an affair, as he could prove to the court.

And now that their daughter was twelve—he smiled involuntarily as he mentally amended that to twelve going on ninety—Lily was legally old enough to know her own mind and speak out for herself.

There had to be something else involved here. Kerry never did anything without a reason and her most common motive was money. Well, he was going to find out what was going on, and if it was humanly possible, he was going to get custody of his daughter.

*   *   *

The front doorbell rang just as Mrs Baxter and Lily were about to go out to the car.

'Who's that.' The old lady went and peeped through the dining room window. 'It's your mother and she looks furious.'

'Oh, no! What are we going to do? You won't let her take me back, will you?'

A grin transformed Mrs Baxter's face briefly into that of a much younger woman. 'Definitely not. Do you think you could ride in the car boot for a few streets?'

'Yes. Anything.'

'Good. Go and get into the boot now. I'll answer the door, fob your mother off then drive away. She'll be able to see that you're not in the car with me.' She waited till Lily had gone round to the back door of the garage, then answered the front door. 'Hello.'

Kerry went straight into the attack. 'I think you've got Lily here.'

Mrs Baxter stared at her. 'I did have. She left about half an hour ago.'

'You're admitting it?'

'Yes. I was delighted to help her. I've never seen such an unhappy child—and I don't like the way you and that American have been beating her.'

'We have *not* been beating her.'

'I've seen you do it.'

'That was just the once. You have no idea how infuriating girls of that age can be.' Kerry scowled at her. 'And she *can't* have got away this quickly. We'd have seen her.'

'She went over the back wall behind the bushes and ran off down the walkway. Easy to do. There was a bus due, from what she said. Now, if there's nothing else, I have to go out shopping.'

'I don't believe you.'

'That's up to you. *I* am not dependent on your goodwill, thank goodness.' She tried to close the door and looked down to see what was stopping her. 'Kindly remove your foot from my door.'

Kerry stepped back reluctantly. 'I don't know how Lily got round you, but you haven't heard the last of this.'

Mrs Baxter shut the door in her unwelcome visitor's face and went out to her car. When she drove out of the garage, Kerry was standing in the middle of the drive, arms folded, still looking angry. On a sudden impulse Mrs Baxter clicked the switch to lock all the car doors.

When she got to the gate, she had to stop because Kerry was blocking her way.

The younger woman came round to the side and tried the door, then hammered on the driver's window. 'I want to check the car. Open this door.'

'You can see she's not here,' Mrs Baxter shouted and accelerated off down the street. Her heart was thumping and she was sure that poor child would be black and blue from bouncing about in the boot, but she wasn't handing Lily over to a woman as angry as that.

She went first to the house of a friend she knew to be away and there, screened by the hedge, she got Lily out of the boot and into the back seat. 'You all right?'

'Yes. I heard Mum shouting.'

'She suspects something but she can't say she's seen you in my car. You'd better crouch down till we get out of the area.'

It was all very exciting, like a suspense film, Mrs Baxter thought as she drove off again. Who'd ever have thought she'd get involved in something like this? She'd been a bit of a devil when she was younger, she remembered suddenly. Where did it all go, that feistiness? 'You all right back there?' she called.

'I'm fine, Mrs Baxter.'

But even with her ageing eyesight, she could see in the rear-view mirror that Lily's cheeks were wet again. 'You'll be all right,' she said gently. 'We'll soon be meeting your father.'

278

It took nearly an hour to get to the rendezvous and until they got on to the motorway, Lily refused to get up off the floor. When they pulled into the services on the M40, Mrs Baxter looked for the motorbike.

'It's over there to the right,' Lily said. Her voice went up an octave. 'He's there! He's really there!'

'Remember what I said. Don't get out of the car and make a scene. Someone will be bound to remember it.' She pulled in right next to the big shiny bike. 'Let him come to us and you stay in the car till you've got that helmet on.'

'Who'd have thought you'd make such a good conspirator,' Lily gave her a watery smile.

'An old woman like me,' Mrs Baxter teased, then smiled at her. 'Chin up. You don't want to upset him, do you?'

Cal brought a second helmet and leather jacket across and crouched beside the car to give Lily a quick hug. 'You all right, darling?'

'I am now.'

'Put this on before you get out. That red hair of yours is a bit of a give-away. I'm glad it's stopped raining or it'd have been a miserable journey.' He turned to Mrs Baxter. 'I can't thank you enough for helping Lily.'

'They've been beating her. I never could stand people who thump children.'

He gaped at her. 'That's not like Kerry!'

'I saw it with my own eyes—more than once. Don't let them take her back.' She shook his hand and reached into her handbag for a piece of paper. 'This is my phone number. I'd appreciate it if you'd let me know that you're all right. You do have somewhere to go?'

'I think so. If not, I'll find somewhere else. Believe me, I won't let them hurt Lily again.'

'Dear me, the weekend is going to seem very tame now.' But she was talking to herself.

As the deep growl of the engine pulsed away into the distance, Mrs Baxter locked her car and went towards the café area. 'A cup of strong coffee *and* a cake, I think. I've certainly earned them.' She smiled, pleased with herself.

*   *   *

Mitch insisted on taking a quick walk up on the tops before they set off, going on his own because Judith's knee still ached if she challenged it too much. He came back half an hour later with glowing cheeks.

'That was great! I haven't been out in the countryside since you left home. Dad is such an urban animal and Gran's not into walking.'

'Glad you enjoyed it. Now, if you'll tidy yourself up quickly, we'll set off.' Judith loved her son's enthusiasm for anything and everything, and it occurred to her, not for the first time, that he was completely uninhibited in her company, which he never was with his father.

They arrived at Saltern House in the late morning and as they drove through the big gateway, Mitch turned his head from side to side, trying to see everything at once. When the house came in full sight, framed by large old trees and flowerbeds overflowing with colour, he whistled. 'It's *beautiful*. I like traditional houses much more than Dad's place.'

'Me too. Now remember, no staring at her.'

He groaned. 'Mum, you've already said that a million times.'

'Because it's important.'

The door opened and Andy came out to greet them. He kissed Judith's cheek, shook hands with Mitch and made no secret of the fact that he was studying the boy with great interest.

'I see that red hair prevails in this generation, too. Your cousin Kate from Australia arrived yesterday and the resemblance is amazing. You could be brother and sister.'

'I didn't know I even had a cousin Kate. Dad never talked about his brother.'

'You'll meet her later. Now, come in, do. Maeve is waiting impatiently to see you.'

As they walked into the sitting room, he held Judith back and let Mitch go first.

Maeve was sitting near the window, very upright but looking frail. Her hair was starting to grow back now, but it was more like silver down at the moment. She stared at Mitch not trying to hide her surprise. 'You look just like your father when he was that age!' She indicated her own hair with a smile. 'I used to have red hair as well. You'll probably go grey quite young, redheads often do, so make the most of it while you can.' She patted the window seat beside her. 'Come and talk to me. Judith, will you lend me Mitch for an hour?'

'Of course.' She walked out with Andy.

He smiled at her. 'Come and meet Kate.'

In the sitting room Maeve leaned back and studied Mitch. 'You're the second of your generation to come and visit me this week. Makes me wish I'd had children.'

'Why didn't you?'

'Couldn't. And I didn't want to adopt.'

'Dad's more than made up for your lack. Did you know his girlfriend is expecting? And he's nearly sixty!'

'No, I didn't know. Goodness, that's another to add to my list. Did *you* know he has an illegitimate daughter called Lily?'

'I knew about her vaguely, not what she was called, though. How old is she?'

'Twelve. I don't know much more about her, but I shall.' She led him on to talk about himself and his hopes, nodding encouragement and asking an occasional question.

He found it easy to talk to her, enjoying her astute answers and comments, the way she treated him as an adult. 'You've more sense about business than Dad, Aunt Maeve. Is it all right to call you that? Good. Dad goes off at tangents for no reason and he likes to throw his money around. If he hadn't been so lucky early on, he'd not have made it in business nowadays. And he leaves too much to Raymond Tate. I don't like that man.'

When Lena popped her head round the door to remind Maeve that it was time for a rest, they were both disappointed.

'I'm sorry to say she's right,' Maeve admitted. 'I'll see you before you go, Mitch—and you'll come another time, I hope.'

'I hope so too.'

He was quiet as they walked out into the hall and before she went upstairs, he suddenly gave her a hug. 'I wish I'd known you years ago, Aunt Maeve.'

She smiled at him, but her eyes were bright with unshed tears. 'So do I. Don't ever start a family feud. It isn't worth it.'

'You don't have to keep it going, if you don't want to.'

She looked at him and murmured, 'Out of the mouths . . .' Then she walked slowly up the stairs.

*　　　*　　　*

Mitch followed the sound of voices and found his mother with Andy and someone who had to be his cousin in the conservatory. 'Is that tea—and are those scones going begging?'

'It'd be more polite to say hello to your cousin Kate first,' Judith chided him.

He grinned at the young woman sitting near a palm tree. 'I didn't mean to sound rude, but I'm absolutely famished. Hello, cousin Kate.' He went over to shake her hand. 'I see you've got the family hair.'

'Have any others of our generation got it? My brother hasn't.'

'My half-sisters haven't, either. They've got brown hair. Apparently my other half-sister has red hair, though I've never met her. She's called Lily.'

'I don't think *she* knows she's a Corrigan,' Judith said. 'She's been brought up thinking another man was her father. And Des never tried to see her.'

Mitch looked at his mother in surprise. 'Do you know her?'

'I've never met her, but I know her father—the one who brought her up.'

He noticed that she flushed as she spoke, and wondered why. Then Kate said something and he turned to answer her with a smile and ask his own

283

questions. 'What's Australia like? It's high on my list of places to visit.'

They held an animated conversation, during which time he finished all the scones.

'You'll not have any appetite for lunch,' Judith scolded.

'Watch me.'

Kate leaned her head back with a sigh. 'I'm sorry, but I fade pretty quickly still.' She saw Mitch looking puzzled and explained, 'I've got ME. Maeve sent me to a specialist and even after the first visit, I'm feeling better, but I've a long way to go still.'

'That's rotten luck. A friend of mine had it.'

'Why don't we leave you in peace for a few minutes and walk round the gardens?' Judith suggested. 'I've never seen such beautiful displays of flowers.'

'There's a Japanese garden round the side. It's a lovely place to sit and think.'

'I'll show you where it is,' Andy offered.

They met Kate again for lunch and it was a lively meal. After that both Kate and Mitch went to sit with Maeve. From the laughter echoing in that room, they were all enjoying themselves.

'It'll tire Maeve, but it'll do her good, too,' Andy said. 'Pity Mitch can't come and stay for a while. That'd really cheer her up. She always did get on well with our younger workers.'

'Des would throw a fit if he knew we'd been here today.'

'It's about time he and Maeve buried the hatchet, Kate's father as well. Life's too short for feuding.'

Twenty-One

Greater Manchester: busy roads thread like ribbons through a posy of small towns, with only the signposts to show where one ends and the next begins.

On the way home, Mitch was very quiet.

'Are you all right?' Judith asked.

'Yes. I was just thinking about Aunt Maeve. It's rotten that she's so ill. I really like her and now I'll not have time to get to know her properly before she dies. She was telling us about her childhood—and Dad's. *He* won't ever talk about that sort of thing.'

'She probably still has a few months left. You can come up and visit her any time you want. I'll always drive you over.'

'We both know what Dad'll say to that, the fuss he'll make.' He didn't say 'the threats' but they both knew Des would use any means he could to get his own way.

'We'll do it somehow,' she said softly as they drove through the village. 'I haven't enjoyed a day out so much for a very long time.'

'Me neither. And Kate seems OK, though she's a bit quiet. She's very thin and pale, isn't she?'

'She's been ill for several months.'

As they were pulling into the drive of her house Judith braked suddenly. 'Cal's here!'

'Wow, look at that!' Mitch was staring at the big motor cycle, but at her words he turned to stare at her instead. 'Who's Cal?'

'A friend. I—um—hadn't expected to see him

285

this weekend. And don't look at me like that!'

'Like what?'

'All knowing.'

'Mum, if you've found yourself a guy, that's cool as far as I'm concerned.'

'I haven't. I mean, I'm not sure. It's early days yet.' Even as she was speaking Cal walked out of the rear quarters he'd used when her aunt was alive and started towards them. 'You go inside and let me speak to him in private first.'

Mitch grabbed her forearm and held her back for a second or two. 'Don't send him away because of me. It's about time you found someone to love. It's been over between you and Dad for a while, even I could tell that.'

She patted his hand, but in spite of his encouragement, she felt flustered as she got out of the car. She introduced her son to her lover and watched them assess each other for a few seconds before Mitch turned away. After waiting till the kitchen door had closed behind him, she turned to look questioningly at Cal.

'I didn't know you had your son with you. The thing is . . . I've got Lily with me. She's run away from her mother and we had to leave in a hurry. I didn't know where else to take her to keep her safe.'

'Keep her *safe*?' She stared at him. 'What do you mean?'

'They were going to take her forcibly out of the country and when she refused to go, that sod my wife is shacked up with said he'd tranquillize her. He's got a private jet and as far as I can tell, no morals at all.'

Judith stared at him open-mouthed. 'You're

286

certain she hasn't made this up?'

'I'd stake my life on it.' He looked over his shoulder as if checking that his daughter wasn't within earshot. 'She's very upset. They've been thumping her, keeping her a prisoner, bullying her.' There was a catch in his voice as he added, 'She's normally so lively and cheeky.'

'Oh, Cal!'

'I know I'm presuming on our friendship, only they'd never find her here . . . But if that's too much to ask, at least let us stay for tonight in the shed and we'll leave first thing in the morning.'

She hated to think of a child being treated like that. 'Don't be silly. I'm happy to have you both stay, but there's just one thing: Maeve has told Mitch about his half-sister Lily. Does *she* know who her real father is?'

Cal stared at her aghast. 'No.'

'Well, what do you want to do? If you're staying, you'll have to tell her about Des before you bring her in. And I'll have to tell Mitch she's *the* Lily. It's a good thing Des has stopped having me watched or who knows what he'd have done about the situation.'

Cal ran one hand through his hair. 'Hell, this is even more complicated than I'd expected.' Then he looked at Judith, his eyes softening. 'I'm sorry for neglecting you this week. It's been—bad. I did try to phone you yesterday, but all I got was an answering service, so I emailed you instead. Did you get my message?'

'I haven't had time to read my emails. Mitch and I only got back from London yesterday evening and we've been out all day today.'

'Then in that case, perhaps I'd better remind

287

you of one important thing.'

She didn't protest when he pulled her to him and gave her a long, lingering kiss which warmed her to the core. She held him for a minute, searching his face and feeling as if she'd found some sort of answer to her unspoken question in the warmth of his gaze. But when he pulled away, she let him go, because this wasn't the time for them, they both had children to look after. 'I reckon if we can get through crises like this together, we can get through anything.'

His gaze remained steady, the smile didn't fade. 'That's a good thought.' He caressed her cheek briefly with the knuckles of his right hand then took a step backwards. 'I'll go and tell Lily, then bring her in from the shed.'

She walked slowly inside to Mitch, hoping he'd understand.

*   *   *

Des spent Friday afternoon with Raymond Tate and his accountant, John Welby, trying to find ways to slash his personal and business expenditure dramatically to get them over the cashflow problems they'd face during the next year or two.

'Every detail mounts up,' John said severely. 'I know you don't usually worry about details, Des, but until this gets sorted out, you'll have to, unless you want to go under. One of the details you can adjust almost immediately is the amount of maintenance you pay Kerry Foster for your daughter. I never did understand why you agreed to pay her so generously—as I've mentioned before.'

'You don't know Kerry. And anyway, I didn't want a child of mine being short of anything.'

'Believe me, she'll never have gone short. If Ms Foster has any sense, she'll probably have a comfortable nest egg saved by now. You have a good case for halving the amount, I'd say—if she takes you to court about it, which I doubt she will.'

Des sighed. He knew exactly what Kerry would say to any reduction. 'I'll give her a ring, discuss it.'

'And you've no need to keep a full-time chauffeur and housekeeper, or run three cars. In fact, I'd advise you to close down that huge house of yours and sell it. It'd bring in three or four million, I should think.'

'It won't look good to sell. People will guess something is wrong.'

Raymond intervened. 'I doubt it, Des. Your marriage has just broken up, so no one will think twice about you wanting to buy a flat instead.'

'I'm getting married again as soon as I can, so I'll need another house, not a flat.'

John looked at him, screwing his mouth up in disapproval. 'Is that wise?'

Des shrugged. 'Tiff's pregnant.'

Raymond grinned. 'Congratulations. You've hit the jackpot again, you old ram.'

Des ignored him. 'Tiff won't want to live in my present house—well, I'm fed up with it myself—so maybe I can sell it and downsize a bit.'

'With a cashflow problem like yours,' John reiterated, 'every bit helps. *Every single bit.* Even reducing the number of meals out at fancy restaurants. You always did spend up to the hilt. Go somewhere cheaper from now on.'

'What's the point in being rich if you don't

enjoy it?'

'You've certainly done that.'

Des felt depressed as his chauffeur drove him back to Tiff's flat, even more depressed when he found the place empty. He debated going home, but without Judith and Mitch the place seemed to echo round him like a big white aircraft hangar. It'd be no loss to sell it. He suddenly remembered Saltern House. He'd only lived there for a few years with his family, after his dad made some money, but he'd loved it, they all had. The old house had had character *and* cosiness. He sighed. It was the thing Leo had resented most, Maeve getting the house.

When Tiff came home, Des was asleep on the sofa. He looked tired so she put away her shopping before waking him gently. 'Have you eaten?'

'What? Oh, you're back.' He pulled her to him for a kiss. 'Mmm. You smell wonderful. I think I'll move in here permanently.'

She realized he meant it and pushed him to arm's length. 'Not wise, Des. This flat's too small and I'm not set up for looking after you. You're a high maintenance guy and you'll be wanting shirts ironed, meals prepared, stuff like that. I don't do domestic if I can help it.'

He opened his mouth to remind her that he was the one who paid for this place so had a right to expect something back, but decided that would be less than tactful. When Tiff decided on something, that was that. 'You're right. It *is* too small. But I'm selling the other place so we'll have to find somewhere to live after we're married.'

'Des, I'm still not sure it's a good idea for us to get married.'

There was silence and it went on for a long time. He swallowed hard. 'But I *really* want to marry you, Tiff. It's not just because you're pregnant.'

'Why?'

'Because I love you, of course. Because we're good together.' He saw her expression soften and pressed his advantage. 'And there's the baby to think of too.' As he watched her hand go up instinctively to her belly, in that age-old gesture, it suddenly occurred to him that he'd had four children by other women and he'd not been around any of them much, not even Mitch. 'Maybe it's time I got involved more, acted the father. I was too busy when I had the other children. I'd like to slow down a bit and enjoy some family life this time.'

'Well, there's no rush to make a decision. You're still married to Judith. We'll talk about it later, see what we can work out.' She could see he wasn't convinced so tried to explain. 'I'm a bit of a loner, Des. I'm not sure I could give up my freedom.'

'You talk as if you'd be in prison.' He went to pour himself a drink because it was that sort of day. Then, feeling hurt, he sat at the kitchen counter and sipped it as he watched her put together a quick meal. Salad again! Did she ever eat anything that wasn't green? He sighed. Things were getting worse and worse. It had never occurred to him that Tiff was serious about not getting married.

'It's not like you to be so quiet.' She put a plate in front of him and flicked a finger towards his whisky glass. 'And you're drinking too much of the hard stuff.'

'I've a lot on my mind. Business problems.' He

didn't usually tell her the details, but tonight he needed to share his troubles so he explained about the trouble that buying Maeve out had landed him in.

'Which just goes to show it's more than time you ended that silly feud with your sister,' Tiff said when he'd finished. 'This would never have happened if you'd stayed friends with her.'

'*Stayed friends!* When she stole the family business from me and Leo.'

'You didn't need it. You made good all on your own. I admire that more than if you'd inherited your money.'

He was too tired to argue and his head was aching. 'Can I stay here just for a few nights then? I don't want to go back to rattle around that big place on my own.'

She smiled at him. 'Poor Des. I've never seen you look so down. Of course you can stay. Only you're in charge of your own washing and ironing, and you can do some of the shopping and cooking too.'

In spite of having her warm soft body to cuddle, he slept badly that night, lying awake worrying. Was he past it? Growing old? What if he didn't pull the business out of this tight patch? What if he went under, lost everything?

She definitely wouldn't want him then.

He didn't want to lose her as well as everything else.

*　　　*　　　*

After Judith and Mitch had left, Maeve gave in to her body's demands and went up to her room to rest. Kate sat down in the conservatory with the same purpose. She came out of a doze to find Mark sitting opposite her, smiling.

'Shall I pour you something to drink, Sleepyhead?' He gestured to a tray with a carafe of orange juice and some glasses on it. 'You didn't even stir when I brought this in.'

'Please.' She felt shy, wondered how long he'd been watching her, hoped she hadn't drooled or snored.

He picked up a glass and began to fill it. 'So— how are you feeling?'

She yawned and stretched, then accepted the glass, enjoying the juice's tangy, refreshing taste. 'My head isn't nearly as fuzzy. Dr Upson must have been right about the wheat intolerance, though it's going to be a nuisance avoiding the stuff. Lena and I were looking at the food labels and it's in nearly everything, even coating the frozen chips.'

'We'll manage.'

She looked at him doubtfully. *We?* What did he mean by that?

'I came to arrange to pick you up on Monday afternoon to take you back to London for our appointment on Tuesday.'

She was surprised because he could easily have phoned to arrange that. Her doubts must have shown in her face.

'I also wanted to see for myself how you were,' he said quietly. 'And . . . I wondered whether you'd like to do a little more sightseeing tomorrow. We could go into Chester or drive out on to the moors.'

'I'd love that. And the moors would be nice. I like wide-open spaces. England feels a bit closed in

293

after the Australian countryside.' She paused, then had to ask, 'Is entertaining the clients part of your duties? Did Andy ask you to do this?'

He set his glass down and leaned forward. 'No. I want it very clearly understood that if we go out tomorrow, it'll come under personal initiatives. My choice. Is that all right by you?'

For the first time in months a small swirl of attraction curled round her belly. She looked at him and felt shy all over again. 'Yes. It's fine by me.' And it was. She knew somehow that this man wouldn't run away if the going got tough, as Joe had.

'I live nearby, you know. I have a flat in Knutsford. I don't spend as much time there as I'd like, though. And I reckon I'm getting too old for racketing around investigating people.'

'It must be an interesting job.'

'Sometimes it is. At other times, it's just plain boring. What was your job like?'

'The same. Both good and bad. Bad because my contracts were with public sector organisations and people aren't kidding when they talk about the mountains of red tape and paperwork the government makes you wade through. But it was good to be dealing with people. I really liked that and I miss it dreadfully. When I was living at home again, I spent so much time in my bedroom fiddling with my computer that I felt as if I were slowly stifling to death. I'm sorry if it sounds ungrateful, but you've met my father and seen how he expects everyone in the family to jump to his bidding. So I kept out of his way as much as I could.'

'Must have been hard for you.'

'Yes. I never thought something like ME would hit me, because I'd always been fairly healthy and energetic before. When you don't have much money, you're very limited in what you can do, as well as being limited by the fatigue.'

'I feel fairly optimistic that this specialist will help you get your zing back.'

Kate smiled. 'She's made a good start. But even if she does restore me to full health, I don't think I'll ever go back to working so frenetically. I had tunnel vision about my career, you know. I was far too ambitious.'

They sat chatting for over an hour before Mark went home. It had been so pleasant, Kate thought as she waved him goodbye. He was easy to talk to and there had been no awkward pauses, none at all. It was as if they were old friends.

In fact, she marvelled as she thought about how promising her life was now.

*   *   *

As Cal went back towards the shed the door opened and Lily asked anxiously, 'What did she say?'

'She said yes.'

She gave a huge sigh and put her arms round him. 'That's good. I like being with you, Dad. I feel safe.'

He put his arm round her and guided her back into the shed. 'There's something I have to tell you before we go into the house. Let's sit down.'

'A problem?'

The anxious, old-woman look reappeared on her face and he cursed Kerry mentally for putting it there. 'Not exactly.' He paused, not sure how to continue, then took a deep breath and said it bluntly, 'It's about your biological father.'

She grew very still, staring at him wide-eyed.

'I've found out who he is.' Cal paused again, trying to gauge her reaction.

'I don't *care* who he is. He's never bothered to see me, so I don't want to see him.'

'You don't need to see him, but something's cropped up and you need to know about it. It involves Judith. In fact, her ex-husband is your father, but we didn't know until recently. And that means her son . . .' He watched comprehension dawn in her face.

'. . . is my half-brother,' she finished for him. 'I have a *brother*!'

They both knew she'd always regretted being an only child. 'Good news, eh?'

'Oh, yes, Dad! Very good news.'

'Well, here's some more. He's staying here at the moment with his mother.'

She clutched his arm. 'What if he doesn't like me?'

'Then he's a fool.'

'Or I don't like him.'

'If he's anything like his mother, he'll be OK.'

Silence, which he didn't dare interrupt, then she said gruffly, 'Let's get the introductions over with then.'

'All right. But one other thing . . . I hope you like Judith, because *I* like her very much.'

She smiled, a shadow of her old self returning briefly. 'Well, duh! As if I hadn't worked that out already!'

Definitely twelve going on ninety, he thought as

they walked towards the house.

*   *   *

Judith took a deep breath. 'Mitch, there's something I need to tell you before Cal brings his daughter in.'

'What?' He looked at her, his expression sunny and relaxed.

'Cal's daughter is called Lily—and—well, she's *that* Lily, your half-sister.'

'*What?*' There was a moment's silence, then, 'Did he bring her here specially to meet me?'

'No. She's running away from her mother.' Judith explained the situation.

'Poor kid. I'd hate to be taken completely away from you. It must be pretty bad for Cal, too.'

He said it so casually she didn't make a fuss, but his comment made her feel warm inside. 'You'll be nice to Lily?'

He grinned. 'I like my other sisters. Why wouldn't I like this one? It's you who has problems with them.'

She flushed. 'I didn't want to have anything to do with Liz, that's why I didn't encourage you to get together with Lacey and Emma. Liz can be a real bitch when she wants to, and from the way she still behaves towards me, you'd think I was the one who broke up her marriage.' She swung round as she heard footsteps outside.

Cal knocked and came in, his hand resting lightly on his daughter's shoulder. 'Lily, I'd like you to meet Mitch and Judith.'

Mitch gaped at his sister. 'Wow! You look just like my—I mean, *our* cousin Kate!'

Lily looked at his red hair and fingered her own. 'I guess redheads must run in my biological family. But I want it understood from the start that I consider Cal my father.' She looked at them all challengingly.

Mitch shrugged. 'It's fine by me. You're not missing much, anyway. Your biological father isn't exactly a family man. His main interests are business and having affairs with younger women.'

Judith glanced quickly in her son's direction, wondering about the bitter tone. She caught Cal's sympathetic gaze and knew he hadn't missed that, so gave him a quick smile. 'Cup of tea or coffee, anyone? Or a can of lemonade?'

'I'd love a lemonade.' Lily's voice was very polite.

'We're both hungry,' Cal said. 'How about I go into the village and pick up a few supplies?'

Judith took a quick decision. 'I'll come with you. The minimart stays open quite late.'

'We can go on the Hog, if you like.'

She stopped, smiling at him. 'I'd like that. I've never ridden a Harley-Davidson before.'

When they'd gone, Mitch found the biscuit tin and offered it to Lily. 'Weird, isn't it? Us being brother and sister, I mean.'

She took one. 'Very weird. I've only just found out you exist. Do you mind about me?'

He shook his head. 'Nah. I—or rather *we* have two other half-sisters, Lacey and Emma.'

'Two more?' She gaped at him. 'I can't get my head round this. I was just, like, an only child and now I've got *three* brothers and sisters.'

'You might get nieces and nephews soon as well, because Lacey's got married a week ago. You'll

298

like her and Emma.'

She beamed at him. 'This is wicked. Tell me about them.'

'Let's go and sit down.' He led the way into the front room, bringing the tin of biscuits and absent-mindedly eating them as he sketched out a rough family tree for Lily on his mother's phone notepad.

'I'd like to meet your father one day,' she admitted. 'Out of sheer curiosity. But at the moment, Dad and I are in hiding from my mother and her new guy.'

'Tell me about it.'

By the time Judith and Cal got back, the two younger folk were chatting comfortably, Lily sitting cross-legged on the sofa, Mitch sprawled on the floor, the biscuit tin between them, empty.

'I can't believe this,' Judith muttered as she glanced through the doorway and took in the cosy scene in the sitting room. 'What were we worrying about?' She waved a greeting and led the way back into the kitchen to put away the food.

Cal set down the bags he was carrying. 'I'd help you with that, but I don't know yet where things go.'

She smiled. 'I'm not used to a man who's domesticated. Des wasn't, not in the slightest.'

There was the sound of laughter from the sitting room and Cal looked in that direction with a smile. 'Lily usually gets on with people.'

'And Mitch is quite used to sisters.'

Cal's smile was replaced by a frown. 'I'm a bit worried about what Kerry will do next. I'm praying she won't set the police after us.'

'Is that likely?'

He considered this for a moment. 'Not sure.

299

She's changed since she met Wayne. I think he's influencing her in this. Big macho fellow. I'd guess he hates to be bested by a child. He doesn't want to live with Lily. She says he was talking about putting her in a boarding school in the States. He was extremely uncivil to me the few times we met when I was picking Lily up.'

'Sounds a nasty type. I'll put some frozen chips in the oven, then I'd better go and make up the beds before I feed that every-hungry son of mine.'

'Do you mind if I ring Mrs Baxter first, then I'll help you. She'll be worrying about us.'

Later, when she and her dad were alone together, Lily whispered, 'I like your new woman. And it's great having a brother like Mitch. My friends would flip over him.'

Mitch stopped his mother in the kitchen as he got a final drink before bed. 'I like Lily. We must introduce her to Lacey and Emma.' He picked up a plum and took a bite out of it, saying indistinctly, 'It'd be funny if Tiffany had a daughter as well, wouldn't it? I'd have four half-sisters then.'

She ruffled his hair. 'Heaven help them all! Now, isn't it about time you went to bed? We have to get you back to London tomorrow.'

'Do we? I want to get to know Lily a bit better. Surely, a new sister is more important than school? It's not as if I'm behind in my work or anything.'

She hesitated. 'I don't know. I'll think about it.'

But she was thrilled to see how well he and Lily got on.

When Judith went into the sitting room, Cal was standing by the bookcase. He turned, holding out his arms to her and she walked straight into them, feeling very much at home there. Strange how easy it was to love this man.

Love! She blinked and stilled against him, looking up at his face. And then said it without thinking twice. 'I think I'm in love with you, Cal Richmond.'

'Good, because I'm definitely in love with you, Judith Horrocks.'

'So quickly?'

'Yes.' He cocked one eyebrow at her then looked upwards. 'Do we sleep together tonight?'

She hesitated, tempted, but shook her head. 'Mitch won't be asleep for ages, and it doesn't set a good example, does it?'

'I think they're both more liberal about those things than you are.' He grinned. 'Good thing I'm tired or I'd have trouble sleeping.'

She wasn't tired and she had great trouble sleeping. She nearly went along to Cal's room, but the fear of waking up either of the children held her back. They were both old enough to be fully aware of what it would mean. And if they heard anything . . . She shuddered at the thought.

*　　　*　　　*

Kerry looked at Wayne. 'We can't leave for America without Lily.'

'I know how you feel, honey. I've already postponed our flight.' He slapped one hand down on his thigh. 'Damn! I hate being bested by a twelve-year-old girl!'

'Me too. But if she's so determined, perhaps we should consider letting her stay with Cal.'

He gave her one of his icy looks. 'I've *never* backed off from a fight and I don't intend to do so

301

now.'

'But we've looked for her everywhere. She must be with Cal, the way he gave you the slip, only I can't think where he could have taken her.'

'We need to have a brainstorming session. I'll get some paper.'

She smiled as she waited for him. His masterful behaviour might be considered old-fashioned by some, but she enjoyed the way he looked after her and made her life easy. It was good to have someone to turn to again. She hadn't had anyone permanent in her life for a long time and would be glad to be settled. Maybe she was growing older, getting tired of chasing around.

He came back and sat down beside her, putting a cushion on his knee to hold the pad in place. 'Right, let's go through everything you know about your ex's past, where he grew up, who his friends are, what he likes to do in his spare time. I'm sure we'll find a clue somewhere in there.'

An hour later she felt wrung out and more like having a glass of wine than continuing to work on the puzzle of where Cal could have gone, but Wayne was still going strong. He was staring at the paper as if one of the neatly listed place or people names would leap off and declare itself to be sheltering Cal and Lily.

He tapped one name. 'I think this is the clue.'

She fought back a yawn and tried to concentrate. 'What is?'

'This. His childhood. The way he loves to go back to the north and walk on the moors.' He nodded slowly and emphatically. 'If you ask me, that's where he's gone. And the best of it is, with that big bike of his, he'll be far easier to track than he would in a car. How you came to choose a loser like him, I can't figure, Kerry. He doesn't even try to make real money and he could in the IT industry.' He tapped the paper again. 'If nothing's cropped up by tomorrow morning, we'll take a little run up north to the place where he was born and poke around.'

'But he has no family left there.' She hesitated. "Shouldn't we call the police now?"

'No. I'd rather settle things myself. We know she's safe with Cal.' Wayne tapped his nose. 'Anyway, I've got a feeling about this. We'll get up early and I'll see if it still seems a hot trail to me. I'm at my best after a good night's sleep. Now, that's enough of your daughter.' He swung her up into his arms. 'Let's go to bed. We have the place to ourselves tonight.'

Excitement ran through her and she put her arm round his neck as he carried her upstairs. His caveman approach was definitely a turn-on. She'd never met a man who gave her such pleasure in bed.

Twenty-Two

Dawn transforms a sepia landscape into full technicolour, invites birds to strut their stuff, sends insects into a whirring frenzy.

Kate woke with a feeling of happy expectation and a totally clear head for the first time in months. She went down for breakfast and found some special rice bread set out by the toaster and beyond it, gluten-free cereal in a labelled jar.

Lena peered through the door. 'Bacon and scrambled eggs?'

'Yes, please. Lovely.'

Andy came in as she was starting to eat. 'You look better today.'

'I feel better. I'm even hungry. I'm really looking forward to going out sightseeing with Mark. I'm even looking forward to getting the results of the tests and finding out what's wrong with my body's biochemistry.'

'Maeve will want to see you before you go out. She likes to keep tabs on us, even now.'

Kate stopped eating for a moment. 'How ill is she, Andy?'

'Very.'

'Terminally?' He nodded, looking so sad she could have wept for him.

'We think we've bought her a little extra time with this new treatment, though.'

She'd said it before she'd time to consider whether it was wise. 'You love her, don't you?'

He nodded. 'She's more like an aunt than an

304

employer.'

'It shows in how you look at her and talk about her. And you just said, "we" when you talked about buying time.'

'You go straight to the point, don't you?'

She grinned. 'I'm an Aussie. We don't pussy-foot around. Besides, I like her too. She's such fun, so alive in the head. I wish my Dad hadn't kept us apart.' She picked up her knife and fork again and picked up a piece of bacon. 'I haven't been so hungry for ages.'

'That's good.'

Kate went up to see her aunt just before she left. 'How are you?'

'Resting. It feels to be the right thing to do at the moment. I got angry the other day and that tired me out too much, made me feel—' She waved one hand about as if searching for the right word '—strange.'

'Aunt Maeve . . .'

'Yes?'

'I don't know how to thank you, but I just want you to know that I'm truly grateful for your help. I feel better already, just by giving up wheat. Why did no one even consider that before, when it's so simple?' Her voice came out a little choked. 'I thought I was going to be an invalid all my life. I even wondered if I had Alzheimer's, my brain got so cloudy.'

Maeve smiled and held out her arms, hugging her niece, something which also felt very right to her. 'The only thing that's certain in this life is that things change, for better as well as for worse. And look—if you want to ring your parents, go ahead. Don't stay estranged from them.'

'I might ring at a time when Mum is on her own. I think it's too soon for Dad and he'd put the phone down. He's good at holding grudges.'

'Typical Corrigan stubbornness. My grandfather was famous for it.'

'What other traits do we Corrigans inherit? Dad's always refused to talk about his family.'

'Red hair, obviously. I had it too once. We're strong-willed, rather too fond of getting our own way, generous, lusty in bed,' she winked. 'Some of us are good at making money but not always as good at keeping it. I'm the exception there. My father made plenty of money and if he hadn't died young, would have lost every penny again, was well on the way to doing so. As it was, I inherited an ailing business, which he left mainly to me because he knew I might be able to pull it together again. I think Des takes after him where money is concerned. Your father's more like my mother, though—a plodder, not at all money hungry.'

'I think he's most upset about not getting this house. He loved it.'

'Is he still upset about that?'

'Yes. It all came out just before I left.'

'I hadn't realized he felt so bad about it. Not that it'd have made a difference. I love it too, you see, and was determined to get it.' She gave one of her wry smiles. 'I'm as selfish as the next person.'

'What about my grandparents? They both died young, didn't they? I hope that's not another Corrigan legacy.'

'Not unless you think car crashes can be inherited. My Corrigan grandparents lived well into their eighties. You could have met them when you were young if your father had kept in touch.

They were always sad about that.' She sighed and got lost in her thoughts for a moment, then shook her head as if to banish the sad memories and smiled at Kate again. 'Well, we can't change the past, only the future. Today you should go out and enjoy yourself with Mark.'

'Do you mind?'

'What?'

'Me having a date with him?'

'No, of course not. Good luck to you both. It's about time he found himself a woman. Just don't rush into anything. You're fairly vulnerable at the moment.'

Kate found herself humming and walking in rhythm to the tune as she went downstairs. She felt as if a load of worry had been taken off her shoulders. Hope was very—invigorating.

And this was all thanks to Maeve. If the worst happened and Maeve died, that gift of better health would be her aunt's best legacy to her.

*   *   *

Des got up to find his dirty clothes still scattered over the floor. Tiff wasn't around, so he stepped over them and went looking for her. She was in her office typing, didn't even hear him come up behind her and jumped like a startled rabbit when he asked the question nearest his heart, 'What's for breakfast?'

'Whatever you get for yourself.' She got up and pushed him gently out of the room. 'Des, morning is my best writing time, so please, just let me get on with it.'

'But you won't need to write once we're

married. I'll have enough money for both of us.'

'That attitude is what I'm afraid of. Let's get this straight from the very start: whatever we decide to do, I'm not giving up writing. I love doing it. And I'm *not* turning into a glorified housekeeper and social secretary.'

Their eyes met in a challenge and it was he who looked away first.

She closed the door in his face and he stood for a moment scowling at it then tied his dressing gown more tightly at the waist and went into the kitchen. When he inspected the fridge he found nothing there except fruit and yoghurt and a loaf of heavy, dark bread. His eyes brightened when he saw a jar of honey in the cupboard and a few minutes later he sat down to enjoy six slices of the most delicious toast he'd ever eaten, licking the runny trails of honey off his fingers. He'd enjoyed it far more than his usual full cooked breakfast. There was, he decided, something to be said for getting your own food and choosing what to eat.

He was just about to go and get dressed when he noticed how untidy the kitchen now was. After hesitating for a moment, he cleared the mess up, muttering under his breath about paying for a woman then having to do things himself.

His thoughts now focused on what he had to do that day, he got ready, putting on the spare shirt he kept here. He'd have to bring some more clothes and get these dirty ones washed.

Surely Tiff could sling them in the washing machine with her own things?

He remembered how firmly she'd dismissed him this morning and grinned. She always had been decisive about what she wanted, both in their life together and in bed. She'd made him sign a legal contract before she'd agreed to live here as his permanent mistress, with specified redundancy payments in case he tired of her. Well, he hadn't tired of her because she wasn't at all like any of the other women he'd had.

And they *were* going to get married. He was quite determined about that.

But everything depended on him getting out of this financial hole. He didn't know what he'd do if his business went under.

* * *

Kerry woke with a start as Wayne shook her. 'Wassa matter?'

'You need to get up. I told you last night, I have a gut feeling about your ex. He's gone back to his roots, I know he has. Where else *could* he take Lily that's out of our way? This is a small island and we can drive to Lancashire in a few hours. It's not even worth taking the plane. Come on.' He flung off the covers and leaped out of bed.

She groaned and covered her eyes with her forearm. She hated early mornings.

He chuckled as he yanked her upright. 'Come *on!* We have to get going.'

'I need coffee.'

'It's waiting for you in the kitchen.'

She stumbled downstairs and took a big gulp of coffee, then another. 'But how will we know where to look?'

'You said Cal came from a village called Blackfold, didn't you? Quite a small place. There's bound to be someone there who's noticed a

Harley-Davidson. They don't exactly blend in with the scenery, you know.'

It made sense, it really did. She set the empty cup down. 'Give me fifteen minutes. And put some toast on.'

But she felt guilty, as if she was hounding her daughter. She'd never dreamed Lily would go to such lengths to get away.

*   *   *

On Monday Judith sneaked a look at her emails before she went to get breakfast, smiling as she read Cal's email of two days ago. He was very eloquent and although she'd worried during the night at being the first to express her love, she could see that she needn't have, because he'd said it in the email, and very tenderly too. She couldn't imagine Des writing anything like this, she thought as she printed it out and put it in her top drawer.

Just before lunch Lily came into the kitchen as Judith was finishing putting the top layer of pastry on an apple pie. Glancing from time to time at her half-brother, Lily wiped and put away the breakfast dishes without being asked to, then fiddled around with a bowl of apples.

Mitch sat and chatted cheerfully to them, clearly not intending to go anywhere, so in the end Judith put the pie in the oven, set the timer then went over and pulled him to his feet. 'Go and do something for half an hour, darling. We need to have some girls' talk.'

'Oh, sorry!' He ambled out and up the stairs to where Cal was working on Judith's computer and soon the two of them were deep in a technical discussion.

The huge relief on Lily's face told Judith she'd guessed right, so she shut the kitchen door. 'You do need to talk privately, don't you?'

'Yes. Look, I'm just about to start my period and I've nothing with me. Could we go out and buy something, do you think? Dad will give you the money. I need some more knickers too. I've only got what I was wearing when I ran away and a couple of pairs he brought with him.'

'I should have thought of that. Get your coat and we'll nip into Rochdale. The men can watch the apple pie. I'll just tell them we're going out.'

*　　　*　　　*

When he heard the sound of a car pulling up outside the house, Mitch looked out of the window. 'I thought it didn't sound like Mum's car. There's a big Landcruiser just pulled into the drive.'

Cal shoved his chair back and went to join him just as two people got out of the vehicle. 'Oh, hell, it's Kerry and Wayne. How could they possibly have tracked me here?'

'Who?'

'Lily's mother and her new guy.'

'She doesn't take after her mother, does she? She's much more like our side of the family. I don't like the looks of that man—he has a brutal face.'

The visitors disappeared from view and the doorbell rang twice.

Cal sighed and braced himself. 'I'd better go down. You might like to stay up here.'

'Give you space? OK.'

311

The bell rang again as Cal reached the bottom of the stairs. As he opened the door, Kerry moved forward into the house.

'I've come for Lily.'

'She isn't here.'

'You won't mind if I do a quick search, will you?' Kerry moved towards the stairs.

Mitch, who had gone to the top of the stairs to listen, moved to block the head of the stairs. 'This is my mother's house and you have no right here.'

Closely followed by Wayne, Cal ran up the stairs. 'Let them look. They'll not find her.'

'They still have no right to do this.'

'Any more than *he* has a right to kidnap Lily,' Wayne snapped.

Mitch swung round to glare at him. 'He didn't kidnap her. *She* ran away—from *you*. And I can see why.'

Wayne simply pushed the boy aside and went to help Kerry search.

Cal held Mitch back. 'It's not worth it. They won't find her here, but it'll keep them occupied. Let's go and put the kettle on.'

When they got back to the kitchen, Mitch said, 'We should just tell them to leave.'

'I'd rather keep my eye on them.'

'But what are we going to do when Lily gets back?'

'We're going to hope she'll see his car and tell Judith to drive past. If they don't, I'll tackle him and give you a chance to run out and tell them to get away.' He grimaced. 'Though I'm not a good fighter and he looks as if he is.'

'He does look like brute force on wheels, doesn't he?'

Footsteps on the stairs heralded the return of their unwanted visitors. Without a word, Wayne went out into the garden and began searching the sheds.

'She's not here, you know,' Cal said to Kerry.

'I prefer to make sure of that. And she's been here. We found some of her clothes.'

'Coffee?'

She hesitated.

'I'd like to be civilized about this.'

'You're too soft for your own good, you always were,' she snapped. 'Why are you doing this to me, Cal?'

'I might ask you the same question, though what matters most is why you're doing it to Lily. I've never seen her so unhappy and jumpy.'

Kerry swung away from him. 'Black, no sugar, if you remember. The same for both of us.'

He watched her for a minute, shaking his head at how intransigent she could be when she'd set her mind on something, then began to make the coffee.

Wayne came in a few minutes later. 'Not out there.'

Kerry looked at Cal. 'We're staying till she gets back.'

'Whatever.'

She sat down opposite Mitch, glanced at him, then looked again. 'Who *are* you?'

'I'm Lily's half-brother. We look alike, don't we? This hair comes from the Corrigan side of the family.'

She gaped at him, then glanced at Cal. 'How the hell did you find out?'

'From Mitch's mother. She's Des's ex-wife and

had her husband investigated.'

Kerry pressed her lips together, but her eyes kept straying towards Mitch and she didn't look happy.

Cal passed a mug to Wayne. 'Coffee?'

'Thanks.' He stood up. 'We'll go into that room at the front if you don't mind. Be able to see them return then. My guess is they've gone shopping and won't be long.'

The only thing Cal could do was choose a chair nearer the door than Wayne and pray he'd hold the man back for long enough to allow Judith and Lily to get away again.

But he was pinning his hopes on one of them seeing the car and driving past.

*   *   *

Des sighed and rubbed his chest absent-mindedly as his accountant droned on and Raymond nodded, looking as if he understood every word. The two of them had done nothing but talk figures and cost-cutting at him today and he had a touch of indigestion. It must be that bread. It'd been very heavy, was sitting like a stone in his chest.

In the end he could stand the discomfort no longer and stood up, pressing one hand against his chest. 'I'm not feeling—' And that was as far as he got, because a vice seemed to tighten on his chest and he groaned with the pain of it, fighting against the blackness and failing to hold it back.

Raymond jumped to his feet as his boss crumpled to the floor, twitched a little and lay still.

John went to kneel by Des, feeling for a pulse and loosening his tie and shirt collar. 'Call an

314

ambulance. Looks like a heart attack to me.'

For a moment Raymond stood there, open-mouthed, then jumped into action.

It took the ambulance only five minutes to arrive. He knew that, because he kept glancing at his watch. But those five minutes were the worst of his life because John had gone down to hold a lift at the ready and bring the ambulance crew up here.

When there was a sound in the corridor, Raymond let out a grunt of relief and stood up, moving back to let the paramedics deal with Des. They had him on the trolley very quickly and were out again before he realized someone would have to go with them to the hospital. 'You go with them.' He said to John. 'I'll call his family.'

He saw all the staff peering out of their offices and yelled, 'Get back to work.' After a moment's thought he rang Tiffany first, because she seemed as near family as Des had at the moment.

'Bad news, I'm afraid. Des has just had a heart attack.'

'He's not—'

'No, he's not dead, but he was unconscious. They said they were taking him to St Rita's. It's the closest.'

'I'll go straight there.'

'Take it easy. He won't want you to lose the baby.' Then he went outside to ask the secretary to ring Des's son and mother-in-law, before going to the hospital himself.

What a sod of a thing to happen! Just when they needed all their wits about them. Just when he had a few plans of his own that needed his attention.

Tiffany took a minute or two to breathe deeply and get control of herself. It wouldn't help Des if she panicked and lost the baby. Then she called a taxi and got ready to go out.

When she arrived at the hospital, she introduced herself as Des Corrigan's fiancée and was shown into a waiting room to one side, where she found Raymond and a man he introduced as the company accountant, both of them looking gloomy.

They stood up and Raymond came across to her. 'Des is holding his own but he hasn't regained consciousness.'

She went all shuddery for a moment or two and clutched his arm, letting him help her to a seat.

'I'll leave you to keep an eye on things here,' the accountant said, 'and I'll go back to the office. We want to quell panic there.'

'Right.' Raymond hesitated, then went to sit two chairs away from Tiffany, keeping a wary eye on her.

'I'm not going to faint, Mr Tate.'

'Just worried, given the circumstances.'

She looked at him coolly. 'I've done yoga and meditation. I can control my own stress. Which is more than we can say about Des. Can you manage the firm in his absence?'

'Yes.'

'Has someone rung his son and mother-in-law?'

'I told his secretary to do that.'

'Are you staying on here?'

'Till I know he's out of danger.'

'Good.' She folded her hands in her lap and

closed her lips firmly. She did have skills to minimize stress, but that didn't mean she wasn't worried sick about Des. If—no, *when* he recovered, she was going to make a few changes in his unhealthy lifestyle.

She couldn't bear it if he never even saw his child.

*　　*　　*

In Rochdale Judith and Lily started shopping with great enthusiasm. They'd agreed on the way into town to buy Lily some new jeans and a couple of tee shirts as well as the knickers.

When they went to pay at the first shop, however, Judith discovered she'd forgotten her credit card. 'I had it next to the computer, paying a bill online,' she remembered. 'Oh, damn! I'm really sorry about this, Lily. I can't get you the jeans today, just the stuff you need and maybe one tee shirt and a couple of pairs of knickers.' She counted the money in her purse and they did some very careful shopping which used up most of her cash then set off home. Even that much shopping was fun and made her wish she'd had a daughter.

As they were nearing the house, her thoughts turned to what she was going to make for lunch and it took her a minute to realize what Lily was shrieking in her ear.

'*Drive on past!* That's Wayne's car.'

By the time that registered, Lily had undone her seat belt and slid down on to the floor, repeating, 'Drive past! *Please!*'

Judith did as she'd asked, speeding up again as she gave one glance at her house. If it had not been

317

for Lily's quick reaction, she'd have turned into the drive without thinking about why a large four-wheel drive was parked in front of the house.

As they continued along the road, which led up to the moors, Lily looked up from a crouching position on the floor. 'How did they find us?'

It didn't take much thought to work that out. 'Cal came from round here originally, so it's a logical place to search. And the motorbike is very distinctive. We shouldn't have gone to the minimart on it last night.' She saw a turning space ahead and drew to a halt in it.

'I'm not going back to Mum. She'll only drag me off to America with her and Wayne.' Lily's voice became shrill as she added, 'I don't care what you say, I won't go back.'

Judith hated to see the unhappiness and tension in her companion, who had been laughing with her only a few minutes earlier.

'Isn't there somewhere else we can go? *Please.*' Lily pleaded.

And suddenly Judith realized that there was. 'Yes.' But as she started up the car, she groaned and turned to Lily.

'The petrol gauge shows nearly empty. I meant to fill the car in town. How are we going to buy petrol without my credit card?'

Twenty-Three

A kestrel hovers over the upper slopes of the moors then folds its wings and dives on its prey, rising triumphant with a mouse dangling from its talons.

After an hour had passed very slowly, Wayne fixed Cal with a lowering gaze and said, 'As custodial parent, Kerry wants her daughter back and you have no leg to stand on legally about this, Richmond . . . not now.'

'I've consulted a lawyer and I think you're wrong.' Cal ignored Wayne. 'You've been trying to fool me about the legalities, Kerry, so that you could take my daughter away from me. Why?'

'Because I don't want her growing up soft like you.'

'You want her like Rambo here?'

Wayne scowled at him and half-rose in his seat. 'Look here, fellow—'

Kerry tugged him down again. 'Don't let him provoke you. He's good at twisting words around, not so good at action.' She turned her head to spear Cal with one of the scornful looks he remembered so well. 'You've only got the ability to delay things, you know. And if you do, that'll put Lily in the middle of a tug of war situation. Can you blame me for trying to avoid that? If you do care about her as much as you claim, you'll let us take her to America and let *her* move on.'

'Never. She's as much mine as if I'd created her and anyway, she'd be unhappy with *him*.'

With a muffled grunt of annoyance, Wayne

stood up and went to the window, fists rammed into his pockets, staring out.

Kerry stayed where she was, but Cal knew her well enough to sense that she was uneasy underneath her anger, as if she wasn't totally comfortable with all this.

After that the only sound in the room for some time was the ticking of a massive old clock on the mantelpiece, and the shuffling sounds Mitch made as he fidgeted in his seat near the door. From time to time he looked at Cal and offered the unspoken support and comfort of a half-smile.

*　　　*　　　*

Tiffany glanced up as someone came into the waiting room. 'Hello.'

Hilary came across to sit next to her. 'How is he?'

'Holding his own. That's all they'll say. Isn't Mitch with you?'

'No. He's still in Lancashire but I've left a message for his mother.' She hesitated then took Tiffany's hand. 'Are you all right, dear?'

'Yes. Just—worried.'

A nurse came in. 'Mr Corrigan has regained consciousness, is asking for someone called Tiffany.'

She stood up. 'That's me. I'm his fiancée.'

'You can have five minutes with him, then he has to rest. He won't settle without seeing you. Is he always so difficult?'

'That's Des.' It gave Tiffany hope, somehow, to hear that he was still being his old awkward self.

He was lying on a bed, with a monitor beeping

320

beside him and wires attached to his body. He looked pale and drawn, and limp, as if he hadn't the energy to lift a finger, but he still smiled faintly when he saw her.

She pulled a chair up to the bed and sat down. 'What a silly thing to do, Des Corrigan.'

He clutched her hand. 'Sorry. I'll try not to do it again.'

'I've got your mother-in-law here, but Mitch is still out of town.'

'It's you I want. The business—'

'—can be left to Raymond. He's very capable or you'd not have had him working for you so long.'

'Yes.' He sighed and looked at their joined hands. 'You will marry me when I get over this, Tiff, won't you? I need you.'

'You never miss a trick, do you?'

'Not if I can help it.'

'All right. I'll marry you.' She'd have a few conditions to make first, but now wasn't the time to mention those. 'They said only five minutes and we've had six.' Standing up she bent to kiss his cheek.

'I do love you, Tiff.'

'I don't know why, but I love you too.'

The nurse came in, her eyes on Des, assessing. She seemed to approve of what she saw and nodded at Tiffany. 'He really does need to rest now.'

'All right.'

The nurse left with her. 'If things go well for the next day or two, he should be out by the weekend. Is there someone to look after him?'

'Me. We live together.'

'Good.'

When Tiffany went back into the waiting room, she felt things in the room waver around her and put out one hand on the wall for support. Hilary jumped up and put an arm round her, so she clutched the older woman instead, grateful not to be alone. 'I don't know why I'm being so silly. Des is looking tired, but he's alive.' Her voice broke on the last word.

'It's quite a normal reaction to feel wobbly once the worst is over,' Hilary said in her comfortable way. 'Did you have any lunch?'

'No.'

'Let's go and get something to eat and drink, then. You can't function without fuel, especially in your condition.'

'I'm not hungry.'

'Just a snack, to please me.'

'All right. It's really kind of you—given the circumstances.'

'I don't blame you for what Des has done, and nor will Judith. Their marriage hasn't been— sound for a long time.'

Tiffany had to swallow hard to hold back the tears. She turned to Raymond who was hovering behind Hilary, looking uncomfortable. 'I told Des you'd see to things at work and he's happy with that.'

He looked relieved. 'Right then. I'll get back to the office. Tell him I'm on to things. Will you be all right?'

'I'll stay with her and see her home,' Hilary said.

He nodded and walked out.

'I want to stay here, be with Des,' Tiffany protested.

'I'll go and ask someone about that.' She bustled

off and Tiffany sat down, closing her eyes.

When the older woman came back, she said, 'They suggest you go home. They're going to sedate him and he won't make much sense until tomorrow. I've given them my phone number. You will come to my house, won't you? You shouldn't be on your own. I need to ring Judith.'

'She won't want to see me.'

'She'll understand. And you really shouldn't be left on your own, not in your condition.'

As they were getting into her car, Hilary shook her head, a wry expression on her face. 'I don't know how Des does it.'

'Does what?'

'What do they call it nowadays? . . . I know: *pulls the chicks.*'

Tiffany stared at her in surprise, then chuckled. 'I'm a bit old to call a chick.'

'You seem pretty young to me. Come on. Let me take you home and look after you.'

*   *   *

'I have some money. I don't know if it'll be enough, though, because they took everything they could find away from me.' Lily tipped out her purse and they counted the coins together.

'It may just buy enough petrol. We'll have to go back through the village and fill up there, because this road only leads up to a pub on the moors, but I can avoid passing the house.'

They were both on edge as they stopped to fill up the car in the village. Lily stayed hunched up in the back, an old scarf of Judith's tied round her bright hair, pretending to read a magazine.

Then, driving in the most conservative way she knew in order to conserve petrol, Judith headed for Cheshire. A few miles from Maeve's house the car began to sputter and jerked to a halt.

'Oh, no!' Lily looked at her fearfully.

Judith smiled and reached out to hug the girl. 'It's all right. We're not far from Saltern House. I'll give Andy a ring and explain the situation.'

She was relieved when he answered the phone on the third ring and explained only that she'd run out of both petrol and money on the way to see Maeve.

'Where are you exactly? Right then, stay there and I'll bring some petrol out to you.'

He was there within half an hour, during which time Lily bit her nails and jerked round if any car slowed down nearby.

'They won't find us here,' Judith said several times. But it didn't seem to get through to the girl, who continued to wear the headscarf and sit slumped in her seat, watching the traffic warily.

When a large blue Mercedes slowed down and stopped next to them, she looked at Judith with such fear on her face that Judith took hold of her hand. 'It's all right. This is Andy, your Aunt Maeve's PA.'

'But what if they don't want to help me?'

'They will, I promise you.' She opened the car door and got out. 'Andy, I've never been so glad to see anyone in my life. Do you have some petrol?'

He nodded. 'I've also brought Reg, who looks after Maeve's cars. He'll fill yours up and bring it back to the house. You can ride home in my car.' He looked at Lily and then back questioningly at Judith. 'If you'd rung, I'd have sent a car to pick you up at home, you know.'

'We—um—had to leave unexpectedly and I didn't realize I hadn't brought my credit card. We need Maeve's help.'

'Who's the girl?'

'Lily. Another of Maeve's nieces. She's running away from her mother and we need your help.'

'This is Des's other daughter?'

'Yes.'

He laughed. 'Strangely enough, we were trying to find her. Maeve wants to meet her.'

Judith could see the girl's white, anxious face pressed against the car window. 'Look, I'll explain when we get there. Lily's very upset, so please don't ask her any questions.' She sat with Lily in the back of the big, luxurious car, holding her hand.

'What shall we do if she won't help me?' Lily whispered as they slowed down to turn into the drive.

'She will, I promise you.'

*   *   *

Maeve felt restless and went to sit in the conservatory as she waited for Andy to return. He said Judith had been very guarded on the phone, but had promised to explain fully when she arrived.

When she couldn't settle, Maeve wound up in the kitchen sitting on one of the high stools chatting to her housekeeper.

'You're looking a bit better today,' Lena said. 'There's more colour in your cheeks.'

Maeve considered this, head on one side. 'Yes. I'm feeling a bit better too—well, I think I am—

though I'm still much weaker than usual. I've to go in soon for another check-up.' She grimaced. 'I'm so tired of hospitals.'

'We're all human, even you, and sometimes we need them. Will you try one of these little rice-flour cakes for me? It's a new recipe and I'm not sure if there's enough sugar.'

Maeve picked one up and nibbled at it absent-mindedly. 'I wonder why Judith didn't let us know she was coming? Was that a car?' She put down the half-eaten cake and went back towards the front of the house.

Lena watched her go, a frown on her face. She hoped this visit didn't mean Des was causing trouble again. But at least she'd got a bit more food into Maeve, who was hardly eating enough to feed a bird.

*   *   *

Hilary picked up the phone, took a deep breath and dialled Judith's number. It rang several times and she was just about to put it down when someone picked it up. The person at the other end was a man and she didn't recognize his voice. 'Could I speak to Judith, please? It's her mother and it's very important.'

Cal stared at Wayne, who had moved closer and was listening carefully. 'Judith's out shopping. Can I take a message?'

'When do you expect her back?'

'I'm not certain.'

Hilary hesitated. 'Would you be Cal?'

'Yes.'

'Ah, she told me about you. Look, it's bad news,

I'm afraid. Des, her ex, has had a heart attack. He's been taken to St Rita's and will be in for a few days. I think he'll be all right, they got to him quite quickly. But Mitch should come back and see him—just in case.'

'I'm sorry to hear that. I'll tell Mitch myself. Are you at home? Give me your number. Right, got it. I'm sure Judith will ring you when she comes back.'

He put the phone down. 'I need to speak to Mitch privately.'

Wayne stared at him, eyes narrowed, fairly bristling with suspicion.

Cal gestured to Mitch to follow him out and led the way into the kitchen.

'Who was that?'

'Your grandmother.'

'It's not Mum, then.' He let out a long shuddering breath. 'I was afraid she'd had an accident.'

'No. It's your father. And it is bad news. He's had a heart attack.'

'*Dad*? Is he—'

'They think he'll be all right, but you'll want to go and see him, I'm sure. They're keeping him in hospital for a few days.'

'I need to get back to London straight away.' He lowered his voice. 'Where do you think Mum and Lily are? It doesn't take this long to nip into Rochdale and back.'

'I'm hoping they saw the car and drove past. Now, I'd better go and tell *them* what's happened. Don't forget, Kerry was once your father's mistress. Maybe this will make them go away and leave us alone.'

'*He* doesn't look like he'd care about anyone.'

'But she will, for all her faults. She's not all bad, Mitch. She's been a good mother in her own way. She's just—a bit sharp.'

Mitch made a scornful noise in his throat and sat down suddenly at the table, fists clenched, eyes closed.

Cal went back into the front room. 'Mitch's father's had a heart attack. He's in hospital. I need to get the boy to London.'

Kerry looked across at Cal in shock. 'Is Des going to be OK?'

'They think so, but they're keeping him in hospital for a few days.'

'Well, you can't leave until *they* get back, can you,' Wayne said, with a sneering sort of smile.

'He can leave any time he wants,' Kerry said. 'I'm not keeping a son from his father at a time like this.'

'It could be a trick, honey, probably is.'

She shook her head. 'Cal isn't into tricks and lies. He's too honest for his own good, always doing people favours instead of charging them for his services. That's one of the things that drove me mad about him.'

Mitch came back into the room as she was speaking and looked at Cal. 'I'm all right now. I think we ought to wait a bit longer, see if Mum gets in touch. If she doesn't, will you take me to London? I need to see Dad, be there. You know.'

'Yes, of course.' He went and put his arm round Mitch's shoulders and the boy didn't shrug the arm off.

Cal saw Kerry watching them with a sympathetic look on her face.

She stood up. 'Shall I make us all some

sandwiches? If you're going on a long drive, you'll want something to eat.'

'Thanks. That'd be a big help.' Cal pulled Mitch across to a chair. 'Your father will be all right,' he said. 'Your grandmother said they got help for him quickly and he's not old, can afford the best treatment.'

'Yeah.'

Wayne said nothing, just sat frowning and occasionally glancing out of the window.

*   *   *

Maeve heard the front door go and called, 'I'm in the conservatory.'

Andy came in. 'I've got a surprise for you, Maeve, a pleasant one too. You wanted to meet Des's daughter Lily—well, here she is.'

He gestured to someone in the hall and Maeve watched two people walk towards her. Her eyes flickered quickly over Judith and settled on the girl. What she saw made her draw in her breath sharply. 'Dear heaven! There's no doubt she's one of us.'

Judith drew Lily forward. 'Maeve, I've brought your niece to meet you—and she needs your help.'

'Come here, child, and be sure that whatever I can do for you, I will.'

Lily studied the woman. 'Even if it means going against my mother?'

'I don't know your mother, but you're the spitting image of myself at your age and you're a Corrigan, so I'm on your side from the start.'

Lily relaxed visibly. 'Mitch said you were nice.'

'I must remember to thank him when I see him.

329

And I'll find some photos of me as a child later and show you. You'll be surprised how alike we look. I gather no one's told you about me?'

'No. I didn't even know who my father was until yesterday.' She looked at Judith. 'Will you tell her why we're here? I get too upset when I talk about it.' She went across to the window, to stand with her back to them, looking out.

Judith went and sat beside Maeve, explaining what she knew about why Lily had run away from home. Only then did the girl come and join them again, her eyes suspiciously bright.

'What's he like, this Cal Richmond?' Maeve asked.

'He's a great guy,' Judith smiled involuntarily at the thought of him.

'He's the best dad that ever was,' Lily added. 'I don't care if your brother *is* my biological father. He never tried to see me, so I don't care about him.'

Maeve looked at her sadly. 'He always was a fool where people were concerned. He's done better with the money side of things. I think the first thing to do is phone your dad and let him know you're safe. He'll be worrying about you.'

'I don't want my mother to find out where I am,' Lily said at once.

'Not until I've seen my lawyers, no. Andy, have you got your mobile handy? Let her use that.'

He unclipped it from his belt and passed it to her. 'Know how to use it?'

She threw him a scornful look as if to say that was a stupid question, then hesitated and looked at Judith again. 'Will you deal with whoever answers first? I don't want to speak to my mother.'

'Of course I will.'

*   *   *

When the phone rang again Mitch jumped forward, hand outstretched.

'Let me take it.' Cal picked it up. 'Hello?'

'Cal, it's me, Judith.'

'Wayne and Kerry are here,' he warned quickly.

Wayne immediately moved forward and Kerry stopped in the doorway, her eyes on the phone.

Cal watched them warily as he listened to Judith.

'We saw their car so we drove on past. I'm using a mobile, so they won't be able to trace this call. I just wanted you to know that I have Lily in a very safe place.'

He watched Wayne warily. 'Good. Keep her there. It's not safe for her to come back here yet.'

'I'll put her on the phone, shall I?'

'Wait a minute. There's a bit of bad news for you, I'm afraid. Your mother just rang. It seems Des has had a heart attack.'

'What?'

'He's in hospital. They think he's going to be all right.'

'Mitch will want to go to him and I'd like to see him too. I'd better come back.' She hesitated, then added, 'I'm with Lily's aunt.'

'Ah. That's great.'

'Is it all right if I leave Lily here and come to London?'

'Yes, of course.' He thought through the logistics quickly. 'You'd be better going straight there. I can take Mitch on the Hog.'

331

'All right. But could you pack me a few clothes and underclothes?'

'Sure. As long as you don't complain about my selection.'

'Thanks. I'll put Lily on for a quick word now.'

'Great.' He waited then Lily came on, sounding breathless and worried.

'Dad? Are you all right?'

'I'm fine, darling. It's you I'm worried about.'

'I like it here. I feel safe.'

Kerry moved forward. She mimed begging to speak to Lily.

'Good. Look, your mother is here with me and wants a quick word. I think it'd be good to reassure her that you're all right.'

'No! I don't want to speak to her. She'll be furious.'

'She's more worried than furious at the moment. She won't shout at you. Trust me, kid. If she does, I'll take the phone away from her.' He covered it with his other hand for a minute. 'No threatening her. Promise.'

Kerry nodded and took the phone. 'Lily? Are you all right?'

'Yes, I'm fine. Judith's looked after me. But I'm not coming home. I'm not going to America with you. I'm *not!*'

'But you're OK?'

Kerry heard her daughter start to cry and a woman came on the phone, an older woman, from the sound of her voice.

'Ms Foster, isn't it? I'm sorry, but Lily's extremely upset.'

'So am I.'

'Then stop hounding her.' There was a pause,

then the woman's voice lost its crisp tone. 'She'll be looked after very carefully, I promise you, till this mess can be sorted out.'

'Thank you.' Kerry hesitated, then added, 'I do love her.'

'Not enough to let her have what *she* wants—and needs,' that cool voice said. 'Now, I think Judith needs to speak to Cal again.'

They made arrangements to meet in London at Hilary's house, then Judith cut the connection and smiled at Maeve. 'Thank you.'

'It's nice to be of use.' She looked at the girl, who was scrubbing her eyes. 'I'll get the best lawyers, but it'll be what Lily wants that they try for, not what you or her father want.'

'That's fine by me.'

*   *   *

When Cal turned round, he was surprised to see Kerry huddled against Wayne, weeping. 'Kerry?' She looked at him resentfully but didn't say anything. 'Look, Mitch and I have to leave now.'

'Do *you* know where she is?'

'Roughly. I know *who* she's with, which is the main thing.'

'They can be trusted to look after her properly?'

'Undoubtedly.' He turned to Mitch. 'Let's get ready. Dress warmly.'

Kerry looked up at Wayne. 'Take me home, darling. Oh, just a minute, Cal. Which hospital is Des in? I'll want to ring and check that he's all right.'

'St Rita's.'

'Lily was born there. Strange how things work

333

out sometimes.'

Wayne put his arm round her shoulders, scowled at Cal and walked her out, tossing over his shoulder, 'You'll be hearing from our lawyers.'

'Kerry will be hearing from ours as well,' Cal said, in a more temperate tone.

*   *   *

Maeve went to hold her niece as Judith finished her phone call. The child sobbed against her, clearly worn out by all the hassles. 'We'll sort it out, I promise you,' she murmured against the damp cheek pressed against hers.

'Wayne's rich. He owns aeroplanes and has millions of dollars. My dad hasn't got much money because he doesn't care about it. How can we fight someone like that?'

'I'll help you as well.'

Lily looked up and smeared away a tear with the back of one hand. She looked round at the beautiful room then back at Maeve. 'Are you rich too?'

'Yes, very.'

'If you can help me and Dad, we'd both be very grateful.' Her breath caught on a sob and she sniffed.

Maeve pushed a handkerchief into her hand. 'Use that, then come and sit next to me. As soon as Judith leaves, you and I will have a council of war with Andy.'

As Lily sat down and used the handkerchief, Judith mouthed, 'Thank you' to Maeve from across the room.

The older woman smiled and made a shooing

movement. 'Andy, get Judith sorted out with some food and then a car. Better if someone else drives her down to London, I think. Oh, and give her some money to tide her over.'

With a smile Judith let Andy show her to a guest suite, where she could freshen up, then she went down to find him waiting at the foot of the stairs.

'I've got Lena to put something together for you to eat in the car. I didn't think you'd want to linger.'

'You're right.'

She went to say goodbye to Lily and was relieved to see that the girl had calmed down and was chatting animatedly to her aunt. What a pity Maeve had never had any children. She was marvellous with young people. Mitch had said she was 'one cool dame' and he was right.

'You're sure you'll be all right, Lily?'

'Yes.' She came to give Judith a hug. 'Thank you for rescuing me.'

'Any time.'

'Tell Dad I love him and I'll see him soon.'

'I will.'

Lily looked at her slyly. 'I think you're fond of him too, aren't you?'

'Yes. Do you mind?'

'Not as long as you make him happy. I read somewhere that men live longer when they're happily married.'

Judith had trouble holding back a laugh at this piece of wisdom as she caught Maeve's amused gaze from across the room. 'Well, we haven't got as far as discussing marriage yet, but I'll—um—bear that in mind.'

'We'll look after her,' Maeve said. 'You look

after her father for her. Tell him not to worry. I have some excellent lawyers. Oh, and give my regards to Des if you see him.'

Twenty-Four

Sunshine and showers pursue drivers down the motorways, foxes hunt small prey along verges, birds chase insects among foliage and flowers. No creature today is standing still.

Judith sat in the back of the big Mercedes, glad the driver wasn't the chatty sort and she could have some thinking time. She couldn't believe how much had happened in the past few months, or how greatly her life had changed, still felt breathless when she thought about that.

She wondered how Des was, needed to know he was all right before she could move on. You couldn't live with a man for nearly twenty years without having some residual feeling for him. It wasn't as if he'd meant to be unkind, he was just— selfish, full of testosterone, full of exuberance too, which was what had attracted her to him in the first place. It had been an accident that he had knocked her down the stairs, though not accidental that he'd played tricks on her. Perhaps his rages and spite had been symptoms of whatever caused his high blood pressure and the heart attack.

But the main reason she still cared about him was because he'd given her Mitch and because she knew he loved his son dearly in his own selfish way—and that was something Mitch still needed.

Was this Kerry person missing Lily as much as Judith had missed Mitch? How must she be feeling not even to know where her daughter was? Was the woman stupid or self-absorbed not to see how close the bond was between Cal and Lily? Judith envied him that strong link, hoped to forge a closer one with Mitch in the time she had before he flew the nest completely. Then perhaps he'd keep coming back. Mitch had accused her of not giving fully of herself, but that had changed, she had changed.

Rain rattled against the car window and she looked up briefly, closing her eyes again almost immediately and continuing to sift through her own thoughts.

And on the whole they were happy ones now.

*   *   *

Kate looked up as the phone in their hotel suite rang, but Mark was closer to it so she let him pick it up.

'Andy. Hi. Everything all right? . . . Yeah, we got here with no trouble . . . We're going for the results today . . . No, she stood up to the journey well.' He winked at Kate, then his expression grew solemn and he looked surprised as he picked up a pen and sat down to write, murmuring 'Mm-hmm' at intervals.

When the call ended he looked across the room. 'We missed out on a bit of excitement. Des's daughter Lily has taken refuge with Maeve after running away from her mother, who wanted to take her to live in the States. The lawyers think it best that Maeve brings the girl to London and allows her mother to have access—they think they can swing it for her to stay with the man she considers her father till the case is settled, because she's over twelve. So as Maeve has to go for one of

338

'You're welcome to visit any time. I think it'll be good for the baby to have a brother like you.'

Mitch blushed and nodded, his eyes still bright with tears.

Judith could feel herself flushing at what he'd said. 'What about the funeral?'

'You won't try to keep me away?' Tiffany asked.

'Of course not. I meant—do you want to help plan it?'

Tiffany thought for a moment, then shook her head. 'No. I don't know anything about funerals. All I care about is being there to say a final farewell to Des.' She gulped and pressed one hand to her mouth, tears rolling down her cheeks.

'I'll take you down to find a taxi, Tiffany,' Cal said when she'd pulled herself together a bit. 'Will you and Mitch be all right for a minute or two, Judith?'

'Yes, of course.'

As she was speaking a nurse came in. 'Mrs Corrigan? There are some papers we need you to sign.'

Later, as the three of them were leaving the hospital, Cal said, 'Had we better go and see Maeve? She may want to be involved too. He was her brother, after all.'

'I suppose so.'

'You look exhausted.'

'I do feel tired. And it's only mid-afternoon. Mitch, we didn't have lunch. You must be hungry.'

He shook his head.

'Then we'll go and see your aunt now, get it over with.'

*   *   *

At the hotel they found Maeve sitting on her own in the suite.

'I'm glad you came. Do sit down. Lily's talking to a psychologist.' She gestured to a closed door.

Cal stopped dead. 'What's wrong with her?'

'She's upset about a lot of things. It seemed a good idea to get her some counselling, and also it should give you ammunition for keeping her with you, Mr Richmond. Do sit down.'

'Call me Cal, please. I'm not one for formality, Miss Corrigan.' But his eyes were on the closed door.

'Nor am I, especially in the circumstances. Now, I have to go into hospital tomorrow for some tests, but it'd still be best if we used this hotel as a central meeting point. I've hired another suite here and suggest we use it as a place to gather.'

She picked up a pad from the small table next to her. 'Now, what else is there? Oh, yes. I've arranged for a lawyer to talk to you and Lily tomorrow morning, Cal. He's coming here. Lily's afraid her mother will try to snatch her if she goes out. Is that all right with you? Good. And Judith, can we postpone Des's funeral for a few days? It'd be good to wait for Leo and his wife to arrive from Australia. Mitch and Lily will want to meet their Australian aunt and uncle, I think. And there are Mitch's other two sisters to think of. Could you break the news to them, please?'

Judith nodded, feeling as if she'd been picked up by a gentle whirlwind and wondering what Des's sister had been like when she was in full health.

Maeve looked into the distance for a minute or

two. 'It looks as if Des's death has brought about a big reunion of the Corrigans. I hope you'll all be involved. A lot of fences can be mended at a funeral. And Lily should know her brother and sisters, her cousins, don't you think? Do you want me to arrange the funeral, Judith, or shall you?'

'I'll do it. My mother and I have some experience in that area. My father died a couple of years ago.'

'Then I hope you'll let me host a gathering afterwards? Good. We'll have it here, of course. It's quite my favourite London hotel.'

As Judith and Mitch rode back in a taxi to her mother's, he said, 'I'd like to be the one who tells Lacey and Emma, and their mother, about Dad.'

'All right, darling.'

After a pause, he added thoughtfully, 'She's an amazing person, Aunt Maeve, isn't she? I'm glad I've got to know her before the cancer takes over. I'll never forget her.'

Twenty-Six

Sunshine spills over everything, defying death and darkness. Golden light dazzles the eye, warms the skin, winks from window panes and gilds the flowers.

When she got back to Cal's, Judith contacted the same funeral company they'd used for her father. They'd been both sensitive and efficient. Tired as she was, she agreed to see a representative within the hour and went through the main details with him. Cal sat quietly to one side, saying nothing, but as he'd said, 'Being there in case'.

His presence was a comfort she needed just then, because she still hadn't come to terms with Des's sudden death. It wasn't fair when he'd always been so full of life!

The following morning Cal helped her make a list of tasks and prioritize them. First of all, Corrigan International, which she'd put off till today. Someone had to keep an eye on Des's business, which was now, presumably, Mitch's inheritance. She knew nothing about the company, because Des hadn't wanted her involved in any way, but she could at least make sure it was being managed carefully during this interim period.

Cal took hold of her hand. 'I won't be much help, I'm afraid, but I'm here if you need me.'

'Thank you.' She rang head office, using the direct line to Des's secretary.

Pamela greeted her cheerfully. 'I'm so sorry about Mr Corrigan's heart attack. I hope he gets better soon.'

Judith hadn't realized she'd be breaking the sad news, had expected it to have filtered through to the office, as these things usually did. 'I'm afraid my husband died yesterday.'

There was dead silence, then, 'Oh, no! I'm so sorry! I didn't know.'

'How could you have? Is Mr Tate there?'

'He hasn't come in yet, Mrs Corrigan. He was here till very late last night, the security guard says. It looks as if he was going through the papers in your husband's office. I do wish he'd put things away. It took me over an hour to tidy up this morning.'

'I'd better come in, I think. Things are so much easier to arrange face to face. Perhaps you could give Mr Tate a ring at home and tell him about Des, ask him to come in as soon as he can.'

'He has an appointment with the accountant at eleven. Shall I cancel it?'

'No. I'll need to see Mr Welby myself. Will you let everyone know—about Des, I mean.'

'Yes, of course, Mrs Corrigan.'

When Judith arrived at the office, Pamela said, 'I rang Mr Tate, but there's no answer. Perhaps he's on his way here.'

'I hope so. I don't really know where to start.'

Half an hour later John Welby arrived, but there was still no sign of Raymond. Judith heard voices whispering in the outer office before the accountant was shown in and was relieved to be spared the task of explaining yet again that Des was dead. It didn't get any easier.

John came across the office to hold her hand for a moment. 'Pamela told me about Des. I can't believe it! He was so full of life, so enthusiastic, even now.'

'Why do you say "even now"?'

'Oh. I forgot you two were separated. He won't have told you—but I suppose you'll have to know. The company is experiencing a serious cashflow problem and Des was having to make economies, sell the house, you know the sort of thing. It was buying that engineering works in Cheshire that did it. I told him at the time it was a foolish move.'

'I thought he was financially stable, set up for life.'

Welby shook his head. 'Des enjoyed taking risks—and I have to say, many of them paid off. But in the past year or two, he's not been as lucky and there's been a considerable drain on our reserves, much of it going to that new company we're setting up.'

'Corrigan Engineering?'

'No, another one, Delferen.'

'I don't know anything about that.'

'Raymond was dealing with it. I was supposed to see him today to go over the accounts. Where is he?'

'No one knows. He was here till quite late, apparently. Pamela said he'd made a terrible mess of the office.'

'Strange. He told me two days ago that everything was ready for my inspection.'

There was a silence, then she took a quick decision. 'I think we'd better send someone round to Raymond's flat. He may just have slept in after working late, but we need him here now.' She gave Pamela instructions, then started going through the overall figures that John produced, trying to get a feel for how bad a position the company was in financially. What he had to tell her made her more depressed by the minute. All through their married life she'd felt so secure financially with Des, had never realized what a gambler he was. She didn't care about that for herself but would there be anything left for Mitch, who had his heart set on running the company one day?

There was a knock on the office door and Pamela poked her head inside. 'Peter's back from Mr Tate's and—well, I think you should hear what he found, Mrs Corrigan.'

The uneasiness that had been skittering through Judith collected suddenly into a hard lump in her belly. Something was very wrong here, she knew it.

*   *   *

Since Judith was busy, Cal went round to see his daughter. He ran into Kerry in the hotel lobby. She was standing tapping her toe impatiently by the reception desk but when she saw him, she snapped something to the harassed looking clerk and came striding across the shining expanse of marble.

'They won't let me up to see Lily,' she said by way of a greeting. 'Is this your doing? If so, you're going to be in trouble with my lawyers.'

'It's Maeve's doing, actually. Her lawyers think a responsible relative is a good person to look after Lily until you and I get things sorted out.'

'Well, I want to see her for myself, make sure she's all right.'

'You'll only upset her.'

Kerry took a deep breath, half-closing her eyes, then opened them and said, 'Doesn't anyone think it's possible that *I* may be upset too?'

He looked at her and saw the strain in her eyes. 'Give me ten minutes. I'll go up and see Lily, talk to her then come back down for you. You could wait in that café over there.'

'Ten minutes, not a second longer!'

He went to the reception desk and asked them to ring Miss Corrigan's suite and let her know he was on the way up.

A young woman opened the door to him and Lily came hurtling across the room to fling herself in his arms.

'Dad!' She peered down the corridor. 'Mum isn't with you, is she?' She pulled him inside and her companion shut the door. 'They rang from reception, said Mum wanted to come up but Kate told them no. Oh, you've not met, have you? This is my cousin Kate from Australia. This is my dad. You won't let Mum come up here, will you?'

'It's only natural that she would want to see you.'

'Well, I don't want to see her and Jerome—he's my counsellor—said I didn't have to if it upset me.'

'Kerry's on her own today, no sign of Wayne. If I stayed with you, don't you think you could spend five minutes in her company?'

Lily shook her head and began sobbing. 'I don't want to, Dad. Please don't make me.'

'All right, darling. I'll go down and explain. I'll be up again in a few minutes.'

He went across to the café and as Kerry started to get up, he shook his head and sat down opposite her.

'What did you say to her?'

'I suggested she see you for five minutes in my presence. Kerry, wait, listen!' As she sat down

366

again, he said, 'She started crying at the mere thought of it. Kerry, you and Wayne have seriously screwed that child up.'

She looked at him as if he'd slapped her face. 'You're just saying that.'

'I'm telling you the literal truth. You know I'd not lie about something so important.'

She bent her head for a moment, fiddling with her coffee cup. 'I didn't mean to upset her that much. I do love her, you know.'

'I know. In your own way. But it's not the way she wants or needs at the moment.'

'Would she see me if I promised not to shout or nag her to come to America . . . or anything like that?'

He bit his lip then looked at her levelly. 'She's too upset this morning. I give you my solemn word that I'll try to set up a meeting. Please go home, Kerry. This has gone beyond you and me, now. It's Lily who's shattered by it all.'

'I only wanted the best for her, and Wayne could have given her that.'

'*You* care about money. I don't think she does.'

'No. You've certainly shaped her, haven't you?' She stood up. 'Very well. I'll go home. Tell her . . . Oh, hell, tell her she can stay with you from now on. But I need to see her first before we get into the legalities, to make sure she's all right. And I want to see her regularly after that.'

He felt as if all the lights in the world were blazing brightly round him. 'You'll let me have custody of Lily?'

'Yes, damn you.' She got up without a word and walked out, not turning to look back at him, though he stood and watched her go. When she'd disappeared from sight, he went across to the lift and along to the suite. This time when the door opened, he found himself facing a man.

'I'm Mark Felton.' He stuck out his hand. 'I work for Miss Corrigan. Lily's still a bit upset.' He gestured towards the couch, where Lily was sitting with her cousin.

Cal went across to hug his daughter, then looked apologetically at the others. 'I need to speak to Lily privately.' Without waiting for an answer, he led her into her bedroom.

She sat on the bed, shoulders hunched, looking at him apprehensively. 'What did Mum say?'

'She was upset, had tears in her eyes.'

'*Mum did?*'

'Yes. She does love you in her own way, you know. I have good news, Lily-Pilly. Your mother told me she's prepared to give me custody—for your sake, not because she wants to. But she needs to see you first.'

'She'll get mad at me.'

'I don't think she will. But if she does, I'll bundle her out quick smart.' He made two fists, waved them in the air and tried to look macho.

Lily was surprised into a gurgle of laughter. 'You couldn't fight your way out of a paper bag, Dad.'

'For you, I'd try.' He gave her another hug. 'I think you'll have to face her sometime, darling. But you can have the psychologist or a lawyer or whoever you want with you when you do. Your mother's gone home and I'll ring her when we've decided on a time.'

She sighed and sagged against him. For a few moments they just sat there, then she said in a husky voice, which sounded to be near tears, 'It's

368

been bad, hasn't it?'

'Yes, darling. But the bad part's almost over now.'

'I hope so. I don't want to feel like this again as long as I live. I was so frightened I'd lose you, Dad.'

He cuddled her for a long time, then said, 'Right. That's enough soppy stuff.'

She gave him a tearful smile and sat up straighter.

'What have you got to wear that looks good? We want to knock your mother's socks off this afternoon.'

'I've only got old jeans and tops here.'

'Then I think we should go shopping and buy you some new clothes.'

A smile crept over her face. 'Could Judith come and help us?'

'She'll be busy, darling. She's got a funeral to plan.'

'I forgot about her husband.'

'Don't forget about him. He was your father.'

'No, he wasn't.'

Cal was glad to see that stubborn look back on her face, to hear her speaking more like her old self.

She looked at him sideways, a smile on her face now. 'I like Judith. Are you going to marry her?'

'I hope so.'

'That's wicked. It means I'll see Mitch all the time. I never thought I'd get a brother.'

'And two sisters.'

'Yeah. Cool, isn't it?'

'Definitely cool. Now, how about washing your face and I'll just have a word with Andy. He'll help us arrange the meeting.'

*   *   *

Maeve stared at the specialist in shock. 'Are you sure?'

'Yes.'

She tried to hold them back, but the tears wouldn't be denied and she suddenly began sobbing. He left the hospital room, where she'd been resting after an arduous round of tests. A nurse slipped in and began patting her back.

Maeve pulled away. 'Can't you—leave me alone?'

'Not while you're so upset, Miss Corrigan.'

'Haven't I a right to be upset?'

'You have indeed. Look, I'll wait just outside the door if it'll make you feel better. Take your time.'

Maeve cried more quietly then lay back, feeling washed out, bewildered, for once not in control of herself.

It was over an hour before she felt ready to face the world, an hour during which the kindly nurse several times peered into her room, giving her an encouraging smile.

Maeve wished desperately that she could get away from nurses and well-meaning friends for a few days and take some time to get used to her news. But she couldn't, she knew that. There was Des's funeral to face, Lily's future to sort out, and other plans to be made.

*   *   *

Peter came into the big office and sat

uncomfortably on the edge of a chair.

'Well,' Welby prompted, 'what did you find?'

'I spoke to the new tenant. Mr Tate hasn't lived at that address for several months.'

'*What?*'

'He moved out, told everyone he'd bought himself a house, didn't leave a forwarding address but no mail ever arrived for him. So I rang Personnel, thinking they'd have his new address. They said he hadn't told them he'd moved.' Peter looked from one to the other. 'So I came back.'

'Keep this to yourself,' Welby muttered. 'Thank you. You've done well.' When the door had closed, he turned to Judith. 'This doesn't look good.' He stared round the room. 'I wonder what he was looking for last night? I wish that woman hadn't cleared everything up.' He went to the door. 'Pamela, can you tell me the names of the files that were out of place this morning?'

'There were a lot of papers scattered around. I can remember some of them.'

'Thank you. Can you do that now, write them down? If you have to look in the filing cabinets to jog your memory, do it. We'll go somewhere else. Just don't tell anyone else what's going on. We'll go into Tate's office.' He gestured to Judith to follow him.

Once they were sitting in another luxurious office, John sighed and began to fiddle with his pen. 'I hope I'm wrong, but it sounds as if he's— well, this has all the signs of embezzlement. Tate has introduced a lot of new business lately through the new company, and we've paid out some large amounts of money. That's why I insisted on an audit of those accounts, something we were going to start on today. Des okayed them, but I'm not sure whether he looked into them or just took Tate's word that they were OK. That may be why he's gone missing. It sounds as if he's been planning it for months, moving house so secretively, siphoning money off.' He spread his hands in a helpless gesture. 'You read about such cases, but you don't expect to be involved in one.'

'I still can't believe it.'

'I hope I'm wrong, but if I'm not, we'll have to call in the fraud squad.' He gave a quick shake of his head. 'I'm afraid that lately Des has been more interested in long lunches and his mistress, and he's been leaving too much to other people.'

She sat for a moment or two, then stood up. 'I'll be no use here. I'm going to ask a friend for help. In the meantime, do what you can, John. I'm grateful you're here.'

Outside she hailed a taxi and went straight to the hotel. Maeve or Andy were the only people she could think of to advise her.

When she got there, she met Cal and Lily at the entrance, about to go out shopping. One look at her face and he turned back.

'What's the matter?'

She explained. 'I've got to see Maeve.'

'This is her day for the big tests. Andy's gone to fetch her back, but she'll be very tired.'

'I'd forgotten. What am I going to do?'

'Doesn't sound as if *you* can do much at all. Are you worrying about your own money? If so, you don't need to. I earn a fair amount, enough to support both of us, and I can easily earn more.'

She smiled at him and for a moment the world seemed to recede as she kissed his cheek. 'I love you, Cal Richmond.'

Then she realized they were standing in the hotel lobby, with the concierge smiling at them from behind his nearby desk, and Cal's daughter beaming at them from nearby.

'Don't mind me,' Lily said. 'I approve. Kiss her again, Dad, if you like. I'm not in a hurry.'

Cal laughed and tousled her hair. 'We'd better go back up with Judith. She might need help.'

'That's OK. Mum's seen me in these things anyway.' She looked at Judith. 'We were going to get me something special to wear for my meeting with her this afternoon.'

'In that case, since Maeve isn't here, let me come with you. There's a boutique just down the road that has some very with-it clothes.'

As they walked along the street, it felt to her as if they were already a family. It was a good feeling, something to give her hope for the future in the midst of all this trouble.

*   *   *

When Maeve got back to her room, Kate was waiting for her.

'Where's Lily?'

'Out with her dad. She's meeting her mother this afternoon—Andy arranged for it to take place at the lawyer's rooms. Didn't he tell you? They've gone to buy her something smart to wear.'

'She's all right?'

'Her mother says Cal can have custody. As for Lily, she brightens up the minute her father appears.'

'Good.'

'How are you, Aunt Maeve? You look exhausted.'

'I am a bit tired. I'll just have a lie down, I think.'

When she'd gone into her bedroom, Kate looked at Andy. 'She looks as if she's been crying.'

'Don't tell her you guessed. She'd hate that. I assume the test results weren't good, but I didn't ask her because it was obvious she didn't want to talk. We've known her chances weren't good for a while and if anyone can cope with bad news, she can. Give her a little time. What about you? How are you feeling today?'

'Not too bad, a bit washed out after the transfusion, but they said I would be today.'

Half an hour later there was a knock on the door and Lily came back, accompanied by her father and Judith, carrying a couple of plastic bags with elegant gold labels on them. 'Is Aunt Maeve back? I've got some really cool new clothes to show her.'

'She's a bit tired, probably dozing,' Andy said. 'Can it wait?'

'Oh. Yes. She's all right, isn't she? I mean, the tests didn't show anything bad, did they?'

'I don't know. She hasn't said. But it's all very tiring for her.'

'OK. I'm going to change.' She vanished into her room with the bags.

'In the meantime,' Judith said, 'I wonder if I can ask your advice, Andy . . .'

*　　*　　*

That afternoon, Kerry looked at Wayne and grimaced. 'I'm feeling nervous about meeting my

374

own daughter. Is that stupid or what?'

'Want me to come with you?'

'Better not. We don't want Lily to feel threatened.'

He let out a scornful snort. 'That young woman *should* feel threatened, the way she's treated you.'

Kerry knew she'd never convince him differently. He saw things in black and white and to him, a child owed obedience to its parents, whatever they decided about its future. She didn't mind. It gave him strength and she was tired of being the strong one.

When she got to the lawyer's offices, she put up her chin and marched inside.

They showed her into a room with a large oval table. Lily was sitting at one of the longer sides, flanked by Cal and the lawyer, with another man sitting at the head of the table.

It was he who stood up. 'If you'd like to sit opposite your daughter, Ms Foster? I'm Jerome Thane, Lily's counsellor, and she's asked me to facilitate this session.'

Kerry did as she was told, shocked at how thin and worn her daughter was, how dark the rings round her eyes were. She didn't know what to say, except, 'Hi, Lily.'

'Hi, Mum.'

'I like your top. It's new, isn't it?'

'Dad and Judith bought it for me yesterday.'

'Judith?'

'Mitch's mother.'

'I'd like to meet Mitch again under happier circumstances one day.'

Lily nodded, still looking wary.

Kerry looked across at Cal and abandoned

formality. 'Let's get it over with. Look, Lily, you can live with your dad from now on. I won't nag you any more about coming to America.'

'What about Wayne?'

'He'll do as I wish where you're concerned.'

Lily let out a huge sigh. 'Cross your heart.'

Blushing slightly, Kerry crossed her heart, muttering, 'It's something we do.'

'It's a good thing to do,' Jerome said in that soft, careful tone counsellors often use.

Lily sniffed, tried to hold it together but failed and began to cry. 'I can't believe it's all over,' she sobbed against her father's chest. 'I can't believe I'm safe.'

'*Safe!*' That word hurt Kerry. She caught Jerome's watchful gaze and a hot protest died unspoken.

'She'll be all right,' he said. 'It's just relief. Better leave it at that for today.'

The lawyer stood up. 'I have some papers for you to sign, Ms Foster, if you'll come into my office?'

She nodded but didn't stand up to leave for a moment or two. As she watched Cal pat Lily on the back and murmur to her, she felt a pang of envy and anger sear through her, but it was no use giving in to it. Forcing a smile to her face, she said, 'I'm still hoping you'll come and visit me in America, Lily.'

Lily raised her head but the wary look was back on her face.

'We'll discuss that later,' Cal said. 'Maybe Judith and I can bring her out to visit you some time. I like America.'

'Judith again?'

'She and I are an item.'

'Congratulations. About time you found someone. If ever a man had *domesticated* tattooed on his soul, you do.' She stood up. 'Well, I have to get going. I'll email you and send you photos of our new home, Lily. You will keep in touch?'

Lily stood up and nodded as Cal whispered something to her. She came round the table, looked at her mother uncertainly, then gave her a quick hug.

Kerry pulled her daughter back into her arms and made it a long hug, then set her at arm's length. 'You *will* keep in touch?' she asked again.

'Yes, Mum.'

'I do love you.'

'I love you, Mum, but I don't want to move away from Dad.'

'I know. You've made that very clear.' She blinked furiously. 'Well, I haven't all day. I'll pack your things and send them across to your Dad's. Where are these papers I need to sign?'

She and the lawyer walked out together.

'She was crying again,' Lily said wonderingly. '*Mum!* She never cries.'

'Maybe she cares about you more than you realize,' Cal suggested.

Lily nodded. 'I know she cares, but she wants me to be like her and I'm not. Can we go back to the hotel now? Please, Dad. I want to pack my bag and come home.' She turned to the counsellor. 'Thank you for helping me, Jerome.'

'I'll see you soon. I think we've a few things to talk about still.'

'Yes, whatever. Dad?' She tugged at her father's arm.

'Judith's staying with us,' he said as they packed her clothes at the hotel.

She paused and looked at him. 'Will she mind me being there?' Her voice quavered. 'Do you need to be alone together?'

'Not if you need me. Would you like me to ask her to move out for a few days, to give you time to settle in?'

She hesitated.

'I'm sure Judith will understand.'

He gave her another hug and she sighed as she rested against him.

'I don't want to mess things up for you, but if we can just hang out together for a bit, I'll know it's real.'

Twenty-Seven

A gentle breeze blows across the cemetery. Faded plastic flowers stand in stiff salute on nearby graves and in the distance black limousines sit quietly respectful in a tidy row.

As the mourners walked away from the grave, Judith found herself next to Cal, who'd been invited to bring Lily, at Maeve's suggestion.

'How are things?'

'Better. She's not as jumpy, and is starting to boss me around like she used to.'

She looked behind to where Lily and her son were walking. 'That's good. I think she's more comfort to Mitch than anyone else at the moment. They seem like brother and sister already.' Mitch had been hungry for kin and he'd got his wish. He was surrounded by relatives now, as well as having three sisters.

'Funerals are so depressing,' Hilary muttered as they all got into the limousine. 'I don't know why we put ourselves through this.'

'Because we want to say goodbye properly,' Tiffany said.

She looked strained today, Judith thought. It was sad that she was now left to bear and raise Des's child alone.

As they filed into the hotel, Andy summoned a wheelchair for Maeve, who pulled a face at him but sank down on it. She was looking exhausted but was very much the matriarch of the family on this occasion. Beside her, Leo seemed colourless, though he was pleasant enough, as was his wife.

On the functions floor they were directed to an elegant room with a few small tables, and a lavish buffet. There was no sign of Maeve.

When they were all there, Andy came in and clapped his hands for everyone's attention. 'I hope you'll excuse Maeve, but she needs a rest now. She hopes you enjoy the meal and invites you to join her for a financial discussion at three o'clock. We have a sitting room booked and you can go there after you've eaten.'

Which was enough to keep people talking as they ate the superb food.

'What's that young woman doing here today? I gather she was Des's mistress. It's a bit off inviting her,' Leo muttered to his wife.

Mark overheard them. 'Apart from the fact that Tiffany was going to marry Des, she's carrying his child. She has a right to join the mourners, don't you think?'

Leo goggled at him. 'How many children did my brother have?'

Mark smiled. 'Four that we know of and this baby.'

'I never did understand what women saw in him.'

Mark decided to change the subject. 'Don't you think your daughter is looking better?'

Jean nodded. 'Better than she's looked for ages.' She nudged her husband. 'Isn't she, Leo?'

His expression softened as he caught Kate's eye. 'Yes. I'm glad you're on the mend, love.'

She returned her father's smile. She knew that was as near as she'd get to an apology for his behaviour towards her, but somehow she didn't

380

care. Today she hadn't woken foggy-brained. That filled her with joy and hope. She had about fifteen tablets to take every day now to boost her immune system and start leaching some chemical overloads from her system, but she'd take a hundred tablets a day if it'd get her better.

Judith put some food on her plate and tried to force down a few mouthfuls, then gave up the attempt and pushed the remaining bits and pieces neatly into a pile at the side. She was more interested in watching Mitch, sitting at a nearby table with his three sisters, all of them talking animatedly.

'Aren't you eating?' Cal asked.

'I'm not hungry.' She gestured. 'Look at them. It's lovely to see the next generation so full of life at a time like this, isn't it?'

'Yes.' He hesitated. Since she'd moved back to her mother's they hadn't really had a chance to talk because Lily had been very demanding. 'Have you sorted things out at the business, found any sign of Tate?'

She shook her head. 'No. The police are involved now, but the accountant thinks we'll have to file for bankruptcy. Tate embezzled a lot of the firm's money and he seems to have planned his escape very cleverly. If that happens, Mitch won't get his dream of going to Harvard, and I'll have to find a job to help pay his way through university. Then there's my mother. Des gave her an allowance and bought that house she's living in, but it's part of the estate and she'll probably have to move back to her old unit, which is a poky little place.'

'Are things that bad at Corrigan International?'

'It sounds like it.'

'I'm sorry.' He took her hand for a moment. 'It won't make any difference to us, will it?'

'I hope not. But I can't seem to think of myself just now. I'm spending all day at the office, trying to help.'

*　　　*　　　*

As three o'clock approached, conversation faltered in the private suite they had adjourned to after the meal. When Maeve came in on Andy's arm, it died out completely. He led her across to an easy chair and waited until she was seated before taking a chair slightly behind hers, placing himself outside the circle of Des's relatives.

'There are,' Maeve began, 'several things which need discussing. Firstly, Des's will, or rather the lack of one. I'm sorry to tell you that my dear brother died intestate, which leaves us with some interesting decisions to make.'

There was a babble of noise.

'Did you know?' Cal asked Judith.

'I wasn't sure. He hated the thought of making a will but I hoped he'd done something about it after I left. If it wasn't for Mitch, I wouldn't care.'

Maeve tapped the side of her water glass to regain their attention. 'The second thing we need to discuss is Des's business, which is in serious trouble. It appears that his Director of Finances has absconded with a great deal of money and if the company is not to go bankrupt, something needs doing.' She paused. 'I hope, Judith, that you and Mitch will let me help you through this patch, both financially and with my experience of business.'

Judith stared at her in shock. 'Are you sure? It'll take a lot of money to set matters right. And—surely you have better things to do?'

Maeve waved one hand in a dismissive gesture. 'I'm not short of money. But there is a condition to my helping you. I think Mitch should take a gap year before he goes to university and be involved in the restructuring. He'll then be able to base his studies on a sound, practical understanding.'

One look at Mitch's beaming face was enough for Judith. 'We can't thank you enough.'

Maeve nodded. 'The third thing we have to deal with is what to do with Des's estate once we've salvaged it. We have four of his children here and one unborn child, represented by its mother. Can we all agree that any money should go to Judith and to them.'

'Typical of Des to leave a mess for everyone to sort out,' Leo said into the silence. 'Will there be anything left, do you think?'

She smiled. 'Oh, yes. I'll make sure of that.'

'Will you have time, though?'

There was silence as Jean exclaimed 'Leo! What a thing to say!'

'You always were a plain speaker,' Maeve said, 'so I'll be equally plain. It's been discovered that I am in remission, thanks to a radical new treatment for my sort of cancer. So even though there are no guarantees about how long I'll last, I should have more than enough time to rescue Corrigan International and make sure Des's children have something worth inheriting.'

The room erupted in cheers, with Mitch and Lily reaching her first, to clip her up in a hug, only to be superseded by Andy, who spun her round until she ordered him to put her down.

'Why didn't you tell me?' he demanded.

'I couldn't talk about it at first, had to get used to it. Strange how hard it is to face life after you've prepared yourself for death. Now, let me sit down, you fool!'

But she was smiling as she took her place again. 'I think that this would be a good time for the champagne I ordered, and I hope that no one will stop even our youngest Corrigan joining us in a toast.'

Lily looked across at Cal and he nodded and waved a hand in permission.

Andy picked up the phone and a few minutes later two waiters brought in a trolley with bottles of chilled champagne waiting to be poured. When everyone had a glass, Maeve stood up.

'The champagne is for two very special toasts. The first one is, of course, to Des!'

They all echoed that name and raised their glasses.

'And I'd like you to bear with me a few minutes longer before we make the second toast, because I want to explain it to you. Ever since I was first diagnosed with cancer, I've been trying to decide who I should leave my money to. Since I'm childless, it seemed appropriate to leave it to my five nephews and nieces, so I tried to find out more about them, because I'm a practical woman and I didn't want to give it to someone who'd waste it. I decided that each of them should receive something, but I wanted to keep my business intact and leave that to one person only. It was a difficult decision to make and now—well, there isn't the same urgency.'

Everyone's eyes are on her, Judith thought, looking round the room. She's got us in the palm of her hand. No wonder she's been so successful.

Maeve smiled across the room at Lily. 'During the investigations we found that I had another niece—welcome to the family, Lily—and as if that wasn't enough, Tiffany is expecting Des's child. So that will make seven in the next generation of Corrigans, whether they bear the name or not. And there's also Andy, who has not only been my right hand man for some years, but has become like a nephew to me. I couldn't in all fairness leave him out. So there will be eight of them to inherit *my* money. I used to think of it as the Corrigan legacy.'

She stared into the distance for a moment or two. 'However, my thinking about legacies has changed completely over the past few weeks. I think that it's Des and Leo who have given the family the best legacy of all, a wonderful bunch of youngsters, and not a bad apple among them.'

Leo stared at her in surprise.

'You're a fortunate man, Leo Corrigan,' she said. 'But I hope you'll share your good fortune with me and let me get to know my Australian niece and nephew.'

Her brother was clearly too emotional to speak, so she raised her glass. 'So we come to the second formal toast. I'd like to drink to the Corrigans.'

'The Corrigans.' Everyone raised their glasses and sipped.

'And now I'll let you enjoy the rest of your champagne in peace.' She sat down, looking exhausted.

But as Leo stood up and made his way across the room, his expression grimly determined, the noise faded and everyone turned to watch him.

Worried about what Leo intended, Andy stood up protectively.

When he got to his sister, however, Leo bent down and pulled her into his arms. 'A good toast,' he said in a voice thickened by emotion. He patted her on the back several times then said gruffly, 'I'm glad we're speaking to one another again, Maeve.'

'Then perhaps you and Jean will come and stay with me at Saltern House before you go back to Australia? And perhaps you'll send your son and his family out to stay later?'

He nodded and put an arm round his wife, who had followed him across the room. 'Yes. Yes, we will.'

Judith sniffed and hunted in vain for a tissue.

'More happy tears?' Cal pressed a handkerchief into her hand. 'Here you are.' Then he turned a bit pink, took a deep breath and got down on one knee. 'Will you marry me, Judith?' His voice rang out and people stopped talking to stare at them.

She gaped at him, astonished by the public nature of his proposal, then forgot about the other people and pulled him to his feet. 'Of course I will.' She went into his arms for a lingering kiss.

Lily nudged Mitch. 'I didn't feel safe till I knew Mum had gone to America, but now she's gone without me I can get on with my life. I told Dad he should propose to your mum today and he said it was too soon. So I bet him it wasn't and dared him to get down on his knee and do it in front of everyone. She's said yes, and look at her face, how happy she is. So I win ten pounds off Dad.' Then

Lily turned to her brother. 'You don't mind, do you?'

He grinned. 'I suppose that means I'll have to put up with living with you, brat. But I reckon I can do that.'

Cal looked across the room at the two youngsters and raised one thumb as a sign of victory.

'Told you so!' Lily mouthed at him.

'While we're all here . . .' Cal called out and then waited for silence before saying, 'We have another announcement to make. Judith and I intend to get married as soon as it can be arranged and we'd like everyone to attend the wedding.'

Once again the room erupted into noisy cheers and applause. Andy went round filling the glasses with more champagne and another toast was drunk, though Mitch removed the second glass of champagne from a protesting Lily.

CHIVERS LARGE PRINT *-direct-*

If you have enjoyed this Large Print book and would like to build up your own collection of Large Print books, please contact

Chivers Large Print Direct

Chivers Large Print Direct offers you a full service:

• Prompt mail order service

• Easy-to-read type

• The very best authors

• Special low prices

For further details either call Customer Services on (01225) 336552 or write to us at Chivers Large Print Direct, **FREEPOST**, Bath BA1 3ZZ

Telephone Orders: **FREEPHONE** 08081 72 74 75